BELINDA POLLARD

POISON BAY

SMALL BLUE DOG
PUBLISHING

Copyright © Belinda Pollard 2014

The moral right of the author has been asserted.

First published in Australia in 2014 by Small Blue Dog Publishing,
PO Box 310, Lawnton, Queensland 4501, Australia

ISBN

Paperback: 978-0-9942098-0-1

Epub: 978-0-9942098-1-8

Mobi: 978-0-9942098-2-5

Cataloguing-in-Publication entry is available from the
National Library of Australia http://catalogue.nla.gov.au

The characters in this book are fictitious, and any resemblance to real persons,
living or dead, is purely coincidental.

Typeset in 12/17.5 pt Adobe Garamond Pro

Cover images via Bigstock copyright © fcarucci, nhm1, Mr. Alliance, yuran-78,
© lg0rZh – Fotolia and © Solomin Viktor – Deposit Photos

For my parents Jim and Barbara,
who taught me to love both Creation
and the One who made it

Acknowledgments

IT TAKES A VILLAGE TO RAISE A CHILD, AND A GLOBAL VILLAGE TO produce a book. Thank you to my dear friends, family and blog readers around the world who have encouraged and challenged me through the process of creating this debut novel.

The people of Te Anau, New Zealand were generous with information, hot chocolate, venison pies—and some good-natured teasing—while I undertook my research. Lloyd Matheson and Alan Johnston explained Search and Rescue operations in Fiordland National Park. Fishing boat operators Steve and David told me their experiences of the real Poison Bay. To those who can tell when I have taken liberties with geography and topography for plot purposes, I apologize; writers make stuff up!

Helen and Nita of Ultimate Hikes were a key reason that I and my eccentric knees completed the Milford Track without needing to be rescued.

Varuna, The Writers House gave me more than an award—their Publisher Fellowship was that first crucial validation, a catalyst that helped me persevere. Varuna manuscript consultant Carol Major guided me in the discovery of both flaws and possibilities.

I honor the amazing beta readers who critiqued my manuscript, and who deserve medals for their skill, patience, generosity, encouragement and wise suggestions. They are:

- Dawn Dicker, content strategist and writer.
- Molly Greene, author of the Gen Delacourt mystery series.
- Karin Cox, editor and multi-published author of both non-fiction and fiction, including the Cruxim dark fantasy series.

- Sophie Cayeux, author of the upcoming Mauritius Migrants women's fiction series.

Journalist, author of *Sell Your Books!* and Type 1 diabetes advocate Debbie Young corrected my many misunderstandings about both the physical and emotional impacts of the survival situation for Rachel and her mother. Her attention to detail was extraordinary. Nurse and writer Sarah Edgecumbe tutored me in the use of insulin pens and blood sugar monitors. If you have been touched by the Type 1 diabetes storyline, please consider supporting the work of JDRF, the leading charitable funder of the search for a cure.

Retired NZ police inspector Grant Middlemiss not only corrected and enhanced my understanding of police procedures and likely behaviors, he offered savvy suggestions for how to get around plot problems and when to boldly take literary license. Grant is also the author of *Waikato River Gunboats*.

Any mistakes that persist after the feedback of these experts are of course my own.

My editor Jo Swinney was much more than a typo corrector. She shared my vision for this book in a way that lifted me. She tightened my prose and strengthened my story through intelligent feedback full of grace and humor.

I honor my parents Jim and Barbara Pollard, who believed I could write a novel even on the days when I wasn't so sure, and who helped me in countless practical ways, from feeding me during training hikes for my research expedition, to correcting my drafts. Dad, I wish you were still here to see this; Mum, thank you so much for everything.

Finally, my heartfelt thanks to the Creator, who first imagined the beauty of Fiordland, and decided to share it with us.

1

CALLIE BROWN WAS FIRST TO SEE THE SHOTGUN AND THE fragile hands that held it, framed in the viewfinder of her ancient second-hand film camera.

The gang had gathered to celebrate the end of high school with one last pool party, on a Brisbane night so humid it felt like February instead of November.

Tomorrow, they would scatter to universities and apprenticeships. Tonight, they seized one final opportunity for the boisterous to bomb-dive, the beautiful to preen near-naked, and the diffident to camouflage the physical consequences of too much junk food and too little exercise.

Callie gave a self-conscious tweak to her faded sarong, straightened to her full considerable height, and tried to look like a photojournalist, not a stalker. She lined up a shot of Jack and Kain attempting to be pleasant to each other. Jack slouched, his butt propped against the armrest of the leather sofa.

Kain stood straight, arms crossed, lord of his square meter of floor.

Tonight she would finally tell him how she felt. What did she have to lose?

The shout went up, "Pizza's here!" and both guys looked towards the voice, changing the composition of the shot. *Nice.* She snapped the shutter, advanced the film and waited, eye to viewfinder, for them to turn back.

Someone jolted her arm. When Callie's left hand rotated to refocus the lens, she saw it. Crystal clear, yet impossible. Instinctively, she pressed the shutter.

And lowered the camera and stared.

Jack must have been next to see. "Liana, what are you doing?" His voice was sharp over the laughter. Others jostled for pizza, oblivious to the girl with the gun.

The room became still, as each noticed others staring.

Pizza slices dangled from limp hands.

A mosquito buzzed its way up the wall.

Liana said, "No, keep eating. I wouldn't want to keep you from anything important."

Callie's stomach squirmed like it was full of spiders. Was this another of Liana's games? It wasn't funny.

"Liana, put that down at once." The voice sounded so strangled Callie had to glance aside to be sure who'd said it. Bryan, Liana's boyfriend.

"I don't take orders from you anymore." Liana's lips barely moved.

Bryan took a step towards her. Across the room Kain moved too, wearing a look so desperate it told Callie more than she could bear to know. Liana raised the weapon and pointed it from one to the other. Both hesitated, then fell back.

Callie tried to speak clearly around a tongue suddenly thick. "What's wrong, Liana? Let's talk about it." She found herself looking down the double barrels of the gun, and into eyes alight with fury.

"Oh, you've got time to talk now, have you Callie? Well, I haven't."

She turned the weapon towards herself.

***

Nine years, eleven months and two weeks later

CALLIE TRIED TO IGNORE THE FEELING THAT SOMETHING WAS NOT quite right.

The squeak of her hiking boots on the tiles at Christchurch International unnerved her. Her usual soundtrack on an airport concourse was the click-clack of the high heels she hated but had learned to endure. The plastic "beauty" required for television work was a curse to a closet tomboy, and yet it seemed this was going to be one of those moments when she couldn't bear to be without it. *My version of Stockholm syndrome,* she thought.

Her big wheeled suitcase was also absent. As instructed, she had only a cabin bag containing a few items of kit, and her camera gear. Bryan would supply everything else.

She felt ill-equipped to meet a bunch of people she'd avoided ever since that awful funeral a decade ago.

When the invitation arrived, it had seemed like a solution— something dramatic to talk about with the ruthless gossips at work, taking the focus off William Green's holiday to Italy. The whole newsroom knew he'd booked that holiday with Callie, but taken a cute little blonde instead. While she'd been indulging the fantasy of a lifetime of jokes about a couple named Green & Brown, he'd been making other plans.

Well, anyone could go to Italy. To rouse the curiosity of a bunch of hardened hacks, trek Middle Earth instead.

She'd discovered years ago that drawing attention to herself was the best way to hide, and the scheme had certainly eased her passage through the past six weeks. But today she faced the ominous reality. Ten days in remote New Zealand, far from phone signals and baristas. A deranged place for a high school reunion. *Why can't Bryan organize a dinner party like normal people?*

"Callie!" Advancing towards her, arms wide, was the only bright spot in her gathering gloom. Rachel Carpenter had been her best friend since they were pig-tailed six year olds.

After a hug, Rachel stood back and looked her up and down. "That's a nice look for our glamorous television reporter."

Callie wore trousers that zipped off into shorts, but they were only the beginning of the horror. "Wait till you see my rain jacket. It's fluorescent orange."

"You're not serious."

"At forty percent off, how could I resist? Besides, it matches my hair."

As they linked arms and walked, Rachel said, "I'm still in shock that you decided to come. Even Mum was laughing at the thought of Callie Brown having to carry her own bag any further than the nearest taxi."

"I'm not that lazy." They exchanged a glance. "Oh, all right, I am. But on the plus side, I've got an excuse to look a mess for days on end."

"I see you made an effort this morning though. I wonder why?" Rachel's mouth curved into an impish smile.

Callie had risen uncomfortably early to straighten her frizzy strawberry curls into a glossy curtain, and even applied a touch of makeup, but found it best to answer: "How's your Mum?"

Rachel grimaced. "She's fine, but I hated leaving her. It's my first time away since Dad died."

Before Callie could think of a comforting reply, they reached the food-court, where people were standing from a table, moving towards them.

Her glance skittered across faces she hadn't seen since high school. Too many, all at once. She didn't know whether to offer a handshake or a hug or a hula dance.

The two blonde women were first to approach. Dumpy, kind Sharon alongside the slender and petite Erica, who had always made Callie feel like a lurching giant. She exchanged a warm hug with Sharon and a less-sincere embrace with Erica.

Next, the men. Kain was as gorgeous and self-assured as she remembered, although his smile seemed, if possible, a little whiter. She fumbled in her portfolio of facial expressions for one that might say Pleased To See You, But Not To Any Foolish Extent. His quick, relaxed hug left an after-image of hard chest and expensive cologne.

Finally, there was Jack. Good old Jack. Not very tall, not very good-looking, not very anything. They'd studied journalism together, long ago and far away. He tripped on someone's bag, and his hug became a collision. "Nice to bump into you again," she said, and he laughed, his face red.

She had just worked out who was missing when she saw Adam walking towards the table, obviously just arrived on a separate flight. His lanky frame looked at home in the hiking paraphernalia.

"Hey team!" he bellowed, grinning. He made a boisterous round of greetings, collapsed into a chair, and launched into the tale of the beautiful "Scottish lassie" who ran hunting safaris in the Northern Territory with him—and the engagement ring that had two payments to go. The previous awkwardness round the table dissipated as he blathered.

Callie returned with coffee just in time to hear Adam ask Jack, "So what are you reporting on these days, Scoop?"

Kain said, "He isn't reporting on anything. He's at Bible college, studying how to be better than us. We're calling him the Reverend now."

Callie was stunned. *So, Jack hasn't grown out of the religion thing.* Adam hooted with laughter, but unlike Kain's his teasing showed no malice. He shoved Jack's shoulder. "Ripper, mate! You can be Team Chaplain." He pointed at Kain. "Team Lawyer, if we need to sue each other, or Team Lifeguard if we fall in the drink. Erica: Team Nurse, for when we scrape our knees. Sharon: Team Hairdresser, to keep us gorgeous. Callie: Team Reporter, because we're superstars." He paused at Rachel, losing traction. "Rachel…?"

She said, "I doubt we'll need a scientist."

"Team Sweetheart!"

Callie said, "What about you, Adam?"

Kain answered for him. "Team Navigator, if Attila gets us lost in the mountains." Needless to say, their old nickname for Bryan was not one they used to his face.

Sharon said, "Don't you think it's amazing that every last one of us came?" She beamed.

People smiled, but Callie noticed that no one said anything. *Most of us are not hiking fanatics, so why are we here?*

2

IN THE PRE-DAWN GRAYNESS, SERGEANT PETER HUBBLE WATCHED the tow-truck pull away, dragging a mangled car, then took a moment to gaze out over the silent water. After eight years in Te Anau, the mighty lake still had the power to move him.

He heard muted voices, and saw a tourist boat being prepped. There wasn't much point returning to his empty house, so he wandered over. It would be someone he knew; it always was, in this tiny town.

He was surprised, however, to see one of his constables aboard.

Tom Granton raised a hand in greeting. "Just helping get the boat ready. Don't worry, I'm still coming to work today." Tom was always helping people at odd hours.

The man's big grin seemed a few watts dimmer than usual. *I hope he wasn't up in the night with the child. I must remember to check if Lily is still in remission.*

"Fishing party?"

"Trampers. Bunch of Aussies heading for the track to George Sound."

Peter heard voices approaching and turned. Even in the half-light, there was no mistaking Bryan Smithton's dreadlocks and wiry physique. His walk was distinctive too, with the slightly flexed knees of a man ready to respond to a flash flood or a charging wapiti bull. His biggest challenge at the moment, however, was the asphalt roadway.

The young Australian man had lived in Te Anau longer than Peter, and was probably as familiar to the locals. Well-known didn't necessarily mean well-liked, however.

Behind him trailed a gaggle of young people. Peter automatically did a head count: eight, counting Bryan—four women, four men.

Peter greeted Bryan with a nod. "So you're off to George Sound?"

One of the party answered, "Nah, Milford!" Peter glanced at the speaker: tall, around six foot, blond, athletic build. The national park contained only a handful of marked trails, and the George and Milford Tracks were in vastly different sections. Peter mentally filed the contradiction in case it turned out to be important later.

The man received a quelling look from Bryan, who said to Peter, "Yes, George Sound." So the lad was probably just confused because Milford was the more famous track.

Peter said, "Good weather today."

"Yes."

The atmosphere was uncomfortable—probably the Smithton-factor. Peter decided it would be more fun to go to his cold, empty office and write his report on the car accident.

3

JACK METCALF WATCHED HIS OLD FRIENDS REACT TO THEIR FIRST view of the Fiordland mountains, as the launch chuntered its way across the lake. They didn't say much, but they stared. Maybe it was dawning on them what they were getting themselves into. To be frank, he felt a twinge of concern himself.

These were professional mountains. If they were buildings, they'd be at least four hundred stories high. They were impossibly steep, rising suddenly from ground level; sharp-topped, crowding close together.

Jack had expected immunity to the scale of Fiordland. He'd seen it before, on a visit years ago when he'd helped Bryan bury his parents. They'd even taken a day hike on one of the popular trails. And yet these peaks astonished him all over again. "An astonishment of mountains." Perhaps he should offer that to Callie. She liked to invent collective nouns.

He'd managed to score a seat beside her on the boat, without even trying. At least, he was pretty sure he hadn't tried. It hardly mattered, since he now had the dubious pleasure of watching her watching Kain, opposite them.

He returned his attention to the view through his little video camera. No photo could capture the scale of this place, but he was going to give it a shot. Only two weeks till summer, and there was still snow on the jagged mountain tops, which perforated both sky and lake, their reflection so perfect a man needed gravity to tell him which way was up. The breeze teasing the back of his neck came from the momentum of the launch. The morning air wouldn't have been moving at all if it didn't have to get out of their way. Perhaps it was half-asleep like the rest of them.

Yesterday, they'd endured a nine-hour drive from Christchurch, crammed into a rattly mini-bus, and followed it with a hard night on a hard floor at Bryan's tiny house. They had been brusquely woken in the dark, and ordered to eat oatmeal and toast, which they'd had to do standing because there were no chairs. What a weird house Bryan had chosen. It had shocked his old friends; they'd been expecting something more like the riverside mansion that had been their playground as teenagers.

Jack panned the camera back towards the town they'd just left, squatting on the south eastern shore. Sunrise tickled the tops of the taller trees. To the north, the lake disappeared into misty distance. Sixty-five kilometers long, according to Bryan, their guide, leader and protector. And completely uninhabited on the side they were heading for, a national park of 12,500 square kilometers. No roads. No phone signal. They would be like ants out there.

"This lake is twelve degrees Celsius," announced Bryan over the chugging of the engine. "If you fall overboard, you can only survive a few minutes. It's half a kilometer deep—the bottom is below sea level and covered in ice. No one will ever see you again."

Jack noticed Callie, beside him, flinch at the strident voice. A Botticelli-angel smile appeared on her face and just as quickly dissolved. When he caught her eye, she flushed. Whatever amusing thoughts Bryan's words had prompted, they probably weren't kind.

"Hey," she said in a stage whisper camouflaged by the engine noise, "what do you make of his hair? Are you tempted to try dreads yourself?"

Jack surveyed the dreadlocks protruding through the gap on the back of Bryan's cap. "I think I liked his old short-back-and-sides better."

"Me too. It wasn't pretty, but you at least knew where you were with that haircut. The new do is too whimsical for his head. Like his hair is having a party on a tombstone." She paused and grimaced. "An insensitive thing to say about someone who's been to so many funerals, I guess. Is this where his parents died?"

"Yep. They're in a little cemetery south of town."

"I remember when you took time off uni to fly over for the funeral."

"At the time I wondered why he didn't take their bodies home to Brisbane, but afterwards when he moved here to live, it made sense. Sort of."

"He worshiped the ground they walked on. Weird that he doesn't have any photos of them in his house."

Jack nodded. Next to Kain, he saw Sharon bend her feet up and back, looking at her cheap boots. "Do you know why Sharon didn't buy the stuff on Bryan's list?"

"Apparently she used Bryan's check to pay her credit card bill before she discovered how much this gear costs."

"Understandable, when she's got a little kid and no husband."

"Yeah." The tired eyes became lively. "I could have punched Bryan when he made her cry about it last night, carrying on as though her life depended on a few clothes."

"I know what you mean. But I guess he's under pressure to keep us safe. It's dangerous out here—avalanches, blizzards, wind storms, flash floods, the works. Did you know they get about seven meters of rain a year? It's one of the wettest places on earth."

"Really?" She raised an eyebrow. "Not something Bryan bothered to mention in his invitation."

He laughed. "Enjoy the sunshine. You might not see it for a while." He became serious. "What do you think of the trek he's planned for us?"

In last night's briefing, Bryan had given almost no details about their route, except that it would take ten days to reach world-famous Milford Sound but stray far from any existing tracks. They would begin on the rarely-used track to George Sound, and that was the destination they would mention to anyone who asked. After a couple of days, they would head off-track into deep wilderness. Bryan wanted to create a brand new trail in honor of his dead parents. He'd tested the route himself, and now it was time for a group of hikers to confirm it. They'd been ordered to keep their goal confidential.

Jack said, "Why choose us to test something like this? We're not exactly trailblazers. And why does it need to be hush-hush?"

"He must be trying to protect the naming rights or something. Can you imagine if we asked him to change the itinerary now? He'd probably grab an ax and kill us all. I'm hoping it won't be as hard as we think. But at least we're carrying our own body bags if we need them."

Jack grimaced. Apart from providing waterproof storage, the huge orange plastic bag in each of their kits was big enough to contain an adult in an array of scenarios, the color designed to catch the eye of searchers. He said, "They're very useful looking bags, but Bryan didn't need to be quite so grim."

"Never fear, I've got duct tape if anything goes wrong."

Jack smiled. "You too?"

"I'm a seasoned traveler. But seriously, we've got the satellite phone and emergency beacon—and he did notify the authorities. Surely that's a safety net."

Bryan had told them he'd registered at the Department of Conservation office. Someone would start looking if they didn't come home.

***

THEIR "TRACK" WAS NOTHING LIKE THE ONE HE'D HIKED WITH Bryan all those years ago. At the time, he'd thought it rough compared to Australian trails. But that scrappy gap in the rainforest seemed like a city footpath in comparison to what they were walking today.

The occasional orange triangle nailed to a tree was the only way to tell they were even in the right part of the valley.

Most of it was an undergrowth-infested bog. Some of it was ankle deep in water. Today's weather might be glorious, but it had obviously rained yesterday. Hard. And probably the day before and the day before that.

They clambered over fallen trees and boulders the size of cars. Not for the first time in his life, Jack wished he was taller. To scale the larger rocks, he had to reach up so far his arms were almost fully extended, then lift the combined weight of his body and rucksack. The women were being helped—a leg up from below, a hand reaching down from above. But he couldn't ask for that. The other blokes were managing.

Long tendrils of hairy lichen hung from the trees, glowing in slivers of sunlight. They tugged at his arms, slapped his face.

Waterfalls hurled themselves down slopes so steep they were virtually forested cliffs. The group ate lunch near a place where the vegetation had apparently lost its courage and let go, laying bare a strip of granite wide as a freeway and one hundred stories high.

"What caused that?" Jack said to Bryan.

"Tree avalanche. They happen after heavy rain."

Later, they crossed the river on an instrument of torture some joker had deemed a bridge: three steel cables suspended above rushing water, one to walk on, two higher ones to steady yourself. The drop to the sharp boulders and rushing water were bad enough, without the wobble in the wire as he edged across. Even worse, he was forced to wait till last, having been appointed by Bryan as today's "sweeper", watching to make sure no one was left behind.

As they made camp in the soft evening light so many agonizing hours later, Jack watched Callie laugh with Kain, and drew ungracious comfort from the suspicion that the other man was hurting from the day's ordeal.

Kain helped Callie and Erica set out their tent, while they discussed the pleasures of a wilderness without spiders or snakes. Kain said, "No bosses, either. It was the sweetest thing being able to tell him there's no phone signal out here as I left the office. You should have seen his face."

Erica said, with a hint of snarkiness, "Why do you stay in that job if you hate it so much?"

"Maybe I won't. Those 'golden handcuffs' might lose their power any day now."

Jack wondered how often those rippling muscles did anything useful. He had always privately thought Kain's voluntary work as a surf lifesaver was mostly about being a hero in front of women in bikinis.

And he was going to have to share a two-man tent with him tonight. Rather than use bunks in a conservation hut, their fearless leader insisted they get into practice for the rest of the trek.

Today's ordeal by jungle counted as a "marked track", even if it was rarely used. Where they were going, there were no huts. No track. No shelter other than what they carried or nature provided.

Bryan called for their attention. "A trace of mud in your tent each day will become a pig sty by the time ten days are up. The cloth in your kit is to keep everything clean. Use it. Thoroughly. Every night. Wash it in the river each day and hang it on the back of your pack to dry as we walk."

"Yes sir!" Adam saluted, drawing a few giggles.

Bryan gave him a cold stare, then continued. "Leave nothing outside your tents. When you go to bed, wipe down your boots and take them inside, or you'll be walking barefoot tomorrow."

"Why?" said Sharon, wide-eyed. "Will someone steal them?"

It was a strange question, since they'd seen no other human since the boat that brought them across the lake turned back to Te Anau, breaking any connection with civilization.

Bryan harrumphed. "Keas. Mountain parrots."

Everyone waited for him to elaborate, but Bryan returned to the dinner preparations.

Jack moved to a vantage point, his camera capturing soft colors and moody mists in the distance.

"You're taking a lot of video." Callie was suddenly beside him, her own camera pressed to her eye as she rotated the zoom on the big lens.

"I'm thinking about making a documentary."

"For the web?"

He shrugged. "Web. Television. Haven't decided."

"Not for television."

The energy of his answer surprised even him. "And why not? Is mediocrity illegal now?"

She blushed. "You can't make a television documentary with a little camera like that."

"What do you think freelance journos who go into closed areas do? They don't take fourteen technicians and a makeup artist. They take a camera any tourist might carry, so no one will stop them at the border. They shoot their own pieces to camera by sitting on the ground and holding it with their feet if they have to. I'm not trying to be Attenborough, just tell a story." He shoved the camera in his jacket pocket and turned back to the campsite, embarrassed and off-kilter.

Later, the weary group made quiet conversation around the campfire, a fingernail clipping of moon hanging overhead. With a warm meal of reconstituted food in their bellies, snug tents awaiting them, and their weight off their feet, the contentment was tangible.

Jack said, "I had no idea those dehydrated things could taste so good."

"Sure beats crocodile," drawled Adam.

Sharon said, "Have you really eaten crocodile? Yuck!"

"No, but I had to shoot one last month, to stop it eating a customer. We didn't put it on the menu. They eat rotting meat. Store it underwater somewhere until it's ripe."

A groan of revulsion rippled round the circle.

"I ate crocodile once," Kain said. "Big overseas client. One of those posh restaurants with main courses for $100, emu and ostrich, that sort of thing."

"What did it taste like?" Erica said.

"Actually, it tasted a lot like chicken."

Jack muttered, "Probably was chicken." Callie apparently overheard him, and stifled a laugh. Their eyes met and Jack felt the awkwardness between them ease.

The sky was clear, the air crisp. Eight people alone in the universe.

Bryan said, "The Maori call this place Ata Whenua—Shadow Land."

Rachel said, "Why is that?"

"The mountains are so steep that in winter some of the valleys never get the sun."

Like many of Bryan's comments, this one shifted the tone. "Great," Callie said. "Does anyone else feel like those mountains are watching us?"

Adam said, "Nah. It's not the mountains, just the mountain parrots."

Jack chuckled, but stopped when he caught a glare from Bryan.

Before long, the hikers dispersed to their assigned tents. Bryan had separated friends and combined people who didn't get along, but whether he'd done it as a mixer or for less cuddly reasons, who could tell? Jack was sure Callie would have preferred Rachel to Erica. As for him, despite being housed with Kain, he wriggled into his sleeping bag with a vast sigh of relief. It was bliss just to lie down.

***

MORNING BROUGHT SULLEN SKIES, SCUDDING RAIN, AND EVEN flurries of snow. Jack found the cold amplified yesterday's muscle strains as he forced himself to walk again.

Adam was about to cross a creek ahead of him when a rain squall hit them full in the face, sending them fumbling to raise jacket hoods. The other man turned back to say, "Great holiday, huh?"

"Yeah. Who'd go to the beach when you could do this?"

Hours later, they prepared to lunch on the last of the sad little sandwiches made yesterday morning. With difficulty, Jack persuaded Bryan to authorize the gas stove for instant soup, to help comfort them in the bleak weather. The meal was eaten huddled under thick tree cover that stopped much of the rain, or at least broke its fall.

Jack sheltered Rachel's hands with part of his jacket while she checked her blood sugar, and beside her, Erica strapped her knee, using a first-aid kit she'd brought from home. "Are you okay?" he said.

She shrugged. "It's the twisting and turning. I'll be okay."

He was impressed by the discreet way she went on to dress Sharon's blistered feet. Sharon didn't need Bryan's criticism for buying the wrong shoes, to add to her physical pain.

Later, his respect for Erica dissolved. She flirted with Kain all afternoon, and Kain reciprocated. They were welcome to each other, but Jack was pretty sure they were doing it to taunt Callie. She'd become unusually quiet.

When the time came for lights out, he went to the tent he was to share with Kain, but his pack had been dumped in the rain. Erica had taken his place inside.

"Where am I supposed to sleep?" He felt a ridiculous desire to report them to Bryan.

Kain said, "Go and share with Callie, Reverend. You've always wanted to do that anyway." He tossed Jack's sleeping bag out, and pulled the tent flap down in his face.

Jack stomped over to Callie's tent. "Knock, knock."

"Who's there?" She stuck her head out.

"Your new roommate. Erica's taken my spot."

"I wondered where she'd got to."

"I'm sure it's going to be a very deep relationship, for about eight more days."

"Well you can't sleep under the stars in this weather, so you'd better get in here."

Jack crawled in after her, and wrestled with his rain-spattered sleeping bag. By the time he'd got himself settled, he'd become philosophical. "This might be better anyway. Kain snores."

"Wait till Erica finds out," she said, her voice muffled by her sleeping bag. "Better still, wait till Bryan catches them."

"Do you think they'll get detention?"

"At the very least."

"Hey, what if Bryan catches *us*?"

"We're not going to do anything. Trust me."

"Yes, but if he sees us coming out in the morning, how will he know?"

"Bryan is weird, Jack, not a moron. He's had to watch those two all afternoon, same as the rest of us."

"I suppose so. But don't you try anything. I'm a good Christian boy y'know."

Callie giggled. "Oh shut up and go to sleep."

After a few minutes silence, she spoke again, her voice soft. "Jack, about those foreign correspondents… you might be right. I'm sorry I was dismissive about your camera."

He blushed in the darkness. "Don't worry about it."

"It's just that I've been used to different production standards. My doccos are always about things that happen in nice, safe places." She snorted in self-deprecation. "With electricity and plumbing."

"I'm sorry I lost my temper. I guess I'm not sure I know what I'm doing."

"I never had any doubts about you, only the camera. Everything you did when we were at school and uni was excellent."

"Flattery doesn't work with me, Cal."

"It's the truth. If you believed in yourself more, you could do anything." She sighed. "I always felt inadequate around you, to be honest. It's all smoke and mirrors with me. Day after never-ending day."

He fought the urge to reach for her hand in the darkness.

4

ELLEN CARPENTER WAS WORKING LATE AGAIN, BECAUSE WORK filled the hours. She knew she must go home, or run the gauntlet of the muggers that populated her imagination when the university campus grew dark and creepy.

But her Brisbane home was silent too, tonight. And so she lingered.

On her desk, three faces smiled out of a photo frame; her own between Roger's and Rachel's, a family holiday at the Great Barrier Reef. Was it only two years ago? Before they even knew anything was wrong. Before she noticed the dark blotch on her husband's back.

Thanks to Ellen's encouragement, her only child was on the other side of the Tasman Sea tonight, engulfed by wilderness, while her mother tried not to worry about the dangers and whether she'd packed enough supplies to manage her diabetes.

And Roger was so much further away than that.

Ellen turned to her calendar and calculated the number of days before Rachel came home.

5

WITH EVERY DAY THAT PASSED, CALLIE'S ANXIETY GREW. WHY had she agreed to come? It was so much harder than she'd imagined back in the lunchroom at work, telling her colleagues stories of daring and danger, while not really believing them herself.

Now she was living the reality of her foolish decision. There were times she wondered if she would survive. She had followed Bryan's instructions and trained till her body ached, weekend after weekend in the Blue Mountains near Sydney. But she was no athlete, and now her body was betraying her. Every muscle and ligament seemed to be debating its level of commitment to her bones. Her thighs turned to jelly on the downhills. On the uphills, her heart roared in her chest, to the point that she wondered how many twenty-seven-year-old women had heart attacks. Her shoulders and neck throbbed from the dragging weight of the rucksack. She counted down the hours and minutes till the next break, when she could ease it off her back and plonk it into the mud for short-lived relief.

At lunch on Day Three, she tried to talk to Rachel about it.

"I'm not coping. I don't know what to do."

Rachel frowned. "What do you mean? You just put one foot in front of the other, that's all."

"I'm afraid, Rachel. We're not even halfway there." She felt tears gathering.

"Don't be silly. You'll be fine. It's just walking."

Callie felt abandoned. Dismissed. Misunderstood. Rachel had always been exercise crazy—her way of keeping a sense of control over her diabetes. She was forever at the gym, or cycling, or swimming, or hiking—she was a *machine*. She obviously didn't have a clue what it meant to be inside Callie's skin right now.

Callie was engulfed in a longing for home—not Sydney and its emerald harbor, the city she'd lived in for the past five years, but Brisbane. The refuge of childhood. In her mind, she saw its gently rounded hills, dusty gum trees, the sleepy brown river.

But most of all, she longed for its great big sky. There was no sky in this place. Just a narrow gap between granite cliffs overhead, and even that disappeared when the clouds fell down.

And fall they did.

The storm that descended later that afternoon had been busy beforehand, up in the tops.

Callie watched Sharon ahead of her soldiering onwards on ruined feet, sloshing through water shin-deep from the swollen river. Every step must be an ordeal for the poor girl, but Callie had yet to hear a complaint pass Sharon's lips.

I'm such a coward. Tears slid down her face, and she didn't care. In these conditions, who would see?

Rain pounded on her jacket hood, bounced off her rucksack's rain cover. She became aware of a roaring noise, even above the sound of the rain. There were shouts from up ahead. Through the downpour she dimly saw people running. Uphill. Away from the river.

When the wave of water hit Sharon, it lifted her off her feet and threw her at Callie. They both fell, and were swept for meters before a tree snagged Callie's rucksack. She instinctively reached out and grabbed the slender trunk with her left hand, wrapping the other arm under Sharon's armpit. She struggled to maintain her grasp on either. Slowly, she found purchase under the torrent, her boot connecting with rock, and she worked her way forward till she could get the tree wedged into the crook of her left elbow, and bring her hands together to grip each other across Sharon's chest. It was a fight to keep the other woman's face out of the water. If Callie tipped back too far while trying to help her friend breathe, they'd both be swept away.

"Sharon! Callie!" It was Adam. He'd shed his rucksack somewhere and clambered towards them, a rope in his hands. Behind him came Kain.

Adam looped the rope around his chest and passed the other end to Kain. Callie couldn't hear their conversation over the roar of the water, but Adam's gestures to Kain made the plan clear. Kain would brace the rope around a sturdy tree, playing it out as Adam needed it, and help haul them back in when the moment came.

Adam shouted, "Callie, you'll need to let go of Sharon the moment we start pulling, and grab the tree at the same time. Can you do that?"

"I think so." What else could she say? She tried to wedge her boot more firmly into the notch in the rock below.

"Sharon, give me your hands! On three. Ready? One. Two. Three. Let go!"

Callie released and Sharon was free. The force of water swung Callie backwards but she fought her way back, renewing her grip on the narrow trunk.

A few more moments and she too was up and out of the flood. She huddled with Sharon in the mud, holding her tight as the rain poured down, both of them weeping aloud. And she didn't care who saw her tears this time.

***

CALLIE LOOKED FOR A CHANCE TO TALK TO JACK ALONE. SHE GOT IT the next day, as the group lunched on crispbread and peanut butter, sitting in tussock grass on a mountain pass. They'd been climbing steeply upwards for hours, and she knew Bryan would crack the whip and drive them onwards again before she'd had nearly enough time to recover. At least it wasn't raining.

A fat and fluffy green and brown parrot walked right up to Jack's rucksack when he was distracted, and used its hooked beak to explore and then grasp his boot-cleaning cloth where it dangled from the straps, drying. It tugged the cloth free, and waddled away with it. Jack crept after the kea, apparently hoping to trade a piece of his lunch (precious) for the cloth (irreplaceable).

Callie waited till the hostage-ransom exchange had taken place, then walked over quietly to join man and bird, who were now "chatting". The kea turned its head from side to side as Jack explained how much trouble he'd be in with his expedition leader if he couldn't clean his boots at night.

Callie smiled. "You're a nutcase, Jack."

"Yeah, but you've gotta admit he's cute."

She laughed. "He's a thief and a vandal."

"He reminds me of Rufus. My dog." When she gave him an incredulous look, he added, "It's the head tilts. Rufus does that. It's like kryptonite, I'm powerless before it. He might have just shredded the bath mat, and I'm trying to tell him off, but three head tilts and all is forgiven."

She laughed again, and felt some of the tension ease out of her shoulders.

Jack said, "Oops. Attila alert."

She glanced around. About ten meters away, Bryan glared at them. For a conservationist, he had a patchy attitude to wildlife. He'd made his intolerance of the cheeky and destructive parrots quite clear during several previous encounters.

Callie sat down on a rock. "Speaking of Attila... does he worry you?"

"Yes." He held her gaze, his face serious. "Something's not right."

"He was always weird, but this is… different. Like he's barely keeping his anger under control. And he just keeps pushing us, like recruits at boot camp, who need to be humiliated." She looked at the ground. "I'm having trouble. Not fit enough."

"Me too. I expected a challenge, but there's nothing like this terrain at home." She could have kissed him for the admission.

"I'm worried about Sharon," she continued. "She needs rest. Her jeans are still damp from yesterday. Her thighs must be red-raw by now."

The two women had been sodden after the flash flood. As they were designed to do, Callie's hi-tech garments had dried quickly, and they were wearable and warming even while wet. Sharon's cheaper versions didn't perform so well, and her jeans were hopeless. An hour steaming over the campfire hadn't dried them.

Jack said, "Erica's knees are a mess too. It's the downhills. She's never been anywhere you have to descend so steeply for so long."

"Could you talk to Bryan? Ask him to slow down? You were always closest to him at school." She saw Jack tense at that statement, and wondered why.

"I'll try."

She watched him have a discreet conversation with Bryan as they prepared to depart a short time later. Judging by Bryan's posture, it wasn't going well.

***

DAYS PASSED, AND NOTHING IMPROVED. CALLIE FOUND DISTRACtion in helping Jack with his documentary. Here at least was something she was good at. She wangled interviews, set up shots, smoothed irritations when people resented the camera. They gradually grew immune to its watchful eye, as people do with any sustained intrusion.

The camera was waterproof and shockproof—and it needed to be. She watched him mount it on a head strap to record his own eye view, hold it by hand, use a mini tripod with bendy legs to stand it on a rock, or attach it to a tree branch. The raw footage previewed on the tiny screen looked surprisingly good.

***

As they made camp on Day Five, Callie listened to Kain and Erica bickering, and tried not to be pleased.

She saw Adam head to the river for water. Jack followed, an intensity in his bearing. Callie decided she needed to see something down at the river too.

As she approached them, Adam was saying, "I agree." His expression was serious.

Jack nodded to acknowledge her presence, but continued addressing Adam. "If we turned back, do you think you could find the way?"

"The Northern Territory is nothing like here," Adam said. "Maybe I'd find the way back, or maybe we'd cross into the wrong valley and go round in circles for weeks. Sharon wouldn't cope with that, and Rachel would run out of insulin. That rain is unbelievable. It destroys our tracks."

Jack sighed, and shrugged.

Adam said, "Today is the half-way point. Maybe we're better off sticking with Bryan."

***

On Day Seven, the issue became more urgent when Sharon fell and struggled to get up again.

This time, Erica joined the huddle. "Sharon needs to be airlifted out of here," she said. "At the very least, she needs a rest day."

Callie nodded. "Somehow, we need to get Bryan to listen. He doesn't understand what it's like to be us."

Jack said, "But if we all gang up on him, he'll probably dig his heels in."

Adam said, "How about you and I go talk to him, Jack?"

Callie stayed beside Erica and watched what followed, trying not to be too obvious. Bryan kept his arms folded across his chest as the deputation made its case.

When the men returned to them, Adam shrugged in frustration. "He says a helicopter wouldn't be authorized unless her condition was life-threatening. And the best thing to do for her is to get to where we're going."

Jack said, "I wouldn't be surprised if he pushes us even harder now."

Erica huffed. "Why don't you guys just hold him down while Callie and I dig that damn satellite phone out of his rucksack." Her face was red with anger.

Callie's eyes went to the rucksack in question, and she saw the others looking too. But nobody acted.

6

SINGLE FILE, THEY TRUDGED ALONG A GRITTY BEACH UNDER A sky the color of hammered pewter. It was almost over.

In the middle of the line-up, Callie's ankle throbbed from a twisting skid on moss. She'd lost so much weight in the past ten days that her clothes were loose. This had thrilled her, one consolation on the dismal "holiday". But now she'd consider trading a kidney for a greasy plate of hot chips.

A hot shower. A steak. A soft bed. Soon.

Ahead, Rachel was taking her turn to support Sharon as she limped along valiantly. They'd redistributed most of her load.

The final challenge was to make their boat connection in time to beat the storm building offshore. Rolling swells heaved onto the beach and sucked back out into the long horseshoe-shaped bay, its sides steep and dark. They'd begun at a lake and finished at the ocean, water to water.

Bryan turned to look back at the group. "Hurry. We must reach our target by eight o'clock."

Callie guessed they must have hiked two or three kilometers along the waterline, from sand to shingle and now jagged rocks, and yet the headland where the bay met the ocean seemed just as far away. Her thighs were strong after so many days of trekking, and yet they ached from the long descent. Her sore ankle notified her of every false step on the haphazard surface.

"How will they ever get us on a boat in this sea?" she said to Adam behind her.

"They can't. We'll have to find somewhere to camp for the night and hope they come back in the morning."

"So why do we keep on marching like maniacs?"

"Because when Bryan says march, we march. That's the way it works, apparently. I don't care anymore."

Bryan strode onwards, surefooted through fallen boulders and striated granite. They followed numbly, dipping close to the water-line, skidding on the slime. He led them in a last exhausting up-ward scramble onto a huge, elevated slab of granite that jutted out into the water, moved confidently to the seaward edge and turned to face them. Glancing over her shoulder, Callie checked that Jack's camera was rolling as he clambered up behind the others. He had it clamped in the head-strap, and nodded at her.

The walkers jostled for a safe perch. The granite surface was difficult for their boots to grip and sloped gently but meaningfully towards the pumping sea. The platform on which they stood had commenced life as part of the mountain somewhere far above, and apparently had ambitions to one day become part of the ocean floor. Behind Bryan, the restless bay made a monochrome back-drop in the dull light—black water, white foam, steely sky. One careless step backwards would be enough to take him off the edge, dropping at least the height of a two-story building into that de-mented water. Part of her was tempted to give him a shove, after the horror he'd put them through. The other part knew they couldn't afford to lose the safety and navigational gear that he carried—not just yet.

Callie could see she wasn't the only one who found the setting intimidating. Erica was breathing hard. Kain looked uneasy. Sharon teetered and gasped, almost losing her balance. Rachel grabbed the hand she thrust out sideways, steadying her. Behind them, the for-tress of forested rock rose steeply above, offering no refuge.

"Where's the boat?" said Sharon. "Have we missed it?"

"We're at the end of our journey," Bryan announced.

Cold fingers of foreboding ran down Callie's spine. He was

much too close to the edge. And how could anything but a very large vessel collect them from this high platform?

"Welcome to Poison Bay." Bryan's voice was like dry ice.

Kain said, "What do you mean? Why is it poison?"

Bryan flushed. "That's its name: Poison Bay."

"Why is it called that?"

Jack said, "Kain, I think the point is why Bryan has brought us here instead of to Milford Sound."

"Why have you brought us here, Bryan?" said Callie. She used her television voice, calm and strong. Her insides felt more like the sea.

"Because the Shadow Land told me that I must bring you to the bay of poison."

He sounded like a Tolkien character, but no one teased him.

"This day and this hour is ten years, the time of completion. My suffering is ending, and yours is beginning. I have earned my release. It has been a battle to get you all here at the appointed time. But it is finished, and now the Shadow Land will purify us all."

They stared, speechless, and then Jack spoke. "Purify us from what?"

"How can you be so complacent that you forget what you owe? You must pay for the murder of Liana and her baby!"

"Bryan, we didn't murder Liana," Callie said. "We all let her down in different ways. We were gutted by her death, and we will see it in our heads forever. But we didn't kill Liana, and neither did you. Liana killed Liana."

"You did kill her! Some of you did wicked things. Others avoided doing the right things. You all know the secrets you carry. For ten years Liana and her baby have lain in the cemetery, waiting for justice. I have paid and paid, and now you will too." He paused and stared at them, one by one. Callie found herself transfixed by the way his nostrils flared in and out with each breath. "You know what you deserve. Not one of you will leave the Shadow Land alive!"

He took a decisive step backwards, the arch of his sole connecting firmly with the angled edge of the rock. He pushed hard, launching his body up and out. The weight of the rucksack tipped him as he fell, so that he hit the ocean spreadeagled. The black water rose up and swallowed him whole.

7

THE OXYGEN WAS SUCKED OUT OF THE UNIVERSE AND TIME stopped for one second, two seconds, three seconds.

Callie started as Jack and Adam moved simultaneously. In swift silence, they unclipped harnesses, piled packs against the rock wall with jackets, followed by boots. Jack shoved his camera, still rolling, into Callie's hand and she stared at it, her mind stuck. It only dislodged itself as the two men leaped off that awful edge, following Bryan into the water.

"Jack! Adam!" she screamed. "The water's too cold. You won't survive!" Twelve degrees, that's all she could think of. With ice on the bottom, and Bryan's mouth frozen open eternally. And she had made it happen by imagining it that first day.

The men dived frantically after Bryan, again and again, disappearing for eternal seconds before bobbing up to gulp air.

The whole time, pressed hard against the rock wall, Sharon screamed—thin, terrified, animal noises. Rachel tried to quieten her, an arm around Sharon's shoulders, rubbing her arm, rubbing, rubbing.

Kain and Erica stood like pillars of salt, watching with their mouths open. Callie ditched her pack and scrabbled back down the brutal rocks they'd climbed just minutes ago, her goal the slippery section near the waterline, low enough and wide enough for the swimmers to come ashore. She stood panting, pointing the camera in their general direction, but couldn't bring herself to focus on the viewfinder.

The two men were tiring.

"Adam! Jack! You have to come in," she yelled, but the wind grabbed her words and flung them into the mountains.

Finally the two men began to swim for the position where she stood, and she was glad of her orange jacket to guide them to shore in the failing light. Her heart hammered against her ribcage. The sea was still rising, sometimes slopping across her boots, but she ignored it.

Adam drew close, but he couldn't grip the slimy rock. Each time, the sea sucked him away. She shoved the camera in her pocket and tried to grab him, but he was pulled from her grasp, and she felt her back muscles scream.

"Kain!" Callie screamed. Still on the platform above, he stared at her, eyes wide. "Help me get him in!"

Finally his paralysis broke. He shouldered out of his pack and clambered down to where she stood. His strong arms grabbed Adam's hand on the next heave of water, and hauled him ashore over the rock.

Adam lay gasping, and Callie looked back to Jack. She grabbed the camera again and pointed it towards him, out of some inexplicable instinct to honor his wishes, and thought: *Am I filming his death?* He was maybe twenty meters from shore now, caught in the current. He was trying to swim, but his arms slopped feebly against the waves.

Kain's voice boomed, startling Callie. "Swim across the current, Jack! Don't swim against it!"

Jack seemed to hear and struck out in a different direction. After just a few strokes, he disappeared under a huge swell. When he finally came up, he sputtered and looked around desperately.

Callie realized she was weeping aloud. *Oh God, save him.*

Kain cast his boots and jacket aside and dived into the water, striking out smoothly towards Jack. Even his effortless strokes weren't fast enough, and Jack disappeared again.

The tawny head reappeared, mouth gaping to suck in air, just as

Kain reached him. In one fluid movement Kain tucked him under his arm in the lifesaving position. He pulled him back across the heaving water with efficient, practiced strokes.

Drawing near to Callie, Kain trod water, and judged his approach. He swept ashore on the peak of the wave, dragging Jack with him, their clothes and flesh tearing against the rock. The two lay tangled, Kain catching his breath while Jack vomited seawater and heaved with shock and exhaustion.

Kain clambered upright and began a first-aid assessment of Jack, while glancing over his shoulder at Adam, who was shivering violently and weeping in gasps.

"Where was Kain when Bryan was sinking?" Erica said, materializing at Callie's shoulder. "Surely if anyone could have saved him, he was the one."

Callie snapped, "Everyone reacts differently to shock." But disturbingly similar questions were swirling in her own mind.

8

WE WERE SUPPOSED TO BE EATING AT A RESTAURANT TONIGHT. THAT was all Jack could think of as a small part of his brain listened to Callie and Rachel rummaging in packs behind him. Not much food left—why would there be? They were meant to be in a hotel.

A friend was dead, seven lives were on the line, and all he could think about was the food he was meant to be eating. Beef maybe, or some succulent NZ lamb. Something hot and fresh and real, and not decreed for him by another. A thought that he could almost taste.

Callie had started it. "There's a steak with my name on it at Milford Sound," she'd said, when they stopped for a break so long ago, before Bryan jumped. "That's all that's keeping me going now."

The promise had sustained him all the way down that last grinding river valley and out along the side of the bay. And now it was like a mind-worm, infesting his head. All he could think about was food.

Retracing their path all the way back around the curve of the bay had been agony, but they didn't know what else to do. Staying out there would have been fatal. The sea hurled itself against the rocks as they walked, and it was even higher now.

Behind him, the group huddled under a flapping tarpaulin, an inadequate refuge from the storm that had fallen like an avalanche. In their midst, a hesitant campfire smoked. Usually, they faced each other round the flames, but not this time, collecting instead in haphazard ones and twos, facing every which way. He could hear some of Callie and Rachel's conversation about getting hot coffee, but the only other human sound was Adam's sobbing, so loud it was audible over the storm. He could think of no reason to turn around and talk to anyone.

They all thought he was such a religious person. Of all the times in his life this was the moment to pray, and yet he couldn't summon a single word to his Maker.

So Jack stared at the sea, seething out there in the gloom. Although he'd traded his wet clothing for thermals and waterproofs, the cold still reached the center of his soul. His body was seized by wave after wave of uncontrollable shivering.

Lightning sheeted overhead every few seconds, its flash freeze-framing the water in yet another brutal contortion. *Frothing at the mouth. It wants to tear us to pieces if the mountains don't manage to do it.*

Callie came to sit beside him, two weak cups of coffee in her hands. He made room but didn't look at her. The cup registered warm between his hands, but didn't cheer him. He brought it to his lips, because that was what you did with a cup, and because he knew at some intellectual level that he needed its heat. It scalded his mouth and throat.

He spoke quietly, just to her. "You know we're all dead now, don't you."

"You can think that if you want, but don't you dare say it in front of the others." There was heat in her answer. "I'm not putting on my positive face because I feel terrific. I'm doing it because misery will kill us faster than anything. I need you Jack. I can't do it by myself. Don't let me down now."

He stared at his feet. *Great, she chases pretty boys forever and finally turns to me when I've got nothing to give.*

"I want to think the best, Cal, but the maps, the GPS, the emergency beacon, the satellite phone—they were all in Bryan's backpack that is now somewhere out there." He pointed at the ocean.

"Even if we could retrace our route, which is unlikely, and by some miracle do it in the same time, we've got people who can't last another ten days." He didn't have to be explicit about Rachel and Sharon. "We haven't seen another human being. We're exhausted and frightened. Soon we'll be very hungry. It's like you said: Bryan is crazy, not stupid. He's planned this execution carefully. His murder weapon is his blasted Shadow Land."

She took a long time to reply. "That's not the whole truth. You haven't mentioned the things in our favor."

"Such as?"

"We have ten days hands-on bush craft training from a man who knew these mountains intimately, and probably didn't even realize he was teaching us. We have shelter and specialist clothing. We're hardly going to die of thirst." She gestured towards the rainwater streaming from the edges of the tarp. Jack rolled his eyes, but it was true: water was always the biggest issue in any survival situation. "We have two strong men over there, even if one of them is a basket case at the moment. We have a nurse on the team. We have a couple of peacemakers who'll stop us being too nasty to each other." She paused a moment and added, deadpan: "And right here on this rock we have a couple of the best brains in the world."

The joke was corny but he appreciated the effort, and gave her half a smile.

She continued, "As for food, there's deer, birds, fish. And plenty of vegetation. Surely we can find something edible. In fact you can help me look for something now if you like."

"Who gets to be the taste-tester, to see if it's poisonous? I vote for Kain." He was only half-joking.

"That's nice, considering he just saved your life."

Jack felt the rebuke all the more strongly because it was justified. He stood, snapped his jacket hood up over his head, and stomped off into the rain. He was embarrassed to have been so ungracious, especially in front of Callie, but there was an undercurrent within him about Kain. It would be childish to resent owing his life to a rival, but something sinister niggled at his brain. Why did the proud surf lifesaver take so long to come and get him out there in the roiling bay? It seemed like hours he'd been under that dark water, desperate for air, eternity reaching out for him.

They'd always grated on each other, but it was a big leap from there to letting someone die. As the future disintegrated around them, would he be able to trust Kain?

9

CALLIE BEGAN THE LABORIOUS PROCESS OF MAKING PACKET soup, and wondered about Jack. It wasn't like him to walk off in a huff. Usually he would stand and fight. *Who cares? He shouldn't have spoken like that about Kain.* But she did care. Of all these people, he was the one she needed, although she couldn't have said why.

The dehydrated main meals were all gone, something that had surprised her last night when she'd realized it. Bryan had provisioned the hike only for the exact number of days required to bring them to this point. She had thought a good expedition leader would surely pack extra food in case of unforeseen circumstances. But now she knew that while Bryan was an expert leader, he was not a "good" one. The aroma of evil was rising from every recollection of how Bryan had behaved.

At least he had allowed a little surplus in soups, powdered milk, sugar, tea and coffee. Working out how to ration these now would be a challenge. Who knew how long they might have to last?

First ingredient for the soup was water, and the river was raging thanks to the deluge. The rocks were slick with rain, slimy with moss, and wobbled under her boots. It took several attempts to get the billycan full of water, but she didn't lose it or herself into the torrent. *My strength and balance have improved exponentially.* Instinct told her that keeping sight of the positives would be vital to survival.

As she struggled back with the loaded billycan, half-blinded by the driving rain, Callie was pleased to discover that Rachel had hunted out the remaining soup packets.

"Perhaps we'd better just use one tonight," Callie said. "It'll make a pretty weak soup for eight, but our food will last longer."

Rachel said, "There are only seven of us now." Her eyes brimmed, and she wiped away tears with a jerky movement.

Callie gave her a hug, but kept it brief. Rachel had already been forced to use some of her precious insulin to deal with her body's reaction to the shock of Bryan's leap. Callie tried not to think about how many adrenalin surges might lie ahead for her friend, before this was over. She made her voice as calm and confident as she could. "I can manage here, if you'd like to go and sit with Adam."

Rachel glanced at Adam, hunched on the ground near the edge of the shelter in his waterproofs, as the swirling rain made rivulets down his exposed shoulder. She nodded, sat down wordlessly beside him in the mud, and moved up close, hooking her arm through his, and leaning against his shoulder. He didn't acknowledge her presence, but when Callie looked again later, he was leaning his head on Rachel's, and the sobs had subsided to hiccups.

It took an eternity to heat the icy river water over that petulant campfire. They had used the stove for the urgently-needed hot drinks, but Callie was anxious to preserve what little gas remained.

The billy finally hit the boil just as Jack returned, water cascading from his jacket and streaming down his waterproof trousers. He held the bottom of the jacket out in front of him, and there was something piled up in it. Something curly. In the dim light, Callie couldn't figure out what it was.

"Fern fronds," Jack said, looking pleased with himself.

"Why?"

"You told me to get something we could eat."

"Oh." She stared at them, then at him, then at the fern fronds again. So he wasn't going to resent their last conversation. *Good old Jack. Skin like a rhinoceros.*

"I remember reading somewhere that most ferns are edible, if you get the young curly tips." He shrugged. "At least, I'm pretty sure it was ferns."

"And how do we know that these are not some of the few that aren't edible?" She picked one up and turned it over in her hand.

"Well I ate one, and I'm not dead yet."

"What did it taste like?"

He grinned. "It tasted like chicken."

"Idiot!" She could have kissed Jack for the dumb joke. The knots of tension in her back eased a fraction. She held the fern to her mouth and nibbled cautiously. It wasn't too bad, so she popped the rest in whole, and chewed hard. It was crunchy, with a sweet taste somewhere between lettuce and water chestnut.

She started scooping handfuls of the fern tips into the billycan of watery soup.

"What's the worst that can happen?" she said recklessly, and then became somber as she thought of the many "worsts" that might lie ahead.

Jack rubbed his face vigorously, then shoved his hands hard into his pockets. "I was thinking while I was up there gathering ferns. You were right. We have lots of resources." He tilted his head, one eyebrow raised. "Heck, we've even got duct tape." Callie smiled against her will.

He said, "We got in here; we can get out. Bryan might have planned it to the last tiny detail, but he didn't have much faith in the human spirit. Even we don't know what we're capable of. This is my suggestion: tonight we eat, we sleep, and in the morning we come up with a plan. We can do this, Callie." His expression was earnest and determined.

She held his eyes for a long moment, then nodded, in decision as much as agreement. "Okay. Food, sleep, and then it begins."

***

ONCE THE OTHERS SAW CALLIE AND JACK EATING HUNGRILY, ONE by one they joined in. The first apparent success with bush tucker introduced a tiny ray of hope.

No one mentioned Bryan. It was as if they'd slid into an alternate reality where he had never existed.

They waited as long as they could to make camp, hoping the rain would ease. But as they finally pitched tents, water still coursed from their waterproof clothing and threatened to flood their battered shelters. They lost momentum with the realization that they had only three tents; the fourth was on the bottom of Poison Bay in Bryan's pack. Callie decided to squeeze in with Rachel and Sharon. Jack shared with Adam. The lovebirds remained together in the third. They worked mechanically in the fitful light of their headlamps. The thought flitted through Callie's mind: *We need to conserve these batteries.*

The three women's overloaded tent was unequal to the extreme weather, and leaked wherever they brushed against it. Entombed in their sleeping bags inside the big orange plastic bags, none of them commented on the dampness.

Callie became aware of another sound over the pounding rain. Sobbing. It was Sharon, lying between her and Rachel. Callie felt rather than saw Rachel's arm emerge from her own sleeping bag to enclose Sharon in a hug, and the sobbing increased.

"I loved him. And now he's dead."

"Who?" said Callie.

"Bry-y-an..." she wailed, frustrated.

Rachel's hand paused from hugging just long enough to jab Callie on the shoulder, hard, and she knew she'd be getting glared at if there was enough light to see by.

"Sorry, just being dense." *But seriously, how could anyone fancy a weirdo like Bryan?*

"I always loved him. But he never looked at me. He just wanted Liana."

Rachel said gently, "None of us got a look-in with any of the guys while she was around."

"I hated her so much, and it's my fault she died, and now I'm going to pay for it, like Bryan said I should."

Callie had trouble imagining gentle, smiling Sharon hating anyone. But if anyone could coax unworthy emotions out of someone so sweet, Liana would have been the person for the job. "How can it be your fault?" she said.

"Do you remember how I'd saved up all year, so I could go to the Whitsunday Islands after graduation? She wanted me to give her that money, so she could get an abortion."

"I can see how that would make you feel bad," Rachel said. "But she asked me for money too, and I said no."

"You don't understand. She said she'd kill herself if I didn't help her, and I said, 'Good! Go and kill yourself.' I actually said that to her! She had Bryan all to herself and she didn't care how that made me feel. I would have loved to have his baby, and she just wanted to get rid of it—and even make me pay for it. I couldn't stand it!"

There was a pause before Rachel spoke again. "Lots of people say terrible things when they're angry. You probably didn't think she'd do it. She was always being dramatic."

"I guess so. But I did have this daydream about what it might be like if she wasn't around anymore—not dead exactly, but somehow just not there—so that Bryan forgot about her and noticed me. But then she really did it, and it wasn't anything like the daydream. It was so awful. And all these years… I felt so hor-r-rible…" She dissolved into tears, long spasms of sobbing from deep in her chest.

Rachel rocked her, making soothing noises, and Callie wished there was enough light so she could make eye contact with her friend, and gauge her reaction to these revelations. Had Bryan somehow known about that conversation? Did Liana tell him, or write it in a diary?

Gradually, Sharon's weeping exhausted itself. When she spoke again, her voice was flat. "Liana could have had any of the boys, but she went for Bryan because he had money. She didn't love him. I never cared about his money. And I came on this horrible hike because I thought, maybe… But he still never thought about me. And now he'll never think anything at all, ever again."

Bryan, someone in the world really and truly loved you, thought Callie, tears slipping across her face. *If only you'd seen the value of this woman, and loved her back, how different might your life have been?*

10

Sunday, One Day Lost

THE STORM HAD BLOWN ITSELF OUT AND A NON-COMMITTAL sun lit patches of pale sky.

As the camp came to life, bleary and subdued, Callie thought how much she had been dreading the all-day drive back to Christchurch scheduled for today. How much would she give now to be on that bus, folded into a seat too small for her height? She headed to the river for water, and Jack followed.

"I've been thinking about which way we could go from here," he said. "There was another creek running down into this bay. We could head up there, see what we find."

"We probably should sit down and brainstorm it as a group."

"I wanted to have a plan ready first."

"So we're just pretending to involve the others in the decision, are we?" She was irritated. Jack often seemed to think he knew best.

He answered calmly. "Cal, these people couldn't organize their way out of a wet paper bag right now. If no one has any ideas, they'll be devastated."

Oh. That makes sense. She looked up the side valley, and could see part of a mountain. Cloud hid its peak. She swung around and looked back towards the bay. "What if we walk to the point and try to hail a passing boat?"

"We went as far as we could yesterday. The rock was sheer after that. Rock climber territory."

"How about the other side?"

"Same problem."

Crunching stones alerted them to someone approaching. It was Adam.

"Are you talking about where we should go today?" He was hesitant, his voice nasal from last night's crying. Callie hated to see him reduced in this way. Under normal conditions, Adam the Outdoorsman would have been their default trailblazer.

Jack said, "It seems like going back the way we came would take too long for Rachel, even if we could do it in the same time. I wondered if we should follow the other creek and see if we can get over that mountain to the north. What do you reckon?"

Callie puzzled why the confident Jack of a moment ago had become passive. It hit her that he was deferring to Adam on purpose. Giving the man a chance to be himself again. *Good on you, Jack.*

Adam cleared his throat. "I agree it wouldn't be smart to try to go back. It's the type of terrain that could keep us lost for weeks on end... But what makes you think we should head over that mountain?"

Jack said, "We've been heading roughly north. Milford Sound is in the north of the national park—I did some research at home— and it's big, at least ten or fifteen kilometers long. If we stayed as close to the coast as we could, surely we'd get to it eventually? There'd be people at Milford Sound. We might even intersect the Milford Track, and find some other hikers. It's a popular track— there are dozens of people hiking it every day over the summer."

Adam raised his eyebrows. "On the first day, I wrote 'Milford Sound' as our destination in that guest book at the conservation hut, when Bryan wasn't looking. And I told the cop that's where we were headed, when we were getting in the boat. I thought people should know where we were really going." He sighed. "But Bryan brought us here instead, so it's probably not much use."

"Yes, it is. When they realize we're lost, they'll send someone to check that book. So if we head north, we might get into the search path."

Callie said, "How can we be sure it's not another ten days walk?

Bryan wouldn't have left us near help."

"Whatever we do has risks."

"He might have assumed we'd think the way we came in was the only way out," she said. "He didn't credit us with much initiative."

Adam looked morose. "We haven't shown much, have we? From the beginning, I didn't like Bryan's secrecy about the route. It was strange, and dangerous. The more people who know exactly where you are in a wilderness, the better. But I thought that whoever was supposed to pick us up at Milford Sound must at least know where we were meant to end up, so I let it ride. And now we find out that person doesn't exist. I assumed that even if Bryan didn't want the whole world to know, he would have to outline the real route when he filed his 'intentions form', since it was an official document—but he obviously didn't. Then we should've turned back five days ago when we talked about it. Our tracks were much fresher then. I probably could've found them. And if we'd tackled him as soon as he started talking like a loony last night, we probably could have stopped him jumping."

Jack said, "Or we might just have fallen into the water with him, and lost a couple more of us, or at least had to abandon our packs to save ourselves."

Callie said, "There's no point in 'what ifs'. If we'd known Bryan wanted us dead, we wouldn't have come in the first place. But now we have to find a way to live with reality. What if you two go up the mountain today, see if it's passable? We don't want to waste Rachel's medication on a wild goose chase."

"Sure. If you like," Jack said. He seemed hesitant. "But we all need meaningful activity today. Sitting and waiting won't keep people's spirits up."

Adam said, "The ones who stay behind could look for things to eat."

Jack raised his eyebrows and nodded. "Good idea. Time for a team meeting."

11

WHAT JACK DIDN'T WANT TO SAY, AND DEFINITELY NOT IN front of Callie, was that if anyone was going to test the mountain, it probably shouldn't be him. Rock climbing was hardly in his resume. It tended to involve heights. And heights made all the blood drain from his brain.

For a moment he'd expected a reprieve when Kain seemed affronted that he wasn't the one accompanying Adam. But the idea of "looking after the girls" pacified him and Jack lost his chance.

And so he found himself toiling up the side valley in Adam's wake. The terrain was as difficult as they'd come to expect, with slippery boulders, cloying undergrowth, and deep mud from last night's rain underfoot. They shared one pack for the expedition, containing only water and the emergency warmth and rain-sheltering gear they'd learned to keep near them always. Jack had taken first turn to carry it. Its lightness was a relief. Nevertheless, hiking with little more than fern shoots in his belly made a noticeable difference to his strength.

But there was no shortage of water. Jack decided to be thankful for it, as they stopped for a breather and a drink.

"I was hoping the head of the valley would look easier the closer we got," he said. "But it doesn't."

"No, it looks like a bit of a mongrel. But we have to try, now we've come this far."

"Yeah, I know."

"You know why I came on this blasted hike? Sheena, my girlfriend—she wanted me to. So I could check out a tourist lodge we were thinking of working at in Darwin's off-season, and do it at

Bryan's expense. Stupid, hey?"

"Not really. It makes sense to do it while you're over here."

"I didn't want to see it without her. And I didn't want to see Bryan again or think about Liana and all that rot." He paused. "I had a bit of a thing with Liana, did you know?"

"No, I didn't. Before Bryan?"

"During."

"Oh."

Adam seemed to be deciding whether to speak again. "I even helped her get the gun."

"What!"

"Yep. One of the proudest moments of my life," he said, his tone bitterly sarcastic, his expression grim. "She told me she was pregnant and it was mine. And she'd kill herself if I didn't help her get an abortion. Bryan had refused, apparently. She'd slept with half the school, so I figured she was trying the same line on half a dozen other guys."

"But how did the gun come into it?"

He looked into the distance. "When I wouldn't give her money for an abortion, she asked if she could have enough to buy a gun. I thought she was just being Liana—being a drama queen, and trying to scare me into giving her the bigger amount. So I gave her enough money for a gun, and even told her where to get a cheap one, and how to use it for the best results. I wanted to show her what I thought of her stupid games."

Jack stared at him, gobsmacked.

Adam saw Jack's reaction, and nodded. "You can imagine how good I've felt about that for the past decade. I've never told Sheena, of course. So she couldn't figure out why I wasn't excited about the chance to do our research trip at someone else's expense. I came so I wouldn't have to explain to her what an awful person I was before she ever knew me." His eyes looked suspiciously moist. "Should've proposed to her weeks ago, instead of waiting for Christmas. Now she'll probably never know how I feel."

"You can talk to her on the video if you like, just in case. I'll record it." It didn't occur to Jack to make soothing reassurances that might not be true.

"Really? Thanks. I'll think about it."

"No worries."

"So why did *you* come on the hike from hell?"

"Callie." He hadn't meant to tell the truth, it just slipped out into the confessional pool they seemed to be wading through together.

"Have you told her?"

"No point. She likes beautiful men who are taller than her."

"Bloody women," Adam said. "We do so many stupid things for them." He resumed climbing.

***

THE TEMPERATURE HAD TO BE CLOSE TO FREEZING AT THIS ALTI-tude despite the sunshine, but Jack's face was moist with sweat and his shirt clung to his back. He reached upwards, fingers probing for a handhold as Adam had instructed. A thin trickle of blood crept down his arm from cuts in his palm.

After a long uphill hike to the head of the valley, the hoped-for series of traversable ledges hadn't materialized. Jagged granite fell sheer below him, and he was thankful for the mist beneath them, so that he almost couldn't see how far he had to fall.

He prayed continually and incoherently: *God help me God help me God help me.*

He wanted to live. And he wanted Callie to include him in the "strong men" category. It was foolish to fret about her comment.

But every time his head span and he wanted to feel his feet firm on solid ground, her words did another circuit through his mind. *Yesterday's failure in the ocean was bad enough. I can't give up.*

Adam was above him and to the right. He must have been able to see that Jack was struggling, but he didn't say so.

Their shared rucksack lay far below, in a natural half-cave indented into the base of the cliff. Below that, a long, steep scree of rubble-strewn glacial moraine.

The camera was in his pocket. He'd had it in the head strap at first, until he realized it could only record granite an inch from the lens, to a soundtrack of his gasping breaths.

He stopped and leaned his forehead against the rock face, trying to rest. When he reached up again with a trembling arm, he saw Adam watching him.

"Jack, it's a no go. We'll have to go back down."

"Are you sure?"

"There's not enough handholds, we'll never do it."

Or is it just that you know I'll never do it? Jack pressed his forehead against the rock again. "I don't know if I *can* go back down," he admitted, hating himself.

"I'll find a way past you, and direct you from below."

When they eventually sat resting beside the rucksack, Jack's arms and legs trembled so much that Adam must be able to see it. The full weight of his failure sat on his chest.

Adam said, "It's not exactly the rock climbing wall down at the Y, is it."

"I wouldn't know. I was always too scared to try it."

"Yeah, well, you've been brilliant today. It's just too hard. How would the girls manage? They'd never do it, especially not Shaz. And absolutely not with the rucksacks."

"I guess you're right. Rachel and Callie might manage, but Erica probably hasn't got the upper body strength. If we could only see what's on the other side."

"I might get there eventually, but there's no guarantee I'd find anything useful. And if I fell and killed myself on the other side, how would you know? You'd all wait for help that never came. It was a good idea Jack, but we're going to have to chuck it and try something else."

As he stood on wobbly legs to begin the long trek back to camp, Jack heard a rumbling noise his tired brain could make no sense of. He glanced at Adam in inquiry, but Adam, further out on the platform, was looking up. And then Adam was hurling himself bodily at Jack.

It was like being hit by a train. Jack felt stunning pain down the length of his back as he slammed into the hollow in the cliff face. There was only a nanosecond to wonder why Adam had gone mad, before he was pummeled again, this time by an explosive rush of air. A series of monstrous booms followed, and still Adam had him pinned to the rock face.

As the noise died away, Adam leaned back against the rock wall beside Jack, panting and swallowing hard. Both remained under the shelter of their semi-cave. Jack instinctively fumbled in his pocket for the camera, hoping it had survived the impact of Adam, as his sluggish mind registered that the white puffs in the air before them were made of snow. Snow that, seconds before, had encrusted the top of the mountain hundreds of meters above.

The camera still worked, although the vision jittered from the fierce tremor in the operator's hands. *Thank you God*, thought Jack. He glanced at Adam. "If we'd still been up there…"

Adam said, "As soon as I get my breath back, I'll get you to record that message for Sheena."

***

JACK'S BACK THROBBED WHERE HE'D HIT THE CLIFF FACE. THE downhill run had been quicker than the ascent despite the deep snow now obstructing the upper section, and he hoped they were only about an hour from camp. He could do with a rest. And a square meal too, but that was a thought for another day.

Emerging from a dense rainforest thicket into a small boulder-strewn clearing, Adam close behind him, he saw Callie and Rachel emerging from the bush barely ten meters away. They stopped and stared, and then scrambled towards the men.

"Oh, thank God!"

"You're okay! We didn't know…"

"We heard the boom and saw the avalanche…"

They were enfolded in hugs, and there was a judicious amount of weeping, mostly from the women. Jack couldn't avoid a slight gasp when Callie's hug grabbed his bruised back a little too hard.

"What's wrong?" she said.

Adam answered for him. "He was on the receiving end of a rugby tackle when the snow came down, that's all."

"Your hands! They're bleeding!"

"They're okay," said Jack, shrugging it off manfully, but making no attempt to withdraw from Callie's tender examination. Behind her, Adam grinned at him.

"What about everyone else?" said Jack.

Callie and Rachel exchanged a glance.

Rachel said, "They're fine."

"There was a debate over the best thing to do. Kain said we should wait, in case the search party missed you coming down as we were going up."

"Logical, I s'pose," Adam said.

"But we couldn't bear to think of you lying there injured or trapped, and no one coming to help," said Rachel.

"And I figured we'd see enough of your footprints, and you'd most likely come back down the way you went up," Callie said.

"So we agreed to disagree."

"That's one way of putting it," said Callie with a pert smile. "But tell us, any luck with the mountain?"

They frowned when they heard the route was impassable, but the disappointment was softened by the avalanche: no one wanted to put themselves in the path of another one.

The atmosphere was a mix of tension and relief when they arrived in camp, but Adam was back on form, and soon smoothed things over with some teasing.

The foraging party had come up with fern tips and seaweed to eat, and it didn't even taste too bad, Jack thought, if you squinted and imagined you were somewhere nice, like a tropical island or your own veranda at home with a dog and a slobber-covered tennis ball.

The seaweed had been Erica's idea. "Well, the Japanese eat a lot of it." It didn't mean every variety was safe, but there were no immediate signs of illness, and the saltiness added seasoning to the ferns.

Kain's find had been less popular: a tree loaded with tiny dark berries Bryan had recommended to him days earlier as good "bush tucker". No one was eager to trust Bryan's menu recommendations, but Kain had grabbed as many as he could carry, and displayed them now to Jack and Adam. The berries stood out on stalks like tiny mutant grapes. Apparently, Bryan had eaten one in front of him. Kain said, "How can they be poisonous if Bryan ate one? I tried one, and I'm okay."

Jack put a berry in his mouth, afraid to chew too hard. It was bitter and disgusting. When he felt his tongue start to tingle he spat it out instantly, racing to the river to cup water to his mouth, rinsing and spitting until the vile taste was all gone.

But Kain refused to discard his find. He stripped the berries from their stalks and packed them into one of the ubiquitous snap lock plastic bags they all carried. "They're not ripe yet, that's all. They might still come in handy."

Around the fire as the light faded, they discussed the next step.

Adam said, "Jack and I talked about it, and we think we should retrace Bryan's route for a while, then look for a valley branching off to the east that might lead us over the mountains."

"That huge lake we crossed the first day runs roughly north-south," added Jack, "and it's sixty-five kilometers long. If we put the ocean behind us and head east, we hope we'll eventually hit another part of that lake. Tourist boats should be on it most days. If we start a fire, someone might see the smoke."

"We're hoping to find a shorter route than the one we used to get here. We have to find a way east that doesn't involve cliffs like the one that stopped us today."

There were questions, but no serious opposition to the plan. Fear of the unknown was outweighed by a unanimous horror of trying to retrace the brutal route by which they'd come.

Kain, however, suggested splitting the group. He argued for leaving the weaker members of the party resting near Poison Bay, with shelter and a share of the cooking equipment, while the others went for help. "Once we reach the outside world, we can send rescuers. And they might be rescued sooner, if a fishing boat comes into the bay."

Jack responded with a characteristic lack of tact, heightened by his disquiet about Kain's reluctance to come looking for him earlier that day. "The girls will be in a mess if we leave them here alone. Are you sure you're not looking for your own best chance to survive, without any liabilities to slow you down?"

Kain's tone became snaky. "If I was wanting to leave liabilities behind, you'd be top of the list. You can't even climb one little mountain to save our lives!"

Jack's face reddened. The taunt hit him hard, because he was afraid it was true. "You didn't even try to climb it, or to come looking for us! You just stayed nice and safe down here and looked after Number One."

Kain stepped closer and was drawing breath for another insult, when Adam interjected.

"Shut up, you two!" he demanded. "Can't you see how this is affecting everyone?" Sharon was staring at the ground. Rachel was weeping quietly. Callie and Erica were looking daggers at both combatants.

Kain shrugged; Jack felt ashamed. "Sorry," he muttered, and looked at his feet. *From hero to zero in a couple of hours.*

Adam said, "I don't think we'd be wise to count on accidental rescue. We need to make a decision based on the worst-case scenario, and we need to do it democratically. Let's vote on it."

Sharon said, "I'll do whatever everyone else wants." She didn't need Kain's or Jack's university education to know what a liability was.

"Yes, me too," said Rachel.

Both Rachel and Sharon abstained from the vote, but it was conclusive nevertheless. Kain was the only one who wanted to split the party.

"And there's something else," Adam said. "After the avalanche, Jack recorded a message from me for Sheena, just in case. Telling her where to find the engagement ring, that sort of thing." He shrugged and cleared his throat. "I thought I'd mention it in case anyone else wanted to do it too."

Even Jack could tell Adam had dropped a clanger; the timing was wrong. There were murmurs and fidgeting, but Kain was first to speak. "How will that help, if none of us survive to take the video home? Or have we decided Jack will be the last man standing, emerging from the wilderness to win awards for his stupid movie?"

Jack didn't rise to the bait, but he did answer, because Kain's logic was flawed. "Actually, I don't have to survive. Only the camera does, and it's pretty tough. Searchers would probably find it one day with my stuff." He copped a glare from Callie. *Oops. Double clanger.*

"Can we please stop talking as though we're going to die?" she said. "We're all getting out of here. We help each other. We focus on the thought of going home. We get up in the morning and get on with it."

12

Monday, Two Days Lost

THEIR PACKS WERE LADEN WITH FERN TIPS AND SEAWEED AS they set off eastwards into the cool early light, leaving Poison Bay behind. The sun had still to emerge over the mountain tops. Today Callie should have been flying home to her little old Sydney flat, and getting herself ready for work tomorrow.

North and the El Dorado of Milford Sound had failed, so they were heading east, towards the sunrise and Lake Te Anau. Somewhere out there.

Seaweed would be off the menu once they left the ocean behind. They were unlikely to run out of ferns any time soon, but the crunchy curly tips seemed to be the most palatable, and they weren't on all ferns at all altitudes, so everyone agreed to gather as many as they could carry when they were easily available. Rachel filled her pockets with them so she could nibble constantly, in an effort to make the most of the sparse carbohydrates they provided.

With the extra distance of another night's sleep between them and Bryan's death, everyone's spirits seemed stronger—everyone other than Sharon. She had drawn Jack aside before they broke camp, to record a message for her son. Callie had tried to talk her out of it, but Rachel had intervened with a fierce look: "Don't you dare stop her!" Callie had felt rebuked and frustrated.

When they stopped for a midday break, Callie watched Sharon with concern. Her movements were sluggish. She mentioned it quietly to Jack.

He said, "She doesn't complain but I reckon she must be in a lot of pain. Her feet and her back are a mess."

"She's in emotional pain as well. She had a crush on Bryan. Did you know?"

Jack raised his eyebrows. "I thought it was just the worry about her child. You should have seen what she said to him on the video this morning. The way she tried to look positive and strong for him would break your heart."

The vexation of the morning resurfaced. "It seems to have broken her heart too. I don't know why you had to do such a thing."

"Steady on, Cal. She asked, and I wasn't going to turn her down. If she doesn't get home, do you want to be the one to explain to her son why you denied him that piece of his mother?"

"Are you sure that's the only reason you did it?"

"What do you mean?"

"That video's going to make a great story."

"So that's what you think of me?" He stared at her, and he looked sterner than she'd ever seen him.

But she still didn't stop. "I guess I'm just hoping you haven't turned into one of those journalists who feast on human suffering. Like carrion."

He stared at her in silence, then turned away. She felt confused and annoyed. And bereft.

13

ELLEN CARPENTER WOKE BATHED IN SWEAT, EARLY MORNING sunlight pouring in the window of her Brisbane bedroom and baking her rumpled sheets. She fumbled for her glasses and looked at her clock radio. Only a couple more hours before she was due to collect Rachel from the airport.

The humidity was suffocating, and a nameless dread sat heavily on Ellen's chest. Her daughter's flight from Christchurch was already in the air. Was she having a premonition of some disaster?

Probably just a hot flush. She sat up and shook her head to try to clear the anxiety, dislodging Mango, the ginger cat, from his place of honor on her bed. The dark hair that usually waved softly round her face was plastered to her neck with sweat, and she flicked it with her hands, trying to get some air onto her skin. Mango stalked off down the hall as she trudged to the bathroom with a cooling shower in mind.

She thought of how the cat was never allowed on the bed when Roger was alive. A shaft of grief hit her as she got in the shower, and she wept. *Oh Roger, I miss you. Rachel, get home safely.*

The weeping was therapeutic, and Ellen was in a much better frame of mind by the time she arrived at the airport. She'd even had a good breakfast, something Roger always insisted on. She saw "LANDED" beside Rachel's flight number on the airport monitor. Premonitions were nonsense.

Over the next two hours, her relief evaporated, one drop at a time. Time after time, the doors from the Customs area swished open complacently, but no Rachel walked through, only more strangers wheeling luggage-laden trolleys. Again and again, Ellen saw delighted recognition as travelers caught sight of their loved ones. But it was never her turn to wave and call out. At first, she was irritated. *Why are they keeping her so long? I'm going to be late for my two o'clock lecture!* But as the morning dragged on, her students were forgotten.

"I'm sorry madam, your daughter wasn't on this morning's flight," confirmed the airline official. "She probably just missed the plane. Do you have a contact number for her in New Zealand?"

Ellen knew it wasn't sensible to get too frightened about Rachel just yet. *I'll go home and wait for her to call,* she told herself firmly, even gathering enough presence of mind to phone the university and cancel her afternoon lecture, so she'd be free to collect Rachel from a later flight. *There's probably already a message waiting for me at home.*

There was no message at home.

The New Zealand contact numbers Rachel had left on a neat list yielded no information, just the disturbing news from the youth hostel that Rachel had not checked in last night, nor did she have a reservation. Ellen gave the names of Rachel's companions. None of them had reservations either, any time this week. It didn't make sense.

14

THEY MADE THEIR WAY STEADILY BACK UP THE VALLEY THEY'D descended two days ago. Callie watched Adam, in the lead, search for a stone impressed into the mud here, a broken branch there, to show which way they'd come. Their tracks had been largely erased by the torrential rain.

After he spent an hour leading six people up and down the same section looking for a passable route, Adam called a team meeting. "When we hit the tricky bits, I'd better go on ahead. It's stupid for us all to be scrambling around and wasting our energy."

In that moment, Callie realized just how much knowledge of these impossible valleys had died with Bryan. She felt their lostness deep in her bones.

Jack had his camera out again during the discussion, and when their eyes met for a moment, she saw no friendship, just cold defiance. She felt even more lost.

Mid-afternoon, Adam stopped and waited for the rest of the group to draw level. They shuffled among mossy tree trunks, slippery rocks and dense undergrowth to find a spot close enough to hear easily.

"Up there," Adam indicated with his arm through a gap in the tree canopy, "I think we might find a way over into the next valley. What does everyone else think?"

There was a murmur of agreement.

Five minutes later as they headed for this new valley, a bird—fluffy, brownish, the size of a small hen—startled from the ground near Adam's feet. He reacted quickly, began to run after it, and chaos ruled as others joined the pursuit. The bird was nowhere to be seen, but there were altogether too many hiking boots pounding the ground, thundering under the weight of loaded rucksacks.

Callie shouted, "Stop running! Don't move." Her voice carried authority, and they all stopped dead and turned to stare.

"That bird was nesting," she said.

"So what?" Erica demanded.

She ignored her, and addressed the group as a whole, her arms stretched wide. "What do birds do on nests?"

It took a moment or two, but Rachel got it. "They lay eggs!"

They stood still as statues while Adam carefully retraced his steps, and began probing the undergrowth where the bird had risen. And there they were. Three beautiful, mottled eggs. There would be protein for dinner tonight.

***

CALLIE WANTED TO CRY OR THROW UP AS SHE ABSORBED THE REport from their scouts, but she tried to look calm instead.

Adam and Kain had looked for a mountain pass to lead them eastwards, from this valley to the next one.

There was no pass. Not for people of their ability.

Adam was limping badly from a fall down part of the rock face, and negativity radiated from both men.

Adam addressed the group. "We have to decide what to do today with the daylight we've got left. And that probably depends on what we're going to do tomorrow."

Kain said, "If everyone is determined to stick together, I think we should either try to find Bryan's route home, or set up a decent camp and wait to be rescued. These mountains are crazy. They're going to kill us."

Callie realized with a start that what she was seeing on Kain's face was fear. For the first time, he was transparently rattled. *Why now? Why not yesterday or the day before? What happened up there?*

"Maybe it would be better if we stayed in one place," Erica said hesitantly. "I didn't think it was such a good idea last night, but I didn't realize how hard it would be to find a way."

Jack said, "We're a million miles from anywhere, we're hard to see from the air, and Bryan would have made sure that if they do look for us, it will be in the wrong place. It could take weeks for them to find us, and Rachel has only a few days' worth of her medical supplies left."

"Yes, but we shouldn't risk everyone else's life for the sake of mine." Rachel's voice broke a little, but she pulled herself together. "We should do what's best for everyone."

"To hell with that!" Callie said. She didn't feel like crying anymore; she felt like punching someone. "Everyone includes you. Even if no one else wants to help you, I'm going to do whatever I can to get you out of here in time to save your life."

"Settle down, Callie," Adam said. "No one wants anyone to die."

Jack sighed in a way Callie recognized as a warning: bluntness was coming. "Look, no one ever likes the way I put it, but it's time to start saying the hard things. We absolutely must see what we're choosing. If we try to go back the way we came, Rachel will die, because even if we can find our tracks, it will take too long. If we make camp and live like castaways, Rachel will still almost certainly die, because it'll take them too long to find us."

Kain said, "No disrespect to Rachel, but there's risks for everyone else too."

"I agree," Jack said. "There are plenty of risks in trying to hike out, especially now we don't have Bryan to help us recognize danger. For most of us it might be less risky to stay put, although we shouldn't kid ourselves that it's 'safe'. This isn't Gilligan's Island.

There's all sorts of hazards, even when we're just looking for food—don't forget yesterday's avalanche."

Adam said, "So what are you suggesting?"

"I volunteer to help Callie try to get Rachel home alive. Most likely, we'd head south in the morning and look for another valley going east, although that's open for discussion. Everyone else must make up their own mind. I'd rather we stick together, because there's more of us to help each other when things go wrong. But I can see the case that Kain is making, too. If we do split the group I think we should keep the sub-groups as big as possible. Erica and Sharon might be better off to go back to Poison Bay and camp near the ocean, but they're not that strong and both injured, so they need at least one man with them to do the heavy lifting."

The silence that followed swirled with uncertainty, but Callie was glad to see Jack and Kain making an effort to work together for once.

"What about this for an idea?" she said. "There's not much light left, so we make camp now, and rest, and decide in the morning when we're fresh." Jack made eye contact with her, and nodded. She felt a tiny surge of joy at the reconnection.

"Yeah, and don't forget we've got eggs for dinner." Adam attempted a smile.

But the thrill of the eggs as a triumph of survival had worn off. They now looked more like a condemned man's last meal.

15

ELLEN DIDN'T GET A CALL FROM RACHEL. AT 2.00 P.M. SHE didn't call. At 3.00 p.m. she didn't call. At 4.00 p.m. she didn't call. At 5.00 p.m. she didn't call.

At 6.00 p.m., Ellen called her local police station.

The constable who answered was pleasant and sympathetic, but Ellen could tell that not much would be done yet. There would be a protocol to follow. People went missing every day, and most of them turned up.

How could she persuade them that Rachel would have found some way to get a message home? That she wouldn't leave her mother waiting and wondering all this time, not after the hellish year they'd had since Roger's death.

But then again, maybe the stress and loneliness of the past year had driven her nuts. Maybe Rachel was actually coming on tomorrow's flight. Maybe Rachel was at this minute laughing with her friends, unaware of her mother's fear. Maybe.

At 2.00 a.m., Ellen went online and bought a ticket on the morning flight direct to Queenstown.

***

ELLEN STARED DOWN AT SNOWY PEAKS FROM HER WINDOW SEAT, 66G, back near the toilets. She and Roger had been to these very mountains long ago, before they were married. Such a chaste holiday, by modern standards. They had slept in separate dorms at the youth hostel, hiked around the impressive lake holding hands, smiled shyly at one another, and declared these to be the most astonishing mountains in the world.

Today they just looked cruel.

She knew, geologically speaking, that they had been thrust upwards through the earth's crust. But from the air, they looked as if they'd been clawed from the earth by the fingernails of a giant hand.

Three hours to go, she thought, counting down to the time she could reasonably expect to present herself at the front counter of the Te Anau police station. The tiny town where Bryan Smithton lived was the closest center of population to the wilderness Rachel had hiked into. Surely the police would find it harder to stick to cold protocol with her standing right in front of them?

As her flight descended, a metallic glint caught her eye. Could it be a search plane? *Patience Ellen. Not yet, but soon.*

***

SERGEANT PETER HUBBLE WILLED HIMSELF TO RELAX HIS WHITE knuckles, to allow his lungs to inflate with air, and then expel it, in and out, in and out. The plane lurched as a thermal updraft caught it, and he grabbed the door handle, even though it was such a stupid thing to do. As if a flimsy metal door handle would save him from becoming a smear on a mountain. More likely he'd accidentally open it.

In his line of work, he knew only too well how many light planes crashed in these crazy-beautiful mountains. He looked with envy at the huge airliner descending into Queenstown. This little thing was smaller than the old Mini Minor he'd driven in his student days, and rattled even more loudly. At least a big plane offered safety in numbers. You could all go down together, singing Kumbaya.

His long legs were folded awkwardly into the cramped footwell, and the narrow seatbelt cut into his beer belly, but he wouldn't have minded making it tighter. *At least this meant I could be at Tahlia's birthday party. It's worth a couple of hours of near-death experience to spend time with my little girl. My little girl who just became an adult, and barely knows I'm alive.*

Ted the pilot turned his way and grinned. "We could fly over the Fiordland mountains too. Great day for thermals. Nice bit of rock'n'roll."

"When we get home I'm going to find some pretense to arrest you. A night in a cell would be just the thing."

Ted chuckled and shook his head. "That's a very dangerous thing to say while you're still in the air."

Peter closed his eyes and groaned.

16

Tuesday, Three Days Lost

THE FIRST SNOWFLAKES DRIFTED OUT OF A LOWERING SKY, landing soft and cold on Jack's face as they struggled out beyond the tree line.

He was at the back of the line again, with six people ahead of him. This morning's decision had ended up being unanimous. They would stick together.

And then they'd discovered this shy little valley, with what looked to be a fairly civilized mountain pass at its head. Everyone's spirits lifted as they made good progress, hopeful of crossing to the next valley before nightfall.

Until the weather closed in.

Now, the temperature was dropping fast and Jack watched Sharon with concern. Every inch of progress over the uneven ground was more of a stumble than a step, and the twisting action on her ankles and knees had to be agonizing, but she just kept moving, seemingly oblivious.

Jack grabbed a strap dangling from Callie's rucksack, just ahead of him, and tugged on it. She turned and looked at him with tired eyes, her breathing audible with the exertion of the steep incline. He nodded in Sharon's direction. Callie turned just in time to see Sharon fall sideways against a large boulder. She slid to the ground and crumpled, defeated.

Callie shouted, "Erica!"

Further up, Erica turned around, took in Sharon's situation at a glance, and began to clamber back down those hard-won meters of mountain. "Sharon!" she called, but there was no response.

Progress stopped. There was now something more urgent than getting over that mountain pass.

***

JACK WATCHED CALLIE AND RACHEL HUDDLE CLOSE TO SHARON, wrapping their arms around the foil first-aid blanket that enveloped her, willing her to warm up. She showed little sign of life other than the staccato shivers that shook her body in waves. Erica and the men discussed the prognosis as though Sharon wasn't there, and in a way, she wasn't.

Erica said, "I'm pretty sure it's hypothermia, plus probably shock. It's serious stuff. We've got to get her warm. Those damp jeans of hers aren't helping."

"She shouldn't be up here at all," Kain said, with a venomous look at Jack.

Adam said, "It wasn't Jack's decision."

"Oh really?" Kain said. "Are you quite sure we'd be here right now if he hadn't said all that stuff about *me* when we were back at Poison Bay? And now we all die because Sharon can't keep going."

"Stop it, Kain!" Erica hissed. "What's *wrong* with you? She's sitting right there!"

Adam said, "Let's figure out an answer that helps us all survive. Will she be warmer if she moves, or does she need to rest?"

"I'm not really sure," Erica said. "I'm no paramedic. In a hospital ward we'd give her warmth and fuel, preferably IV glucose."

Rachel cut in. "What about my glucose tablets? We could give her some of those."

They all turned and stared. Rachel's meager remaining supply could be the difference between life and death for herself.

The group focus shifted to Erica, reluctant team medic. "Maybe if we just gave her one, that might help," she hedged.

Adam said, "And we need to try and get over this mountain. How about I carry her? I'll give her a piggy-back, if she can hang on. If one of you guys takes my pack, and the other takes Sharon's, we can at least keep moving."

Kain said, "It's too dangerous scouting a route in this weather with two packs on. We have to get over that pass. Hurry!" He turned and started back up the mountain, leaving the load-sharing problem behind him.

Jack stared at his retreating back.

Callie said, "It's okay. He's probably right about a scout needing mobility. I can carry Sharon's pack, clipped to the front of mine. Jack, can you manage Adam's as well as your own?"

"I'll give it a go," he replied. "Kain's definitely right about one thing—we need to get over this pass before the snow gets any worse."

***

ANOTHER HOUR, AND THE WIND HAD RISEN, AND THE TOP OF THE pass seemed as far away as ever—what little they could see of it. The snow swirled into their faces, stinging their skin. Jack's eyelashes were working overtime to keep the snow out of his eyes, and he knew they would soon freeze into hard spikes. He longed for his snow goggles, lying in the back of a cupboard at home, souvenir of an ill-judged ski trip seven years ago.

His heart pounded with the effort of supporting the extra dragging weight of Adam's rucksack as well as his own. Attached to his front, it banged forcefully on his knees each time he tried to reach a foot up to the next rock. He'd tried it on his back, but it pulled his center of gravity too far backwards, and threatened to send him tumbling down the mountainside to a messy death.

Ahead of him, Callie labored with Sharon's pack. She'd always complained about how she'd like to be petite, but her strong frame was a godsend today.

A little further up, Adam kept making determined, laborious progress up the mountain with Sharon strapped to his back. He had begun with his arms hooked under her knees, as though piggy-backing a child, but she had been too weak to grip his shoulders effectively, and he'd also had no hands available to steady himself in a stumble on the uneven ground. Rachel had been the one to suggest they use a rope and a small tarp like a large papoose to strap Sharon on, and it was a much better solution.

They hiked close together now, not strung out over a hundred meters or so, as they had done. They needed to be close to each other, and not just for emotional reasons. As the visibility dropped, it became all too easy to lose someone in the whiteout.

17

"Peter!" Amber exclaimed, as he walked in the front door of his tiny police station. He'd been home for a quick shower to wash the anxiety of the flight away, and now he wanted to take the pulse of his station and his team.

"You're back early," she said.

"Quick, better look like you're working." He knew she'd take it as a joke, since she was the least idle person he'd ever met. As well as managing their watch house where offenders were detained before transfer to Invercargill, Amber was his front-desk interceptor and all-round source of the local knowledge no one else would tell him. A duffel bag lying on the floor against the counter caught his eye. "What's this?"

Amber nodded towards a woman sitting in their "waiting room", a glorified name for two upright chairs off to the side. "It belongs to Mrs Carpenter. She's just arrived from Brisbane. She says she's staying here until she can see the officer in charge."

Peter raised one eyebrow at her, and turned to greet the woman in jeans and t-shirt now rising from one of the chairs. A slender, elegant woman, fairly sensible looking, but behind the fashionable glasses her eyes showed signs of recent tears. *Tread carefully, Peter,* he thought.

"Peter Hubble." He held out his hand to her. She shook it firmly and replied, "Ellen Carpenter."

"What seems to be the trouble?"

"My daughter's missing. She was due home in Brisbane yesterday, but she wasn't on the plane, and she hasn't called."

Amber chimed in: "Rachel Carpenter, twenty-seven, on a

tramping expedition led by Bryan Smithton. We got a call from Interpol this morning. Tom checked with DOC and the panic date is two weeks away." Peter read the message in the look Amber gave him. Tom was his right-hand man, and had responsibility for Search And Rescue. He had followed correct procedure, and there were no grounds for action yet, but explaining that to a distraught relative was quite a different matter. Especially a relative determined enough to cross the Tasman Sea within twenty-four hours of a no-show.

Ellen said, "Please take me seriously." Her look was intense. "Rachel is an insulin-dependent diabetic. And she's a thoughtful, compassionate girl. She wouldn't leave me wondering." She rummaged in her handbag, and he could see her fingers tremble. "I've brought the itinerary she left me, just so you can see how careful she is." There was a slight catch at the edge of the last word.

Peter touched her elbow and she looked up at him. "Why don't you come through to my office. Amber, would you mind keeping Mrs Carpenter's luggage behind the counter please. And get me that form from DOC."

After he'd got her seated in his simple office, Peter started making conversation. "So Mrs Carpenter, how far have you come today?"

"Please call me Ellen. I've come from Brisbane. I managed to get a direct flight to Queenstown, and then a shuttle bus down here."

"A busy day then."

"Yes, and not the most restful night's sleep before it." She gave a hint of a wry smile. "I realize I probably sound like a loony. My husband died a year ago, and Rachel has been my support through it all. If she was going to be late, she would find a way let me know. The group had a satellite phone. The fact that she hasn't called must mean she can't. I know there will be rules you have to follow, but I need to convince you that something really is wrong."

She fumbled to pull several sheets of paper out of her handbag and thrust them at Peter. He smoothed them on the desk in front of him, reading quietly. It was a detailed document. Flight arrival and departure times, addresses and phone numbers of Bryan Smithton and the accommodation in Christchurch, where they would be and what they would be doing on different days, a list of the other members of the party and even the contact details of some of their families. If something had happened out there, this list would be a head start for the investigating officers.

"Have you called any of these people?"

"Yes. Callie's mother wasn't certain exactly when she was due back. Jack lives with his parents and they were expecting him yesterday. They're worried. Sharon's parents haven't heard anything either and they're beside themselves. They'd gone to the airport with balloons. She'd never been overseas before so it was a really big deal for them. They're minding her little boy."

"I see."

"What was your officer saying before, about the doctor and panicking?"

"About what?" His frown cleared. "You mean DOC and the panic date. DOC is the Department of Conservation. When tramping parties go into the national park they're required to register their intentions. They list a 'panic date', so that we know when to send the search parties. Sometimes people get delayed a day or two by a flooded river or what-have-you, and sensible trampers have extra supplies to allow for that. Bryan Smithton is definitely a sensible tramper. He would also be able to find food in the environment if necessary. Searches are expensive and difficult. As a rule, we can't launch a proper search until we pass the panic date, and apparently it's still two weeks away." He privately thought it a long panic date, even for someone with Bryan's skill, but he kept that to himself.

"Two weeks! I'm sure Rachel didn't have enough supplies for that long."

"Do you know how much she did have?"

"Not exactly. She definitely took extras of everything, she's very careful—she's been on long hikes before in Tasmania. But I'd be surprised if they'd last her more than a week, less if she can't eat the right things." Her voice was measured, but he saw her swallow hard.

Footsteps approached, and Amber appeared to hand Peter a form.

"Where were they going?" he said.

"George Sound," Amber said.

Memory clicked and he looked at the dates on Ellen's paper-work again. "That's the group I saw leaving the other week. Tom's cousin took them across the lake. Amber, can you check when they're booked to come back? If they're not booked with him, check the others."

"Sure."

"Ten days. Helluva long time to be tramping George Sound." Peter frowned at the form. "Surely five days would be more than enough." *Something doesn't add up in all this, but I don't know what it is.*

"I thought so too. But sometimes he goes off-track to do nature studies or photography or something."

"Possible. I'll pop round to Bryan's house on my way home, see if there's anything going on there, check with the neighbors." He turned to Ellen. "And I'll drop you at your hotel. You need a good meal and a rest."

"So, will you start searching?" Ellen said a few minutes later, as she buckled her seat belt.

"Not today, it's too late. And there's things we need to do first. But I hear your concern. Bear in mind, Bryan Smithton is very experienced. He'd have a mountain radio, emergency beacons, the works. He'll be able to cope with most things."

Ellen drew breath to interrupt, but he cut her off. "No, hear me out. I understand your anxiety—it's possible Bryan didn't know about her diabetes when he filled in the DOC form. So we'll check everything we can, make sure we know what we're dealing with. Okay?"

"Okay. Thank you, Sergeant."

"Call me Peter. We don't go in for formality here."

"Okay, thank you Peter."

He pulled up in front of Ellen's lake-front hotel. It was expensive, but probably the only place she'd been able to get a booking at short notice.

"Now, Ellen, I'm serious about what I'm about to tell you." She nodded solemnly. "You need a proper meal with meat and vegetables, a shower, and then a rest. Lie down, even if you think you'll never sleep. That's a police directive. Okay?"

"Yes sir," she replied with a shaky smile.

"I'll call you here at the hotel when we know something."

***

BRYAN'S HOUSE LOOKED NEAT AND BARE LIKE IT ALWAYS DID, NOT that Peter had ever been invited inside. He was glad of those bald curtainless windows today, and the evening sun slanting in. He didn't want to force entry yet, but most of the rooms were visible anyway. The weirdest thing was the grid pattern on the living room floor. Masking tape, by the look of it. Who knew what that was about.

As he came around the side of the house, he heard the screen door swing and snap into place next door, followed by shuffling footsteps. "Oh it's you Peter," said a thin, warbling voice. "How are you dear? And how was Tahlia's party?"

"Great thanks Doreen, to both questions." He smiled and leaned on the fence. She seemed to have become even thinner in the week he'd been gone. The chemo was taking its toll.

"Are you looking for Bryan?" she asked.

"Yes, have you seen him?"

"He's been gone a week or two. He had a big group of friends here. So lovely to hear young voices and all that laughing. He spends far too much time alone. Arthur!" she called towards the house.

Steady footsteps sounded on the floorboards and a balding head appeared. "Is everything okay?"

"Of course, lovey. Do you remember what day Bryan had all those lovely young people in the house?"

"Oh hello Peter. How was the party?"

"Good thanks."

Arthur looked at least ten years younger than his sick wife, although Peter knew they'd been in the same year at school together.

"I think it must have been Wednesday, week before last. Remember Doreen, we had to go down to Invercargill for your treatment the next day."

"So you haven't seen him since then? Or anything else unusual?" Peter said.

"No, not a squeak out of the place," Arthur said. "But he did have a lot of deliveries over the past few weeks. That was unusual."

"Deliveries?" It didn't seem relevant, but his curiosity was aroused.

"I asked him and he said they were tramping supplies from Dunedin," Doreen said.

"Lots of rucksacks and things," Arthur affirmed. "I saw them all laid out in his living room later on."

"I see. Well thanks for your help."

"Is anything wrong?" Doreen said.

"He's just a bit late back from the tramping trip, that's all."

"Oh well, he's very experienced," Arthur said. "I'm sure they'll be all right. Just a flooded river or something."

"Yes, of course they will," said Doreen, and turned back to Peter. "And how is Tom's little girl?"

"I haven't actually seen Tom yet. I only got back from Auckland an hour ago. But Lily went into remission about six months ago."

Arthur frowned. "I think that might have changed. He was down at Invercargill with her the day we were there. She was having a round of chemo, the poor wee thing."

"That's awful," said Peter, taken aback. *I wonder why he didn't tell me she was having treatment again.* It wasn't like Tom to withhold any news about his treasured family, good or bad. "I've probably been too caught up in my own silly problems to notice." He sighed and scratched his ear.

"I'm sure they're not silly problems," declared Doreen stoutly. "Anyway, we all get distracted by our daily muddle at times." She smiled and headed back towards the house on Arthur's arm. He watched her go, every step a careful one, and found his mind's eye suddenly full of little Lily Granton at last year's office Christmas party. Her eyes much too big in a face far too thin; the quiet carefulness of her older brother, making sure the games didn't get too rough for her—only about nine himself. He should have been pulling his little sister's hair and putting frogs down her dress—not carrying the weight of the world.

Peter sighed again and walked over to peer into Bryan Smithton's living room window again. He did a quick count of the masking-tape grid. Eight spaces. They must have been for the rucksacks and supplies. Ellen Carpenter had mentioned that Bryan paid for all his guests, and supplied their equipment. The grid made sense now, even if it was still pretty weird.

***

PETER'S ROUTE HOME TOOK HIM NEAR TOM GRANTON'S PLACE. ON impulse, he turned into the street and pulled up near the letterbox of number forty-seven. He turned off the engine, and sat for a moment as it ticked and settled. The front door was open, and he could hear faint sounds from a game show on the television inside.

"What am I doing here?" he wondered aloud. He was reaching for the ignition key to restart the car and head home, when a movement at the door caught his eye. It was Nyree, with a pajama-clad toddler perched on her hip. She'd seen him and waved, her face breaking into a huge smile.

He returned the wave, got out of the car and walked across the grass, skirting a blue tricycle being held together mostly by rust.

"Welcome home, Peter. How was your holiday?"

"Good thanks, Nyree. Good to be home though. I don't fancy the big smoke so much these days."

She laughed. "Who would? Come on in for a beer. I'm putting this one to bed, but I'd love to hear how it all went. Ted was just on the phone telling me how much you enjoyed the flight home." She was teasing him now. The pilot was another of Tom's cousins, and lived in the next street.

"Yeah, and I can't wait to throw him in the lockup if I catch him dropping litter or parking his car too far from the curb."

Nyree laughed again. "You go through, Peter, and I'll be out in a minute. Tom will be home soon."

He passed between the kids and their television, but they paid him little attention. He saw Lily slumped at one end of the lounge. She looked even thinner, a pink beanie on her head. Her hair must have fallen out again. Peter's heart ached for her—for all of them.

He walked through the kitchen to the patio, and went to a battered folding camping chair that creaked as he sat. The Granton's big rangy dog materialized from under the house, and flopped down at Peter's feet. His warm flank made contact with Peter's ankle—the ultimate expression of canine approval. "Hello Hank," Peter said, and rubbed the dog's ears. Hank's strong tail thumped the ground, one-two-three.

Nyree emerged juggling not just two beer cans, but a steaming bowl of stew, fork embedded, which she plonked on the folding table at Peter's elbow. Peter looked at it, and then grinned at her. "How did you know I hadn't eaten?" She waved a hand dismissively and sat in the mismatched folding chair next to him.

It was very good stew, Nyree's famous recipe, rich with tomatoes and kumara and other treasures from the overgrown vegetable garden up near the fence, and crammed with tender venison.

"Still working through last season's hunt?"

"There's a heap of it in the deep freeze. Tom did really well this year."

They had a desultory chat about Tahlia's birthday party, the youth of the guests, the loudness of the music. Nyree's mood changed when Peter mentioned the missing trampers he was investigating.

"It's not as though I'd ever want anything bad to happen to him, but I don't much like that Bryan Smithton. He's so negative about everything that it makes life harder for Tom." This was strong criticism, coming from Nyree.

"I didn't know Tom and Bryan were close."

"They know each other through the hunting club. But lately he started going over to Bryan's place all the time, and he's usually tired and tense when he comes home."

"Probably helping organize this tramp."

"Since Lily got sick again the visits to Bryan seemed to really upset him."

"I didn't know about Lily, Nyree."

"Didn't you?" She looked surprised.

"Doreen and Arthur told me this afternoon. Tom never mentioned it." Peter shrugged uncertainly.

"I wonder why not." She looked down the garden, but her eyes were seeing something other than the evening light on the trees. "She was doing so well, and then she started having pains about a month ago. They whacked her straight in for treatment, no mucking around. Chemo and radiotherapy this time. It's really knocking her."

"What have the doctors said?"

She looked at him and shook her head, just once, and then stared at the ground.

"I'm so sorry." He couldn't imagine how he'd cope if it happened to Tahlia. Hank shifted at Peter's feet, and looked from the man to the woman, his ears pricked, sensing something in the atmosphere. "It's no wonder he doesn't want to talk about it," muttered Peter, almost to himself.

"He's not talking much to me about it either. He found some miracle cure on the web, and I was negative. So now he just doesn't tell me what he's thinking at all."

"What miracle cure?"

"Some place in the States. Hundreds of thousands of dollars. Where would we get that kind of money? Perhaps we could sell the car?" The hard, sarcastic tone was unusual for Nyree, and she seemed to repent of it almost immediately. "Well, anyway, the doctor said it was nonsense. He said they'd just take all our money, and we'd have nothing to show for it."

And it'd be much easier to believe the doctor, when you can't do anything about it anyway. He was so engrossed in his thoughts that he jumped as Tom appeared around the corner of the house.

"Sorry, did I frighten you, Mr Big Policeman?" Tom drawled, mischief in his dark eyes.

"I was worlds away. Didn't hear your car arrive. Which is pretty amazing, considering those brakes of yours."

"They're a special feature. You gotta pay extra for that."

Nyree was already heading for the kitchen, as Tom collapsed into another of the folding chairs. She returned with another beer and another bowl of stew, and Lily followed silently in her wake. The little girl crawled into her father's lap, and buried her face in his shirt. He simply held her, his hands gentle, his expression fierce. Steam rose in plump wraiths from the bowl of food, grew thinner, and finally petered out, and still Tom held his daughter.

Peter felt a shaft of the man's pain as if it were his own. He filed away a mental note: he'd ask Bryan Smithton for a donation to the Granton family, once he finally emerged from the wilds. Bryan's wealth was legendary around town, even though no one ever discussed it with the man himself. Surely he could afford to help a sick child.

But he didn't say anything to Tom and Nyree. There was no point getting their hopes up.

18

"STOP!"

Callie looked up, rolling her shoulders under the weight of the two packs she carried.

It was Kain. He had come back down out of the whiteout to rejoin them.

"We can't keep going," he said. "The snow is too thick. I ran into a drift up there that was waist deep, and it took me forever to find a safe way out of it. Even the shallowest snow is knee deep now. We'll fall in a hole and break a leg, or fall off the mountain altogether. There are ledges we'll have to sidle along further up, and the cliffs drop sheer from the edge."

"Well what are we going to do?" Adam said. "We can't go up, and we can't go down."

Callie said, "We'll just have to pitch camp here. We need shelter. And we need to get something warm into Sharon. She's barely conscious."

"Well, there's no wood up here, even if we could get it to light," Jack said. "How much gas have we got left?"

"I think there's enough if we use our water bottles rather than snow. It would take too long for the snow to melt. We've still got seaweed, and the ferns we picked this morning."

"We can huddle under one tarp, with the stove in the middle. Give it the best chance to burn. And put Sharon in the middle of us too, so she can warm up."

"While you're doing that, I'll see if I can find some flattish spaces for the tents," Kain said. "Our best place to ride out this blizzard will be in a tent in a sleeping bag."

"Yep, good idea," Adam said. "And maybe when we wake up, the snow will have finally stopped."

***

THE ZIPPER ON THE TENT FLAP SLOWLY OPENED, ONE CLICK AT A time. Then there was silence, apart from the gentle breathing of the three sleeping women, one breathing more shallowly than the others. Two gloved hands reached carefully inside. One cupped Sharon's chin, the other hand pinched her nostrils closed. She struggled feebly against the restrictions of her sleeping bag. And then she was still. The hands withdrew, and the tent zipper closed. One click at a time.

19

Wednesday, Four Days Lost

CALLIE STOOD FROZEN IN FEAR ON A NARROW ROCK LEDGE, willing her limbs to move. Everyone else was out of sight, and she felt desperately alone. Why had they left her? The ground under her feet began to vibrate, and then to shake violently. Suddenly the ledge crumbled from beneath her and she was pitching forward into an awful void.

She desperately wanted to reach out for a branch, a tuft of grass, anything to halt her fall, but her arms were stuck to her sides; they wouldn't move. She tried to scream, but no noise came. Far away, she could hear Rachel calling her name, over and over, and a branch dug into her shoulder.

"Callie! Wake up!"

The sky was green. She was falling and the sky was green and her heart was pounding with adrenaline. But that wasn't the sky, it was the roof of the tent, sagging inwards with the weight of snow. Her sleeping bag was tangled around her, and everything was okay. It was just a dream.

"Callie," Rachel said, her voice hoarse and strange. "Sharon won't wake up."

Callie propped herself up on her elbow and looked at Sharon. In her disorientation she hoped this was another bad dream. Sharon was an odd color, and her eyes weren't fully closed.

"Rachel, get Erica. Quickly." While Rachel was struggling out of her sleeping bag on the opposite side of the overcrowded tent, Callie sat up properly and began to rub Sharon's face. So cold. How could she be so cold, when they had spent so much time warming her up?

A commotion outside the tent flaps materialized into Erica, quick and purposeful, wearing her professional face. Erica felt under Sharon's chin, first on one side, then the other.

"I can't find a pulse," she said, and then directed her voice back over her shoulder. "You guys, help me get her out of this tent."

Strong hands reached in and slid Sharon and her sleeping bag out onto the mountainside. Callie clambered out after her, fumbling for her boots as she registered the snow burning her bare feet, her eyes aching from the sudden brightness of high-altitude sun in a pale blue sky. Snowy mountains stood back and watched, detached, cool, impersonal.

"It can be hard to find a pulse on a hypothermic person," Erica said to no one in particular, and put her ear to Sharon's chest. "Let's get her out of this sleeping bag and do some CPR. Quickly!"

Jack unzipped Sharon's bag while Adam grabbed her under the armpits to pull her out.

"Wait!" Erica said. "Bend her arm for me."

Adam tried to pull Sharon's elbows, but they were stiff. "She's stuck. Let me try another angle."

"Stop." Everyone looked at Erica, breathing hard, ready to pounce on her next instruction, but her face had changed. Closed.

"I'm sorry guys," she said. "That's rigor mortis."

They kept staring at her, waiting for a solution, unable to comprehend. Refusing to comprehend.

"She's been dead for hours. There's nothing we can do."

Callie felt herself shrinking inside her skin, coming away from the sides of her being. *It's my fault*, she thought. *I didn't keep her warm enough. I shouldn't have gone to sleep.*

"But she was so much warmer," Rachel said, her face blank with shock. "She was doing so much better. Wasn't she Callie?"

But Callie's mouth had lost any connection with the rest of her.

Adam jumped in. "Callie, Rachel, you did everything you could for Sharon. We all did. It's not your fault."

"I don't understand it myself." Erica seemed to be talking mostly to herself. "She *was* improving. I wouldn't have gone to bed otherwise. And rigor has set in so fast."

"Could it be the low temperatures here?" Jack asked, rubbing his face.

"I don't know." Erica shook her head slowly in puzzlement. "I'd expect this level of rigor to take about twelve hours at home."

Rachel erupted. "Could we stop acting like we're in the fresh meat department! This is Sharon we're talking about. There's a little boy in Brisbane who has no mother this morning. And he doesn't even know." She burst into tears.

"Come here, sweetie." Callie moved beside her friend and folded her arms around the trembling shoulders. "They didn't mean it like that, they're just upset and worried like we are."

"I'm sorry, I didn't mean what I said. It's just so awful I can't even breathe. I can't believe I slept. While Sharon died. I lay there and slept. And it's all my fault. She should never have been here. She should have stayed back at Poison Bay."

***

JACK FELT HOLLOW, ECHOING INSIDE. THIS WAS EVEN WORSE THAN Bryan's death. Not just because Bryan had wanted to die and Sharon hadn't. This time there was a body to deal with. They'd all been in the presence of death once before, at Liana's suicide. But that time there had been professionals to handle the practicalities. This time, it was all up to them.

"Well congratulations, Reverend." Kain's voice dripped malice. "Your 'keep the team together' strategy has been an overwhelming success. Perhaps you could tell us what to do next, since you're not only our resident wise man but also our expert on the afterlife."

Jack flinched. Everyone was looking at him. No one defended him, not even Adam, who'd supported him yesterday, or Rachel, who he'd been trying to help. No one said: It's not Jack's fault. And then Callie spoke.

"Kain, if you can't say something helpful, I suggest you just shut up. We're all doing our best to get every single one of us out of here alive, and we all feel gutted that Sharon won't be going home." Her voice broke and she took a deep breath. The others shifted weight, looked somewhere else. "But Jack, do you have ideas about what we could do for a…" she waved her hands uncertainly "…funeral type of thing?"

They were all looking at him again, all except Kain—this time with something like hope. He felt as lost as the rest of them, but apparently he'd drawn the short straw. *Oh God, help me.*

He rubbed his face with both hands, then shoved them deep into his pockets, stalling for thinking time. "How about this. We leave Sharon in her sleeping bag inside her big orange plastic rescue bag. That will protect her from animals and weather, and it'll also help the searchers find her eventually, so she can be returned to her family." More inspiration struck. "We need to go through her pack to see if there's anything that might help the rest of us survive. Whatever is left, we pack it up nice and tight and leave it beside her. Then we have a bit of a funeral, to say goodbye. And then we pack up all our stuff and get the hell off this mountain." He lost it on the last few words, and bent his head to look at the snow, his vision blurring with tears.

"I think that's a good plan, mate," Adam said. Several others nodded.

Soon afterwards, Jack was marveling at this odd group of people, and how they could be at each other's throats and then such a team when the need arose. Adam had tipped out Sharon's pack onto a tarp and was sorting through the contents with Erica's help; Kain was dismantling and packing the tents with silent precision; Callie and Rachel were attending to Sharon's body, trying to make her "comfortable" in the sleeping bag, combing her hair, straightening her clothes. Jack helped them manhandle her into the big orange bag, but he left her face uncovered for the moment. It went against every instinct to cover her with plastic, even though she wasn't breathing any more.

Jack was setting up his mini tripod on a nearby rock when Kain came up behind him. "Tell me you're not going to film this!"

"Yes I am." Jack was quietly sure of himself this time. "One day her son will want to know about what happened to her, and then he can choose whether or not he wants to see it. If I don't video it, he has no choice." He had a sudden thought. "Hey Adam, don't forget Sharon's camera."

"Why would we need that?"

"One day her son might like to see the photos on it."

They gathered around Sharon's body, only six of them now. Jack cleared his throat nervously. "I thought perhaps we could each say something that was special about Sharon. Only those who want to do it of course. And it doesn't have to be the most important thing about her, just something we'll remember. And then, if no one minds, I'll finish off with a prayer." Several people nodded and no one objected. Apparently religion was okay at a time like this. "I'll start if you like."

He cleared his throat again. "Sharon found this hike the hardest of any of us. She's been in pain since Day One, with her feet ripped to pieces, but she never whinged about it. She had a much harder life than any of us, but she just soldiered on. Her husband took off with some eighteen year old, but she didn't expect anyone to rescue her. She went to work, she fed her kid, she took her parents to the doctor and the bowls club and the shops. Sharon, thanks for persevering, and for still being our friend after all these years."

There was a pause.

Adam said, "Shaz, thanks for those fantastic Anzac bikkies you used to make at school." A little smile of remembrance fluttered around the group.

Rachel spoke up. "Sharon, thanks for being such an encouragement to me on this hike. For making me think sheer determination can get a person through anything. And I promise you I'm going to do the best I can to get home to that boy of yours, and tell him what sort of a person his mother was, and to make sure he is looked after and loved the way he should be."

They stood around the big orange bag on that icy mountainside, and said goodbye the best they could.

At the end, Jack cleared his throat and prayed aloud, "God, thanks for Sharon and for everything she's meant to so many people. Forgive us for failing to save her life. Please help her son and her parents to go on when they find out she's gone. And please help us to get through this thing."

A couple of the group said, "Amen." Others nodded respectfully. Kain stared at the ground, silent and withdrawn.

Callie and Rachel gently pulled the sleeping bag hood down over Sharon's face, and tucked the orange plastic over it, tenderly, firmly, sealing out the elements.

And then they all started walking again.

***

CALLIE TOOK ANOTHER STEP, AND THE SNOW'S BRITTLE CRUST cracked under her weight, allowing her to sink through to the mush underneath. Again. The unseen rock below was at a severe

angle, and her ankle twanged as her boot made contact and twisted. Again. Her pants were sodden to knee height, because she just
couldn't stand to wear the waterproof over pants today. Jack had
frowned, but she'd ignored him. The squelching noise of them irritated her beyond all reason. Her lower legs were cold to the point of
numbness, but she managed to feel hot and bothered just the same.
The sun was glaring off the snow, and she thought about removing
her jacket, even though in truth the temperature couldn't have been
much above freezing way up here in the tops. But she was afraid
that if she stopped for any reason, she'd lose all momentum.

Be thankful it's stopped snowing today, Callie, she told herself
sternly. *Be thankful it's not raining for once. Be thankful you can still
walk.*

She was also thankful not to be lugging the extra weight of
Sharon's rucksack this morning. It would have been dragging her
shoulders down, crashing onto her thighs with every agonized step.
But she couldn't bear to think about the reason she didn't have to
carry it.

Nevertheless, her mind had a will of its own, and kept circling
back to Sharon's face. No matter how she tried to redirect her
thoughts onto something nicer, it was like herding cats. They just
slipped past her, and wriggled and wormed their way back to have
another look at Sharon's face. The look of it, the feel of it, as she and
Rachel had prepared their friend's body.

No one should ever have to do that for a friend. Too unbearably
intimate. Too many liberties to be taken with someone who could
no longer give permission.

Trying to tidy Sharon's hair, all lank and oily because, like the
rest of them, she hadn't been able to wash it for many days. It
seemed horrible that they had to leave her looking so awful. *Why*

does the mind latch onto such a trivial thing in the face of such a disaster? thought Callie. Even back in high school, while Callie had been getting around in mismatched tomboy clothes, too lazy to do battle with her cloud of red frizz, Sharon had always been well-groomed.

She didn't wear makeup to school; it was against the rules, and Sharon followed the rules. But outside of school she always had at least mascara and lipstick. There was no color on her face today, where she lay far below them on this mountainside, tucked up inside her orange bag. Callie wondered if she would ever be able to forget the feel of Sharon's pale and blotchy skin—cold, unresponsive, more like marble than human flesh.

And those marks on her face. Something was bothering Callie about those marks. It nibbled away at the back corner of her consciousness like a little mouse; whenever she tried to pounce on it, it darted away.

She didn't want her mind to be filled with Sharon's face. Because it made her want to weep and weep and weep. So she focused with all her might on the burning pain where the melted snow was soaking through to her knees.

And took another step.

And then it hit her, with awful clarity.

***

MIRACULOUSLY, THEY'D FINALLY FOUND A PASS OVER THE MOUNtain's shoulder into the next valley, and were back below the tree line at last, and out of the snowdrifts. Jack had been longing for this moment. Under the trees, there would surely be less snow, less undergrowth, and it would be much easier to walk. Surely.

For two hours they had been fighting snow-laden mountain scrub that ripped at their clothes, snagged on their rucksack straps, dragged them backwards. Sometimes it was knee-high, other times right up to their armpits.

Bringing up the rear, there were times Jack found it easier because the others had trampled the wiry vegetation ahead of him. Sometimes it was harder because they had ground the snow and earth to slippery mud.

Now, under the trees, instead of the clearer path of Jack's daydreams, they encountered even worse conditions. Slippery rocks, tangled tree roots, dangling moss slapping at their faces, ferns and undergrowth clawing their bodies.

And the worst of it was that, for each excruciating fifty meters of mountainside, they didn't even know if they were headed in the right direction.

They could be heading away from help, away from rescue. Away from medical people with fresh medical supplies for Rachel, who was scrambling over a vine-entangled rock just ahead of him. Away from life and into disaster.

Yesterday morning, it had seemed so clear they needed to keep moving, that inactivity was the fastest way to certain death. But now, Sharon lay still and silent in yesterday's valley, and Jack wasn't sure of anything anymore. Maybe it really was his fault that Sharon was dead. He'd been so focused on Rachel he'd forgotten about Sharon. How could he face her motherless little boy? Maybe it would be better if he didn't survive either.

His dark thoughts were interrupted by a shout from up ahead. Adam, today's trailblazer, had found a useful clearing and called a halt for lunch. Not that there was much to eat, just more stupid ferns—but they definitely needed the rest.

Jack also needed a toilet break—the world might be ending, but the body kept processing. He ditched his rucksack and started staggering off into the rainforest. As he tried to cross the small stream whose course they were following, he noticed his leg trembling—with fatigue? Grief? He lost power as he committed his weight to a mossy rock, and skidded sideways, breaking his fall by grabbing a slimy vine on the way through. *Oh God, I need your help. Please get us out of here. Show me what you want me to do.* He became aware of noises behind him, and looked over his shoulder to see Callie following.

"Ladies loo is thataway, Cal," he said, pointing in the general direction of anywhere else.

"I'm not looking for the loo, I'm looking for you." She swayed vaguely for a moment, and said with raised eyebrows, "That rhymed."

"Well, I am looking for the loo, so if you don't mind…" He left a meaningful pause.

"I do mind. I need to talk to you. Now." The vagueness had disappeared.

"What's up?"

"Not here. Walk a bit further."

They struggled over the tangled terrain for several minutes more, until at last Callie was satisfied. The rest of the group was out of sight.

"What is it, Cal?" He sank down onto a fallen tree. She slumped against a slimy boulder and wriggled her shoulders, massaging them. The heavy vegetation hung all around them, eavesdropping.

"Have you got your camera?" She must have seen him tense, because she added, "I just want to see something. From the funeral-thing we did for Sharon."

He pulled the camera from his pocket and began locating the correct recording. "What is it you're looking for?"

"There were marks on her face, and I didn't know why they were bothering me. But now I've realized they were bruises."

"We're all bruised and battered." He didn't feel very patient just now, especially with anything Callie had to say about his video.

And he wanted the loo.

"Not like that. Rachel and I were fixing her hair, trying to make her look nice. The stupid, pointless things we do for someone who doesn't care anymore." She stopped and drew a deep breath. "Anyway, I was looking at her face. Up close. For quite a while. And it had these strange marks on it. I thought they were just the cold, the hypothermia, you know?" She ended on an upward inflection, asking for a sign that he understood.

Jack nodded.

"But it has been bothering me ever since. I couldn't get the picture of her face out of my mind."

"None of us can get Sharon out of our minds, Cal," he said gently.

"No, it's more than that."

"Here it is." He'd reached the shot of Sharon's face as she lay in her bag. A close-up he almost hadn't been able to bring himself to record. But his job in the moment was just to observe the reality. The decisions about how to use it would come later.

"See these marks either side of her nose, and this one under her chin. Her eyelids were kind of red too."

He toggled the controls and zoomed in on the image. "I see what you mean."

"I couldn't figure out why it bothered me, and then suddenly I remembered. Like my brain had been downloading a photo for hours and then suddenly there it was in front of me." She shook her head in amazement, but Jack was still mystified.

"Sorry, I'll try to make more sense. A couple of years ago, I went on a three-day course in forensic pathology, you know, a course for journalists. So we'd know what we were reporting and not write so much nonsense."

"Ye-es."

"They showed us photos of murder victims. Those shots they take up close, showing the gunpowder residue, the angle of the knife cuts. Not just crime scene photos, but the pathology ones as well. Somehow they're even more creepy when all the blood's been washed away. Some people were fascinated, but it made my skin crawl."

"Sounds gruesome. But where are you going with this?"

"They showed us a couple of bodies as well, just people who'd died in hospital, so we could get a feel for what it was like for them to handle dead bodies. And then there was this murder victim. Laid out there on a metal table with a sheet over her. They'd saved her for last, like she was a prize or something. It's half the reason I switched to making documentaries instead of news. I'll never forget it, Jack, I had nightmares for weeks. A young girl, only twelve years old, and she'd been suffocated by some pervert."

Jack stared at Callie, and he felt a trickle of fear run down his spine and hit his adrenal glands with a slap. Tired though his brain may have been, it rebooted and started to make connections that he really didn't want it to make. "You're not saying…" he began, unable to finish the question.

"Jack, that little girl had the same marks that Sharon had on her face. *Exactly* the same marks."

20

ELLEN STARED OUT THE HOTEL WINDOW AT DRIVING RAIN. THE surface of the lake was covered in whitecaps. It looked like whipped lead. A tiny floatplane bobbed erratically at its moorings. The hotel's "No Vacancy" sign swung crazily in the wind. Despite appearances this was the tourist season; she'd been lucky to get this room.

She had actually gone to sleep last night despite her expectations, but it had been a restless, dream-filled slumber, where shadowy figures moved through her room, and she couldn't always judge the boundaries between sleep and wakefulness.

She'd also ordered a full dinner last night as instructed, even though she didn't think she'd be able to eat until she knew Rachel was safe. But the words of the policeman had been so like what Roger would have said, it gave her comfort. They also recalled the command of a wise medical specialist at the beginning of one of Roger's long stints in intensive care: "This will be a marathon. Sleep. Eat. Keep your strength up. It won't help him if you end up in the bed next to him." The doctor had been proven right, and she knew the policeman also would have seen what happened to family members who neglected their own physical needs during an extended crisis. And so she'd obeyed.

Ellen had been ambushed by the appetite that returned in a rush after the first two reluctant bites. She'd wolfed it down, the whole enormous plate of roast lamb and vegetables, and then to her own astonishment ordered apple strudel for dessert. She felt guilty enjoying it, but then imagined Roger in the seat beside her. "Good girl," he would have said with a sharp nod. He encouraged rational behavior in times of tension, the wonderful, stupid, absent man. And so she'd focused her mind on evaluating textures and flavors, forcing all other thoughts out for at least a few minutes.

Sergeant Peter Hubble had phoned this morning, even though he had little to report. He seemed to be telling her everything there was to tell, and that helped.

They hadn't yet found anyone who'd seen Bryan Smithton return from the hike. They had talked to the boatie who'd taken the group across the lake, but he had no booking to bring them back. This was unusual but not unheard-of; they might have been planning to walk out via the southern shore of the lake, a possibility given their time-frame. A group of young people just returned from hiking the same area for the past four days, and now doing laundry in the youth hostel, hadn't seen any of Rachel's group. Peter was going to try some of the various associations that used the wilderness. A group of eight was a good-sized crowd—people would remember it.

Ellen's window was fogged in places. Raindrops ricocheted off the glass like pebbles. Ting ting ting ting. Across the lake, only the foothills were visible, flat and one-dimensional against the low cloud.

Somewhere, Rachel was out in this.

The hotel room was warm and cozy, and Ellen could no longer bear to be so comfortable when Rachel was so cold and so lost. She grabbed her rain jacket and headed out.

She walked blindly for about an hour, along the lake-front at first, and then through residential streets. The raindrops driving into her face felt like slivers of ice. They found their way around the hood of her jacket, insinuating themselves into the collar of her shirt, starting a trickle down her back, one vertebrae at a time. Her cheeks burned with the cold, but then stopped hurting. She realized with a start that her face was numb.

Suddenly, Ellen was outside the police station. The lights inside looked warm and appealing, and being cold and wet didn't seem such a good idea any more.

She dripped onto the entrance floor, teeth chattering. Through glasses that had instantly misted with the sudden temperature change, she saw a foggy facsimile of Peter Hubble walk from the back office. He saw her and stopped dead. "Ellen." As her spectacles cleared, she registered that there was something about him, a tension.

"What's happened?" Her lips were numb. "I'm not drunk, just cold." *Oh good grief, I must sound like a jibbering idiot.*

Peter grabbed her arm and steered her towards his office. "Hey Amber, would you mind getting Ellen a blanket and a coffee—she's frozen!"

A few minutes later Ellen was drinking sickly sweet instant coffee, wrapped in a gray government-issue blanket that was starting to smell like a wet dog.

Her sodden jacket hung askew on a coat-stand, shedding drops of water from its lowest corner, one at a time. Every now and then it would be a double drop: plit-plit. She could hear it in spite of the buzz of the police station, and the electronic hum of Peter's computer. She didn't usually take milk in her coffee and it felt gluggy and thick in her mouth. She didn't usually take sugar either. Sweet drinks were for shock. So they thought she was in shock. Or soon would be.

Her face was burning as the blood started to flow again, and her fingers looked weird around the coffee mug in the fluorescent light. Blotchy.

She had to know what Peter's news was. And yet she could wait about 100 years for it. Until he told her, it wouldn't have to be true.

"It's not Rachel." He began at the most important fact, with the wisdom of a man who's had to give a lot of bad news. "A man's body has been found."

She swallowed and said nothing. It wasn't Rachel. Her heart soared. And then she felt guilty. What had it come to if she could be happy about someone else's grief?

"It was seen washed up on rocks along the coast by a tourist vessel. The rescue chopper is bringing it here now."

"Was it one of Rachel's friends?" Why were they calling the body "it"? Surely it should be "he".

"We don't know who it is yet." He drew a deep breath. Perhaps he couldn't decide how much to tell her. How much he was allowed to tell her. How much she could take, more likely. "It's the body of a man in tramping clothes. With a pack still attached. Nothing much in the pack—it's all fallen out. No ID on him that they could find so far."

A thought coagulated in Ellen's mind. She tried to sound intelligent. "If it's one of Rachel's friends, I might recognize him. It's been a few years since I've seen most of them, but maybe I can help." Inside, she recoiled from the thought of having to look at a dead man, especially one so young. But if it might help her daughter...

Peter paused. He seemed to be making a decision again. "It seems he's been in the water a few days. He won't be easy to identify."

Apparently, Peter was trying not to be gruesome. "Oh. Will you... will you do a post mortem here?"

"Invercargill. But they're bringing him here first in case he's a local and we can make a preliminary identification."

"He" now. Not "it". But how could they identify him if he wasn't recognizable?

"Peter, please tell me the truth. Believe me, I'm not as crazy as I seem, and there is nothing you can tell me that will be worse than what I can imagine all by myself."

He sucked in a breath through his teeth, and then shrugged. "Okay Ellen, I'm trusting you to take this in strictest confidence. I'm being open with you because if it was my kid out there, I'd want to know what was going on." She nodded.

"The body is a tall, thin man with dreadlocks. It may take several days to get a positive ID, and we may be wrong but... there's a possibility it's Bryan Smithton. That's why they're bringing the body here first. We may be able to tell, to a reasonable degree of certainty, whether it could be Bryan, as several of us know him fairly well."

Ellen let the words filter through her consciousness. Her mind ran aground on a piece of verbal debris. Dreadlocks. Straggly, messy thing to do with perfectly nice hair. Long was okay. She was at uni in the seventies after all. But since when did clean cut Bryan Smithton go in for dreadlocks? *The facts, Ellen.* "If it did turn out to be Bryan," she said, careful to use the same kind of indirect, non-committal language Peter was using, "then that would probably mean the rest of the party were still out there, because otherwise they would have reported the death."

"Yes."

"They would be in difficult and unfamiliar terrain, without a guide."

"Yes."

"They may not have been able to contact us because the communications equipment was in Bryan's rucksack."

"Yes. Or they might not know how to operate it."

"And whatever event caused Bryan to fall into the water could have affected other members of the party."

He looked straight at her. "Yes, it would be a matter for serious concern. But on the upside it would also release us to start some serious search and rescue."

Ellen wrapped her hands around the coffee mug. She absolutely must stay calm, and so she studied the way the light from the window was hitting the mug, a chunky graceless thing in mustard yellow, with a chip out of the rim right where you wanted to put your lips. She took a sip and felt the heat run down her throat and pool in her stomach. Sweet and milky. She concentrated on the sensation of it until the fear steadied.

"So we wait for that helicopter," she said.

"Yes. And then we'll know what to do next."

21

CALLIE HAD MANEUVERED HERSELF NEAR THE BACK OF THE lineup, right in front of Jack, as they continued their rainforest scramble. She slowed her pace so the others would pull ahead of her, as she looked for an opportunity to talk to him alone again. When she stopped and turned, he looked at her intently.

"Are you very, very sure about those marks on Sharon's face?" he said.

"I wish I was just imagining it. But I'm absolutely certain now that they match what I saw on that girl. Someone deliberately suffocated Sharon. While I slept right there beside her."

Jack rubbed his face vigorously. "Do you have any theories about who might have done it?"

"None that make me happy."

"Let's hear them."

"It's one of us. Or it's someone else, maybe someone acting on Bryan's orders. Or it could even be Bryan, I guess."

Jack tilted his head and gave her a funny look. "Are we being chased by the undead now?"

"Hardly, Jack. But what if he—I don't know—had an oxygen tank ready where he jumped in. Something like that." She lifted her arms in a large shrug. The suggestion was foolish, embarrassing almost, and yet it had to be said.

Jack opened his mouth to speak, and she could tell his instinct was to say it was a crazy idea, but then his face changed, and he paused. "I suppose he was pretty organized. It's not completely impossible. Not that much crazier than everything else that's happened."

He was silent for a minute, thoughtful. "So… Bryan, if he had the oxygen tank thingy, would have done it because he wanted us all dead. Wouldn't it be better though to leave her alive to slow us down?"

"Look at how her death has affected us. It's slowed us down emotionally. When we were trying to save her, we at least had a united purpose."

"And someone he set up to do it might have done it because…?"

"He could have paid them. Money is a powerful motivator."

He nodded and chewed his bottom lip. "Bryan certainly has access to plenty of motivation. And one of us… why would we do it?"

"Because she was a liability," said Callie, softly. "She was slowing us down, making it harder for the rest of us to survive."

"I could have done it, you know. Did you think of that, before you came to me?"

"I did, actually. But the fact is, I just don't believe it was you. I don't know if I'm being irrational, but if you ever decided to kill someone, I can't imagine you bothering to hide it."

He gave a wry smile. "Yeah, if I'm always belting people over the head metaphorically, why not physically?"

She laughed, and then became earnest again, with an edge of awkwardness. "Anyway, I'm willing to trust my gut on you. For what it's worth. I do trust you, Jack. And I'm sorry about those things I said about your video."

"Yeah." He looked her in the eye. "That hurt like hell."

"I know. I just don't get it, the way you can do it, because I'm different. I get too caught up in the emotion of the moment."

He shrugged. "Makes you good at the human interest stories."

"Whereas you'd make a good war reporter, like those ones embedded with the troops back in World War I. You're the real thing. I know so many journos who feed on other people's pain, and for a minute I was afraid you'd become one of them. But that was stupid. There's nothing cynical about you."

He shrugged again, but his look was warm. "I just think the truth is worth telling. Whether I like it or not."

"And you have to keep telling it, Jack. If we don't get out alive, that video is our message to our families and the world. They have to know what really happened out here and why."

***

THERE WERE STILL SEVERAL HOURS OF DAYLIGHT LEFT, BUT THE rock bivvy they'd found on the side of the valley was just too perfect to pass up. A dry and flat platform for six sleeping bags, no need to set up the tents. Extra undercover space for their cooking fire, and even some dry twigs and leaves, caught in the crevices, that they could use to get a fire started and dry out some wood. The gas was all gone now, but they still had matches.

Ironically, it was Bryan, the man who wanted them dead, who'd trained the group to recognize a good natural camp when they saw it. Callie caught herself wondering yet again: *Did he train us so we'd have a sporting chance, or could he just not stop himself from teaching? If Ranger Bryan and Murderer Bryan were to arm-wrestle, which one would win?*

Kain was silent as he laid out his sleeping bag, radiating frustration. He'd argued they should keep going while the light and the weather were good, but he'd been outvoted. Again.

Everyone was exhausted, and wanted an end to this woeful day. And it was so much harder to keep on going, when they didn't even really know where they were going. Another tree, another log, another rock. Were they closer to the end, or just circling?

Maybe sleep would erase the mental pictures Callie wanted to delete. Sharon in her orange body bag. So still and so alone, as they all trudged off and left her with only the indifferent mountain for company.

Callie was longing to speak to Jack again, to work out what they were going to do with her discovery about Sharon's death. Most particularly, whether they would tell the others. But Jack had gone off with Adam to look for wood and perhaps, maybe, hopefully, something to eat. They'd taken the spear that Adam had fashioned yesterday, sharpening a long, straight stick to a vicious point with his hunting knife. So far, he'd not managed to skewer anything on it, despite several lunges at startled birdlife. But there were fish in the river. They'd seen them, a silver glimmer here and there in the sunlight. The water was too deep at that point, but there must be some shallower parts. And if anyone could catch some food, it had to be Adam the outdoorsman. Callie sent up a message to whoever might be listening: *Please let us be lucky today.*

They would need some greenery to go with whatever the two men brought back. "Anyone wanna help me go choose some veggies?" Callie asked. "The lads have gone to the meat department." She wasn't sure she should ask Rachel to move again, with carbs in such short supply. However, she also wasn't sure if she should leave her there alone to play gooseberry with Kain and Erica. Even if the lovebirds were still sharing a tent, the flirting had stopped and they were not that nice to be around. Sore feet and chronic B.O. were a bit of a romance killer, apparently.

In the end, both Rachel and Erica went with Callie, leaving Kain to his dark thoughts. Ferns were plentiful at this altitude, so they gathered a good supply, including some for tomorrow.

"I'm getting pretty tired of these, three meals a day," Erica commented, as she snapped off another tip.

"I know what you mean," Callie replied. "But the risk of trying something else just doesn't seem worth it, if we're only doing it for variety. At least we know these give us something in the tummy without killing us."

Erica inspected a couple of the curly tips lying in her hand. "There must be at least a few carbohydrates in them, since we've got a certain amount of energy each day. But they're hardly a balanced diet."

"They say people can survive for weeks without food, so long as they've got water," Callie said.

"Hopefully we'll be found before we get too skinny," broke in Rachel, a sharp edge to her voice.

"What's wrong?" said Callie in quick concern.

"I'm sorry. It's just that... well... I can't survive for weeks on nothing." Her eyes filled with tears. "And I've had to use so many test strips to keep track of my blood sugar since we stopped having regular food... If they run out..."

Callie had been best friend to a diabetic for many years, so she didn't need Rachel to spell out how dangerous that was. "I'm sorry, sweetie." She gathered her friend into a hug, a muddle of arms and coats and lumpy ferns. "I wasn't thinking. As usual."

"I worry about how it will affect Mum if I don't come back. She's been through so much already..." She started to sob against Callie's shoulder.

Erica stood a little aloof for a moment, and then spoke up. "How about you give me those ferns to take back to camp, and you two have a good blub. Get it out of your system. It'll do you good. Nurse's orders."

Callie smiled gratefully at her, and disentangled the ferns from their jackets as Rachel wiped at her teary face. Erica clambered off up the hill with their cargo, while Callie led Rachel to a fallen tree just the right height for sitting side-by-side.

"It's been such a horrible day," Callie said, and Rachel's face crumpled again. She really cried then, without inhibition, wailing like a small child. Callie put her arm round her shoulders and rocked her gently back and forth, her own face streaked with tears. Rachel's energy was soon spent, and she grew quiet.

When she finally spoke, Callie had to strain to hear her. "It really was my fault, you know. Bryan was right. If I die, I deserve it."

"What are you talking about?"

"Liana. She asked for my help to get an abortion, and I refused. In fact, I wasn't very nice to her about it."

"You never told me!"

"It was such a crazy time, with all our final exams and everything. And besides, you were so vocal about 'Choice'. I figured we'd have an argument, and I didn't want to deal with that just then."

"Do you mean you're against abortion?" She tried not to sound incredulous.

"Yes, I do. It has nothing to do with religion. I'd seen embryos under the microscope at my dad's lab—and lots more since then. It's a distinct, self-directing life from the time it's only three cells, and to me it's human and worth protecting. I've never told you what I think about it, because I didn't feel like I could stand up to you and your ideals on that particular topic."

Callie felt chastened. "So we've been best friends and yet you couldn't tell me what you really thought, all these years. I can't believe I've been so pushy and overbearing."

"Not pushy, exactly." She smiled. "Just enthusiastic and passionate and hard to disagree with."

"I'm sorry, Rachel. I'll try to respect your different opinion on this one. Truly." They both stared into the trees. "What exactly did you say to Liana?"

"I told her to talk to her parents. Her father was so traditional she was terrified to admit to him that she'd been sleeping with

Bryan. But I told her they loved her and they'd all figure it out together."

"That sounds like pretty good advice."

"Yeah. It was excellent advice. But there was an undercurrent for me. I tried to be sympathetic but I was impatient with her for getting herself into that situation. She was always flirting with the boys—like she was testing her 'magical powers' or something—instead of doing her schoolwork. I knew I needed a good score to get into the science degree, and I couldn't take any shortcuts like she was trying to do. She used her beauty like a password, but all I could do was study hard. I had no time or energy for distractions from her. I'm sure she sensed that. It's part of the reason I came on this awful hike. To try to make amends somehow. And when she blew her brains out it felt like a direct challenge to my commitment to brains over heart."

"I doubt she did it that way for that particular reason. Although I can see how it made you feel, when you describe it like that. I've always thought of the way she looked straight at me. Accused me of never having time for her. I've wondered a thousand times why she didn't ask me for help. Surely she'd have known I'd be supportive."

"You'd just spent all your savings on that stupid car that you had to belt with a spanner just to get it to start. You didn't have any money."

"Oh. I'd forgotten about that."

"Plus Kain was always looking at her instead of you, and she'd have known you didn't like her for that."

"Was I that transparent?"

"Yes, my dear, you were." Her tone was kind, and they smiled in a moment of shared remembrance of the pressures of adolescence. And then Rachel became somber again.

"Do you know what's worse? A couple of times today I wished

I hadn't given any of my glucose to Sharon, since she died anyway. What sort of a person am I to think such a thing?"

Callie sighed. "A normal one, I suspect. I thought of exactly the same thing."

"If I'd stayed back at Poison Bay, like Kain said, Sharon might still be alive."

"Maybe, maybe not. We'll never know. But there's no way I was leaving you alone back there."

"I'm either holding everybody up, or making them walk when they'd rather stay put. It's only going to get worse now. What happens if I pass out?"

"We carry you." Callie stated it baldly and with determination.

Rachel pulled back so she could look Callie in the eye. Callie returned her gaze without wavering. Rachel seemed to come to a decision, and nodded. "Well, we'd better get back to camp then."

They were clambering back up the hill when shouting broke out further along the mountainside. They looked at each other in alarm, and increased speed, entering the camp short-of-breath just as Adam burst from the bush, waving something over his head.

At first, Callie thought it was some kind of weapon, and that Adam had gone mad, was possibly even the killer, and where was Jack? What had he done to Jack? But then Jack stepped in after him, and her vision cleared, and she realized that in fact Adam was holding aloft not a weapon but something soft. And feathery. Some kind of bird was dangling limply in his hand. A relatively plump bird, not unlike a small hen. A smile started to gather at the corners of her mouth, and she glanced at Rachel, who was holding her hands to her lips and staring at Adam's trophy in amazement.

"Waddaya reckon, kids?" he demanded, a note of triumph in his voice, and a huge grin on his face. "What am I bet that it tastes just like *chicken*?"

22

IT WAS A MAJOR CONCESSION TO BE ALLOWED INTO THE SEARCH room, and Ellen knew she'd have to be careful not to make Peter regret it. The opportunity to do something useful was a gift she didn't want to lose.

"You already know Tom," Peter said, beginning the introductions. "He's my senior man, but he's also our police liaison with the search team." Tom smiled and nodded at her, but his manner was more reserved than previously. She had the sense that he didn't think she should be there.

"This is Hawk, our search coordinator," Peter continued. "He's also the best chopper pilot you'll find anywhere." Peter spoke in a matter-of-fact tone, and she'd already learned that he wasn't given to exaggeration, so she looked at the man with interest as she shook his hand. Lean and tough-looking with a military bearing. The skin on his heavily tattooed arms was leathery, and what hair he had left was gray. Hard to pick his age—he could have been anywhere between fifty and seventy. He nodded, unsmiling, and said nothing, but his eyes were kind.

The third man in the room might have been Hawk's antonym. Probably only in his twenties, almost as wide as he was tall, his body shaped like a large, half-empty potato sack, and somewhat chaotically dressed.

"Hemi is our local paramedic, but when he volunteers for search and rescue he brings a lot of other skills as well. Tracking, experience with aerial searches and high altitude rescues, you name it. He's even an exceptionally good shot."

"Yeah mate," Hemi said to Ellen. "I'm a superhero." His face split into a beaming grin as he took Ellen's proffered hand. "I tried wearing tights but they look like hell on me."

Ellen laughed, her troubles forgotten for a nanosecond. Hemi was still holding her hand, and he folded his other hand around it, a warm expression in his dark eyes. "Don't you worry, mama, we'll find your girl."

***

Peter cut in, before Ellen could weep at Hemi's kindness. "I'd like to show you something."

He put a piece of jewelry in her hand and said, "Formal identification will be difficult, but this gives me enough certainty to proceed." There might be two tall thin men with dreadlocks currently tramping in Fiordland. They might both own the same color and brand of weathered rain jacket that Bryan always got around town in. But they couldn't both be wearing a woman's locket. The necklace with its elaborate swirls was Bryan's trademark. Everyone had seen it, even if they didn't say anything about it to his face. You didn't tease Bryan Smithton.

Ellen turned it over a few times, and opened it. The locket had been sealed so well that the photographs inside weren't even damp. Did manufacturing jewelers think about the day a locket's wearer might drown?

Ellen said, "Those are Bryan's parents. They were quite famous anthropologists. Do you want me to track down a photo for comparison?"

"Yes please." He wasn't sure if it would make that much difference, but it would give her something to do. The more tasks he could assign to her, the better he could control Tom's uneasiness about a relative in the search room.

Tom Granton was a stickler for rules. His forms were always

filled in correctly and on time, and his hair and uniform conformed exactly to regulations. The pleasant shambles at his home had startled Peter the first time he'd seen it. He'd thought it must be Nyree who made it so, but he was no longer so sure. People weren't cut out of cardboard. They were a mixture of a lot of different things.

Peter had allowed Ellen to help because he had a hunch it would help her—and he was right. Anyone could see the difference in her now she had a job to do. Like someone had taken jumper leads to her brain. And that was the other reason he'd let her join in—that brain. Her ability to comprehend and analyze the data coming in could be an asset in this search, and her knowledge of some of the players was handy too.

Peter's flexibility about rules had got him into trouble before. He hoped it wouldn't get him into trouble again now.

The provisional identification of the body was enough for Peter to order a search of Bryan's house. Tom had volunteered to do it. It wasn't a big house, so he let him go alone, to keep other staff free for other tasks.

He'd also sent requests via Interpol in Wellington, asking for the homes of the missing trampers to be checked for anything that might prove relevant to the search. It wasn't regular procedure, but his gut told him something wasn't regular about this case.

A general alert had gone out via phone and mountain radio. The tour lodges and guides on the Milford Track, the settlement at Milford Sound, every ranger at every manned hut, and several informal groups of trampers up and down Fiordland were now on the lookout for a group of seven people in trouble. The wapiti hunters were getting word out to their people, even though it was off season. And fishermen checking their crayfish pots were watching for anything in the water or washed up on the coastline.

It didn't make sense that they'd still be near the track they'd started on after two weeks, but it was the only logical place to start in all that chaotic emptiness. From there, they'd follow Tom's inside information.

"This is the area Bryan was talking about," Tom said, pointing to a section of the map. "Depending on how long he's been dead, they might have strayed outside this zone. But the southern section of the national park is the best place to start looking."

Amber had joined the briefing. "But the body was found up here," she said. "Doesn't it make more sense that he went into the water further to the north, up towards Poison Bay or Milford Sound?"

"The ocean currents are unpredictable. Bryan showed me the route he was planning to take. It was all around this region. It would be foolish to look anywhere else."

"We'll start in that southern zone," said Hawk. "It would explain why they have no booking to come back across the lake." Tom looked pleased, but then reddened slightly at the next instruction. "And perhaps Amber could check with the search advisors and find out about currents and winds in the past few days. See if you can get someone to narrow down a likely drop zone for that body."

Someone had written "Milford Sound" as the group's destination in the first hut on the George Sound track, but it was probably just the same clown Peter had spoken to the morning he saw them leaving. No one in their right mind would go to Milford via the George track.

Peter was thankful now that Tom had spent so much time with Bryan in the past couple of months, despite Nyree's reservations. It could turn out to make all the difference.

**

PETER WAS ITCHING FOR THE INTERIM REPORT FROM THE FORENSIC pathologist. At last the phone call came.

"I can't confirm cause of death yet, obviously. But there was water and foam in his lungs."

"So he was alive when he went into the water?"

"Seems like it. And the fish have been busy, but the SOCOs managed to get two full fingerprints, and one partial."

"Good, we're dusting his house first thing tomorrow. It's going to be hard to find anything that only Bryan touched. But we'll find something. Any idea of the time of death?"

"Hard to tell. Maybe two or three days."

"Jonesy, those wounds on the body—any chance he was attacked?"

"Quite a lot of them appear to be post-mortem. Probably from being thrown against the rocks. There were some good storms out there in the last few days. What do you have in mind?"

"I'm not sure. I'm just suspicious. This man was maniacally careful. I know the fittest and best can make a mistake, but I'm... uneasy."

"I'll take the magnifying glass to any head trauma, or anything that could be a stab wound. Last thing I want is an uneasy copper. But if he was simply pushed, rather than clobbered, there won't necessarily be any forensic proof."

Ellen was at his elbow as he hung up the phone. "Katrina and Philip Smithton," she said, and placed a single page printout containing several photographs in front of him.

"That was quick!"

"I rang Bryan's aunt and asked for them. I've just picked them up off my webmail."

"You did what?" *Ten minutes on her own and she's contacted the next of kin—why did I let this woman help?*

"I told her it was for a project someone's working on at the university," she said calmly. "She'll hate me later for keeping her in the dark, but I'll just have to wear that."

"Oh, okay then." Maybe not a mistake after all.

He gave his attention to the photographs, and placed the open locket beside them. There was no doubt they were the same people. But it didn't constitute formal identification of the corpse.

"Bryan's aunt was basically a mother to him while his parents were working overseas," added Ellen. "Don't keep her out of the loop any longer than you have to. She needs to know."

23

Thursday, Five Days Lost

WATER BLASTED FROM THE SKY LIKE IT WAS BEING SHOT OUT of a fire hose, thumping onto the hood of Jack's coat. The drumming noise on his head and backpack was hypnotic.

The good weather had ended with a thundering crash at four in the morning, and conditions today were worse than any they'd experienced so far on this rain-soaked expedition into hell. Even the blizzard was child's play by comparison. Cliffs had become thundering waterfalls, the ground a series of fast-flowing streams, ankle deep. Visibility was almost zero.

Jack's boots squelched with every step, the weight dragging on his legs. Yes, the boots were waterproof. But that became academic once the water level rose above the height of the boots and spilled over. Now the fancy waterproofing was keeping the flood in. Like walking with a bucket of water on the end of each leg.

Slosh, slide, slither. Lose your footing, teeter sideways, put out a hand to save yourself, slip on the slimy thing you grabbed, jar your shoulder, wrench your knee. On and on it went. Like hiking through one great big jungle-infested storm water drain while someone poured gravel over you from a height and your spirits sank into oblivion.

No one had wanted to leave their sleeping bags this morning and venture into this maelstrom, and who could blame them? The bald facts were these: they'd have stayed put today, ridden out the storm in their rock-walled sanctuary, if it wasn't for Rachel. She had very few medical supplies left. They had to keep moving. They needed to find rescuers, and fast.

What made it even harder to accept today's struggle was that they'd had such a good night. So warm and comfortable in the rock bivvy, their stomachs satisfied thanks to the bird. The rise in morale around the campfire last night had been so tangible you could almost have used it as furniture. They'd laughed their way through Jack and Adam's colorful story of the failed fishing expedition, the lunging into the river that looked ankle-deep and turned out to be thigh-high, the loss of the precious spear. The dismal wander back to camp, empty-handed, only to see the bird scratching in the undergrowth, complacent and barely aware of their presence. The frantic chase and how Adam had finally been the one to nab the fugitive and bring it home.

But Jack had said nothing about what he'd seen in Adam's eyes. The wiliness and skill and power of him. The clinical way he swiftly wrung the bird's neck. Jack knew Adam killed things for a living—big game fish, wild buffalo, feral pigs, even crocodiles when necessary. And he'd been more than pleased to have someone with his skill on their team in this survival situation.

But when the crux point actually came, there had been something in Adam's eyes that unnerved Jack, something cold and pragmatic—a killer instinct. It seemed utterly contrary to the kind and protective face Adam had worn so far. *Perhaps it's just that I'm a wuss*, thought Jack. *Maybe every "real man" looks like that when they're killing food.* Or maybe not.

Previously, Jack had found it impossible to cast Adam in the role of Sharon's murderer, but a tiny, niggling seed of distrust had been planted, and he was wondering how much to let it grow. As he labored through today's watery nightmare, Adam haunted his thoughts.

He hated suspecting a mate, but someone had killed Sharon. Jack would like to believe Callie was mistaken, but she was no fool, and besides, it actually made sense of the death. Sharon had been so very much improved before they went to bed that horrible night, much warmer, more responsive, and able to answer basic questions, even though she was still weak as a kitten. It didn't make sense that she'd improve so much and then die of cold in a warm, sheltered sleeping bag. It was possible, but not likely.

His mind roiled with the question of who might have helped Sharon into the hereafter.

The oxygen tank scenario was possible, but not probable. Bryan's heavy pack would have acted like a diver's belt, helping him sink. But the sea was so rough that day it would have been hard to control his descent through the water. And he would have been trying to find the oxygen by touch in the underwater darkness.

As for someone shadowing them, an assassin paid to clean up, that was feasible given Bryan's immense wealth. And the group would be hardly likely to notice a skillful and stealthy tracker as they blundered their way around the mountains, trampling undergrowth and pillaging the ferneries.

But the most likely killer was someone among them. Someone who wanted to survive, and could best do that by removing any source of drag on the team. *One of us.*

24

Sergeant Peter Hubble stood in the living room of Bryan Smithton's tiny house, listening to the timbers creak, almost sure he could hear his own breathing echoing off the hard naked walls and floors. He'd come here hoping the house might tell him something about Bryan, a technique he'd sometimes used in his days as a city detective in Christchurch, before the marriage collapse and everything else had gotten on top of him, and sent him to the country for refuge.

He knew his ex-wife and her friends talked about it like it was some kind of demotion—they couldn't imagine a bright star from the CIB going back to uniform voluntarily—but it had in fact been his choice. His instincts had been right. Immersion in the kind of country community he'd grown up in had been just what he'd needed. After eight years, he had trouble imagining he'd ever enjoyed a different life.

The death of Bryan Smithton stirred those old habits from the back of the mental cupboard. He felt a strong, slow dragging of suspicion underneath this death. And the fingerprint report had only intensified it.

Hardly any prints in the house at all—none on the light switches or handles in the bedroom or office; a few in the kitchen and bathroom, but none belonging to the deceased. It was the sort of thing he'd expect to see at a scene where someone was trying to remove evidence. *This place was wiped. Why?*

Peter could have put it all down to obsessive compulsive disorder—Bryan seemed a classic candidate—except for the laptop. Who puts a top-of-the-range, late model laptop in a tub of water outside the back door? There were no signs of a break-in, so the most likely explanation was that Bryan did it himself. *Why?*

Someone trying to remove evidence. The words roamed restlessly around Peter's mind, looking for a place to settle comfortably, but everything had sharp edges and awkward corners. If Bryan was a murder victim, why would he be the one hiding evidence? And who was he hiding it from? An enemy? The police?

And then there was the ongoing thorny problem of making a formal identification. Being ninety-nine percent sure wasn't enough. Dental records were proving elusive. Bryan didn't seem to have visited a dentist or doctor for years. DNA could have helped, if they could only find something to match it with. Hairbrush and toothbrush were both impossibly clean and smelled of bleach. It looked as though Bryan had been trying to delay his own identification, if that didn't sound so far-fetched.

Peter puffed out his cheeks, and slowly blew out the air, thinking, staring at that grid of masking tape on the living room floor. He had a sudden inspiration, and went to the patrol car for the fingerprint kit.

Five minutes later, the fingerprinting dust had revealed what he had hoped for: multiple clear impressions on the masking tape, at least two different fingers, and even a couple of thumb prints. *Whoever cleaned up missed this.*

He lifted the prints carefully, left the case near the front door and headed down the hall. The room Smithton had clearly used as an office was barely big enough for a desk. Nothing but a local nature calendar on the wall, with one date precisely outlined in heavy black marker pen—last Saturday. Peter frowned and plumbed his memory of the tramping schedule Ellen had given him. That would be the day they were to leave the wilderness. Why mark that, but not the date they all arrived? He made a mental note to review the thought later and turned to the desk.

A few neat office supplies in the top drawer. The will that Tom had found yesterday must have been in the next drawer down. A plain vanilla will, leaving everything to the aunt who raised him. A woman who was both bereaved and very wealthy today, but knew nothing of either because Peter was unwilling to contact her till they could pin down the formal identification. He sighed, thinking of her loss and her gain.

His gaze roamed around the room, but found nothing illuminating other than the bare bulb in the light socket overhead. The film of fingerprinting dust on the light switch near the door revealed not a single ridge or whorl.

He continued down the hall to the bedroom, as bare and charmless as the rest of the house. No family photos, no rug, no curtains or blinds. The bed was a single. Clearly Bryan didn't entertain overnight visitors on a regular basis. Peter crouched and looked under the bed. Nothing. Not even a dust bunny to make the man seem human. He pulled back the blanket and sheets one by one— all old and utilitarian—then lifted the thin mattress and looked under it. Still nothing. It seemed oddly disrespectful to leave it in that mess, so he found himself putting it back together, sheets and then blanket. "I'm not doing hospital corners," he muttered to the disapproving room.

He stepped over to the quaint old wardrobe and pulled out a drawer, riffling through a thin selection of jocks and socks, finding nothing. Same with a second drawer containing t-shirts.

And then he opened the wardrobe door.

And stood rooted to the floor, stunned.

He pulled out his cell phone. This was not a conversation he wanted to have over the two-way radio. "Tom, did you search Bryan's bedroom?"

"Yes, sure." The voice was wary. He must be picking up an undercurrent in Peter's tone.

"Did you open the wardrobe?"

"I think so."

"Would you come to the Smithton house please. Right now."

***

PETER HAD TO KNOW IF HIS MOST EXPERIENCED CONSTABLE WAS incompetent or something worse. He couldn't decide what that "worse" might be, but the recent odd friendship between the police officer and the dead man made Peter's thoughts circle uneasily. It was laughable to think Tom could have been out pushing Bryan into a fiord a couple of days ago, but the friendship plus today's discovery raised a red flag in his mind. Either way, if he needed relief sent out from Invercargill, the morning was drawing on, and he had to get on it. The way things were unfolding, he couldn't afford to be understaffed.

"Peter?" Tom called from the front door.

"Bedroom." Peter shut the wardrobe door and waited.

Tom entered the room, his face guarded.

"You searched this room yesterday?"

"Yes."

"Did you open the wardrobe?"

"Yes, I think so. I can't remember exactly."

"There's not a lot of places to look in this room, Tom. Did you open the wardrobe door or not?"

"I can't remember."

Peter had his hand on the wardrobe door handle, and he swung it wide, keeping close watch on Tom's face. "Do you remember now?"

Tom stared at what was revealed. Peter was pretty sure that Tom was seeing it for the first time.

"I guess I mustn't have opened it. Unless that's appeared there since then."

Peter said nothing, just crossed his arms and looked steadily at the other man.

Tom's face changed. "I'm sorry. I seem to have missed it. I've been a bit distracted, with Lily and everything."

Peter was full of compassion, but he rebelled against having a sick child played as a "get out of jail free" card. It wasn't the first time Tom had done it.

"Maybe you should take a couple of days off."

"No! If I sit around at home all day I'll go mad. And I want to help. I want to know who did this to Bryan and get that body identified."

There was something not quite right about the last statement, but Peter couldn't put his finger on it. He could, however, understand the need for distraction in an unsolvable crisis. And so he relented. "All right then, we'll see how you go. But I want everything checked and double-checked. This is turning into a big case, and this oversight," he nodded towards the wardrobe door, "has set us back a whole day. If you have even the smallest doubt about your work, ask someone else to check it for you. People's lives could depend upon it." He added silently to himself: *And I will be watching you like a hawk.*

***

ELLEN LINGERED OVER BREAKFAST, GAZING DOWN OVER THE GREEN lawns to the lake, and sipping hot, strong, black coffee. She'd eaten the full heart-attack meal—bacon and eggs and toast and mushrooms and hash browns—as well as fruit and a blueberry muffin. It would keep her going all day if necessary. The whole expertly-prepared feast tasted no better than dry bran in her mouth, but she knew she should eat it, that Roger would want her to eat it, and so she did. "The machine needs fuel," he always said, "no matter how the heart feels." And so she fueled the machine.

The coffee was good though, and so she focused on the mellow flavor of it, and the way the heat felt, traveling down her throat. Mindfulness, that's what the psychologist had called it. Being entirely present in the moment, refusing to let the fearful future hijack right now. Who could have known the grief counselor's training would come in handy for a whole new crisis so very soon? She had spent some time both last night and this morning doing her deep breathing exercises, even though it was hard. And every time the panic threatened to rise up and choke her, she did the in-for-three, out-for-three crisis breathing she'd been taught, until it subsided to somewhere just below her breastbone. She was determined to stay useful, to do everything she could to save her child, even if it meant forfeiting a mother's right to lie on the bed and scream and scream and scream.

She'd slept incredibly well, in the circumstances. The commencement of a proper search for Rachel and her friends had lifted the crushing weight that had been sitting on Ellen's chest since her daughter failed to step off that plane two days ago. She hadn't needed the discovery of Bryan's body to tell her that something had gone wrong; she'd known straight away. The discovery of the remains, though hideous and tragic and terrifying, had actually been freeing for Ellen, because now she had someone to worry with her. The police were no longer just humoring her. They were concerned. It was professional concentration rather than loved-one-in-danger worry, but she found it immensely comforting just the same. She no longer had to do all the worrying herself. And she trusted Peter Hubble.

Ellen walked outside onto the springy grass, closed her eyes as the warm sunshine caressed her back, and inhaled deeply from the cool breeze blowing off the lake. The weather was so much better today, and it gave her hope. Rachel couldn't die on such a beautiful day as this.

***

THE FINGERPRINTS ON THE FLOOR TAPE WERE A MATCH. IT STILL wasn't absolute identification of the body, but it was enough for Peter to make the difficult call to Bryan's aunt in Brisbane.

Despite her shock and grief, she was able to think clearly enough to tell Peter about the umbilical cord blood stored at Bryan's birth by his scientific parents. Only a day or two now, and they would have firm DNA confirmation of the body's identity.

25

JACK WAS BRINGING UP THE REAR IN HIS NOW-DEFAULT POSITION as sweeper. They were strung out across the jungle-clad mountainside, Kain pushing far ahead as scout. Kain's ties to the group were becoming more frayed each time another of his suggestions was rejected.

Callie had indicated she wanted to talk to him again, about Sharon. They needed to allow a good gap to open between them and the rest of the group, since the pounding rain that masked their voices from eavesdroppers also forced them to speak more loudly to each other. They found a large boulder with an overhanging tree fern that provided a measure of shelter.

Jack began. "Horrible as it is, I think it's most likely the culprit is one of us, even though the other two ideas are possible. I've been looking at everyone differently today. And I don't like the way that feels."

"I even had a moment's thought about Rachel," Callie said, "because she was right on the spot—even though I can't believe she would ever actually do such a thing. She's got such a soft heart."

"Sharon was in the middle near the tent opening. Easy to reach. We all knew that, because we'd been helping get her settled and warm. Sneaking around the camp wouldn't be that hard for any of us. Just leave your tent for a toilet break and do the deed on the way back. And we're all so used to the sound of a tent zipping in the middle of the night now. It might have woken one of us the first few nights, but not now."

"We were so outrageously tired as well," Callie agreed. "A herd of elephants could have been break dancing out there and we wouldn't have known."

He smiled at the image, in spite of himself. "I reckon we'd all have been physically capable of the job. She was so weak, a five-year-old could have done it. And it would have been even harder for her to struggle, swaddled in the sleeping bag."

"And wedged between me and Rachel. That was one very crowded tent."

"We end up having to decide which of us is most likely based on what we know of everyone's character, and that's hardly a scientific way to investigate a murder."

"Ugh, that word." Callie grimaced. "Murder. I'd rather call it almost anything else. I find it hard even to say it in my head, let alone out loud."

"Yeah, I know. But no one's hands 'accidentally' went round Sharon's face and held her mouth and nose closed."

"Ugh," Callie said again, raising her shoulders in a shiver. "So, do you think we should tell the others?"

"I've rolled that one round and round in my head. On the plus side, it would put everyone on their guard. But it could also plunge the team into despair. And do serious damage to our relationships with each other—suspicion, competition, survival of the fittest, who knows what else. We don't want this turning into *Lord of the Flies*. It's bad enough as it is."

"But what if they do it again?"

"If anyone is weeding out the weak, that would make Rachel the next target. She's okay right now, but how long can that last, now that she's so low on insulin?"

"Oh God." Callie put her head in her hands. It wasn't until her shoulders shook with a small sob that it dawned on Jack that she was crying.

Stupid fool, he thought, wincing at his careless words. So focused on analyzing the facts he'd forgotten people's feelings, as usual. Aloud he said, "I'm sorry. I'm sure I could have put that a lot better."

He reached out awkwardly to squeeze her arm in an attempt at comfort, and then wondered if she even felt it under the squeaky wet sleeve of her rain jacket. She must have done, because she looked at him with eyes full of tears.

"It's just that Rachel has been such a good friend for such a long time—my only true friend, if I'm honest—and I really, really, really don't want her to die. And this whole thing is so draining. I keep trying to think sensibly—be objective, don't let it get on top of me, work towards a positive outcome. But sometimes it seems to have sucked the whole 'me' out of me. Like I don't even know who I am anymore." She wiped the tears from her face with the back of her hands. "As if it wasn't hard enough already, without a murderer in our midst."

"I know. And I don't think it helps that because we've been around bad people and dangerous situations before with our work, we expect ourselves to cope with this. But reporting the news isn't the same thing as *being* the news."

Callie looked thoughtful. "I think you've hit on something. The first time I covered a murder, I couldn't sleep for days—but gradually you find mechanisms for dealing with it. Distance yourself from the events… refuse to absorb the relative's emotions… hang out with other people who know what it's like. But I don't think I'd realized that wouldn't work with this one."

"The events and the emotions are happening to us, not someone else."

"So it's okay, really, if I can't cope some of the time." She smiled a watery smile at him.

"We just need to keep on trying to encourage each other, and work together."

"And keep an eye on Rachel. I'll find a way to booby-trap the doorway to our tent, so that they have to make enough noise to wake me if they want to get at her."

"Good idea. Hopefully no one will try anything in daylight, but just in case, we can make sure she doesn't get cut off from the rest of the group."

"So I guess that's our project for today then: try to keep Rachel safe."

"We'd better hurry and catch up with her. We can't keep her safe if she's miles ahead!"

26

E LLEN TOOK THE SCENIC ROUTE TO THE POLICE STATION—A long, brisk walk along the shores of the lake to blow the cobwebs out of her brain. She tried to make it last as long as possible, so that it would fill some of the seconds and minutes and hours that stood between her and news of her daughter. She even stopped in a little church along the way. She knelt for a while in one of the pews, unsure what or how to pray, but comforted nevertheless by the quiet calm of the place. Since Roger's death, she'd been finding herself drawn back to spiritual memories from childhood.

"Hello Ellen." Peter Hubble loomed large in the crowded search room. "Good to see you looking better today."

"I've had sleep and food and exercise. It's amazing what it can do for the human body."

Peter nodded in agreement and gave her a meaningful look. "And the human mind."

She smiled. "It doesn't hurt that the weather is so much better today, too. It's hard to imagine bad things happening on a day like this."

"Yes," said Peter after a microscopic pause, and then his eyes slid away from hers. She was instantly alert.

"What is it?"

He seemed to be thinking about how to answer. That couldn't be good.

She decided to take the proactive approach. "Peter, would it be possible to have a private chat with you? I know you're very busy but I promise it wouldn't take long."

He lifted an arm to indicate back along the hallway. "Let's go to my office."

When they were seated either side of his desk, Ellen drew her thoughts together and summoned her most sensible and credible face, the one she used when she was nervous about giving a major presentation at a conference.

"Peter, I'm aware that it's extremely unorthodox to have the 'frantic mother' involved with your search team, and I appreciate the problems that could cause for you if I abused the situation. I also know that… well, that I must have seemed deranged when I came in here that first day. I'd had no sleep, and I was desperate to get someone to take me seriously." She paused and pursed her mouth. "And yes, I probably looked like a bit of a loon again yesterday. But that was caused by an excess of rain and imagination."

She saw the corners of his lips twitch to suppress a smile. Heartened, she went on.

"I respect your right and duty as a professional to manage the investigation in whatever way you see fit, and so I recognize that you could refuse the request I'm about to make. But I'd like to ask you to tell me the truth about the things you discover about Rachel and her friends, even if it's bad news. I'll handle it better if I actually know the details—it's something about my personality. I'm asking you to do this for my own sake, but I also hope it might benefit you. I do have skills and knowledge that I can contribute to the investigation, if you're willing to treat me as one of the volunteers instead of as an hysterical relative who needs to be managed."

She sat back and waited.

Peter leaned his elbows on his desk, and bent his head to look at a paper clip he was pushing around on the notepad that lay there. He was using his poker face—a useful skill in his line of work—but Ellen could almost hear the mental cogs whirring.

After a few moments, he looked up at her from under his eyebrows, a long stare. She didn't flinch. He sat back. "Okay."

She smiled. "Thank you. So…" She raised one eyebrow. "What's wrong with the weather?"

He smiled slightly at her perceptiveness, and then became serious. "It's good this side of the range. If they're on the west, it's a different story. There are weather warnings out for that region. Very severe and sustained rainfall predicted, with the possibility of flash flooding and landslides."

"I see." She looked out the window at the dappled shade being cast by a tree in the warm sunlight. "It's very weird country this, isn't it? If you don't like the weather, drive for a minute."

"But on the plus side, yesterday the western side had great weather while it was pouring here."

"And we have no way of knowing which side they're on."

"No, but we do know that they're well equipped. We've checked the items on the purchasing list that your daughter received, and tracked down what Bryan himself ordered for the expedition from a place in Dunedin. They had the full survival kit for extreme conditions. And it seems likely that Bryan would have had time to teach them how to use it all before he died."

Peter scratched his ear, and Ellen instantly recognized the "tell". "What is it?"

"Well… in the interests of full disclosure, there were some blizzards in the tops a couple of days ago."

"Blizzards? It's nearly summer!"

"We can get blizzards in high summer up there. It's not that unusual. But they were equipped for those too. As you say, interesting country."

"Heavens above. You know that old Chinese curse: may you live in interesting times? Perhaps it should be: may you live in interesting country."

"Perhaps. But let's get back to that search room and find you a job to do."

27

It happened so quickly that Jack struggled to take it in. One moment he was clambering over a fallen tree in Callie's wake as they struggled to catch up with the others now so far ahead of them up the valley. The next moment the ground was shuddering and a noise like apocalyptic thunder filled his senses.

"Is it an earthquake?" Callie cried, looking back at him with fearful eyes, clutching at a bush to try to keep her balance.

Jack looked up towards the top of the mountain, and what he saw was impossible. His mind was suddenly and absurdly flung back into high-school Macbeth: Birnam Wood was on the move. And headed straight at them. The tree tops he could see were writhing, and through their trunks he glimpsed a moving wall of mud. Beneath their feet, the very earth was sliding.

"Callie! Run!"

He grabbed her hand, leapt past her and began dragging her, clanging his shins painfully on a fallen log. Behind him, she tripped and fell, but he just kept pulling until he wondered how her arm was still in its socket and his heart hadn't burst with the effort.

She regained her footing and staggered awkwardly behind him. His fingers stayed locked around her hand like a vice, and he pulled and ran and leapt and ran. Time slowed to the speed of treacle, and they seemed to gain no ground no matter how much they tried. The noise was now enormous, and yet somehow Jack could still hear his own breathing, ragged and violent in his throat.

Fractions of a second passed like hours, and they gained two meters, three meters, four meters, though the ground was like jelly. They were finally in rhythm, and as Jack launched his weight off a rock, Callie's boot landed in its place.

Jack could see a clear spot ahead where the mountain didn't appear to be moving, and he dragged Callie towards it in desperate, mindless fear. Run and pull and leap and gasp for air. And again.

Nearly there. Don't stop.

And then he felt a powerful jerk through his shoulder and swung around in time to see Callie's hand wrenched from his grasp, her eyes wide with terror, her mouth open in a scream that he couldn't hear over the roaring monster. Tree branches and tendrils closed over her face like evil fingers, and she was swallowed whole by the falling mountain.

***

SURFING. LIKE THAT HORRIBLE DAY, HER THIRTEENTH CHRISTMAS, back before Callie was afraid. A girl her age should never have been in that malevolent, cyclone-whipped sea. Flung from her surfboard, tumbled and pulverized and dragged across sand and rocks, her lungs aching for oxygen, her equilibrium struggling to find Up.

Her mind exploded with the pain of a sickening blow across the side of her head.

And everything went black.

***

THE RAIN HAD NOT STOPPED FALLING, BUT THE MOUNTAIN HAD stopped moving, more or less. Jack's brain could not accept what his eyes were seeing. Where dense rainforest had filled the mountainside moments earlier, there was now bare rock. A vertical strip wide as a football field, and possibly hundreds of stories high—the low cloud made it hard to judge. Ahead, where the rest of the team were presumably still walking unaware, everything looked normal. Behind, a steep and heartless rock face, being washed shiny clean by the torrent from the sky. A deep gash in the mountain, all the way to the bone.

This had to be one of the tree avalanches described by Bryan on the first day. The rainforest now lay below him in a massive ugly pile of tangled tree limbs, mud and shredded vegetation. Parts of it were still settling, and as he watched, a mighty tree that had been perched precariously on top of the mound slowly, regally tilted sideways to a 45-degree angle, and slid from sight beneath the mess. Nearer to him, he saw mud shift and begin oozing downhill, lured by gravity, searching for a way to insinuate itself into the debris. The rain was so heavy he couldn't see the far end of the landslide, let alone the other side of the valley.

Jack lay askew on top of the muddle of rocks and battered greenery where his downhill slide had finally ended, staring at the chaos, his heart pounding in his ears, his lungs burning in his chest. Somewhere down there, Callie was caught in all that. He had to find her, before the mass shifted any further. But he also had to breathe. He had to find her, but he had to get some fluid into his searing throat.

He groped behind for the water bottle in the side of his pack, shoving the rain cover aside. As he gulped thirstily, it gradually registered that his hood had come loose in the fall, and the downpour was now flooding down his back, inside the jacket, drenching his clothing, making him cold. Cold. His sluggish mind finally grasped that this was not a good thing for a man in shock, and he fumbled to reinstate the hood.

Jack's right shoulder throbbed and his left knee seemed to be on fire as he began the difficult descent down the slope. As he went, he searched for a relatively firm and safe place to discard his rucksack, and at length found a large flat boulder a few meters from the edge of the slip zone. It would have to do. He fumbled with the harness clip with fingers that had lost all dexterity, and finally shed the load

with relief. The screaming in his shoulder lowered about five deci-
bels. As an afterthought he grabbed the water bottle and shoved it
in his pocket before setting off again. He felt the camera in there,
and pulled it out, started it recording, pulling the head strap into
position so it captured more or less what he was seeing.

Lighter now, he could move more swiftly down the mountain
into the danger zone. He crept on all fours, crab-like, eyes seeking
out the next reliable hand- or foot-hold, while constantly glancing
down the mountain at his goal. The whole enormous landslip was
still desperately unstable, and he could see trees and boulders shift-
ing, now just a small nudge, now as much as a meter in one big jolt.

He thanked God for Callie's revolting orange rain jacket that
she'd joked about back at Bryan's house in Te Anau. It seemed like
centuries ago. "Orange is the color of fear, Jack," she'd teased him.
"Are you afraid, Jack?" *Yes, Callie, I'm so very afraid. But if anything
will help me find you in all this mess, it's that awful jacket.*

He drew level with the heap of displaced mountain, and began
searching in earnest. *God help me. Where is she?* If he couldn't see her
near the surface, he couldn't imagine knowing where to start. Even
a bulldozer would take days to shift the immense pile of debris.
He moved gingerly onto the unstable mass, still on all fours, and
peered down through any gap or cavity he could find.

Within two minutes he saw it just ahead: a glimpse of orange.
It was the sleeve of Callie's jacket, emerging from a muddle of torn
branches and mud, flung across a pile of tattered vegetation. The
fingers of the protruding hand were completely still. Jack maneuvered carefully and discovered he could also see one of her boots
and part of her leg. Yes, she had come to rest near the surface! She
appeared to be lying face down, partially buried to a depth of no
more than about thirty centimeters.

He adjusted his balance and started lifting rainforest trash from where her head and upper body must be, working fast, carefully, always looking around to check what the mound was doing. *Please God, let her be alive.* He kept repeating the words in his head like a silent chant, his breath coming fast and shallow. As he lifted one of the larger branches to toss it aside, his vision was engulfed by gray fog, and he nearly toppled.

He paused a moment, closed his eyes, and breathed out long and slow. *Stop hyperventilating, Jack. You're no use to anyone if you pass out.* One more shredded branch out of the way, and her head was free. She had it turned to the side so he could see her face in profile. Her nostrils seemed clear—hopefully she'd been able to breathe—but the top of her face and eyes were covered in the slippery mud. Jack grabbed his water bottle and started gently washing the muck away, trying to clear enough so that she could at least open her eyes and see. For once, the rain was helping instead of hindering.

She still didn't move, and in those conditions there was no way to see whether she was breathing. "Callie! Can you hear me?" *Please God, don't let her die.* "Callie!"

He saw her mouth move, the tiniest fraction. Or was it just the pressure of the rain? "Callie! You have to wake up!" Her fingers moved now, a slight clenching. That was real, not his imagination. She was still in there, somewhere. "Thank you God," he whispered. "Help me!"

He set to the rest of the debris with renewed zeal, steadily uncovering her torso, both legs, and then her other arm. Incredibly, her rucksack was still firmly attached. None of her limbs lay at an unnatural angle; hopefully nothing was broken. He felt relief welling inside him, until an abrupt jolt through the depths of the mound dropped them a sudden meter down the mountainside and sent Jack's heart vaulting into his mouth. Callie cried out, but he couldn't tell whether it was from pain or fear.

"Callie, can you hear me?" His voice was urgent; he had to get her out of there before the whole mess shifted again and swallowed them both. She didn't respond.

"Callie, say something. You have to answer me!"

"Ja-ack. Help me…" Her voice was small and hoarse, and he had to struggle to hear her over the pounding of the rain and the roaring of the river below. She began to weep aloud, a soft guttural keening that tore his heart into a hundred bruised pieces.

Jack's own eyes filled with tears. "Callie, we have to move from here. There's been a landslide and we have to get you to stable ground. Can you move at all? I know it's hard, but Callie, you have to try." He longed to let her recover quietly while he tried to assess the extent of her injuries, but they just didn't have the luxury of that sort of time. And throwing her over his shoulder in a fireman's lift could make things worse if she was bleeding internally. Imprecise though it was, asking her to move her own body seemed the safest way to find out how badly she was hurt before he tried anything else.

Slowly and hesitantly, Callie pulled her arms in and rolled onto her side. The movement dragged her hood from her head, and Jack winced as he glimpsed blood matting her strawberry curls. "Do you think you can sit up, Cal? We can't stay here. I wish we could, but we just can't."

As he spoke, he glanced at the mound again, and saw something beyond that horrified him. The river they'd been following through this valley, now in full raging flood from the implacable rain, had been dammed by the landslide. And it wasn't happy about it. Upstream, the river was rising fast, and they were on the upstream side. Though they were still a good distance above the water level, the monstrous force of the water was pushing and shoving, determined to blast the obstruction out of its way. If it succeeded, it would undermine the foundation of the heap on which they were perched, and send them plunging dozens of meters down the mountainside.

"Take my hands, and I'll help you sit up." She reached for him and managed to close her fingers around his, though her grip was weak. Gradually he levered her upright, releasing one hand to reach around behind her rucksack and support her back. "That's good Cal, you're doing well." He tried to keep the panic out of his voice, while also monitoring the threat beyond.

"I'm going to lift you now, okay?" He slipped his other arm under her bent knees, and lurched upright. Callie groaned with the jolt of it, and lay in his arms, a dead weight. She turned her face into his shoulder and continued to weep. Jack began the staggering journey across to the stable part of the mountainside, his shoulder and knee screaming in two-part discord. With her pack she must have weighed at least eighty kilos, probably more, but he tried not to think about that. The mound shifted suddenly under his feet, but he dared not slow down or look back.

As he reached relative safety, he glanced up the mountain. The rain had eased a little, enough that he could see nearly to the top, the full height of that astonishing vertical gash. Bare rock, long and straight and wide, like some kind of giant's laundry chute.

Jack didn't know if he'd be able to lift Callie again if he put her down, so he kept going, climbing the mountain back to where he'd left his rucksack, pushing on up that forty-five degree slope. A crashing behind him made him pause and look back; the mini-mountain had slid at least another twenty meters down the slope.

The perch where he'd found Callie just minutes ago was gone, mashed into the jumble of rocks and trees.

28

As they walked in the front door, the coldness hit Ellen like a slap in the face. It wasn't just the temperature. The house was bare, but not like an empty house awaiting new residents. An absence. Or even a presence. Their heels echoed obscenely on the timber.

"What's with the masking tape on the floor?" she asked Peter as they moved through the living room with its two rows of four rectangles marked under their feet. There seemed to be a narrow walkway between them, and there were a few discarded duffel bags against the walls.

He paused near the hallway and looked at the floor. "Apparently he put all their rucksacks and supplies there. One rectangle for each person." He lifted his hand in the direction of the hallway, inviting her to go ahead of him. "The thing we need you to see is down here."

She was still staring at the floor. Each rectangle was marked with a name, in the format of surname and then initials. Girls one side, boys the other, in alphabetical order. "Like plots in a cemetery," she muttered. She wriggled her shoulders and shook her head, trying to dispel the sinister thought.

As she stepped into the hallway, she saw him glance back at the masking tape grid, his eyes narrowed.

"The bedroom." He nodded in its direction as she paused at the end of the hall.

She walked into what could have been a monastic cell, except there was no crucifix on the wall. In fact, there was nothing at all on the walls. No curtains on the windows. Just a narrow bed with a small table beside it, and an old, cheap timber wardrobe, the kind sold at charity shops.

"Now Ellen," Peter began, his voice firm, "you are going to find this upsetting, so I would like you to sit down, and do whatever it is you do to prepare yourself for things that are upsetting. There are some photos on the back of the cupboard door—a sort of shrine, I guess. I wouldn't ask you to look at it, but the fastest way to identify some of the faces is to ask you, and we need to get some answers quickly so we know how to proceed. Do you understand?"

She nodded, perched on the edge of the hard bed, and took several deep breaths, exhaling long and slow. Outwardly at least, she was calm, but she could feel the terror fighting to crawl up into her mouth. Peter was watching her. "Ready as I'll ever be."

The long creak jarred her nerves as he swung the door open, and then he came to sit beside her on the bed, his long legs crossed loosely at the ankles, his hands clasped in a relaxed position in front of him. He sat so close she could feel the warmth of his upper arm only millimeters from hers, and the almost-contact was comforting.

Her eyes were drawn straight towards the top of the door, where a studio portrait of a beautiful young woman took pride of place, her features delicate, makeup perfect and hair glamorously-styled. "That's Liana," she said, pointing. It looked like a photo the girl would have used to audition for acting and modeling jobs. "She was his girlfriend who committed suicide. On the last day of high school. They had a party at Bryan's place that night, and she shot herself. In front of them all. In his living room. It was unbelievably traumatic." She glanced at him. "She was pregnant, too."

He nodded, slowly, obviously thinking. "We'll need more on that, but later will do. What about the others?"

She looked back at the door, her eyes moving to the images circling Liana—a collection of photos cut from nature magazines, and a faded print of a young boy blowing out candles on a cake, a smiling man and woman behind him. She gestured in a circular motion. "Those are Bryan's parents, but I guess you know that."

He nodded. "I thought so."

Her gaze now moved down the door. Eight photos cut into perfect squares, aligned into two rows—four men across the top, four women across the bottom. She gasped and her hand went to her throat as she saw Rachel. A heavy black cross had been drawn across the photo with marker pen, going from corner to corner with mathematical precision, just as with the other seven images. Transfixed, it took a moment for Ellen to speak. She drew a deep breath and fought the desire to scream. She swallowed hard. "That's my daughter. Second from the left." She looked at Peter, frowning. "I've never seen that photo before, and it's recent—she's only had that hairstyle this year. I wonder where he got it. We live in the same house and she's always enjoyed showing me her photos."

He spoke calmly. "Except for the shot of Bryan, they're all taken with a long lens. We think they're probably surveillance photos."

"But why...? I don't understand." She shook her head. But she did understand. At least enough to know that she was looking at the product of a very disturbed mind.

"Would you like a drink of water?" Peter's hands were still relaxed, the heat of his upper arm still near enough to hers to give support without professional impropriety.

"No, let's get this done and get out of this place." She shivered and wrapped her arms around herself, one hand each side of her waist. One by one she identified the other photographs. They were older now, but still recognizable as Rachel's high school friends. "And I guess that must be Bryan. He looks so different with that hair. I wouldn't have recognized him in the street."

"Thank you, Ellen." He stood and closed the cupboard door,

hiding its images—although they remained burnt on her retinas. "Let's get you out of here."

He reached for her elbow and helped her to her feet, maintaining the hold as they walked back down the hallway. She was glad of the human touch, and the physical support—her legs felt rubbery, her throat dry. It was a visceral relief to emerge into the sunshine again, and gulp fresh air as Peter locked the house's horrors within it.

29

CALLIE STRUGGLED UP FROM DEEP INSIDE THE EARTH. IT WAS warm and dark down there, and she wanted to curl into the fetal position till the end of the world, but for some reason she wasn't to be allowed to do so. Up. She had to come up. There was a murmur of voices, and someone was flicking her face. Something cold. Water. They were flicking her face with water.

She opened her eyes a crack, and the vicious light pierced her brain like a rapier. Callie instinctively turned from it, and at the movement her head exploded with pain.

"Callie! Are you okay?" That was Jack's voice.

"Stop flicking me," she muttered. Or she thought she said it. So hard to be sure if her tongue had actually shaped any sounds.

"Callie! Can you hear us?" That wasn't Jack. A woman. Rachel? Yes, she sounded odd, but it must be Rachel.

Callie cracked her eyes open again, and looked up towards that horrible light. Three shapes. She closed her eyes, and tried to pull her thoughts back from the corners of the universe where they had fled. A slapping noise. Slap, sla-slap. Rain. They weren't flicking her.

"It's raining."

"Yes, sweetie, it's raining, but not nearly as bad as before." That was Rachel again. She sounded anxious. *I wonder what's happened to make her anxious?*

"Callie, can you open your eyes?" Someone else. Callie's mind roamed around awkwardly, then settled on an answer. Erica, and she was wearing her professional voice. *Why?*

"Callie, you need to open your eyes and talk to us." Erica again, and quite bossy this time. "Callie! Open your eyes!"

"Bossy-boots."

A short gust of laughter. That was Jack.

"What did she say?" Erica again.

"She called you a bossy-boots. That has to mean she's still in there somewhere."

"Come on, sweetie." Rachel's voice again. "See if you can open your eyes for us. I know it's hard, but you just have to do it. Please Callie."

Something in the timbre of Rachel's voice pierced the fog. Anxiety, insistence, pleading. Callie struggled to raise her eyelids, so thick and heavy. This time the light didn't hurt quite so much. The shapes around her took form. Jack beside her in the tent, Erica and Rachel crouched awkwardly in the opening, rain spattering through the gaps between them.

"Well, hello there." Rachel was smiling at her, but her eyes looked teary. Or was it just the rain moistening her face?

"Can you move, Callie?" asked Erica. "Just see if you can roll onto your side for me."

Not for you, but I might give it a crack for Rachel. Laboriously, she began to move, and the pain radiated out from her head and started grabbing her limbs, now a shoulder, there a knee. Even her hand and wrist didn't like it. She moaned. "Why does it hurt so much?"

She must have said that one clearly enough, because Jack replied. "You've been through a blender, love. Keep going. You're doing well."

Eternal minutes later, they had Callie more or less sitting upright in the cramped tent. They'd tried to explain the landslide, and her tumble down the mountain, but her brain didn't want to absorb the information. Jack had moved out into the rain to let Erica in to tend to Callie's head wound from her mini first aid kit. The disinfectant applied from Erica's small, precious bottle felt like razors slicing into Callie's scalp, and she gasped with the agony of it, her eyes wet.

While Erica worked, Callie gazed thick-headedly at the puzzling clutter down the end of the tent. Her eyes seemed to have forgotten how to focus. Finally, the orange mound resolved itself into her wet-weather gear, the jacket slung, arms akimbo, over her rucksack. Jack's gear was down there too, except for his blue rain jacket, which must be on him. Filthy boots were mixed in among it.

Their sleeping bags had been set up side by side, each inside its big orange plastic waterproof bag, as required in this sort of weather, but they were lumpy, twisted and misshapen. The roof of the tent sagged lopsidedly, and there seemed to be almost as much mud inside as out. She puzzled over an oblong shape above her head, then realized it must be duct tape—Jack had repaired a tear. It looked like a camp set up by a blind and drunken madman. It was a far cry from the shipshape order enforced by Ranger Bryan from Day One of this march, and robotically perpetuated by his reluctant acolytes even after he was gone, for the simple reason that it worked.

Callie looked round for Jack. Rachel still crouched in the opening, watching her closely, but Jack must be standing up taking a look around. All she could see was his legs from the knee down, bare toes sticking out the bottom of his pants. So that's why there were so many boots in the tent.

"Hey, Jack!" she called, and the sound resonating in her head only hurt a moderate amount.

The toes changed direction on the rock, the knees bent, and in a moment Jack was peering in at her, his concerned face aligned with Rachel's. "What's up?" he asked.

"I just wanted to say: I love what you've done with the place. Bryan would be so proud."

His face split into a grin. "Oh shut up! You try doing any better in these conditions. It was like trying to wrestle an elephant in a car wash!"

"Who are you calling an elephant?" she demanded, and erupted into giggles. Jack joined in and then even Rachel started a little muffled snorting, her hand over her mouth as she looked with new eyes at the chaos inside the tent. Each shake of Callie's body pounded her bruised ribcage and thumped inside her head, but it felt good in spite of all that. *Never underestimate the value of laughter.*

It became one of those spells of uncontrolled laughter that sometimes happen among old friends who've been too tired and too stressed for too long—a moment of release.

As they grew calm again, Callie realized Erica had not joined in. She turned to look at her; lines of strain were showing on the other woman's face. "What's wrong?" Her heart leapt into her mouth as she realized Erica somehow might have diagnosed the severity of her injuries; though she could move and talk and even laugh right now, her life might yet be slipping away. She'd seen it before when covering road accidents: people talking to their rescuers, alive and breathing, but when she called the police later to follow up, she'd find out the person had died in the ambulance.

Callie saw a look pass between the other three, and Erica seemed close to tears. Her anxiety levels rose. Jackson sighed, and looked at the ground. He might have been formulating words, but it was Rachel who broke the silence. When she did, it took a moment for Callie to absorb that it wasn't her they were concerned about.

"There was another landslide further along, Cal," she said. "Up where we were walking. Much smaller and narrower than this one, but not good, just the same."

Callie gave her a questioning look. "What happened?"

"Well, it's just that..." Rachel shrugged helplessly, and looked at the other two for help. They were both looking somewhere else by now. Her eyes went back to Callie's and her expression was gentle.

"Callie, we can't find Adam or Kain."

30

THE VOICE DOWN THE PHONE LINE WAS AS DRY AND SIBILANT AS two pieces of paper rubbing together. It conjured up in Peter's mind visions of a dusty old law office with high windows, and a hunched figure at a gloomy desk. It seemed perfectly appropriate that the man's name was Dickens.

"I am not authorized to release Mr Smithton's will until thirty days after his death has been formally declared." There was no apology in the tone. The owner of the voice was smugly assured of his legally superior position.

Peter was working hard at holding down the edges of his temper. "I understand your situation, Mr Dickens. Are you able to confirm for me the date on which the most recent will was signed?" He looked at the document in his hand, arrived via Interpol so recently that the paper was still warm from their laser printer. A copy of a will that was catastrophically different to the older one found in Bryan's house. A will found locked inside a safe at the home of Kain Vindico.

There was a moment's silence while the lawyer considered Peter's request. "The document we hold is dated the thirteenth of October this year."

Peter inhaled sharply. "The thirteenth did you say? Not the third?"

"The thirteenth."

"Mr Dickens, that will is relevant to an ongoing police investigation. It is imperative that we see the content of it."

"Then I am very much afraid, sergeant, that you will have to get yourself a warrant."

31

CALLIE WASN'T SURE IF HER VISION HAD BEEN DAMAGED, OR IF the mist really did keep pulling in and out of the trees as though it was doing a hula dance. The rain had eased, but the vegetation they pushed through was heavy with rainwater, and the ground so waterlogged that some sections were like quicksand. It sucked down on a boot, only letting go with huge reluctance and an angry slurping noise. Every step was painful already without that complication. Her rucksack seemed about ten kilograms heavier than it had this morning, even though the others had taken some of her load. Callie wondered, again, if she should have argued so hard.

She had been determined not to remain alone at the slapdash campsite, while the others went searching. Yes, she wanted to do her bit to help, but her display of team spirit had been cloaking a kernel of fear. What if the mountainside gave way again, with her on it, trapped inside the tent, with no way to escape, and no one to help? Tumbled downwards inside a giant cement mixer, and then slowly and inexorably flattened, trying to draw breath in the dark, with the weight of scrambled rainforest pressing down and down and down, and no one even to hold her hand while the last molecules of oxygen left her body.

Even worse, what if there was another slide between Callie and the searchers, and they couldn't get back to her, and the afternoon drew on into evening and night and the next day, and she was the only person in the universe?

No, she couldn't stay in the tent on the rock. She'd been even more mutinously determined when she saw the bossy look on Erica's face. "You need to stay here," Nurse had declared with complacent finality. "Sure, you don't seem to have any broken arms or legs, which is great. But we have no accurate way to tell what your internal injuries might be, and I'd be very surprised if that head wound of yours hasn't given you concussion. You need to rest."

"You're right. I also need a long hot bath. And a big plate of steak and chips. But they don't seem to have a Holiday Inn out here, so I'll just have to put all that on hold for another day."

Rachel had wavered between the two points of view, but ultimately Jack had been the one to see the issues for what they were, and to state them with his customary candor.

"Whatever we do from here, we must stay together. We can't risk getting separated again. It's too dangerous." He'd started ticking off a list on his fingers. "We also have to take our gear with us; we can't risk getting separated from our tents or sleeping bags or cooking equipment by any further landslide or something else we haven't thought of. We also can't spend the night here—there's not enough room for more tents on this rock, and I don't trust its stability anyway, this close to the slip zone. It would be lovely to get back to last night's rock bivvy, but we can't because the mountain we hiked across earlier is in a big pile down there." He'd indicated the foot of the landslip, and they'd all looked at it, and then above it at the sheer rock face it had revealed, too steep and too slippery for their meager rock-climbing skills.

"So that means tonight's camp is somewhere up ahead." He'd shrugged. "She has to come with us. It's not ideal, but there's no real alternative."

Now they seemed to have somehow split into two groups anyway. Jack was in the lead, forging on, anxious to find Adam as soon as possible, and Callie was in his slipstream. The group had agreed Kain had been striking out so far ahead today he was probably a kilometer or more beyond the slip zone when the mountain fell, and hadn't even seen it. Callie would be glad when they caught up with him and she knew he was safe, just the same. What if there had been a third landslide further up?

But Adam was the urgent problem. He had been walking with Rachel and Erica, even though they seemed to have become slightly separated. He would surely have found them by now if he could. Whatever had stopped their jungle warrior, it wouldn't be pretty.

Despite the distraction of her own injuries, Callie had seen enough of Jack's form to know he was hurting too. Every time he bent his left knee, there was a slight jerking twist to the follow-through. She paused a moment for a breather, and looked back through the trees. The mist had become so dense that she couldn't even see the other two women behind her.

Her mind flitted back to this morning's conversation—was it only this morning?—about keeping an eye on Rachel. "Jack!"

He stopped and turned. "What's up, Cal? Are you okay?" He came the few steps back, and peered at her while absentmindedly massaging his shoulder.

"Yeah, I'm okay, but I can't see the others. I think they've fallen back a bit. I can't even hear them now."

He looked beyond her to the foggy trees. "It's just the mist. It deadens the sound. They're probably not that far behind. We need to find Adam urgently. If he was injured by that slide, he's been lying there at least two or three hours now. In heavy rain, for most of it."

"It's just that… about a thousand years ago, we were talking about not letting Rachel out of our sight. It's so hard to know what's most important now."

Jack chewed his lower lip, and rubbed his shoulder again. "We should wait for them; we can't afford to get separated again." He sagged against a tree, and Callie found a log to prop against.

Jack went on, "Callie, have you thought about…" He trailed off, and grimaced. Clearly, whatever it was, he didn't want to say it out loud. She waited. "Well, it's crazy, but what if Adam is, you know… hiding, rather than lost. Had you thought about that, or is it just me going nuts?"

She stared at him, speechless.

"Yeah, okay," he said, nodding. "It's just me going nuts. It's virtually impossible to see him killing Sharon—especially when he had a golden opportunity to shove me off that cliff right back near Poison Bay, if he wanted to improve his odds. I hate what I'm becoming out here. The things I'm thinking." He shook his head and stared at the ground. "I never in a million years would've thought of Adam as one of the bad guys, but last night, when he killed that bird… there was something in his eyes I'd never seen before. It freaked me out."

"I don't think you're nuts. It's just a shocking thought. I've been having my own confusing little thoughts about Erica. Something didn't seem quite right about her reaction to Adam's disappearance. I couldn't put my finger on it."

"I could," said Jack with emphasis. "But then, you've got to remember how paranoid I've become and take it with a grain of salt. I noticed that Rachel was really precise about what she was doing when the landslide started. She'd stopped to eat ferns and measure her blood sugar, and she described what she saw and how she felt. But Erica seemed a bit vague and abrupt about it. And why did they let themselves get so far away from one another? That's one of the things that made me wonder if Adam had been deliberately trying to lose them." He frowned. "And yet, the rain was so incredibly heavy, you could hardly see your own hand in front of you. Plus the mudslide we experienced ourselves was disorientating. I guess it's reasonable to have trouble remembering the details."

Callie said, "I'd hate to think of Adam against us. He'd make a pretty scary enemy, with his strength and skill, and that hunter's instinct."

"Thinking of Adam not-for-us is almost as bad. If he's been injured or killed, we've lost probably our biggest asset, our best chance out here." He rubbed his face with both hands and stared down the valley into the fog. "Kain doesn't seem to be around when we need him. You're probably the next strongest and you've just been pulverized by the mountain. Erica's tougher than she looks, but very small and her knees are playing up, and Rachel can't stay strong much longer."

"And what about you?"

He gave a derisive snort. "I'm just the Reverend. You call me if you want someone to pray, or possibly to cry like a little girl."

"What a load of rubbish! I don't need my brain to be working very well to figure out you did something pretty amazing to get me out of that mess back there."

He waved a hand dismissively. "I just did what had to be done."

"You saved my life," Callie declared. "Thank you, Jack. I'm very glad to still be alive."

He looked sideways at her and shrugged, but his eyes had changed, and she knew he was touched by what she'd said. She continued, thoughtful this time: "And doing what has to be done seems to be something you're good at. I'm discovering that you're actually a very good leader in a crisis, which I'd never noticed before, in all the time I've known you. We can be very blind, sometimes, to the strengths of people we know well."

He looked a little puzzled. "I'd have thought you were the leader among us."

"No Jack," she replied with a mischievous smile, "I'm just loud. There is a difference, you know. I know how to get people's attention; you have the clarity and conviction to show people the right path to take."

Jack raised one eyebrow. "What a bore I must be. And what a burden for me to carry."

"Clarity isn't boring for people who are confused. But yes, you do have to be careful how you use it."

They heard noises behind them, and the sporadic murmur of voices, and turned to see Rachel and Erica emerging from the mist. Rachel was puffing, but she mustered up a smile when she saw them looking back at her.

"Gosh, that mud's a killer, isn't it?" she said.

"Haven't you heard the joke before?" Callie said. "There's no such thing as gravity; this planet sucks."

Rachel smiled. "It does, doesn't it?—quite literally today."

Erica didn't smile, she just looked tense, and Callie found herself wondering about her again.

Jack said, "I think we might be getting close to the next landslide. The mist lifted for a minute before and it's lighter up ahead, less tree cover. Are you guys okay to keep moving?"

"Yes, let's keep going," Rachel said. "We have to find Adam."

Erica said nothing, so they took her silence for assent, and began scrambling again through the clinging mud.

***

As they drew near to the tangle of trees and rocks of the next landslide, the mist lifted, and Jack could see the full height of the slip despite lowering clouds. It wasn't nearly as comprehensive as the one that had engulfed him and Callie, and had not stripped the mountain down to rock, yet it was still messy and possibly unstable down near the roaring river.

"I can see how you couldn't find anything in that really heavy rain," Jack said back over his shoulder to Rachel and Erica. He scanned the heap, looking for anything non-rainforest. He mentally cursed Adam's green rain jacket. If only they'd all worn Callie's hideous orange.

"We tried so hard," said Rachel.

"I'm sure you did." Callie squeezed her friend's arm. "Don't worry, we'll find him."

"Who's coming with me?" Jack spoke briskly, steering them away from the emotional undercurrents. He was already unbuckling his harness.

"I'll come with you," said Callie.

"I'll stay here with Rachel and look after the rucksacks," Erica said.

She propped her rucksack against a rock and sat down. Jack shot a quick look at Callie, and started climbing down the slope. She followed, putting each foot where his had been. When they were about fifteen meters down the mountain, Jack stopped to scan the mound of debris.

Callie drew alongside him. "What was all that about?" she said. "Surely she's had more experience of death and injury than any of us?"

"I don't know." He gave a small shrug. "We need to find Adam."

They moved carefully, looking for footholds, and then peering into the rubble.

"Is that...?" Callie pointed.

Jack nodded, with a quick expulsion of breath. "It's a boot."

The rain started again, and Jack pulled his hood up. He looked at Callie, waiting for her to do the same. She ignored him, and started moving out onto the mound, in the direction of that boot.

"Calliope, put your hood up."

"I'm okay." She kept moving. "It makes me crazy. No peripheral vision, and that infernal crackling and rustling in your ears all the time."

"We can't afford to have you with hypothermia on top of everything else. So put it up. Now."

She looked as though she was about to come up with a retort, but apparently reconsidered. She pulled the hood up with a loud "humph", and stuck her tongue out at him. "I tell you you're a good leader, and next thing I know, you're going all Master and Commander on me."

"Whatever." He gave her a searching look. "Callie, how much pain are you in?"

"I'm all right. This has to be done. I can be injured later."

"Are you ready for this?"

Her eyes filled with sudden tears, and she shook her head. "No, but we have to do it, don't we?"

He gave her hand a quick squeeze. "Come on. Try to move lightly. We don't want to dislodge the mound."

They picked their way across the jumble of muddy vegetation, headed always towards that boot, thrust into the air like a small and dismal ensign. When they reached it, they could see the rest of the leg, disappearing into the debris at an unnatural angle. They perched each side of where it seemed Adam might lie, and began to lift branches and tattered ferns, digging their way down.

Slowly, his torso emerged, his neck, and his face, until finally his eyes were uncovered. They were wide open, staring sightlessly into the sky, flooded by fat raindrops which pooled and then overflowed down his temples like tears. Jack's eyes became wet too. He felt Adam's face and neck with the back of his fingers. It was as cold and slick as the side of the pool at those horrible winter swimming lessons of his childhood. It didn't matter what they did now. Adam couldn't be anything but dead.

Jack glanced up at Callie, who was weeping without constraint. She held his gaze for a long moment, and then reached out tenderly to move the last clump of leaves from Adam's hair. She gasped and went pale, and Jack looked down at what she'd seen: a puncture wound in Adam's forehead.

"It must have been a stick or something…" he muttered, through lips that seemed to have lost their elasticity.

"No!" Callie's voice was rough. "Oh dear God!" She shook her head, again and again.

"Callie?" Jack reached a hand towards her, and she grasped it across the body of their friend.

"Oh Jack. You don't understand. A stick didn't do that."

"What do you mean, love?" He was confused. It was only natural for her to be upset by what they'd just discovered, but this was something more.

"Oh Jack, I'm so scared." She sobbed, and gripped his hand tight. "This is so much worse than we thought."

"What is it, Callie? Tell me!"

She drew a deep breath. "You remember that pathology course I told you about? Where we looked at the photos and the dead bodies, the victims of crime?"

He nodded. She stared again at the wound on Adam's forehead.

"That's no accident, Jack. That's a bullet hole."

32

PETER WATCHED THE WATER FLICKERING IN THE LATE AFTERNOON light, mesmerized by the patterns. A breeze was coming off the lake, picking up molecules of the wine in the glass before him and wafting them into his nostrils. One glass was all he could afford to drink—he needed to keep his wits about him—so he planned to sip it very slowly. He was waiting on news regarding the death of Liana Rickard. An old friend now working for Interpol had been chasing it for him. The three-hour time difference with Australia's east coast was a blessing in a case like this—they'd be at work for a while yet across the Tasman. But it sure did make for a long day.

An odd movement in his peripheral vision drew his eye. He beheld Ellen Carpenter on the footpath, and she'd apparently stopped in her tracks at the sight of him on his front veranda.

"This is awkward," she said, her tone light. "I'm not stalking you, as it happens. I didn't even know where you lived. I was just walking, yet again. I find it therapeutic."

"The amount of walking you're doing, you were bound to come past my place sooner or later. This is a pretty small town." He nodded in the direction of the wine bottle. "I've got another glass in the cupboard if you want to stop walking for a moment. Won't be for long though. I'm going back to the office shortly."

She looked at the wine bottle, then at him, considering, and nodded. "Thanks. It would be nice to have a bit of company for a few minutes." As she stepped onto the veranda she added, tongue-in-cheek, "Do you often get sloshed while in uniform, and more importantly, does your 'deputy' know?"

He grinned. "I've been trying to teach Tom that rules were

made to be our servants, not our masters, but it doesn't seem to have taken." He pushed down on the armrests and levered himself out of the canvas chair.

"How long have you been trying?"

"Nearly eight years now." He indicated the other chair for her, but she remained standing.

"What will you be having for your dinner?" she asked, her head tilted.

After a brief verbal scuffle covering stress, the nutritional value of wine, and the proper functioning of the human body, he found himself in the kitchen toasting slices of bread excavated from the freezer. Beside him, Ellen was cooking up some kind of omelet involving several not-too-ancient eggs, grated cheese also from the freezer, and the contents of some cans she had evaluated and found acceptable from the motley collection in his cupboard. There had been no time for shopping since he returned from leave. Her domestic activity in his home was rather wonderful, but he forced himself to pull his thoughts back. *She's a relative, Peter old son, that's what she is.*

They ate in companionable silence on the veranda, unembarrassed by the crunching of toast and the scraping of cutlery. The egg creation was surprisingly fragrant and delicious. Ellen took a sip from her glass of wine, and Peter saw her eyebrows go up.

"What did you expect?" he teased. "Battery acid?"

She smiled. "Don't take this the wrong way, Peter, but I'm getting the impression more and more that you're not the typical small-town cop."

He thought about what he might say to that, and opted for the truth. "I used to be a city detective in Christchurch till my marriage went south and I decided to get out of Dodge. It wasn't that much fun hanging around watching some bloke cut me out of my daughter's life." He said it without self-pity.

"Isn't it harder, though, now you're not able to see her regularly?"

"I think it's actually better for both of us this way. I was getting a bit aggro with him, and that wasn't good for my relationship with Tahlia. I've been doing all the work to keep in touch with her, but she's legally an adult now, so hopefully she'll start to reciprocate soon."

"And if she doesn't?"

"Then I'll keep on keeping in touch."

"Do you miss the city work? It must be very different here."

"Everyone up there seems to be drinking caramel lattes and shoving drugs up their nose. Down here it's more community policing. You feel part of something. It was just a place to recover at the beginning, but now I actually prefer it."

"Well I'm glad you're on this case. It's turning out to be more complicated than anyone would have thought. Those photos in Bryan's house, and the fact you've had so much trouble finding fingerprints..." She shook her head, remembering. "If there's been a crime here, it makes him look more and more like the perpetrator instead of the victim. When you put it together with the will you received today, it creates a very strange picture."

He glanced at her from under his eyebrows. "How do you know about the will?" Some things were discussed openly in the search room, and some were not.

"Um..." She smiled sheepishly. "I might have read it on your desk when I went in to give you those printouts."

He stared at her. "So, you can read upside down? I'll have to remember that."

"It was just an automatic reaction, I'm afraid, when I saw those lines highlighted in yellow." She looked uncertain. "Am I in trouble? Are you going to ban me? If you need to do so for the sake of the investigation, you should, but for the sake of my sanity I'm hoping you won't."

He frowned, thoughtful. "I won't ban you just yet, but I may need to. Do you think it's helpful for you to be talking about all these things?"

"Yes, it is. It makes me feel like I'm doing something about it. Relieves some of the psychological pressure. I did the same thing when my husband was dying. I investigated treatments and doctors, assessed options. For some people that would make it even more stressful, but it helped me to cope."

"When did he die?"

"A little over a year ago now. Melanoma." She sighed. "Twelve months from freckle to funeral." The words were flippant, but the tone was not.

"That sucks."

"Yes. It really, really does."

He changed the subject. "Like a quick coffee before I go back to work?"

She smiled. "Can you do a caramel latte? I hear they're very nice."

He grinned. "Sorry, we're all out. But it's not instant, at least."

A couple of minutes later he was pouring from the coffee plunger. "If you feel able to talk about it," he said, "I'd be interested in your perspective on what's going on with Bryan Smithton."

"Well, to be honest I'd like to get some of the thoughts outside my head. It's getting crowded in there. I've obviously thought a lot about that visit to his house today. Bryan was clearly suffering some form of mental illness, and the death of Liana had become his focus. The arrangement of those photos on the cupboard door makes that clear. The death of his parents might be influential too, given the 'happy childhood' circle he'd placed around her, but Liana is the trigger for whatever it is that he's set out to do. The eight photos at the bottom represent everyone who was in that room the night Liana shot herself. And the big black crosses through the photos look like... well, the impression I received from the whole arrangement was that he thought they should all be punished for what happened to Liana. Eliminated, even, if that's not being too dramatic."

"Would he have any reason to think it was their fault?" He knew he was on dangerous ground asking such a thing, when one of the "guilty" was her own daughter. But she seemed able to discuss it, he needed to know, and she was his best available witness.

"Rachel discussed it with us in great detail in the days afterwards. Liana gave a very nasty little speech before she pulled the trigger, blaming them all for failing to support her in her desire for an abortion. Rachel took it very much to heart, and we had to spend a lot of time talking it all through with her. She struggled with guilt over things she could have said or done differently. Any sensible person would, if a friend committed suicide, even without the direct accusation. We finally helped her understand that while we can always be better friends than we are, suicide is ultimately a choice. No one forces it on another person."

"You don't believe there was any kind of conspiracy?"

"Absolutely not. There was no organization about it. Some of them didn't even know she was pregnant till that night, and the ones that did hadn't discussed it with each other. Even Rachel and Callie, who were best friends, hadn't discussed it. At a different time of year, I'm certain that they would have done, but they were so busy with final exams that all their normal routines were in uproar."

"Do you know how it affected Bryan?"

"I do know he was visibly distressed at her funeral, which they all were, and yet Bryan was never given to displays of emotion, so that made it all the more upsetting to watch. I recall discussing with Roger our concerns that Bryan might not work through it the way he needed to. He was inclined to bottle things up."

"You don't know if he talked it over with his parents?"

"His parents were overseas when it happened. They weren't at the funeral, and as far as I know, they didn't see him for several months." There was something steely about her expression as she said it.

"You didn't approve?"

She paused a moment and sighed. "I was a little judgmental, I suppose. It's so easy to criticize someone else's choices when you don't really know what's going on, isn't it? But I always thought they shouldn't have had a child if they had no time for him. You must remember that this happened at the end of high school, just after graduation, so they weren't even present for that milestone in their son's life."

"They weren't interested in him?"

"Oh, they were interested. Like you'd be interested in a long-term experiment that you checked on from time to time. They wanted to see what they'd made."

"But did they make a murderer?" He stared at the lake, ruminating.

She apparently recognized that the question did not require an answer. "The will doesn't make any sense, does it? Why leave your wealth divided between seven people you hate, the very people you blame for your girlfriend's death?"

Peter glanced at her. He probably shouldn't tell her. It would upset her. But he wanted her analysis. "They have to survive Bryan for thirty days in order to inherit, which probably means he doesn't expect them to do so. And the will you saw on my desk is not the one we found at Bryan's house. That one left everything to the aunt, and appears to have been a deliberate decoy. I asked for the Australian police to search Kain Vindico's home because he made multiple phone calls to Bryan in recent weeks, some of them quite long. They found that copy of the will there."

She stared at him and the pause stretched. He could almost hear her mind making connections and rearranging previous assumptions. "So whatever Bryan was up to, Kain was in on it."

"You may be aware, since you have such good radar, that I was never quite convinced Bryan's death was an accident, although previously I'd been inclined to see him as the victim not the criminal. It was just a hunch before today, but the strangeness of that will and the extraordinary fact that it was in Kain's possession has given me some leverage both with my own superiors and the police across the Tasman. They're hacking Kain's laptop right now to see if they can find any emails or other evidence, and they're also checking the computer of Erica Bonkowski, who made a couple of international calls to Bryan. There was nothing suspicious found in her home, so I'm not sure if she was complicit, but it was more contact than the rest of the group had." He shrugged. "She might just be sociable."

"What a tangled web Bryan has woven."

"Indeed." He knew he really should stop now, but he didn't. "I've got a lot of options chasing themselves around my head about Bryan's death. Did Kain push him in the drink to activate his inheritance, or did the group discover what Bryan was up to and overpower him?"

"There's another option. Don't forget that Bryan had put a big black cross through himself. He blames himself as well as them." She drew a long ragged breath, and made a visible effort to center herself. "He could have killed the others, then jumped."

Peter stared at her. She clearly wanted his feedback so much that she could vocalize the unspeakable, so he honored her determination by continuing the discussion. "It's possible. But the second will seems to indicate he expected them to outlive him a little. He could have been relying on the wilderness to kill them, perhaps involving Kain to help that plan along."

She nodded slowly, staring at the lake, and then shook her head. "But there was a cross through Kain as well."

He absolutely shouldn't tell her this part. "That puzzled me too, until I found out that Bryan's Dunedin lawyer has another will, signed ten days later, that Kain probably doesn't know anything about."

"Another one! What's in it?"

"I don't know. The lawyer won't release it. His orders were to withhold it for thirty days after Bryan's death is declared."

She latched onto one word. "*Declared*. So that explains why he made it so hard to formally identify his body. No fingerprints, no DNA traces."

"Of course! Why didn't I think of that? He's a 'clean skin'—he's never been in trouble with the police, so we have no fingerprints or DNA on record. And if he did jump in the ocean… he'd know that the sea rarely gives up its dead out there. It's a freakish thing that we found his body at all. An unusual combination of winds and currents, apparently."

"So it could have been years before anyone benefited from his death."

"Exactly."

"So what's in the third will? Maybe it just transfers the estate back to the aunt. But if that were the case, why hide it? If the second will shows us that Kain was somehow involved in this… 'crime', or whatever we're calling it, it's quite possible the third one could identify another accomplice." She swung in her chair to face him fully, her expression intense. "There could be someone out there following them, or even someone working right alongside us in the search room, who stands to gain from the death of seven more people. We need to know who that is. Urgently."

Peter sighed and scratched his ear. "I know. I'm trying to get a warrant for the will, but it's tied up in red tape."

Ellen turned again to stare at the lake, and her eyes narrowed in thought.

33

"So, what are we going to do?" said Callie. They'd crawled back off the mountain of jungle-rubble, and huddled under the shelter of a large tree fern to regroup. Her legs still felt like they were made of rubber, and Jack looked a bit green. They both needed a nice hot coffee with lots of sugar in it. Callie found herself disappearing into a momentary daydream about the funky pottery mug on her desk at work, souvenir of a Tasmanian holiday, and its texture in her hand, its weight and warmth when it was full of coffee from the barista next to the office…

Jack's voice hauled her back to Fiordland. "Well, there's no doubt we have to tell the others now. And we'll have to tell them about Sharon." His face turned bitter. "If we'd told them sooner, would Adam still be alive? I've made so many stupid decisions the last few days." He stared morosely at the river, still leaping with runoff, even though the rain had eased to mere buckets.

"So it's somehow your fault that someone pulled out a gun and shot Adam, is it?" She shook her head. "I had no idea you were so wicked. Or so important, for that matter."

He rolled his eyes, but his dismal mood did seem to lighten a degree or two. Jack could usually recognize the truth when it was pointed out to him, even in sarcasm. He sighed. "Well, it's just that Adam had been stalked by crocodiles and stuff and lived. If he'd known there was a threat, he may have been able to avoid it. A bullet in the forehead! He must have walked right into an ambush." He started scanning the riverbank upstream, and the opposite side of the steep valley. "I wonder if whoever did it is watching us now? And how close do they have to be to do it again?"

She searched her memory. "I'm almost certain that bullet wound is the kind you get from a small gun, up close. Which would mean, I think, that it isn't a sniper."

"Actually, that would make sense. The best sniper in the world couldn't have shot him from a distance in that really heavy rain. So maybe we don't have to watch the hillsides and mountaintops all the time. But I guess it doesn't necessarily mean the shooter doesn't have another gun. They might be equipped for both." He sighed and rubbed his face with both hands.

Callie went very still. "You know what else it could mean? It could be one of us. A small handgun could easily hide in one of our rucksacks. It's not as though we unpack them fully in front of each other every day."

"I guess so. But why would any of us have come on this hike prepared to kill someone? Why would anyone come at all if they'd known what Bryan was planning? Or they'd need to have a separate agenda to Bryan's, which seems even more unlikely."

"I suppose it doesn't make much sense."

"We'd be foolish to dismiss any possibility, given everything that's happened." He thought a bit more. "The other problem would be: where did they get the gun? You can't bring a gun through customs. So they'd have got it after we arrived in New Zealand. We all arrived on the same plane, except for you and Adam, and then got on the shuttle together, so there wasn't really an opportunity to meet an accomplice." He paused again. "Although, I guess we weren't exactly watching each other every single moment. Who could have had a motive to kill both Adam and Sharon? They live in different states and haven't even seen each other since high school."

"That's if the same person killed both of them."

Jack visibly recoiled, and stared at her. "So there's two homicidal maniacs on our trail? Are you nuts?"

Callie gave a lavish shrug. "This whole thing is preposterous from beginning to end. But I was thinking more that one of us could have killed Sharon—because that killer wanted to live, and Bryan or his goon could have killed Adam—because that killer wants us to die."

"Oh." He stared blankly, thinking. "They're not the same sort of killing, are they? Different methods, and very different victims, tactically speaking—one an asset, and one a liability, putting it bluntly." He sighed, and buried his head in his hands. "Argh! What a mess!"

"In any case, I think we'd be wise to keep in mind there might just possibly be a gun among us, and someone who isn't afraid to use it."

Jack nodded. "Watch out for furtive behavior with rucksacks. If there's a motive we don't know about, it could have been any of the other three—Kain could have come back from Neverland to do it, Erica actually admits to being nearest to Adam at the time, and even Rachel could have circled round past Erica in that useless visibility."

Callie said, "The other three… there's only five of us now, did you realize that? We started with eight." She sighed deeply.

"Yeah. I keep hoping this is a nightmare and I'll wake up back in Brisbane with the ceiling fan on and Rufus nudging my foot with his tennis ball."

"It's funny what we miss, isn't it? I was hankering after my pottery coffee mug a minute ago, with a nice steaming latte inside it…"

Jack smiled. "We can still get through this, if we don't give up. We really need to believe we'll be home soon."

"Yes, and try to support the others when we tell them what we know. Adrenalin from shock is dangerous for Rachel, especially when she's so low on insulin."

He took a deep breath and squared his shoulders. "Well, we can't put it off any longer."

***

JACK GLANCED UP AND SAW THE TWO WOMEN'S FACES AS HE AP-proached: Rachel teary and frightened, Erica… "watchful" seemed the best description. As they'd climbed, he'd been shooting up silent little arrow prayers in time with his footsteps: *God help me, God help me.* And he'd decided to fall back on what came naturally and take the direct approach.

Rachel was the one at immediate risk, so he started speaking straight to her as they drew level. "Rachel, don't you have breathing or something you do to try to avoid an adrenalin rush?" She nodded. "Can you do it now? I know it's hard to be calm with all this going on, but it's worth a try."

Her expression changed, became more determined. "I'll give it a go."

They moved into the denser forest, where a fairly solid tree canopy meant everyone could take their hoods down, making conversation easier.

Jack looked at Callie to see if she wanted to speak first, but she nodded encouragingly at him.

He spoke as gently as he could. "You've probably gathered from watching us down there, and the fact that we didn't rush back, that we found Adam, and yes, unfortunately he has died."

Rachel sighed and nodded. Erica stared at her hands lying in her lap, her fingers interlinked, rhythmically squeezing them together. He made a mental note to watch the reactions of both women. Rachel wasn't the only one who could suffer ill-effects from shock. He'd already made that mistake with Sharon.

"We'll need to work together to move him from there to

somewhere he can be found later. But first of all we need to talk about what killed him." His mind raced as he struggled to find a way to put it that wasn't horrifying. "Adam didn't die in the land-slide, and you need to brace yourselves to hear this, but he was actually shot."

Erica's glance flicked up to his eyes and back to her hands, but her face blanched. Rachel exclaimed, "What!" and put her hands to her mouth, staring from Jack to Callie and back again. "Who could have shot him?" It was almost a whisper, hard to hear over the slapping of the rain on the leaves above.

"You okay, Erica?" asked Jack. Her glance skittered across his face and went back to her twitching hands, but she nodded.

Rachel spoke up. "So what do we think happened? A hunting accident? They hunt deer out here, don't they? Only they call them something else… woppities or something. I remember Bryan saying that." She seemed satisfied with her solution. "But that must mean there are other people out here, and maybe we can find them!"

Jack shot a glance at Callie; she looked back and nodded. He took it as indication he still had the ball. *Darn.* "No, we don't think it was an accident, Rachel, unfortunately."

Erica's glance flew up to his face again, and this time it held, and her fingers stilled. "But how can you say that?" she challenged. "Surely a hunting accident is the most likely explanation. If they were shooting from a distance in these conditions, they probably wouldn't even know they'd hit him."

"I did a pathology course a few years ago for my work," said Callie. "The kind of wound he had is the kind you get from being shot up close. From a small gun, not a rifle."

Erica's face was red now. "I don't know how you can be so sure." Her tone was aggressive. "You're not a scientist."

"I'm not absolutely certain, no. But I remember what I learned, and I know what I saw. Trust me, it wasn't what I was expecting or hoping to see. It took me a while to accept it."

Jack joined in. "Plus, it's not hunting season. Bryan said so. I guess there might be illegal hunters out here. But it's hard to imagine anyone hunting in the appalling visibility we had this morning. And it makes sense to me that a high-powered rifle... well, let's just say I think it would have done more visible damage, that's all."

"You don't really know anything do you? It's just your opinion," Erica retorted. She seemed angry.

He sighed, and leaned on his knees. "There's more, actually. We haven't told you everything yet." He looked at Callie, and indicated with one hand, encouraging her to tell her story.

She took the conversational baton. "This one is about Sharon. Rachel, do you remember how she had those bruises on her face, when we were doing her hair?"

Rachel nodded slowly. Callie went on. "I think they were coming out gradually, over time, because I didn't notice them in the tent when we woke up. Or maybe the light in the tent was a funny color and that made them harder to see. We could look at it on the video, but that's probably more stressful than necessary. But there was a bruise either side of her nose, another one under her chin, and her eye sockets were kind of red."

"Yes, I do remember it. It looked odd, but I thought it must be something to do with the cold."

"So did I, at the time. But it kept bothering me, because I knew it reminded me of something, but I couldn't think what. And then later that day it hit me."

Rachel stared at her.

"Remember back when I did that pathology course, I told you how they showed us a body? That young girl?"

"Yes, I remember it. You couldn't sleep afterwards."

"Yes, that's the one." She turned to include Erica in the explanation. "This poor little girl had been murdered, suffocated by someone who held her nose and mouth closed." Callie focused on Rachel again. "Well, she had the exact same marks on her face as Sharon, the bruises in the same place."

"Are you saying…?" interjected Erica, but she couldn't complete the sentence. "Do you think…?" Her anger had gone; she was pale again, and flustered. "But it can't be." Erica shook her head, and tucked her fidgety hands under her armpits, hunching onto her rock.

Callie continued. "Just think about the shape of those bruises, Rachel." She stood from her log, and maneuvered herself next to Jack in the mud. "Imagine someone reaching in from the tent opening above her head, like so." She placed her hands on Jack's face, thumb and fingers of the right hand either side of his nose, left hand hooked under his chin. She looked at Rachel. "Would it match?"

Jack didn't see Rachel's reaction, because around the obstruction of Callie's hand, he was watching Erica now. She was trembling, and tears were making a trail down her face. He couldn't tell if the reaction was shock, or fear. Or something else. Guilt?

Rachel spoke, and he looked at her again. Her eyes were narrowed, thoughtful. "Yes, it would match. I can't believe I didn't see it sooner."

Callie unhanded Jack and moved back to her log. "Well, why would you think of it being that? I'd seen the exact same thing once before, and even I took hours to think of it."

"Are you okay, Erica?" asked Jack.

Callie and Rachel both turned quickly to look at her; they'd been engrossed in their own discussion. "No, not really. I can't believe I didn't realize. I was the 'medical professional', you know? Everyone was relying on me to help Sharon. And I couldn't believe she'd died after she was getting so much better. I should have twigged that something wasn't right. I remember thinking the bruises were odd, when we were doing the funeral thing, and I was looking at her face from a bit of a distance. I didn't know what they were. But I could see it when you put your hands on Jack's face like that. That's exactly the right shape." She put her head in her hands and started to weep aloud.

"Oh Erica." Rachel got up and moved nearer to Erica. "Shove over." Erica glanced up from behind her hands, and slid to one side of her rock. Rachel perched beside her, and put her arms around the smaller woman. "Don't worry, sweetie, it wasn't your fault. We all thought nature was enough to contend with. We didn't know there was some 'bad guy' out here with us as well." She looked from Jack to Callie. "Because that is what we're saying, isn't it? That there's someone out here following us around?"

Jack shot an inquiring glance at Callie, and she took on the explanation. "Well, we wondered if it could be someone Bryan hired, or even Bryan himself if he was organized with an aqualung or something back at Poison Bay." She shrugged. "An odd idea, I realize."

Rachel was silent and thoughtful, and Erica's sobs gradually subsided. "I suppose it's possible," Rachel said. "Poor Bryan. He'd got so messed up. We should have been there for him, years ago, and maybe none of this would ever have happened." She sighed.

Jack said, "There is one other possibility. We hope it's not right, but we have to consider it."

"What's that?" Rachel said.

If it had been hard to say before, when it was only a discussion between him and Callie, it was even harder now that all but one of the remaining pool of suspects was gathered. He looked at Callie, but she dropped her eyes and chewed on her bottom lip. Clearly he'd be getting no help from that quarter. Jack sighed. There was no escape.

"We have to keep in mind that it could actually be one of us."

Erica dropped her hands from her face and stared at him, her tears apparently forgotten. "Are you saying that after we all worked so hard to get Sharon warm and keep her alive, one of us waited till everyone was asleep, and then killed her? That's crazy! Why would anyone do that to Sharon?" She shook her head in disbelief.

Rachel's eyes clouded, and her gaze dropped. "Actually, Erica, I can see a reason. Sharon was slowing us down, the way she was. Someone could have wanted to get her out of the way. To increase our chances of surviving."

Erica started to speak, and then stopped. She'd apparently thought of someone who might conceivably think that way. Someone she knew pretty well.

Rachel spoke again. "But it doesn't really make sense why anyone would get rid of Adam." She looked at Jack and then at Callie, puzzled. "Did you think about that?"

Callie was still busy chewing her bottom lip, so Jack replied. "Yes, we did. The two murders don't match. So it's possible…" he looked at Callie again for support, but she wasn't looking at him. "It's actually possible they were killed by different people." Rachel inhaled sharply. Jack continued, "It's also possible that Adam's death was some kind of mistake, or he found out something about the killer." He shrugged. "There's lots of possibilities. But basically, we need to keep our minds and our eyes open, and be on our guard. That's all." He shoved his hands into his jacket pockets, stretched his legs out straight in front of him, and stared at his mud-caked boots.

"Well, I personally think it's lunacy," Erica declared, her voice much stronger now. "To think there could be two crazy killers tromping around the mountains after us is just outrageous. It must be one of Bryan's mates. What do any of us know about guns, anyway?" She looked at Callie. "Unless you've had some training in how to use them. For your work, like." Her voice dripped with sarcasm, and Rachel withdrew her arm and moved back to her own rock.

"Come on Erica," Jack said. "We're all on the same team here."

"No we're not," she spat. "You've just as good as accused me and Rachel and Kain of being murderers, because you obviously don't think it's your precious Callie that did it, or you wouldn't have been having such important, grown-up conversations with her behind everybody's back."

"Don't be childish, Erica, we didn't accuse anyone." Jack stood and moved back a few steps, withdrawing slightly from the circle. He was struggling to keep his anger in check.

"It wasn't like that, Erica, really it wasn't." Callie's tone was conciliatory. "I know it must look pretty weird that we didn't say anything before now, but we've been agonizing over whether or not to tell everyone."

"Huh!"

"Honestly, you guys!" Rachel exclaimed. "I coped with the news about Adam and Sharon much better than this horrible argument."

"Oh, poor little delicate flower!" exploded Erica. "It's all about Rachel. Whatever else we do, we mustn't upset you! No one else is suffering here, we're all having a lovely holiday." She stood and stomped off into the rain, whipping her hood up over her head with a sharp snap.

Rachel burst into tears. Callie went to her, hugging her. Jack stood awkwardly, wanting to escape and yet wanting to help. But what could he do?

He caught Callie's eye. "I guess I messed that one right up," he said.

Callie spoke firmly. "You did an amazing job. That was never going to be an easy conversation, so what did you expect?" She raised her eyebrows, her mouth wry. "She'll come back when she gets scared. Or cold. She's left her pack here."

"Oh." He glanced at Erica's rucksack, propped next to Callie's, and then looked up the mountain for a bit, and then down at an angular rock. He started kicking it absentmindedly with the side of his boot. Rachel was still weeping into Callie's shoulder. "Um, it's just that we've got to sort out..." Jack began. He waved vaguely down the hill, not wanting to say "Adam's body" in Rachel's hearing when she was already upset.

"Yeah, I know. We'll get onto that. Just give me a minute. Go and pick some ferns or something, why don't you?"

He left, gratefully.

34

"INTERPOL CALLED," SAID AMBER, AS PETER WALKED BACK INTO the police station. Even his watch house assistant had volunteered for overtime this week. He wished he'd been there to take the call, but the fact was, the conversation with Ellen had been very valuable.

"Any news?"

"Brisbane managed to salvage a couple of suspicious-looking emails that had been deleted from Kain Vindico's computer. I've printed them out and put them on your desk. They don't say that much, but they seem to be referring to promises made in phone calls. Nothing strange on Erica Bonkowski's computer. They've also sent through the coroner's report on that girl who committed suicide. I forwarded it on to the pathologist. Was that the right thing to do?"

She looked uncertain, but Peter nodded in approval. He liked his team members to take initiative. She moved on to her last piece of news. "The records show that someone asked to see that report back in February this year. You'll never guess who."

Peter raised one eyebrow a millimeter and waited.

"Bryan Smithton, that's who."

35

THE STEEP SLOPES WERE ALIVE WITH WATERFALLS, EVEN THOUGH the rain was taking a breather. Jack picked his way carefully around the landslip that held Adam in its grasp, looking for a path the group could use later. They needed to get upstream of the pile of debris before nightfall, and find a stable place to sleep in relative safety.

He paused at the peak of the mound, and looked up the river. The cloud had lifted, and he could see to the full thunderous height of the cirque at the head of the valley, with a lopsided pasting of snow—or was it a glacier?—at its center. The rim of the mountains was in front and to both sides, far above. He swung round to look downstream, taking in the majesty of more steep and lofty slopes marching away into the distance, following the twists and turns of the leaping river, their colors softening the further away they got.

In spite of the pains in his body, the ache in his heart, and the fear that never really subsided even when he was asleep, Jack felt his spirits lift. It was, quite simply, a glorious view. He pulled his shoulders back, filled his lungs with air, and reveled in the uncomplicated joy of being alive and the freedom of a hoodless head after so many hours of claustrophobic rain. *Thank you God.*

Returning to his task with renewed motivation, he continued upstream, looking for a route that was sufficiently elevated in case the river rose any further. He could see what might be a usable camping platform further up, but he needed to make sure they could get there without too difficult a climb.

He clambered across a small field of boulders, and then sidled along a rocky ledge for a few meters. It was manageable—the drop wasn't enormous. As he prepared to round the end of the ledge he glanced at the ground for his next foot placement, and saw something that made the blood drain from his face and his innards contract. A footprint, from a large boot. It could be no more than a couple of hours old—the heavy rain earlier would have washed it away.

Fighting down fear, he peered carefully round the corner of the rock face, dreading the gunshot that might be the last thing he ever heard. That's if he could even hear it over the hammering of his heart in his ears. He could see nothing suspicious, but he didn't have a full view of the rocky platform. He pressed himself in against the rock, and scanned the other side of the valley, and back the way he'd come, searching for anything that didn't seem right. All he saw were rocks and trees and mountain scrub, looking back at him with blank faces. He craned his neck and tried to check above him, but it was pointless—all he could see was more of the rock face curving away upwards—and his head spun with dizziness at that strange angle, threatening to make him fall.

He pulled back in against the rock, and waited for his equilibrium to settle. Peering around the corner again, he dropped to the ground, and edged forward on all fours in the mud, constantly scanning for anything that moved. He peered round a boulder and saw it. A tent. Kain's tent, if he wasn't mistaken. Relief flooded his body, and then sucked back out again like a receding wave as he recalled what had happened to Adam. What if Kain was the shooter? Or he might even have met the same fate.

He stayed behind his boulder and called out. "Kain! Are you in there?"

There was movement at the mouth of the tent, and Kain's face and shoulders appeared. He didn't answer, but stared at Jack silently, his eyes dark and unreadable.

Jack said, "Are you okay?" He stood tentatively and walked towards the tent, trying to see if Kain had anything in his hands while also scanning the mountainside for signs of movement—a nearly-impossible combination of tasks.

"No, I'm not. I've sprained my ankle walking in that quagmire. We should have stayed back at the rock bivvy, like I said."

"Yeah, probably." Jack spoke dismissively, and half turned away. He'd actually been thinking the same thing himself, after the horrors of the past few hours. *But there's no way I'm agreeing with you.*

After a pause, Kain spoke again. "When the cloud lifted, I saw there'd been some landslides down the valley. Everyone okay?"

The question probably represented a concession of sorts, a white flag. But Jack doubted Kain's sincerity, and found himself wanting to shock. His eyes slid back to Kain's face. "No, we're not okay. Callie was hurt, and Adam's dead." For all the reaction the bald statement got, he might have been reciting the train timetable. "Adam was shot," he added.

That did the trick at last. Still crouched in the tent opening, Kain visibly recoiled and his eyes widened. "Shot? Who shot him? Who's got a gun?" He stared at Jack. *Looks like Kain's not the shooter.*

"How should I know? That's what we've been trying to figure out. The girls are terrified." And the boy too, but there was no need to mention that.

Now Kain started to look around him, scanning the slopes and the cliffs above, unsettled. "What are you doing about it?"

"We're being careful. We're looking out for each other. But first of all, we need to get Adam's body off the landslide. Will you come and help me with it?"

"I just told you, I sprained my ankle. I need to rest it." He withdrew inside the tent.

Jack wheeled around, stomping back the way he'd come, so

angry that his fear evaporated in its heat and he didn't even feel the pain in his injured knee. He'd sidled back along the ledge and traversed the boulder field before he'd even registered what he was doing. *Slow down Jack. You'll hurt yourself, or get yourself shot. And you're supposed to be a forgiving person, remember?* "But, God, I don't know *how* to forgive a pratt like that," he shouted at the sky, his hands clenched into fists at his sides. "I know I should forgive him, and I know I've done plenty of things wrong myself, but I'm just *so* tired. How can he not help us?!" He subsided onto a rock, breathing roughly and trying to contain his anger. At last, not exactly tranquil, but capable of being moderately sensible, he continued through the muddy forest above the river.

As he approached the path he'd earlier picked out across the landslide zone, a flicker of light caught his eye, down near the river. Instantly alert, he crouched behind some ferns and watched. As moments passed, it dawned on him what he was seeing. A shaft of pallid sunlight had fought its way through a momentary break in the cloud cover, and hit a shallow pool of water that had been dammed by the landslide debris. The fleeting sunshine was now gone again, but he could see the tiny pond, not much more than a deep puddle, and something flickering within it. Something silvery. Fish! They'd been trapped by the very destruction that had swept Adam away.

Jack worked his way down the incline, now scanning the slopes around, now looking for a foothold, now looking at their prospective dinner. Eventually, perched above the pool with a foot either side, he plunged in a hand and grappled with one of the fish. It slid through his grasp and he teetered and almost fell, jerking his painful knee.

He rearranged his feet, and this time grabbed with both hands. Success! He lifted the fish up, and struggled to keep hold of it as it flipped and whipped in his hands. How to kill it? *And quickly, before I lose the thing altogether!*

He looked around and spied a fairly solid rock within reach among the tangle. Grasping the fish firmly round the tail, he swung it over his head in a sweeping arc and brought it crashing down on the rock. It stopped whipping around, but he couldn't tell if it was dead or merely surprised. Before it had any chance to rethink its position, he needed to catch its friend, and get them both away where he couldn't lose them. He lined up carefully and plunged in after the second fish, repeating the process.

Catch in hand, he walked back to the women, light of step, an uncontrollable grin on his face. As he stepped back onto more-or-less solid ground and drew near to the little ferny grotto where he'd left them, he saw through the trees that Erica had returned, as prophesied.

Callie was facing the other way, but she heard him approaching, and stood to greet him, hands on hips. "Where the hell have you been? We thought you'd been shot or something, you stupid idiot." Her voice was sharp, her face drawn.

He said nothing, just held the fish out at shoulder height in front of him, one in each hand.

"Oh!" She back-pedaled faster than anyone he'd ever seen, her eyes widening in delight. "I take it all back. You wonderful, wonderful man!"

***

JACK ACQUIESCED WITH BAD GRACE WHEN THE WOMEN RESOLVED to share the precious fish with Kain.

"He might be quite badly hurt," Rachel said.

"Maybe he's having trouble walking," Callie said. "But no matter why he's done this or how we feel about it, we should still do what's right."

Jack noticed that Erica did not jump to her boyfriend's defense. Things seemed to have cooled between them.

"It'll be easier to light a cooking fire up there than down in this bog, I suppose," he said, relenting.

That left Adam's body to be dealt with, by an injured not-very-large man, and three women in varying states of diminished health and strength. Their need to get him down off the landslide debris was not purely sentimental. His rucksack, still strapped to his body, contained a significant portion of their survival equipment—not least his hunting knife, which they needed to prepare the fish.

It was hard to know who to excuse from stretcher-bearer duties. Each of the four had limitations that made it difficult. Jack longed to keep Callie out of it, because of the pummeling she'd taken in her fall. But aside from worrying that the others would find his concern for her transparent, one look told him that Callie would not be sidelined, and so he said nothing. Jack felt a quiet rage that Kain did not even care enough to come pay his respects to an old friend.

Perched precariously atop the mountain of shredded rainforest, they worked carefully to separate Adam from his rucksack. Jack saw that while Rachel gazed upon Adam's face and even touched his cheek with tenderness, Erica deliberately did not look at the dead man's face at all. She remained focused on the arm she was extracting from his rucksack harness. He glanced at Callie and she raised one eyebrow at him; she'd noticed it too.

The rucksack was heavy, so they took a corner each and carried it back to stable ground, then extracted Adam's sleeping bag and a couple of ropes to knot at the corners, turning it into a makeshift stretcher. Struggling back down the treacherous mound with their burden a few minutes later, Jack found the thought flitting across his mind: *so that's why they call it a dead weight.* He felt his muscles straining with the load, and heard his companions breathing hard.

The best plan he'd been able to come up with was to place Adam in his orange bag in an open area up towards the top of the landslip, where he'd seen a large flat boulder that seemed to have finished its sliding. The women were deferring to Jack with regard to decisions about the body. Perhaps, after Sharon, "offices for the dead" had become his responsibility. Team chaplain, as Adam had joked so many days ago. He hoped he wouldn't be called upon to do it again.

The simple ceremony they'd conducted for Sharon had been filled with grief, and fear of the mountains. With Adam, everything had changed. They now knew that neither Sharon nor Adam had died of natural causes. Every rock and tree seemed to be watching them, every shadow concealed an assassin. Jack longed to get out of the clearing where he felt so vulnerable, back to where they could hide themselves under the tree cover—not that foliage had saved Adam.

"Don't forget to tape this for Adam's fiancée," Callie said suddenly. "Like you did for Sharon's son. Sheena might want to see it some time."

Before Jack could reply, Erica burst into gusty tears, gulping in air in spasms. Rachel put her arm around Erica's shoulders. "Shhh," she soothed, rubbing Erica's arm. "It'll be okay."

"No it won't." Erica buried her face in her hands. "It won't ever be okay." She eventually got herself under control again, and remained silent, staring at her feet, as each of the others made a short statement in tribute to Adam.

By the time the four of them were sidling along the last section of rock ledge leading to the night's chosen camp, loaded with extras sorted from Adam's pack and the ferns they'd gathered for the evening meal, they were exhausted and dispirited and incapable of taking much care to avoid any possible sniper.

Kain must have heard them coming. He was standing outside his tent, staring at them wordlessly as they rounded the last of the rocky barriers.

Rachel said, "Hello Kain." She was the only one who bothered.

Jack scanned the cliffs and slopes above them, then looked down the narrow valley retreating below, as the river it followed zigged and zagged its way towards the ocean. The overcast skies had lifted slightly, and it was lighter now than it had been at midday, even though the evening was drawing in.

He turned back to the rest of the group, to find they'd all collapsed onto the nearest rock, unspeaking, their rucksacks abandoned askew on the ground. No one was making any move to set up camp. The mood was as damp as the muddy rock underfoot. It had been miserable enough on the trek from Adam's resting place; now Kain's presence seemed to be curdling the atmosphere even more. *Useful activity. That might help.*

Jack rummaged in his pack for Adam's knife, and stood up, extending the fish. "Okay, who knows how to gut a fish?"

All eyes turned to him. Erica's glance hit the knife and skittered away again.

Kain spoke first. "I'd have thought any fool would know how to gut a fish."

"Kain!" Rachel was distressed.

Jack cast the fish on the ground and took a step towards Kain, his body rigid, the vicious knife still held tightly in a clenched fist. "Oh you would, would you? Well, you wanna know what I'd have thought? I'd have thought that any fool would help his friends in a crisis. Adam went surfing with you every weekend when we were kids, and he even got his arm broken rescuing you from bullies, and he died today and we had to bury him and you wouldn't even help!" Kain flinched very slightly before lashing out with some target practice of his own.

"Help? No one wants my help! Everyone listens to you, Jack. Adam's dead because of you, Jack. Sharon's dead because of you, Jack. I said we should leave the girls back at Poison Bay, and this morning I said we should stay at the camp till the rain stopped. But no, you had to keep us all together and keep us moving, and now they're dead." His eyes narrowed to slits. "I hope you're really satisfied with what you've done!"

The words seared Jack's soul for the very reason that he feared it was true, that it was all his fault. He resorted to sarcasm. "Yes, Kain, that's right. I'm the one who put a bullet in Adam's brain, and I'm the one who held his hands over Sharon's face until she choked to death." He flung his arms wide, and several pairs of eyes followed the knife uneasily, probably hoping he didn't accidentally release it into the air. "I confess! Don't ask me where I got the gun though, because I haven't got a clue. But I've got hands haven't I," he waved them in front of himself, and the knife waggled with the hand that held it, "so I could have killed Sharon."

Kain became very still, and stared at Jack. "What are you saying about Sharon?"

Jack realized he had the upper hand over Kain with this one. He muted his fury and made his tone colorless. "Sharon was murdered too, Kain. Someone suffocated her. Callie recognized the bruises on her face. If you'd been around, helping the rest of the team, you'd have been there when we discussed it as a group earlier today." He shifted his weight and tilted his head a little. "Come to think of it Kain, where were you that night? Go for a midnight stroll, did you?"

Kain stepped forward again, and pointed at Jack for emphasis. "You're not pinning this on me!" He glanced at Callie. "That's if it's even true. Bruises on her face! What a load of crap."

"Not nearly as much crap as you and your 'sprained ankle'. How about we make a stretcher for you and we'll carry you tomorrow—the people with the injured knees and shoulders and the diabetic with no insulin. Our suffering is nothing at all compared to yours, you poor little darling!" Jack shook his head in disbelief. "Callie was crushed in a landslide this afternoon, and even she helped with Adam, you stupid moron!" He almost choked on the last few words.

Kain came back at him like a snake, striking again. "You stupid moron!" he mimicked, his voice high pitched like a girl. "Come on, choirboy, *swear* at me!"

"You..! You...!" Jack seemed to have lost the power of speech. He advanced towards Kain, the knife still in his hand, everyone and everything else forgotten in a moment of all-consuming hatred and despair.

"Stop it, you two! Right now!" It was Callie, suddenly standing in the narrowing gap between them, fearless, a hand held up like a stop sign in each direction. Her tone brooked no argument. "Pull yourself together, Jack. This isn't like you. You've got a knife in your hand, for God's sake!" She frowned fiercely at him, and wriggled her fingers towards him. "Give it to me!"

Jack stared at the weapon, and clenched and unclenched his fingers around it, breathing hard. Who knew what was or wasn't like him, anymore?

He turned away abruptly, tossed the knife down alongside the abandoned fish, and headed for the rocky ledge along which they'd come.

36

"PETER, IT'S JONESY. I'VE HAD A LOOK THROUGH THAT coroner's report you sent down, and I thought I'd better ring you straight away."

Peter was instantly alert. "What have you found?"

"The body I've got on ice down here was meant to be the father of the girl's baby, is that right?"

"Yes, that's correct."

"Well, either this body isn't Bryan Smithton after all, or Bryan Smithton wasn't that baby's father."

"How can you be sure without DNA testing?"

"The blood types don't add up. It's simply not possible."

"I see." He paused, thinking. "Bryan Smithton asked to see that coroner's report a few months ago. Could he have realized what it meant?"

"Did he have a medical background?"

"He's from a scientific family."

"Then yes, it's possible. But anyone with average intelligence and a suspicious mind could see that the combination of letters didn't look right, and Google it. So I'd say it's very likely your boy knew he couldn't be the father of that baby."

37

BY THE TIME JACK RETURNED TO THE ROCKY PLATFORM NEARLY an hour later, after an uncomfortable interlude among the boulders a little further down the valley, first pacing like a caged tiger and then sitting in a dejected hunch, he'd had time to cool down and think about what he'd done. He'd been only trying to lift team morale when Kain attacked. *What a success. The morale must be positively stratospheric now.*

He couldn't figure out why he resorted to schoolyard taunts whenever he disagreed with Kain. The man had a knack for bringing out the very worst in him.

Well, Jack would have to suck it up, apologies to everyone, and do his best to get on with Kain and ignore his taunts. Usually he was pretty good at ignoring insults. He'd had to do a lot of it growing up, being a religious nut. He couldn't seem to let anything go past him today.

As he drew near the camp, probably more embarrassed than he'd ever been in his life, he took a deep breath and squared his shoulders. Rounding the last crease in the rock face, he saw tents had been set up and the fire had been lit. He could smell the fish cooking.

Callie looked up as he approached, and gave a small, tight smile. "Oh well," her look seemed to say. Neither Erica nor Rachel looked at him, although they glanced swiftly at each other. The women were sitting around the fire. Kain hadn't left as Jack had thought he might have done, but he definitely wasn't part of the cozy tableau. He was sitting at a distance, his body angled away from the women, staring at the opposite side of the valley.

Jack shuffled towards the other man, hands in pockets. He looked at the ground and then at Kain's face. "I think we need to talk."

Kain shot him a quick glance and then resumed his consideration of the opposite slope. "I don't."

Jack shifted his weight, and tried again. "I'm sorry for the things I said."

"I'm not."

Jack inhaled slowly, silently and held his temper. "Well, that's your choice. But I don't think we can just leave things as they are. It's not good for you or me, or the team."

Kain remained silent, but at least he didn't get up and walk away.

"I've been thinking about the things I said to you when we argued way back at Poison Bay, about you wanting to ditch the liabilities and stuff. I reckon they were pretty hurtful things to say, and I shouldn't have said them. I can see now that they probably made you feel alienated from the rest of us." He added silently: *And I really hope they didn't turn you into a murderer.*

Kain still held his body aloof, but his focus had shifted to somewhere not too far away from Jack's feet.

Heartened by the small sign of response, Jack continued, keeping his voice mild. "I have a tendency to just blurt things out, without thinking about the consequences. It doesn't always occur to me at the time that maybe I'm just plain wrong. Well, I'm sorry I said those things, and I hope you'll forgive me and see if we can start again." He shrugged diffidently. "We're all just doing the best we can out here."

Kain stared at the ground near Jack's feet for a long moment, and then stood. His eyes flicked to Jack's face and then away again. "Okay," was all he said.

Jack thought about trying for a handshake, and decided not to push it that far. He angled his head toward the campfire. "Come and sit by the fire." He had a sudden realization, and quirked his mouth. "That's if they'll let us." He received a variety of quick looks from the women, but the one from Callie was surprisingly warm.

Later that night, he discovered that the accommodation arrangements had changed. At some point, probably when he was having his boulder-field interlude, Erica had obviously decided to separate from Kain and share with Rachel instead. Kain disappeared into his tent with a decisive ri-ip of the zipper closing behind him. That left Jack sharing with Callie again, in the tent that he'd mangled and muddied after the landslide, so long ago and far away. Was it only this morning?

As he wriggled into his sleeping bag, he felt something slimy on his hand, and realized it was mud, still wet. Callie's must be even worse. He recalled the battle to wrestle her barely-conscious body into it after the fall, fully clothed although he'd managed to get the rainproof layer and the boots off, with the rain still thundering down and the tent poorly erected and giving inadequate shelter.

"Should we offer to swap tents and sleeping bags with the others?" he said, keeping his voice quiet. There were no private conversations in a tent; the sound passed straight through. He got a muffled giggle in response. "Surely we could convince them there was something very special about this set up."

"No chance, unfortunately. They saw the state of it in daylight." She snorted. "Looked like a couple of pigs had been mud-wrestling in here."

He sniggered, and then sighed theatrically. "I really hope the dampness of my sleeping bag warms up after a bit."

"Yeah, then you can pretend it's actually a sauna. That's the effect I'm hoping for."

They were silent a moment, and then she spoke very softly to him, her mouth close to his ear. "Jack, I really think Kain would have packed up and left this evening, except we had fish."

He pondered that for a bit. "Can't really blame him, I suppose, with the things I'd said to him."

"Maybe. But I just got a feeling there was more to it than that. He's making me uneasy. I'm… well, I'm scared of him."

The statement went through him like an electric shock. He felt a surge of some kind of caveman emotion, fiercely protective. And he needed to know what Callie had seen and sensed—she was so much more perceptive than he was. Impossible to have this conversation with the others just a meter or two away!

"Do you want to talk about this now? We could go for a walk."

"No. Tomorrow will do. We're okay right now. And we could fall in the dark and kill ourselves." She sighed. "I'm just so tired. I can't bear to stay awake another minute."

He was silent for a while, and then a sudden thought hit. "We were supposed to be watching out for Rachel."

She inhaled sharply. "Damn. I forgot all about it."

"She's in with Erica. Do we even trust Erica?"

"I really don't know. She's definitely been behaving very oddly. But what could she do? Rachel's not as weak as Sharon was. Not yet, anyway."

"I don't see how we can change the setup now." He sighed in frustration. He just wanted to sleep and forget everything. The passivity of exhaustion was setting in. Nothing else seemed important in the face of that all-consuming need. But what if he slept and Rachel was dead when he woke up? Then, vigilance would seem far more important than sleep, but it would be too late. "At least our tents are side by side. We'll just have to listen, from here. I'll take the first watch—you go to sleep."

Callie didn't disagree, and after only a few moments she grew quiet, her breathing even. She was asleep. His ears strained for any suspicious sound. The wind was starting to pick up. How to tell the rustle of a tree branch or tent flap from the footstep of a murderer? He lay staring into the darkness as the night drew on, and longed for morning.

38

JACK WAS JUST STANDING FROM STRAPPING HIS INJURED KNEE with duct tape as a makeshift support when Callie approached him, quiet and intense.

"Have you got Adam's hunting knife? I can't find it."

He shook his head, and then stared at her as an awful thought crept in around the edges of his exhaustion. He hadn't had the heart to wake Callie, and so he'd kept watch the whole night, amazingly managing not to fall asleep. And no one had attacked Rachel. But now as they packed up camp, he was paying for his chivalry with leaden arms and legs and a sluggish brain tickled by paranoid thoughts.

He decided to take a forthright approach to the missing knife. "Has anyone seen Adam's knife?" he asked loudly, feigning unconcern.

Everyone paused in their duties, looked around and shook their heads. The women started looking at the ground, searching for it. Kain cast a glance around the area, but then resumed his packing up.

"Who had it last?" Jack said. "Who gutted the fish?"

"I did," Rachel said. "But I rinsed it off and left it here on this rock to dry. The sheath was over there, I think."

A search of the rocky clearing and even up into the edges of the trees failed to turn up the knife. Jack was left with two equally unpleasant possibilities. Either someone was indeed following them, and had managed to take the knife from right in their midst without being seen—probably in the night, if it had been left out.

Or one of the team had it.

***

"WHAT DO YOU MAKE OF THE KNIFE SITUATION?"

Jack was bringing up the rear again, and Callie had angled the question back over her shoulder, her voice quiet.

They'd moved out above the tree line into alpine scrub that was tearing at their clothing and tangling around their feet. The sky had lifted enough to give a panoramic view of the the lofty rounded cirque at the head of the valley before them and the sharp mountains marching away into the distance behind them. With the rest of the team still in view, the discussion—even the fact they were having one—had to be discreet.

"I guess there are limited options," he replied to her back. "Either, one of us took it, or someone else who's following us. And it was taken either to be used as a weapon, or to stop us being able to use it for food."

"I've been racking my brains, trying to remember when I last saw it. It was on that rock while we were eating, I'm sure of it, because I can see it in my mind, over Erica's shoulder… but when we were rinsing off the dishes, I don't think it was there any more."

"If that's right, it would probably mean one of us has it. But it's hard to know how we prove it, short of insisting that everyone empty their packs."

"And whoever has it could slip it into someone else's pack too. To divert suspicion."

Jack raised his eyebrows. "I hadn't thought of that."

"Probably just me being paranoid anyway. I don't trust anyone now. Even Rachel. My best friend." She stopped a moment and half-turned to look back at him. "Do you know, this morning I was even wondering if she might have more insulin than she said." She lifted her hands up in an expansive gesture. "She could even have some extra energy snacks squirreled away in her pack."

He stared at her, thunderstruck.

"Yeah, I know, crazy stuff." She turned and continued clomping her way up the mountain.

But Jack found the thought taking insidious root in his mind, and beginning, just slightly, to grow. "What if it's not crazy?" he said. "We'd virtually ruled her out because of it—I mean, why would she put herself in mortal danger? But that's based on the assumption that she didn't know about it beforehand. That she wasn't prepared. I think we've got to let go of that idea and rethink the whole situation. Not just for Rachel, for everyone."

She stopped abruptly and turned to look at him again, her mind obviously crowding with thoughts. "You're right! If one of us knew Bryan was going to do it, it changes everything. But why would Bryan tell someone what he was planning, that's what we need to figure out. And who."

Up ahead, Jack saw Kain stop and turn to look back along the line. He'd stayed close to them today, not gone ahead on his own, and Jack hoped that was a positive sign of reconciliation, although sometimes little insinuating thoughts suggested there might be a different reason for it. "Keep moving," he said to Callie. "We're being watched."

She set off again, and soon after, so did Kain further up the mountain, but it was a while before she spoke. "You know what we've got to do, Jack? We've got to go right back to the beginning. The death of Liana started all this. We've got to stop thinking about what we know about everyone now, and trying to interpret little hints and looks which lead us nowhere, and go back to what we knew about everyone ten years ago. If Bryan took someone into his confidence, who would it be, and why? That's where we'll find the answer."

Jack thought for a while. "We'll be stopping for a break soon. Why don't we just ask everyone what they remember?" He was looking at the ground, searching for the next secure foothold among the scrub, so that when Callie stopped and turned he almost cannoned into her. He staggered back a little and looked at her face.

"No Jack, don't do this one your way. The direct approach won't get us what we want this time. They'll just clam up. They already think we're investigating them all. We have to be subtle—make them think it's their idea to talk about it."

He frowned. "You think?"

She nodded. "Yes, I do. Trust me."

39

THE SEARCH RADIO EXPLODED INTO LIFE SO LOUDLY THAT PETER heard it all the way down the corridor in his office, although he couldn't make out the words. When the excited exchange stretched on for several minutes, he decided to investigate. He arrived in the search room in time to hear Hawk saying, "We'll get a chopper out there straight away."

"What have we got?"

"A tourist plane has sighted what could be a body in one of those big orange bags, way up here." He pointed to the colored pin he'd just stuck into the map. The northern section of the map. Nowhere near the search area. Neither mentioned the debate between Amber and Tom two days earlier.

"High elevation."

Hawk nodded. "They flew back over it for a second look. It's lying in fresh snow, with what looks to be a rucksack alongside."

Peter narrowed his eyes in thought. "Yesterday's rain would have washed away any tracks."

"Yep. But they saw a faint track heading south east."

"Are we relocating the search to that area?"

"Already happening."

Amber spoke. "Peter, I finally heard back from the marine search advisor. Bryan Smithton most likely went into the water in the north of the park, possibly Poison Bay or a little south of there."

Peter's mind swirled with possibilities and uncomfortable recollections. Would this nameless body inside the orange bag still be alive if they'd started from the north instead of the south two days ago? "Where's Tom?"

"He went out in a search plane."

40

WHEN THEY STOPPED WITHIN VIEW OF WHAT THEY HOPED was a usable mountain pass, the cloud was beginning to break up and jagged peaks loitered at a discreet distance. Alpine daisies bloomed around them in the tussocky grass, making Callie wonder if Julie Andrews might leap out from behind a bush and start singing. Even Jack was apparently struck by it and his camera was out again. The venue for their snack was glorious; the snack itself, less so. Even shafts of otherworldly sunlight glistening on the scurrying river far below couldn't make up for the taste and texture of yet another handful of crunchy ferns.

"You know," Callie said to no one in particular, "when I was busy neglecting my potted fern at home, I had no idea one could save my life one day. I'll be more respectful after this. Anyone else got ferns at home?"

Erica laughed, but it was not an entirely happy sound. "I've got one on the kitchen bench, but if I get home again, it's going outside." She stared at a fern tip in her hand, turning it over. "You know what they remind me of? That fern Liana used to keep in her bedroom. She made such a fuss of it. She even gave it a name—the sort of name your elderly uncle might have. The stupid things that go through your head out here... just this morning I've been walking along trying to remember the name of that fern."

"Reginald," interjected Rachel.

"Yes! That was it!"

A little smile of shared memory went round the group.

And there it was. The conversational opening. Liana. Jack got so far as to open his mouth, but Callie shot him a warning glance, and he closed it again.

And so Rachel spoke instead in the gap. "I've been thinking such a lot about Liana today. And what Bryan said. Do you think it's our fault she died? Even Liana blamed us." Rachel's eyes became focused on a point a few meters in front of her, but they seemed to be seeing not the alpine scrub of Fiordland, but a Brisbane living room buzzing with mosquitoes on a hot November night, and a small and delicate teenager, holding a shotgun jammed under her chin. " 'None of you will help me', that's what she said."

Silence. Finally, Erica spoke. "I actually think Callie was right in what she said back at Poison Bay, when Bryan was about to jump. It stuck in my mind, and I keep going back to it. We didn't kill Liana. Liana killed Liana." She sighed. "We could have all done better than we did, of course."

"Did she talk to you about the baby?" Callie said.

"Yeah." She sighed and shrugged. "I was supposed to be her best friend, but I was pretty disgusted with the whole situation, to tell the truth. The night she died she made that big speech as though she was in the deepest despair, but she didn't say any of that stuff when she spoke to me. I wish she had. It all just seemed to be about convenience. Her life plans and how they couldn't be messed up. Not missing the start of the year at acting school. Keeping her figure. I couldn't see why it was such a big deal—as if she wouldn't have sprung back into shape anyway, at that age. So I told her she should have thought of all that before she got herself pregnant. And…" She slid Kain a significant look. "Well, Kain probably knows what else I was disgusted about."

He stared at her. "How would I know what you were disgusted about?"

"Are you really going to pretend you don't know?"

He remained silent and became very still.

Erica turned to the others and lifted her hands in a broad shrug, but she seemed to relish the telling. "Liana said she didn't know if the baby was Bryan's or Kain's."

Rachel inhaled sharply, and put her hands over her mouth. Callie stared at Erica, then Kain. His nostrils flared slightly, but he looked away, staring down the valley.

"But she… I thought she loved Bryan," Rachel said. "She said… that night she looked straight at Bryan and said, 'You say you won't love me any more if I don't have this baby.' If she didn't love Bryan anyway, why would she care what he thought?"

"She needed his money to do it," Erica said. "Bryan wouldn't give it to her, and everyone else seems to have said no as well."

After a pause, it was Rachel who spoke. "Did she ask you for money, Kain?"

He was silent so long they all wondered if he'd even heard, but he did answer at last. "No, she didn't. I didn't even know she was pregnant until that night." He raised an eyebrow. "But maybe she asked Adam."

"What do you mean?" Erica's tone was sharp.

"I caught them at it one time. At her place, when her parents were away. On a sleeping bag up the back garden behind the fruit trees."

"Yeah, Adam told me he'd had a fling with Liana," Jack said.

"What a mess," said Rachel.

Callie said, "Can we be certain that she didn't love Bryan? People do funny things sometimes. And from what I've seen, people don't sleep around unless something's a bit messed up in their lives."

"In Liana's case, probably just practicing for future movie roles," said Erica, and Rachel gasped. "Oh come on, didn't you ever wonder what a girl like Liana was doing with a weirdo like Bryan? A *rich* weirdo like Bryan."

Callie said, "Yes, I admit I did wonder. But then, love is blind and all that."

"I've always thought love had its eyes wide open, where Liana was concerned," Erica said. "Bryan was besotted with her, and he could pay her way through college, give her all the things she'd need to get her career started. Maybe I was just jealous of her, but I thought she was a bit of a calculating bitch, to be honest, even though she was my friend. And I still think it, even though it makes me feel horrendously guilty."

Kain said, "She *was* a calculating bitch. The only thing she ever loved was Bryan's money. She just used the rest of us for fun." There was a deep current of bitterness beneath his words, and the thought landed in Callie's mind: *Kain really loved Liana. Is that why money is so important to him? Because it was the thing she wanted that he didn't have?*

"What would you have done if she'd asked you for help, Kain?" said Erica.

"I'd have asked her to keep the baby. I'd have offered to marry her. I was that much of a fool back then." Erica looked like he'd just punched her.

Callie said, "Did she ask you for help, Jack?"

"Hardly. She'd have known what I thought. But Bryan asked my advice. I told him to stand firm." He grimaced. "That worked out well."

"You couldn't have known what was going to happen," Rachel said.

"No, but I could have tempered my ideals with some common sense. And given him a few hints about how to make her feel like it was a blessing instead of the end of everything."

Another silence stretched, until eventually Callie spoke. "I just don't know how to make all of this fit with the picture of someone so desperate they'd blow their brains out."

Jack said, tentatively, "I've wondered, sometimes, if she really meant to do it."

The group stared at him. Rachel said, "Do you think the gun went off by mistake?"

"No, not exactly. It's more that…" He rubbed his face vigorously. "I don't quite know how to put it. I'm not saying she wasn't genuinely upset. But the words she said that night sounded so… scripted. Rehearsed. Not that a different type of person wouldn't practice a statement like that. Anyone would, if it's the last thing you're ever going to say. But it had the edge of the actress in it, somehow. Remember when she'd be a character with us, and just play that character all day, and you couldn't get her out of it, no matter how annoying it got? I just wonder if maybe she was so engrossed in playing the suicidal teenager that she forgot it wasn't a role. Got so caught up in the drama of it all that she just… played the scene out to the end."

A thoughtful silence followed. Callie recalled the scene in Bryan's luxurious living room, and those words, carved into her brain a whole decade ago. The careful laying of blame. The desire to punish. Each look and turn of Liana's head. The inflection of her voice as it rose and fell and paused. It wasn't a stupid idea. What if she'd just wanted to get their attention, but then become carried away?

Callie murmured, "I've always thought it was an odd method for her to choose. Her beauty was so important to her. Why not take some tablets, and still be beautiful?"

"You can't stand in front of a roomful of people and threaten them with a bottle of tablets," Kain said. "We'd have taken it off her."

"And she wouldn't have done it alone—she needed an audience," added Erica. "She needed to see how it made us feel. A bit like being at your own funeral, I guess."

Jack nodded. "And the gun helped her get our attention really quickly. It was a pretty good visual aid. Very theatrical." He found himself miming the movement of holding a shotgun under his chin, seemed to realize what he was doing, and plunged his hands into his pockets, looking awkward.

"I wonder if we could have said or done anything differently that night, and stopped her," Rachel said. "I've wondered and wondered about that, over the years."

Jack reached out and quickly squeezed her arm. "We all did the best we could at the time, Rachel. We were paralyzed when she stood up in front of us with that gun. We didn't know what to do. We were just kids really."

"Do you think Bryan knew?" blurted Callie.

"Knew what?" Jack said, puzzled by the *non sequitur*.

"That Liana was cheating on him."

"Well, they say the injured party always knows," Erica said. "Although, in my experience, that's not necessarily the case."

Callie saw some kind of sub-text flicker between Erica and Kain, but she couldn't read it. What was there between these two that she didn't know about? She filed the thought away to come back to later, but aloud she said, "I'd have to agree with you there. You don't always know. What did Liana say about it?"

"She was trying to keep it from him. So she didn't think he knew. But she could have been wrong, of course."

Callie turned to Kain. "Did you get any sense that he knew about you and Liana? Even just since we came to New Zealand?"

Kain stared at her, his eyes wide. She'd accidentally hit a nerve. "I don't think so. I'm not sure."

It was then that they heard the engine. Somewhere between

a whine and a hum, but definitely mechanical. Jack leapt to his feet and motioned for quiet, straining his ears. Everyone stood and stared into the sky, scouring it in all directions. It was difficult to track the direction of a noise in these encircling mountains.

Jack saw it first. "There!" His finger stabbed at the sky to the south of them. Callie caught the glint of sunlight on metal. It was under the cloud cover, probably a few kilometers away. Distances were hard to estimate when everything was enormous.

"Callie, quick, your jacket!" Jack extended an arm towards her.

She stared at him, uncomprehending.

"It's the brightest thing we've got!" he said.

She unzipped the bright orange garment and wriggled her arms out of it. The wristband on the left sleeve caught on her watch strap, and she flailed the arm in desperation. "Help me!"

"Hold still," ordered Jack, deftly unhitching the sleeve. Then he ran to the edge of their little clearing in the scrub with the sleeves of the jacket gripped firmly in both hands, and started swinging their rescue banner in a wide sweeping arc over his head and to the ground on each side, left then right then left then right.

They had to see it. Surely, if they were searching for them, they had to see it.

"Please God," said Jack, and swung the jacket, over and back, over and back, making the biggest movements he possibly could, an ant in the land of the giants.

"No-oo!" wailed Rachel. "They're going the other way!" She started sobbing, taking great gulps of air, standing rigid, her hands over her mouth.

Jack kept swinging, his breath becoming louder.

Everyone else stood like alpine statues, numb and disbelieving, as they watched the little aircraft fly away, until their senses struggled to register it at all, and they could only imagine the echo of its engine in their ears, the after-image of its fuselage on their retinas.

Rachel collapsed to the ground, weeping without restraint, hunched over her knees, her head buried in her hands. Erica roused herself from paralysis, and went to sit alongside Rachel, reaching her arms around the other woman's body, her own eyes filling with tears.

"Jack," said Callie. Still he swung. "Jack! They've gone. You've got to stop." She walked up behind him and reached for his shoulders, trying to still him, without getting injured by the zips and attachments of the flailing orange jacket. "Jack, stop!" He let his hands fall in front of him, still making small swinging movements, the jacket sleeves still held tightly, his chest heaving.

Callie ran her hands down his upper arms and then reached forward around his chest, gripping her hands together in front of him in a bizarre cross between a straitjacket and a hug. His arms became still against the restraint, and Callie relaxed her grip a little. She rested her cheek along the slope of his shoulder, leaned her weight against his back, and spoke again, her voice barely a whisper now. "Oh Jack."

Kain stood aloof from the others, staring to the south in the direction the plane had gone. He was very still, his expression unreadable.

41

WHEN THEY TOLD HIM THE BODY RETRIEVED FROM THE orange bag on the mountain was a woman, Peter felt a wave of coldness wash over him. And then when they told him the name on the passport tucked carefully alongside, he felt relief. He was being unprofessional. Each life mattered equally, whether or not the mother of the deceased had cooked eggs in his kitchen.

And where was she, all this time?

"Amber, have you seen Ellen today?"

"She was here really early. She borrowed my car."

"*Your* car?" He stared at her. Amber's car was less reliable than the Fiordland weather.

"I did warn her about it." Amber looked uncomfortable.

"Well let's hope we don't need to launch another search before the day is out. Do you know where she was going?"

"She didn't say."

"Wonderful. So when the car breaks down we don't even know where to look."

"She's not helpless you know." There was an edge to Amber's tone. Everyone's nerves were beginning to fray.

"Yes, I know that. I would have liked her to confirm the ID of this body, before we send it on to the pathologist, that's all. He will just have to do his best with the passport photos."

42

THE LOSS OF THE PLANE WAS DEVASTATING. BONE NUMBING. Grinding through their hearts and souls and empty stomachs and weary bone marrow. As they kept slogging up the shoulder blades of this giant mountain, an hour passed, and then another one. No one spoke the question aloud: "Why didn't they see us?"

If we were under tree cover, you could understand it, thought Callie. *Or far down in the valley, just atoms in a jumbled mess of rocks and scrub. But we were held high on the upstretched mountain, in the open, waving a fluoro orange banner. If they can't see us there, how will they ever see us anywhere?*

No one had suggested waiting to see if the plane came back. They had all headed instinctively for Somewhere Else. Anywhere that the plane had not already been, so that they might somehow find themselves in the place where its little plexiglas eyes might look next. And, this time, be seen.

Callie's injuries from yesterday's crushing fall were back with a vengeance. Earlier, the endorphins generated by the morning's vigorous exercise had dulled the sensations of pain, and with feelers of sunshine probing through the high cloud, the grandeur of the panorama had spoken to her soul. But now, each step jarred through bruised and torn muscles and ligaments, and there was a particularly sharp pain in her right side that razored into her lungs with each footfall. There was damage in there, and she was afraid that very bad things might lie ahead for her if it wasn't treated soon.

But mostly, she was terrified of what the lost opportunity may mean. The possibility of a search plane had been an unvoiced hope in her heart, a mini El Dorado that they had been hiking towards, well ahead of the elusive lake they had vowed to seek in the east. Once it became clear that they were overdue, surely searchers would come looking, buzzing round the sky in planes and helicopters. Rappelling down out of heaven like the emergency workers on TV shows, in helmets and safety suits. Stretchering out the injured. Saving them.

It had never occurred to her that the search plane, when it came, might not find them.

The vastness of the landscape was whispering no beautiful sweet nothings now, just evil insinuations with an after-breath of sulfur. *I will hold onto you, no matter what. My concealment is total. You will never leave me alive.*

Ahead of her, Rachel was moving up the mountain step-by-step in Erica's wake, and Callie could hear her breath sometimes catching on a sob. They were out of the scrub and onto a stretch of rocky moraine, each step a different size and at a different angle. The wind was picking up, buffeting them, and making progress even harder. After the search plane, Rachel had pulled herself together and dried her eyes, trying to put a good face on it for everyone else as well as herself. She had been as determined as the rest of them to keep moving. So much fitter than the rest of them at the beginning, her form was beginning to fail. She was still eking out her insulin, but had used her last glucose tablet. Now she had only ferns standing between her and a potentially fatal hypo, and her spirit was breaking. Callie saw each stumble and twist as the other woman's boot hit angled, unstable rock.

She turned her head and spoke quietly to Jack, laboring behind her. "I think Rachel needs a rest."

He looked past her at Rachel, and then his gaze shifted further up the mountainside. Kain, in the lead, had stopped and turned back. He waited near Erica until the others drew near enough to speak without shouting. At least they could stand in a circle in this terrain, unhemmed by vegetation.

"I can't see the way forward," Kain said. "I'm not sure if we're going to find a pass over the mountain up this way after all. We obviously can't get over the summit, in our condition and with our skills. And what looked like a pass from down in the valley isn't so promising now." He shook his head and half turned, indicating with his hand in the direction they'd been heading. "Up there, to the right, we might be able to sidle, and then scramble to the top. But I'm not sure." He turned back to them. "And what's on the other side is another matter, as usual."

Callie looked up and around, scanning the mountain for answers, the same as the rest of them were doing. Which way? They couldn't have spent a whole day climbing only to have to descend again and find another way, another valley. And the mess and the landslides that lay down below. It was unthinkable to have to go back through it.

They'd been leaving it to Kain to choose the route, following passively. Pleased, really, that Kain had stayed near instead of striking out so far ahead. There'd been a change in the man, a thaw. It had become even more pronounced after the talk about Liana. Or the search plane. Something had hit Kain between the eyes.

He spoke again, drawing all eyes back from the mountain tops. "How about we find a spot out of this wind where Rachel can rest, and I'll go on a recce. That way I can leave my pack behind and move a lot faster."

"Perhaps one of us should come with you," Callie said.

"Not you," Jack said. "You're injured."

"We're all injured."

"I'm not," said Kain, his sprained ankle apparently forgotten. "And I won't be out of sight. Jack should stay with you girls, just in case anything happens. There's someone out here with a gun, don't forget."

"And a big knife," added Jack. "Adam's knife is still missing, too."

Callie saw Erica flinch, and wished the men didn't have to speak so bluntly. Everyone was scared and disorientated enough already.

Kain continued, "Yeah, well, they'll have trouble sneaking up on us out here in the open. But now that Adam's dead we've only got two men, so I'll go alone, and that's that."

"Oh, and we're helpless little females are we?" snapped Erica. Kain could be condescending to women, but her voice was much sharper than it needed to be. "No handbags to hit the nasty bogeymen with. Funny how we've managed to get so far without our lipstick, isn't it?" She virtually spat the final words, and Callie was shocked.

Kain's only reply was to stare at her. He then started shouldering out of his pack, preparing to proceed exactly as he had decided.

Erica turned abruptly away, her face red, and started helping Rachel find a spot to rest in the windbreak provided by a large boulder.

Kain set off up the mountain without a backward glance.

***

CALLIE WAS STILL PUZZLING OVER ERICA'S OUTBURST WHEN JACK moved close to her and spoke so that only she could hear. "Were you offended by what Kain said?"

She shook her head. "Kain can be a bit old-fashioned about women, but I don't think that's what caused that. It's just tension between the two of them. And there's something else as well." She glanced across at Erica, busying herself with Rachel's sleeping bag. "She's trying to divert attention at the moment. Like a cat that's done something embarrassing and then starts washing itself." Callie narrowed her eyes and pursed her lips. "I actually have a hunch it was the mention of Adam's death that set her off."

"Really? You think it's grief? What a strange way to show it."

"She could hardly say 'I can't stand it when you talk about Adam', could she? So she said the next thing that came into her head. But I think it's more than just grief. It looks like guilt, to be honest. But whether it's because she actually did something, or just a general feeling of responsibility, I don't know."

He stared at Callie, and then at Erica. "She's certainly been very weird about Adam. Ever since he first went missing, in fact. All that hanging back and long silences. We were all scared, but there was something different about her reaction."

"I know. She knows something, I'm sure of it. But how do we get her to tell us what it is?"

"Why don't we just ask her?"

It was a revolutionary idea to Callie. "But why would she tell us the truth?"

"I have a strong feeling that Erica is longing to tell someone the truth. It's eating her up from the inside. She wants it gone from her body."

And so they waited until Rachel was resting, wrapped in her sleeping bag in the fitful sunshine. They'd already chosen a position about ten meters away, where each could sit on a small boulder, keeping Rachel in sight, while avoiding disturbing her too much with their voices. Erica crouched on a rock adjusting the straps on her rucksack. Callie hung off at a slight distance while Jack walked up to the other woman.

"Erica. Can we talk to you please? It's important."

She looked up at him, and then beyond him at Callie. Both continued to regard her silently. She seemed to sense their serious intentions, and drew a deep breath, but raised no protest. "Okay."

Once they were seated in a circle, Callie looked at Jack, his signal to take charge. Direct confrontation was his gig. She was just waiting to see how it unfolded.

Jack took the hint. "Erica. What happened to Adam?" He looked at her steadily. She blanched visibly and stared at her hands, now twisting in her lap.

"What do you mean: what happened to Adam? Why do you think I know anything you don't?" Her voice quivered. Exhaustion? Anger? Nerves? Fear?

"Erica," he said again, leaning just a little forward. "What happened to Adam?"

She gulped a huge breath, her glance flickering around the mountain slopes, and burst into a torrent of sobs. She hunched over her knees and covered her face with her hands, weeping uncontrollably. Callie began to move, ready to console, but Jack caught her eye and shook his head, just once. She subsided back onto her boulder, even though withholding comfort when another person's grief was so violent was as piercing as a physical pain. She decided to trust him.

Gradually, Erica's sobs softened a little, and Jack spoke again. "Erica." His voice was gentle now. "What happened to Adam?"

The words were wrung from her; little more than a guttural whisper. "It was an accident."

43

CALLIE WAS GLAD ERICA COULDN'T SEE THE EXPRESSION OF utter shock on her face, and she turned her head to stare at Jack. He raised his eyebrows a millimeter.

"I was just checking the gun, and Adam walked up and saw me... and the landslide... and it went off... and I didn't know what happened... and then we couldn't find him." Erica's voice broke into shards on the last words and she fell again into sobs, deep and grating, her eyes squeezed closed, her face awash with tears, her nose a dripping mess.

Jack looked at Callie and inclined his head towards Erica. She took it as a signal to follow her earlier instincts. She moved alongside, and wrapped her arms about the other woman. Erica turned into the embrace and clung like a small child, her weeping becoming even more visceral for a time, and then slowly subsiding.

Jack rummaged in his pocket and fished out a handkerchief, the same one he'd been washing out in streams and drying on a rock ever since they'd entered Fiordland all those eons ago. It was not a pleasant looking square of cloth, and he quirked his mouth at Callie, his eyes questioning. She grinned briefly and reached for it, offering it to Erica. "It ain't beautiful," she said to Erica, "but it might be better than turning into a glazed donut."

Erica snorted a quick laugh despite her distress, and took the proffered hankie gratefully, wiping the worst of the mess off her face, then blowing her nose lavishly. She sat back weakly, her grief spent. "I can't believe you guys are still sitting here, after what I've just told you."

"What else would we do?" Callie asked. "Walk off and leave you?"

Erica raised her eyebrows. "Or throw me in a lake."

"Yeah, well, let's stop talking that sort of rubbish," Jack said. "How about you tell us how you came to have a gun." Callie moved back to her own rock, so she could see Erica's face better, but leaned towards her in wordless support.

Erica sighed. "Bryan gave it to me." She rested her forehead on her right hand, still clasping the sodden hankie, staring at the ground near Jack's boots.

"When?"

"The day before he jumped. He told me to put it in my pack, and use it 'to make sure I was the only one'—and then he'd make sure that I got the money I needed. I had no idea what he was talking about—the only one what?—but I just put it in the bottom of my rucksack. He was completely off his trolley and I figured we'd be in a hotel the next night. And then after he died it dawned on me what he wanted me to do." She shook her head slowly. "Man, that was one crazy guy."

Jack said, "Did you tell him you needed money?"

She nodded. "After I got the invitation, I thought, well... he'd got in touch, and he had money, and, you know, maybe this was a way out of my problem. So I rang him in New Zealand, and asked him to help me. I have... gambling debts. Really big gambling debts."

"How big?" Callie said.

Erica glanced at her face. "About a hundred and thirty thousand, give or take."

Callie inhaled sharply. "Wow."

Erica replied with an ironic tone and a roll of her eyes. "Yeah, tell me about it. At least I excel at something." She stared at the ground again. "And I didn't borrow it from a bank."

"Who then?"

"Some low life I met at the casino. Acted like my best friend. But he wasn't."

Jack pulled the discussion back to the first topic. "So what did Bryan say when you phoned him?"

"He told me he'd think about it, and then he called me back a couple of days later, and he gave me these specifications for a particular type of gun. I had to go to a gun club—he even gave me the details of the club—and practice firing this particular gun. It seemed really creepy at first, like it might be something to do with Liana's death, but it was a completely different kind of gun. So I thought it must be so we could shoot food or something." She rolled her eyes. "I had no idea what it would be like out here, so that seemed the best explanation. And Bryan was always asking us to do such crazy things. Anyway, I had to learn to use the gun and then I had to come on the hike. And then he said he'd give me the money. Or 'that I would be provided for' were the words he used, I think." She raised her hands in a helpless shrug. "I had no idea what he was on about, but I was desperate, so I figured, just do what the rich loony says, and you'll get your money, and everything will be okay." She shrugged again. "And here I am."

Jack said, "So, what exactly happened yesterday?"

Erica sighed. "I'd been trying to figure out if I should tell everyone I had the gun, so we could use it to shoot some food or something. I'm not a very good shot, but I figured Adam would be able to use it. But I just didn't know how to tell everyone why I had it in the first place."

"Had you been tempted to do what Bryan said?" Callie's tone was not judgmental, just curious.

"Well, no... but then there were moments in that first day or so when I wondered if I really could do such a thing..." She looked from Callie to Jack, and shrugged her shoulders again. "I was just so desperate. The guy who lent me the money… he was a very scary guy, and he was getting pretty intense. He told me I could either pay up immediately, or he'd send the boys round. Or I could work it off in his brothel."

"Oh!" Callie was horrified. She reached across and squeezed Erica's arm in sympathy.

"I told him I was expecting money soon, and he gave me a few more weeks, and then when this all happened… I wondered… But after Sharon died, and I saw her lying there so cold, and I thought about her little boy and her parents seeing her off at the airport, I knew that I could never take a life no matter what I had to face back home. I knew it right inside my bones. And so then I had this piece of metal burning a hole in my rucksack, wondering and wondering what to do with it."

"But you'd taken it out, just before the landslide?" Jack pressed for the full details.

"Yes, I'd almost decided to tell everyone, and Adam had gone on ahead, and Rachel was somewhere behind me, so I took the chance to get it out, and I was leaning on a log and I just had it in my hand, looking at it, and I'd been slipping the safety catch on and off, kind of fidgeting with it, and Adam walked up, and it was pouring rain, so it was hard to see very far, and he suddenly saw what I had in my hand, and the look on his face, the *look* on his face... and I was about to explain, and then suddenly the ground just gave way and something hit me in the back, a tree or something maybe, I don't really know, and the gun went off and everything was chaos, and I just couldn't find Adam, or the gun." She was silent for a moment, staring into space, ambushed by remembered trauma. She pulled herself together. "I kind of surfed down the landslide, on the top of it. My rucksack landed quite close to me when everything stopped moving, thankfully, or I'd never have found it again, but I don't know where the gun ended up. It's somewhere back in that horrible mess. And I didn't even really look for it because I didn't ever, ever want to touch it again. Oh, poor Adam. And his girlfriend!" She began to weep again.

Callie moved back alongside Erica and put her arm around her.

But Jack hadn't finished. "Erica," he said, and waited till she looked up. He looked her full in the eye, but spoke gently. "Did you kill Sharon?"

"No!" Her answer was violent. "No way!" She began to splutter and the words got stuck. "I didn't... I couldn't." She shook her head repeatedly. "I tried to save Sharon. I tried so hard."

"Back when we found Adam, you wanted us to believe the same person had killed them both."

"That was so you'd look for Sharon's killer, and not be looking for me. I was so shocked at first, when you said she'd been murdered. But then I realized..." She shrugged. "It could work to my advantage. Stop you finding out about what I'd done. If you thought there was just one killer." She looked him full in the face again. "Because I definitely did not kill Sharon."

He stared at her for a long moment. "Do you know who did?"

She looked away. "How could I know who did?"

"I had a feeling you might have seen something that made you wonder. That's all."

"Well I did. But I don't really know. And I wouldn't want to accuse someone when it might be quite wrong. It just seemed odd, that's all. And then with everything else that's been going on..." She sighed.

Callie said, "What did you see?"

"Well... I woke up that night, when Kain went for a pee. I mean he sometimes goes for a pee in the middle of the night. But..."

Jack said, "Yes?"

"Well it's stupid. I mean, it was freezing that night. The snow had stopped, but it gets even colder when the snow stops."

Callie frowned. "So what did he do that seemed strange?"

"Well, he put his gloves on. That's what woke me up actually, because he was rummaging for them. It's been in my head since you told us, and I couldn't stop thinking about it last night." She shrugged. "I mean, I know it was cold. It's just…" She looked at Jack, questioning, almost hoping he could refute what she was thinking. "Well, you're a bloke. Would you wear gloves, if you were popping outside for a quick pee?"

"Well, no. I wouldn't," he said, looking uncomfortable. "They'd, um, hinder dexterity, shall we say. It's odd. Suspicious even. But it's not proof. I'd suggest we be wary of Kain. But keep our minds open. Assumptions can be deadly out here. If someone else is following us, we don't want to miss it because we're all looking at Kain." He nodded, suddenly realizing something. "But it's good to know there's no sniper after us."

Callie said, "Yes! That's one less complication for us to deal with. But then," she glanced at Erica, "you already knew there was no sniper."

"It wasn't exactly a comfort to me. You can't begin to understand what it feels like to know you've taken someone's life. And they can never ever get it back." She shook her head slowly and sighed. "I hardly slept at all last night. My head was just full of this horrible emptiness where Adam used to be. And pictures of that hole in his head. I tried so hard not to look, but I saw it, and I can't stop seeing it. And it's all my fault. Just because of worthless money."

***

"THAT WAS QUICK," SAID PETER, WHEN HE PICKED UP THE PHONE. He'd been surprised when Amber told him the pathologist had called—he couldn't have had the body more than half an hour at best.

"I haven't done the post mortem yet. But I thought you'd like to know straight away that this girl didn't die naturally."

"How can you be sure?"

"She has bruising on her face that you only get when someone uses their hands to hold your mouth and nose closed and suffocate you."

Peter swore, his tone fierce. "So now I have to figure out who did it, and find a way to prove it. Unless they're all guilty somehow. And if not, I wonder if they knew she'd been murdered when they packaged her up."

"Not necessarily. The bruising doesn't come out straight away. Even if any of them could have recognized what it meant. She was found in snow wasn't she?"

"Yes."

"They could have thought it was just hypothermia. Her gear isn't very good. I wouldn't be surprised if she had some trouble staying warm, the poor little sweetheart."

"And now I've got a murder investigation to run as well, in the middle of the biggest search we've ever had."

***

"I WISH WE COULD FIND THAT KNIFE," JACK SAID. HE LOOKED AT Kain's pack, resting against a rock only a few meters away.

"You think it's in there?" Callie said.

"Don't know." He swung to look at Erica. "Have you got the knife?"

"Absolutely not!" Erica was affronted by the question.

"Don't be precious. You just told us you had a gun until yesterday. We need to be totally open with each other if we're going to survive. And you were the last one to use the knife last night. I didn't see you use it because I was quite busy sulking at the time…"

He shrugged in self-deprecation. "But judging by the results, you must be pretty good with a knife. All that medical training perhaps. You could have taken the knife for security, not necessarily to use it on anyone."

Erica's temper flared. "So now that I've told you the truth about Adam, you're going to suspect me of everything else as well, are you?"

Jack wrinkled his nose thoughtfully, and stayed quite calm. "Well, wouldn't you do the same if the positions were reversed?"

She thought about that for a moment, and her anger subsided. "Well, probably, yes I would. But I seriously didn't want to kill Adam, and I didn't kill Sharon, and I don't have the knife. Truly."

Callie was now staring at Kain's pack. "Do you think we could?"

Erica said, "Could what?"

"Search Kain's pack."

She swung round to look, and now three pairs of eyes were fixed upon it. Wondering.

"How would he react if he knew we'd done it?"

"If there's a knife in there, and we get it back, I don't really care how he reacts," Jack said.

"No, me neither," Callie said. "Although… we probably should think about what he might do. He's pretty strong, even without a knife. If it does turn out that he's dangerous, and we confront him, what might happen?" She looked at Jack, but it was Erica who spoke.

"If we found the knife, we could just take it, and not say anything. He wouldn't even know until he went looking for it later. And he could hardly say anything about it, could he?"

Callie laughed briefly. "Yeah. Who stole the knife I stole earlier? But it might make him a bit weird, when he realized it was gone."

"But would he realize?" Erica said. "It's so hard to find things in these stupid packs. They're so long and narrow. Whatever you want, it's never on the top. He might just think it had slipped down to the bottom. He'd have to take every single thing out to be absolutely sure it wasn't there."

"I don't like the idea," Jack said. "I'd rather be honest about it with him. But then you know what I'm like. Blundering in and just saying what I think." He shook his head. "But think about when he'd be able to check the contents of his pack without us seeing. When he's alone in his tent. At night when we're all asleep, and vulnerable. Surely it's better to get his reaction at a time that we control, when we've got the best chance of managing it."

Callie nodded and sighed. "Of course, we're assuming the knife is in there. What if it's not?"

Erica gasped. "You're right. It might not be Kain at all. It might be someone following us. This whole thing is making me so paranoid. He'd probably be able to tell we'd been through his stuff, and imagine how that would make him feel. He's already feeling left out as it is."

"Has he told you that?" Callie said.

"Not in those exact words. But yes, he feels it." She glanced at Jack. "He knows you don't like him."

Jack felt the rebuke, and it was justified. "I've been trying a bit harder with him since last night."

"Yes, I know," Erica said. "I think he's been trying a bit harder too. What do you think?" The question was for Callie.

"He's been a bit different since the plane," she agreed. "Something changed."

Jack was alert. He'd noticed a difference too. "What did you think it was?"

"I'm not sure. Maybe the conversation about Liana," Callie said. "Or the plane itself? The thought of how hard it is to get rescued out here, and the fact that we need each other if we're going to survive. But he was thrown by my question about whether Bryan knew he'd slept with Liana. The look in his eyes. It was like I'd hit him with a taser."

"I saw that too," said Erica. "I've been wondering, the last couple of hours... Well, you know how Bryan spoke to me before we left Australia? I was part of Bryan's plan somehow, even though I didn't understand it at the time. What if I wasn't the only one? What if he spoke to Kain as well? If he had, what might he have promised Kain? It would make all the difference in the world, if Bryan knew about Kain and Liana. You can't trust a man who knows you've betrayed him." She sighed. "But then, it's probably just more paranoia."

Or maybe not. Jack felt the suspicion flower within him all over again, and longed to search that pack. But, looking up the mountain, he saw Kain returning. Still about twenty minutes away over rocky moraine, but the little group would be fully visible to him. They couldn't search his pack now.

44

Erica's confession had to be shared, and there was no easy way to do it. At least, not one that Jack could think of.

He said, "Just before you tell us about the route, Kain, we need to tell you and Rachel something important we've just found out."

He looked at Rachel. The rest seemed to have revived her, but she was definitely weaker than on previous days. *Then again, aren't we all?*

"The good news is, there's no sniper following us," he said. "The bad news is, Erica shot Adam. Accidentally. With a gun Bryan gave her."

Rachel gasped in shock and turned towards Erica. "No. You didn't! You couldn't!"

Kain stared at Erica, his eyes narrowed. "Why did Bryan give you a gun?" He emphasized the word "you".

Callie gave Jack a look that didn't seem entirely supportive.

Erica struggled under their scrutiny. "It was just... I asked Bryan for money, and he said... Well he gave me... I didn't understand... and then there was the landslide and the gun went off..." She became incoherent and trailed off miserably.

"Money!" Kain exclaimed. "So, you killed Adam for money!"

"I didn't! It was an accident. You don't understand..."

"And you slept with me and said you loved me and all the time you had a gun under your pillow, did you, thinking about how to kill me for money?"

"No! It wasn't like that."

"And you let me hunt for Adam and worry so much about him, and all the time..." Rachel trailed off and stared at Erica, her eyes brimming with tears. "How could you make us all search and wonder, when all the time you'd killed him yourself?"

"I didn't know. I knew the gun went off, but I didn't know it hit him. I didn't." She buried her face in her hands and began to weep without inhibition.

Callie frowned in distaste and stared at Jack. "Well, that went well, Einstein. Perhaps we'll nominate you for a Nobel Peace Prize."

"I was trying to cover the main points quickly," he muttered. "We've got to get back on the trail."

"And now we'll spend twice as long putting the group back together. Ever heard of 'more haste, less speed'?" She stood, and spoke briskly. "Okay, listen up, you lot. Erica, stop blubbing. Rachel and Kain, you've got the wrong end of the pineapple, so stop calling Erica a murderer, and listen." Everyone looked at her, even Erica, though she still sobbed quietly. She pulled Jack's grungy hanky out of her pocket and started to wipe her face.

Callie gave a more detailed explanation of Erica's story, one that covered motivations and feelings. Her embarrassment about the gambling debts. The uncertainty of how to admit she had the gun. The shock of the landslide and its aftermath.

A long silence followed, but Rachel's expression had softened a little. "I guess I can see how you could get yourself into a mess like that."

Erica shot her a thankful glance, and fresh tears began to well in her eyes.

"I can't," Kain said, his face hard. "We only have her word for how it happened. How do we know she didn't shoot Adam on purpose?"

"It's a reasonable question," Callie said, her voice mild. "But then, why would she shoot Adam? He was our best asset, with all his wilderness skills. If I was going to cull this group, and I wanted to make it out of the wilderness alive, I wouldn't start with Adam."

"Maybe not," said Kain, his voice silky and dangerous as he gave Erica a poisonous stare. "But you might start with Sharon."

Rachel inhaled quickly. "Did you kill Sharon?" Her expression was agonized.

"No!" Erica said, desperate. "I swear to you, I'm not the one who killed Sharon. I tried so hard to save her. I did everything I could." She gave Kain a hard stare. "But we could ask where you went that night, Kain."

"Oh, what, so the little murderer wants to blame me now, does she?"

Erica stared at him, her expression intense. "Please look me in the eye and tell me you didn't kill Sharon. Please Kain. I have to know. You went for a pee in the middle of the night, but you wore your gloves."

He huffed. "So what? It was freezing that night."

"I think that's a weird thing for a guy to do, and Jack agreed with me."

Don't bring me into this. Jack cringed internally. But it was too late. Kain turned on him.

"Oh, so you've all been yarning round the campfire and deciding that good old Kain's a murderer have you, just because he gets cold hands?"

Callie said, "Erica, why did you bring Jack into it? It was your idea, so own it. Don't go making even more trouble between Kain and Jack. How are we going to keep this team moving if you stir them up like that?"

"I'm sorry," Erica said. "I didn't mean to…"

Callie turned to Kain. "What actually happened was that Erica mentioned it, because it had been playing on her mind, like lots of things are playing on our minds out here, and when she asked, Jack agreed that he probably would find it inconvenient to wear gloves when going for a quick slash in the middle of the night. Stop thinking you're so important that we can't stop talking about you.

We're all wondering about each other, and it's making us crazy, which is exactly what Bryan wanted. So how about we stop fighting and suspecting each other, and get on and decide what we're going to do next."

There was a long pause while everyone readjusted their minds, and then Callie spoke again. "So, Scout, what did you find up the mountain?"

Kain stared at her for a long moment, his eyes steely, and then apparently relented, at least a little.

"It's a hard climb," he said, his voice flat and controlled. "Very hard for non-climbers carrying rucksacks. Past that cliff-edge we can see, there's a fairly long section where we'll need to sidle along a narrow ledge. I've been right along the ledge and you can get around the end of it onto a boulder field. Some hard scrambling there—pulling ourselves up by our arms, a lot of it. But once we get past that, I can see a section of that tussocky stuff, quite a large area, and I hope it should take us over into the next valley. Or at least give us somewhere reasonably flat to camp the night before we come back down, if we have to."

He'd been looking at all of them during the speech—except, significantly, Erica—his eyes flicking from one to the other, but now his stare settled on Jack.

"So, what's your recommendation?" Jack said.

"I don't make recommendations. I've learned that much."

Rachel frowned, and Erica stared at her feet, but Callie spoke up.

"Oh, stop being such a grump, Kain." She sounded irritable. "We're all just doing the best we can." She looked from him to Jack and back again.

Kain redirected his stare to her, and remained silent.

Jack sighed and rubbed his face with both hands. He felt

constrained, as though he couldn't take part in the decision. But then, that was undoubtedly Kain's goal, so he decided to proceed as though the discussion had been civilized. He struggled for a mild expression to paste onto his face.

"Do you think the ledge is wide enough for us all to manage it?" He kept his voice neutral.

Kain shifted his stare back to Jack, but didn't reply immediately. In the end, he settled for a neutral voice too. Some kind of detente. "If we're careful, we should all be able to do it. There's a bit of a swing to get off the other end of it, which I found easy enough, but it will be harder for a shorter person." He didn't look at Erica, the shortest person there.

Callie joined in. "And the drop from the ledge?"

"Ten meters or so. Not huge."

Jack looked around them at the sweep of cliffs. The shadows were beginning to lengthen, but the long summer twilight and the thinning of the cloud cover gave them extra time. "What are our chances of making it to that grassy area before dark?"

"It looks to me like we could probably do it in two or three hours. But it won't be easy." Kain's eyes slid to Rachel. "And it may tax our strength quite a bit."

"I couldn't bear to go back the way we came," Rachel said, her voice catching. "We have to get out of this valley." Her glance flickered round the group. "Please."

Jack gave her an assessing look, and then glanced at Callie, who raised her eyebrows briefly. They couldn't navigate by emotion if they wanted to reach the lake and safety. But they also couldn't keep going if they were utterly demoralized. Whoever said an army marches on its stomach only had half the story; an army marches on its spirits, especially when there's next to nothing in its stomach. "If we went back, we'd have to go the other side of the river anyway,"

Jack said, squinting down the valley. "That major landslide would be hard to get around. And the ocean is that way. We don't want the ocean, we've been to the ocean. We want the lake."

Callie said, "There could be a pass up there. I'd really love to get over this mountain. I know we won't magically see the lake from the top, it's too far and the valleys twist and turn too much, and there might be more mountains and more valleys yet, but I just feel sure we'll be closer to the lake beyond that peak."

"You need to remember that if it is harder than it looks, and we can't get up this way," added Kain, apparently reconciled to taking part in the discussion now, "we'll have used up most of our daylight. We won't get back to last night's camp in time, even though it's downhill. And the wind's picking up. It's sheltered here, but I got hit by a few serious gusts up there."

"Sheltered?" Erica said, her tone uneasy. The wind was beating at the looser sections of their garments, tossing the hood of Callie's jacket as it lay down her back—flip and snap, flip and snap.

"Is it really strong wind?" said Callie in quick concern. "Will it make it too dangerous on that ledge?"

Kain shrugged. "I got along it and back okay. But if we're going, we probably shouldn't wait too long."

"Well, we need to make a decision, and we don't have a coin to flip," Callie said, her voice brisk. "We've lost confidence in ourselves because of that plane, and the idiot searchers who didn't see us. But we're not dead yet. We can still make it home. I say we go up. What does everyone else think?"

"I'm scared of that ledge. And the wind." Erica looked on the verge of tears. "But I'm even more scared of having to go back the way we came, and lose another whole day."

Callie said, "So what is it? Up or down?"

"Up, I guess."

"Rachel?"

"Up, definitely. I don't want to go back there."

"Jack?"

"You've got three 'ups' already. I don't have to vote." He was uneasy about both options, and part of him didn't want to be responsible for whatever happened next.

"Jack." There was a warning note in her voice.

"Oh all right. Up. We might as well try it."

"Kain?"

He shook his head. "I'm not voting. I'll go along with the majority." When Callie gave him a stern look he simply ignored her, stood and walked over to his rucksack, busying himself with preparations for the climb to come.

Another snack of the endless ferns, gathered that morning and eaten raw, was the best they could do for an energy boost. They didn't sit easily in anxious stomachs. Jack saw Kain fiddling with a bulging plastic bag, but the contents looked dark, not green like everyone else's fern tips. He angled for a closer look. "Not those berries!" The man couldn't be going to eat something Bryan the Serial Killer had recommended, surely. His dislike for Kain didn't extend to wanting him dead. Or disabled, for that matter. The team needed him.

Kain was holding one of the tiny berries in front of him, studying it. "Almost a complete food in itself, Bryan said. And we could certainly do with the energy."

Jack saw the others staring at the berry between Kain's thumb and forefinger, transfixed. Callie looked worried, Erica fearful, but the expression on Rachel's face could only be described as longing. Who could blame her, in her situation? What if it turned out to be true, and the berries were miniature lifesavers but they didn't eat them and died of starvation? And searchers found their bodies in days or years to come, with a little bag of desiccated berries, and wondered why the stupid fools hadn't eaten them?

Callie spoke. "Kain, you can't trust what Bryan said."

"Why not? He told us a lot of things that were true, and that are helping keep us alive. About the weather, and camping. And he told me about the berries way back, on about the second or third day."

"Kain, please don't eat them," Erica said, her voice intense.

He snorted. "As if you care if I die." She put her head in her hands.

Callie frowned in Jack's direction, and mouthed the words "do something".

What and win another peace prize? Jack rubbed his face. "Kain, you're right that Bryan taught us a lot of things about survival. He was a compulsive teacher, and he also wanted to get us all to Poison Bay in good order and condition for his big announcement. But he didn't show us any other 'bush tucker' among all the things there must be to eat out here. Why did he point them out to you, the person Liana cheated on him with? He may have known that, don't forget. And how can a berry be a complete food? His main goal was to kill us, even on the second or third day. It's apparently been his goal for months at least, if not longer."

Kain stared at Jack, holding the eye contact, and put the berry in his mouth, slowly, deliberately, and chewed it, and swallowed. Jack shook his head in frustration and looked away.

"Kain, please!" Erica was close to tears.

He stared at her while he fished another berry out of the bag by touch, and put it into his mouth, chewing deliberately. He stood in a quick fluid movement, shoved the bag of berries in his jacket pocket, and shouldered into his rucksack. Without another word, he set off up the mountain, his hand fishing in his pocket for more berries as he climbed.

45

CALLIE WAS MORE SCARED THAN SHE'D EVER BEEN IN HER LIFE, even counting the terrors of the past few days.

She'd slotted in behind Kain in their little conga line when they set off from the rest stop, mostly to make a buffer between him and Erica, leaving Rachel to be watched by Jack at the rear. And as the minutes passed and dragged and added themselves on top of each other, she regretted the decision more and more, wishing she could talk to Jack about what she was seeing. But she couldn't turn back to reach him on the end of the line, or Kain would get away from her altogether. And she didn't want to frighten Erica.

The berries. She cursed those berries in her head, using every epithet, profanity and blasphemy she could think of. And then she cursed Bryan even more lavishly. His determination to hang on to past hurts like incendiary trophies, fanning their flame until they burnt a hole right through the center of his soul, and turned to charcoal the lives he touched.

It had been a missed foothold here and there at first, as they clambered up the mountainside. By the time they reached the ledge they must traverse, Kain's feet were barely coordinated.

As Kain had promised, the initial drop from this ledge was indeed only short—by Fiordland standards, that is. The ledge below it however—wider, flatter, and yet frustratingly inaccessible from the downhill end—edged into a cliff that fell sheer and straight to the valley far below. A voracious wind swirled along the narrow shelf with battering-ram force.

She tried to stop him stepping out there, called to him, reached out to grab at his arm.

He twisted to look at her, and the desolation in his eyes made her gasp. He seemed to be working hard to form the words clearly, but even so, she struggled to understand his meaning. "He set me up. Make sure you survive, and tell them. He set me up. I can't believe I listened to him. I can't believe what I've done. Tell the little boy…" he swayed, "…I'm so sorry."

"Kain! Please!" She grabbed at his arm again, but he batted her hand away, steadied himself, and launched out onto that awful ledge.

What could she do but follow him?

And everyone followed behind her, Erica too governed by her fear of heights to notice anything else, Jack focused on keeping Rachel on her feet and moving, moving, while trying not to look down himself.

Behind her, she could hear Erica whimpering aloud, apparently no longer able to control her vocal chords, so overwhelmed was she by atavistic fear. Not usually given to vertigo, even Callie could feel the vastness of it pulling her, luring her, out and down, and down and down.

Kain was nearly to the end of the ledge, and Callie was keeping close to him, letting Erica fall behind to battle her demons alone.

Maybe he could make it. Maybe they'd be safe on the boulder field Callie was beginning to see ahead around the curve of the cliff. And he didn't have the strength to fight them off now, so they'd be able to hold onto him, stop him marching upward, and somehow make him vomit. Get those berries out of his system, and perhaps he'd recover.

Kain's boot caught on the uneven surface, and he stumbled and teetered. "Watch out!" she shouted. He half-turned to look back at her, his eyes glazed. His pack scraped on the rock wall alongside him, pitching his upper body outwards, at the very moment his knees bent and gave way beneath him.

Callie grabbed instinctively for the straps dangling from the back of his pack. It was too little to save him, but it was enough to unbalance her. She felt her right boot slip off the edge into nothingness in the same instant that Kain tumbled from her view. She grabbed for the cliff face, but there was nothing to hold her, and she kept sliding. Sliding and falling. Her whole world was sliding and she was going to die. She heard the sickening crunch from below, and she was next, and there was nothing she could do to stop it.

"God! Callie! No!" It was Jack's voice, and suddenly, her fingers found purchase on that edge, and she hung, dangling in space, the great weight of her rucksack pulling her outwards, dragging, dragging, drawing her down.

Now there was screaming, long and hoarse. That was Erica. Useless and screaming. Behind her, Rachel. And Jack trapped behind them both, unable to reach her. "Oh God! Save her!" That was him again, desperate. She didn't want to be one of the ones who didn't make it home. She didn't want to go wherever Kain had just gone.

Callie found strength from somewhere unknown, surging up through her body. She thrust herself upwards, pushing with her feet against the cliff face. She managed to hook the fingers of one hand into a groove near the back of the ledge. Eroded by rain? Who knew. *Thank God for it.* The other hand followed, and she struggled to swing her left leg to the ledge. It wouldn't go high enough, so she used her arms again, every muscle fiber in her chest and shoulders shrieking and howling with the pain as she struggled up onto her elbows, and swung the leg again. *Like getting out of a swimming pool with a gorilla on your back.* This time her leg found purchase on the rim of the ledge, and she pushed and groveled till her other leg could join it, and then lay flat on her face, full length along the ledge, the weight of her rucksack crushing her, the smell of the beautiful, solid granite filling her nostrils as she gasped for oxygen, her lungs rasping, that pain in her side piercing with a vengeance, her torn hands now beginning to make themselves heard above all the other agonies. But, oh sweet Lord, she was alive.

Erica was still screaming, like someone was murdering her in slow and brutal ways. Callie struggled to clear her head enough to think what to do next.

Kain. She edged her head just a little to the right, and saw his outflung hand, thrusting out into that awful void beyond the next ledge. She moved her head a little more, and as the lip of the ledge on which she lay slid from her field of view, like a blind retracting, the rest of him was unveiled. Lying spread eagled across the mound of his rucksack, its harness still firmly buckled. Back painfully arched, legs akimbo. His head at an impossible angle, his beautiful eyes wide and staring straight at her. As she watched and waited for any sign of movement, even the merest hint of life, a thin snake-like trickle, almost black, slid out from under his head, and slithered right off the edge, creating a jagged trail across the rock. Blood.

Poison berries. Broken neck. Head staved in. They were spoiled for choice with cause of death. Callie made a conscious decision to distance herself from the event, defer its emotion, treat it like a news story. *Another one bites the dust.* She would feel the loss and the horror later, the brutal end to a teenage obsession and an adult affection, when there was time and energy for such luxuries. For now, they must survive. She moved her head back in line with her body, and rested her forehead on the cold rock. This ledge had been pure joy in comparison to the recent alternative, but now it was beginning to pall, and the labor of drawing air into lungs compressed by the huge weight strapped to her back was becoming unsustainable. And that terrible noise behind her had to stop.

She levered herself into a sitting position, slowly, painfully and oh so very carefully, her legs dangling off the edge. Erica was a couple of meters away, her left side and rucksack pressed hard against the rock wall, staring down at Kain and screaming, a throaty visceral noise, terrifying all by itself. "Shut up, Erica!" Callie's voice was harsh, sharp, and shocking, and Erica stopped instantly and stared at her with scared-rabbit eyes, her chest heaving, her breathing loud and guttural.

"Do you think you could make it over here to me?" Callie made her voice softer, encouraging. Erica shook her head, and closed her eyes, two fat tears sliding down her flushed cheeks. But Callie persisted. "C'mon, Erica, just try. See if you can move one foot. Your left foot, just move it a centimeter, that's all you need to do."

Erica's eyes opened, and she stared at Callie, but then shook her head—a tiny movement. "I can't. I can't move. I'm so sorry." Her voice was little more than a hoarse whisper, and Callie saw a tremor in her legs. An especially strong gust of wind drummed along the cliff face just at that moment, and Callie knew she'd have to act fast, or they'd lose another one.

She struggled to her feet, precarious on the narrow ledge. "Erica, look at me for a moment. I'm going to get off this ledge, ditch my rucksack, and then come back, and help you off here, one step at a time. Have you got that?" Erica nodded. "Okay, now I want you to shut your eyes, press against the wall just like you're doing now, and think about eating lasagna at your dining table at home, all warm and safe. Just do it." She hoped the diversion would work. Erica loved lasagna back in the day—hopefully the preference still held after ten years. "Smell the crispy cheese," she added over her shoulder as she set off. "Have a nice glass of red with it, too."

Adrenalin gave Callie extra speed, and she was to the end of that ledge like a startled ferret. Kain hadn't lied about the swing-off at the end of the ledge—with her height, she managed it easily enough. The drop immediately below that point wasn't sheer, more of a steep slope down to the second ledge. But it was extremely exposed, the elevation intimidating even for her. It was going to be seventeen different kinds of fun getting Erica off there in a minute.

Without the ungainly pack, it was a much easier journey back to the fear-paralyzed woman. Speaking softly, she persuaded Erica to keep her eyes shut while she unclipped her harness and eased the rucksack from her shoulders, reaching around to wedge it as firmly as she could into the angle of the ledge. And then she just hugged her for a minute, pressed close to the cliff face, while Erica clung and wept.

At last, Callie was able to make eye contact with Jack, about two meters further back. He was crouched on the ledge facing her, Rachel hunched in front of him, and he had his arms around her in a hug—for comfort or to keep her from falling, or both. He held Callie's gaze for a long moment, and then another and another. His face was wet with tears.

The trip back along the ledge was slow and laborious, Callie murmuring coaxing words to Erica, insisting that she keep her eyes closed. That meant Callie had to watch the placement of each foot, so she stayed facing the other woman and moved backwards, shuffling her feet so she could feel the surface, incessantly looking over her own shoulder to check for bumps and dips.

At the end of the ledge, there was no option but for Erica to open her eyes, but before she'd allow her to do so, Callie gave strict instructions that she was only to look uphill, not downhill.

She left the trembling woman safely wrapped in a space blanket from her own rucksack, and went back for Erica's pack. Then it was time to help Rachel and Jack. They formed a train, Rachel hanging onto Callie's waist, and Jack steadying Rachel from behind.

As the four survivors crouched in a circle among those boulders, finding what windbreak they could, the relief to be alive and off that ledge was tangible. There was still maybe two hours walking if they planned to try for the alpine meadow tonight. And they had to deal with Kain yet. But that was a problem they could face soon enough.

And the mountain watched, silent, unyielding.

46

"STAND UP, THOMAS GRANTON, AND FACE ME LIKE A MAN!"
Peter turned to see Ellen Carpenter sweep into the crowded search room like a tornado. He, along with everyone else, froze in shock. "How dare you!" She was trembling with naked fury, and her eyes could have bored holes in concrete. "How *dare* you sit in this room and smile and nod and pretend to be helping, when all the while you're trying to kill my little girl! Explain yourself."

The vision before him reminded Peter of a childhood warning never to get between a vixen and her cubs, but he finally snapped out of it. Stupid to be scared of a woman in his own police station. "Ellen. Calm down and stop shouting. What seems to be the problem?"

"What seems to be the problem? This seems to be the problem." She thrust a sheaf of papers towards him, and shook it. "We wondered who the new beneficiary was. Well, look at that."

A passage was marked on the document, and he read it rapidly, disbelief growing with each word. He looked at his senior constable, now standing by the radio, arms crossed not in self-defense but in defiance. "Tom? What do you have to say about this?"

"I have nothing to say." His voice was flat, toneless.

Ellen launched another attack, and for a moment Peter thought he might have to physically restrain her. "You better have something to say. What have you done? What have you done, to this search, to these families, to my little girl? You cold-blooded scumbag!"

Tom was stung into a reaction and he rounded on her, his hands clenched into fists by his side. "What about that other family that lost their little girl? Your daughter's a grown woman who got away with murder for ten years. Well not any more. She's getting what she deserves! They all are! And then *my* little girl who never hurt anyone might get a chance to live!"

Ellen hurled herself towards him and the search room descended into chaos.

47

"JACK, BE CAREFUL, PLEASE." HE LOOKED BACK OVER HIS shoulder. Callie had followed him towards that awful slope down to the lower ledge. It looked like the playground slide out of a horror movie, ending in hundreds of meters of empty air. Gusts of wind kept punching him, trying to carry him off the mountain. He felt the void drawing him like a magnet, and his blood pressure rose in anxiety, his breath coming fast. It was a relief to turn his back on the fearful view for a moment and face Callie. "I know you want to make sure Kain's body is treated with respect," she said, "and I agree that it's important we do the best we can for him or we'll go mad. But if it comes down to it, don't risk your life. Please. Just leave him where he is if you have to. We need you." Her eyes were intense, with just the slightest brightness of tears.

He closed the gap between them in two steps, and gathered her into a wordless hug for one, two, three seconds. And then he released her and turned back to the task. She was really crying now, but he couldn't watch her do it.

Ten meters or so, not a huge drop. That was how Kain had described the distance between the upper and lower ledges. Not huge, but more than enough to kill a big strong man, his spine snapped, his head smashed. *Not huge*, Jack kept repeating in his head, as he carefully clambered down that steep, exposed slope with its perilous full-stop ending. When a particularly brutal gust whistled past him, pushing and shoving, he flattened himself against the mountain and clung until it passed.

Flooding, that's what psychologists call it, when you do a whole heap of the thing that terrifies you, so you stop fearing it. He'd written an article on it once. About theories, and other people's experiences, distant lives. But it wasn't distant theory any more. Flooding was what he'd been doing all the way along that narrow ledge. Flooding was what he was doing now, and had done so many times on this expedition. Acrophobia: fear of heights. That was Jack's poison.

As if what awaited him on the lower ledge wasn't bad enough, without the added fear of the edge. He knew Callie would have helped him if she could, but though she said nothing, he could see there was pain in her shoulders by the way she'd been carrying herself since they'd left the ledge. Adrenalin had given her the strength to lever herself out of the jaws of the fall, but now her body was paying for it. She needed a rest. In a hospital bed, probably. But a wind-blown mountainside would have to do. Rachel was struggling, and Erica his fellow acrophobic—the team nurse who should have confirmed death for them, felt for a pulse, that sort of thing—was a basket case who simply couldn't face any more flooding today. And so the task had fallen to Jack.

They'd agreed that Kain's body should be covered against the elements if possible, and left on the ledge, as far from the edge as Jack could manhandle it. There was no way to get it back up that slope. And Jack, as "the Reverend", would say some kind of prayer on everyone's behalf, recording what he could on the camera that lay in his pocket. It would be a far cry from the send-off they'd given Sharon, which itself had seemed so inadequate at the time.

What an inappropriate person he was to be doing the "last offices" for this man. Tension had always been there between them, nurtured by Jack's jealous anger that anyone could be loved by Callie and not value it. But it had flowered into naked enmity these last few days. *They'll know you are Christians by your love, that's what Jesus said. Yeah, Jack. Good one. Well done.* Self-hatred seared his soul as he grappled with the remains of Kain's life. Unclipping the rucksack, dragging, pulling, heaving the corpse across that ledge, crossing arms on top, wrestling legs, torso into the big orange plastic sack they each carried for just such a time as this, tugging it up over the sightless staring eyes and tucking it in under the pulpy head. Giving tender care that he'd not shown him in life. Jack wept, loud and uninhibited, with only the sullen mountain and the angry wind to hear him. *Oh God. I'm so sorry.*

And then it was time to empty that rucksack. Suspicion had been so important just one hour, two hours ago. Who cared what was in it now? Emotion told him to kick it off the ledge into space, and never know whether Kain had the knife or not. But rationality said they needed the cooking equipment and other practical stuff, plus it would make sense to take the tent to replace the one damaged after the landslide.

So he moved that rucksack well away from the edge, and started sorting.

***

THEY STARED AT THE ITEMS LYING IN THE CENTER OF THEIR LITTLE circle. Sheltered by the mass of an uphill boulder, they were merely slapped by the still-rising wind instead of pummeled.

No one spoke. Just stared. And tried to process what it meant.

The knife was one thing. They'd had their suspicions about Adam's knife anyway. He could have just wanted that for protection. But the satellite phone, and the GPS. And those energy bars—three of them, lying in a neat row.

It was Jack who finally broke the silence. "He had the emergency beacon too. But it seemed to have been damaged in the fall. I tried to get it to activate, but I couldn't get anything out of it. So I left it down there." He suddenly felt unsure of that decision. "I could go back down and get it, if you want." He looked from one face to another, hesitant. "In case one of you can get it to work." Still no one looked at him; their eyes were locked on the emergency equipment.

The silence that followed stretched long and thin and tight. The stuff that could save their lives—could have saved Sharon and Adam and even Kain—was not on the bottom of Poison Bay with Bryan, but traveling beside them every day, sleeping beside them every night. Kain had it with him, all along, and hadn't told them. Had food that he hadn't shared. How could their spirits recover from a blow like this?

Finally, Rachel spoke. "Can we be certain that he knew he had them? That they weren't hidden in his pack, by Bryan or someone else?" Her voice was flat, toneless, but her words were more articulate than they'd been since the plane missed them, hours earlier.

"They were wrapped inside his sleeping bag." He felt like this needed an explanation. As though that was an odd place to look, a violation. "It seemed heavier than mine, that's why I got it out and unrolled it." Down there on that ledge, with the wind wrestling with him for control of the fabric. Right next to a corpse in a plastic bag.

Rachel nodded, her expression somber. "So, he knew."

"Wrapped in the folds, or actually inside the sleeping bag?" Erica's question had an alertness behind it.

"Actually inside the bag. Right down at the feet."

"That accounts for how he hid them from me. He must have slept with them there." She paused. "Even made love to me with them there."

The euphemism for sex surprised Jack in such a context. He'd have expected harsh words. Profanity. But the look on Erica's face wasn't anger. Kain must have meant more to Erica than he realized.

If that was the case, watching him die would have been especially horrific. Knowing that he was apparently willing to use her and then let her die, so much worse.

Callie must have noticed it too. She reached out and took Erica's hand—a gesture Jack could never have imagined seeing between these two particular women even twenty-four hours ago. And Erica received it readily, actually squeezed the hand in acknowledgment.

"So," said Callie, "do either of them work?"

"I couldn't get anything out of the satellite phone—I don't know if the battery's flat or I'm just doing it wrong—and the GPS will turn on, but it shows an error message. You try it."

They tried everything they could, fiddled with buttons, looked for settings to change, but nothing worked. The phone was dead, the GPS nonsensical. The hopes of rescue that had fluttered to life inside them bled out and died.

48

PETER LEANED HEAVILY ON HIS DESK, THE WEIGHT OF THE WORLD on his shoulders. His senior man was in the lockup, the man's wife was in despair, and the search team was in chaos.

The prisoner should have been transferred immediately to Invercargill, especially since it was one of his own staff. But the city had all hands chasing a series of armed robberies, and they'd asked Peter to hold Tom till morning. Sometimes they took liberties, knowing Peter's previous CIB credentials, and usually he didn't mind. But he could have done without their trust, this time.

He was dog tired and tonight he'd have to sleep on a camp stretcher in his office, because he couldn't leave the watch house unattended, in case the blasted building burnt down and killed the inmate. He couldn't ask Amber to do it. She'd done far more than her fair share of overtime this past week.

Across the desk, Ellen was wrapped in the same gray blanket they'd given her last time. At least she'd stopped weeping, at last.

Peter sighed and leaned back in his chair.

"So, do you mind telling me how you got the estimable Mr Dickens to give you that will?"

"Do you really want to know?"

He groaned. "By the sounds of it, no I don't. But I have to. It's evidence. What did you tell him?"

"I had quite a speech prepared, with various alternative endings depending on how things went. But in the end I didn't tell him anything. He was out at a meeting. Or perhaps on his yacht. It turns out that his assistant has both a daughter and a modicum of common sense."

Peter stared at her and said nothing as the implications jostled in his head.

"I'm sorry Peter, if this creates problems for you. But my instincts were that we absolutely had to see that document, and once I did see it, I knew it was imperative that you get Tom off the search, whether it hurt a court case or not. What might a desperate man do, so that his sick daughter can inherit a fortune he thinks will save her life? She doesn't get a penny unless the rest of them are dead. It seems likely that he has already sabotaged the search, and we can't risk him doing anything else. We simply don't know what he might have arranged with Bryan, and he's refusing to tell you, isn't he?"

He didn't answer that. "I hope the things Tom said in the search room today don't get disallowed in court because they were prompted by my possession of an illegally obtained document. Any other evidence against him is circumstantial."

"The document wasn't illegally obtained. I just asked for it without any deception or duress, and she gave it to me freely. And then I gave it to you. You couldn't get it that way and still be able to use it, but I'm not a policeman conducting an official investigation that has to be covered by warrants. Red tape doesn't bind me like it does you. I'm just a mother acting on my own initiative, and you knew nothing about it until it was done. I made sure of that."

He pondered that. She was probably right. But if the aggrieved lawyer decided to represent Tom, how much trouble would he have on his hands? "I wonder how long that lawyer's assistant will keep her job?"

"I got the feeling I don't need to worry too much about her. Once I told her what had been going on, I was more inclined to have sympathy for Mr Dickens. I suspect he'll be getting an earful tonight. And once the truth of all this is made public, he's not going to want to advertise the fact that he defended the rights of a dead murderer above those of a bunch of innocent people. When he knew what had happened, he must have realized that Tom was a danger."

The phone rang beside Peter and he stared at it, jaded. He answered it on the third ring, discovered it was the pathologist, and realized with a start that Ellen still didn't know about today's discovery. He toyed with the idea of asking her to leave the room, and then decided not to bother. She'd hear it on the news anyway, soon enough.

"The cold has interfered with normal processes, but I'd hazard a guess she died between two and four days ago," said Jonesy. "Suffocation was the cause of death, but she also showed signs of frostbite. If she had hypothermia before she died, it would have weakened her, made it harder to fight back."

"No fingerprints, or anything else useful?"

"The SOCOs found a lot of fingerprints. None in the right places. Most likely left when her friends were packaging her up. But I have got one thing to cheer you up. We found a fiber in her right nostril—the type of thing they make gloves out of."

"So the killer wore gloves. We'll have to hope we can identify which gloves, and who was wearing them at the time."

"That's right."

"Any confirmation on ID?"

"She matches the passport, and doesn't look like any of the others. We're as sure as we can be, without a relative to check."

As Peter put the phone back on its rest, he looked at Ellen. She was alert and watchful. His end of the conversation hadn't given her too many details, but it was enough for her to know someone was dead, and they hadn't died peacefully.

He spoke gently. "We found Sharon Healy today."

"Dead?" Her voice wasn't much more than a whisper.

"Suffocated."

Her eyes filled with tears. "She's got a little boy. Only about three or four years old."

"I know. I've got a fun phone call to make tonight." He sighed.

"Where was she?"

"On a mountain side, in the north western corner of the national park."

"North, not south." They both knew what that meant. Tom had been pushing them south. He probably knew the hikers were actually north.

"We're basing the search on that area now. Depends how far they've traveled since she died. But it's better information than we had before."

If they'd searched north to begin with as Amber had suggested, who knew if Sharon might still be alive?

49

THE WIND HAD PASSED THE POINT OF INSANITY ABOUT FIFTEEN minutes ago when they moved onto an even more exposed section of the mountain's collarbone. They had to get to its shoulder, a level tussocky area they could see above them. Jack silently prayed it would provide a passage into a valley that might lead towards the lake and people. The white-capped peak loomed far overhead on the right, a stream of snow flicking off its top like a flyaway fringe. Staying upright had become a pitched battle against the wind. There was no way to spend the night on this rocky slope, nowhere to pitch a tent, nowhere to light a cooking fire, and even if it didn't rain and they slept under the stars inside their orange plastic bags, there was no reasonable space in which to lay four humans.

The long, slow evening was drawing in. There was no other way. They had to keep going.

Jack was leading, Rachel behind him, her forearms linked through the straps on the rear of his backpack to conserve her energy. The team had devoted Kain's energy bars to Rachel and it was helping her, but they were being rationed—a sliver at a time. No one knew how long they would need them to last.

Callie was bringing up the rear, and leaning hard against Erica's rucksack from behind, but not for her own support. The smallest and lightest one there, Erica was most vulnerable to the force of the wind. Her feet had lifted from the ground on more than one occasion before an even more savage blast hurled her bodily against the rocks. Bruised and disorientated, she'd clung to the granite and pleaded for help.

Every step was grueling for Jack, crouching low and dragging the combined weight of his own body, his rucksack and most of Rachel's bodyweight and load. He concentrated on where to put each step, trying not to think how far he still had to go. Water began to slap him in the face. *Please, not rain again.* He looked up. No, it wasn't coming from the clouds, but off the pass. It took him a while to figure out what it could be. There must be a tarn—a small mountain lake—up there, invisible beyond the lip of the pass, its contents being scooped up by the wind and flung at them, a few buckets-full at a time. The spray became heavier, falling in sheets, and he fumbled to raise his jacket hood, but it was impossible to keep it on his head in that wind, so he gave up and continued bare-headed, wet-haired, step by arduous step. At least it warned him that a tarn lay in their path if they continued this trajectory, so he began to angle to the right, hoping to get beyond its reach, and in due course, pass to the side of it.

When they finally emerged onto the tussock-covered platform that they hoped marked the beginning of a pass, there was no relief. It must have been a hundred meters wide, but being comparatively flat and elevated, it subjected them to the full screaming wrath of the wind. They fell into a huddle on the ground, and clung to each other. Erica was sobbing aloud; that final stretch had intensified the terrors and agonies of a most brutal day.

Jack shouted above the rush of air. "You lot stay here, and I'll look for a campsite."

"How on earth are we going to be able to camp?" said Rachel. She waited for no answer, merely put her face on her arms, lying prone on the ground.

Erica still sobbed, and Jack glanced at Callie. She nodded, and he crawled off on all fours, staying low to the ground. He hadn't even discarded his rucksack for this reconnoiter, but instead kept it on for extra ballast, hoping it might help him not to get blown off the mountain altogether. When he returned he couldn't stop grinning. "You're not gonna believe this! It's perfect!"

***

TWO HOURS LATER, THEY WERE SITTING ROUND A SMALL-BUT-COM-forting campfire as the last light faded from the sky, their bellies full of warm ferns flavored with a slice of energy bar—Rachel had insisted they not keep them all for her. Only a light breeze twitched at the tent flaps. The windstorm still raged overhead, but they felt secure in a little oasis of calm. Jack had found a ridge on the far side of the pass, curving up high above the tussocks into a supremely effective natural windbreak. It was so high that they could even stand up without hitting the windstorm. Underneath them, the lumpy tussocks were like cushions compared to the surfaces they'd slept on recently. The simple pleasures of their alpine campsite felt like five-star comfort after the hellish day they'd endured.

The murmur of conversation among them eventually turned to the emergency equipment again, and Jack retrieved the GPS and phone from his pack, so everyone could have another go at getting them to work. Everyone tried, but there was no joy.

Callie said, "I guess the question is: were they broken in the fall, have the batteries gone flat because Kain's used them up, or were they never working in the first place?"

Jack shrugged, but Erica didn't share his uncertainty. "I'll bet you any money you like it was another of Bryan's horrible little tricks. To make Kain think he was the chosen survivor, going to win the prize, but then giving him equipment to hide from us that doesn't even work." She snorted: derision with an edge of despair. "At least the gun actually *worked*."

"What do you mean by the prize?" Callie said.

Jack answered, not Erica. "Money, I would think."

"What else would Bryan have that Kain might want?" Erica's tone was bitter now. "I mean, think about it. If you were a loony with lots of money, and you wanted to buy some help in making sure all of us died, which of the seven of us would you target?"

They all considered that for a moment. Faces, names, personalities. It was an uncomfortable thought. Kain had worn his poverty like a protest banner as a teenager, and had gloated in his comparative wealth during this reunion.

"Kain hated the fact that money gave Bryan power," Erica said. "And he hated it even more that it gave Bryan Liana. He'd have jumped at the chance to finally win. I don't know if he knew the details of how it was going to unfold. But I believe he was expecting us to die and him to live. Otherwise, why would he have all this gear? And why would he not tell us about it? He didn't even tell me!"

Rachel said, "You didn't tell us about the gun." Erica fell silent.

Jack said, "If Bryan told Erica to make sure no one else survived, he probably told Kain the same thing. He must have offered him pretty big money, to make that seem worthwhile."

Callie nodded. "I guess Kain was hoping nature might do most of the work for him. Or Bryan might have convinced him that it would."

"He'd probably be planning to find a way to outlast us," Jack said. "Use the GPS to make it out to civilization, then toss the equipment in a lake in time to be grateful to his rescuers. And sell his story to the tabloids as the miraculous sole survivor of a big tragic accident."

"Erica, if you didn't know how to tell us, something similar could have happened to Kain," Callie said. "He might have been supposed to get rid of the rest of us, but after Sharon died, he couldn't do it. He might have regretted whatever he'd agreed to do for Bryan, but it had all gone too far by then and he didn't know how to tell us. Got himself painted into a corner." She shrugged.

"Let's hope that's how it was," Jack said. "But they are very different secrets to be keeping. Erica hid a weapon of questionable value. Kain hid emergency equipment he must have thought could bring rescuers within twenty-four hours."

Callie had a sudden insight. "He couldn't test the phone or emergency beacon without drawing attention from the outside world, but he might have tested the GPS, when he was off by himself. And it worked, sort of, so he might have assumed he was doing something wrong with it."

Jack nodded slowly. "But after he heard Adam was shot, he could have tested the other two and found out they were completely dead. He barely reacted when I told him Adam was dead, but then when I said he'd been shot... well, shocked doesn't even begin to cover the expression on his face. That must have been the first hint that Bryan was double-crossing him. He went straight back into his tent when I left to go back to you guys. He was probably ferreting in his sleeping bag before I was even three meters away."

Callie said, "That might be why he reacted so strongly today when we asked if Bryan knew about his affair with Liana. It probably hadn't occurred to him that Bryan approached him for the opposite reasons to the ones he claimed."

"But did he kill Sharon?" Jack said.

"He was terrified the night Sharon died," Erica said. "When he and Adam couldn't get over that mountain the day before... that seemed to be when he first actually realized just how much danger we were in. Up until then, I think he'd been assuming he was big and strong and he'd get out of it okay. But that night he said, 'No one could survive out here on their own.' I told him that's why we were sticking together, but it didn't seem to comfort him. He was really rattled."

Callie looked thoughtful. "He might have thought Sharon was going to die anyway, and decided to give nature a helping hand to save the rest of us."

"Knowing we suspected him of killing Sharon gave him a jolt," Jack said. "If he did kill her, hearing there was a piece of evidence against him would have made him realize how much trouble he was in. Plus he must have started wondering whether whatever reward Bryan had promised him was going to be delivered. Or whether he'd get quite the opposite, like a pile of evidence delivered to the police, or even a direct attempt on his life waiting for him."

Callie nodded. "I wonder if that's why he ate the berries—to test Bryan's veracity. He must have felt the symptoms of the poisoning, realized what was happening to his body, and yet he just kept eating the damn things, one after another." She sighed.

Jack stared at her. "What you're suggesting is… well, it's virtually suicide."

"Can you imagine how Kain would feel about going to jail?" she said.

"He couldn't bear that." Erica shook her head emphatically. "He'd think of all his lawyer friends taunting him. And the shame for his family."

"He said he was set up." Callie instantly had three sets of eyes locked onto hers. "Just before he went onto the ledge, I tried to stop him, and he spoke to me. 'He set me up,' that's what he said. And that he couldn't believe what he'd done and he was sorry about the little boy." It struck her, suddenly and forcibly, what that meant, and she put her head in her hands. "Oh no. He did kill Sharon."

"And he wished he hadn't," said Rachel, her eyes full of tears. "Oh dear God, I can't stand this."

50

Saturday, Seven Days Lost

J ACK SLEPT DEEPLY DESPITE THE THOUGHTS OF KAIN THAT ROILED through his mind as he lay down. Since the previous sleepless night, he'd discovered there was no sniper on their tail, and, with the death of Kain, apparently no smotherer in their midst either. With the number of known mortal enemies reduced to two—the environment and Rachel's diabetes—the anxious hand clutching at his innards relaxed a little. Just enough to seem like freedom by comparison.

In the morning, the windstorm had died of exhaustion, and the sun was presiding in full optimism. The previous night's agonizing conversation round the campfire had receded. They had confronted the unthinkable, and survived. As he and Callie packed their tent, the mood was lighter than it had been for days.

"I have this feeling that we're within reach of the lake," Callie said. "I really hope it's true."

"Me too. And I hope this pass turns out to be manageable." *Please God, take us toward the lake today. We can't possibly turn around and go back into the valley of the shadow of death.* The image of the bodies of the two friends that lay below crept into his mind, but he flicked it away.

They'd formulated a plan for Callie and Erica to take turns monitoring Rachel. With the last of her glucose testing equipment used the night before, they had no scientific way to measure her blood sugar. So they would give her a sliver of energy bar each hour to supplement the ferns she nibbled constantly, and watch for the early warning signs of a hypo. Now that she was out of glucose tablets, with all the exercise they were doing low blood sugar was her biggest danger.

The women stood back and waited for Jack to lead off, a development that took him by surprise, and made him feel needed. Manly, even. He didn't know if they were doing it on purpose, and he didn't care.

The far side of the mountain did not turn out to be the sheer cliff he'd secretly feared. There were several false starts, as they found themselves up against obstacles, and then they were confronted by two possible paths—two different valleys. Jack felt drawn to one of them, but it wasn't something he could explain to the women. "I know this way looks harder," he said, "but I truly believe it's where we need to go." He waited for a discussion, but Rachel and Erica had become passive, and Callie said, "I trust you. Lead on!"

Half an hour's awkward scrambling through a boulder field led them to a steep but doable slope. A couple of sidles along ledges, but none with perilous drops. Some alpine vegetation, some rocky sections. Not too much cloying mud, thanks to last night's drying wind. Visibility was good, so they could see ahead, and modify their route when a barrier was approaching.

They zigged and zagged their way down, for an hour, and another hour, and then the slope moderated, so they could push ahead in a more direct manner. Through ferny tangles and past waterfalls that were beautiful rather than roaring monsters, now that the rain was gone. Across streams only ankle deep in this weather, steadying each other on moss-covered rocks.

A month ago, they'd each have thought today's hike an endurance test. After the experiences of the past three weeks, it seemed as civilized as a city footpath.

By common consent, instead of stopping, they snatched fern tips as they went past, snacking on the go. For an hour and another hour. And then another hour. They were making amazing time.

Around midday, they came upon a clearing along the side of the valley's river, a stony beach jutting out into the crystal flow. So they stopped and lit a fire, and cooked more ferns. Opposite, cliffs rose sheer from the river, and their mirrored image fell back into the water at the opposite angle. Jack saw the glimmer of fish, and wondered what he might or might not be able to do with Adam's knife and a stick.

With the twists and turns of the long valley, he could no longer even see the peak above last night's campsite. He could pretend the horrors they'd left behind there had never existed.

***

A MOUNTAIN PARROT LANDED ON A HIGH LEDGE, AND POKED around the large bundle that lay there. Orange plastic, very bright. He was curious, persistent, but ultimately unsatisfied. The big green canvas thing alongside it looked more promising. He tugged at the straps, pulled at flaps, looked for a zipper—they were fun! But there wasn't one on this so he kept pecking until he was through the canvas, and started pulling through the hole the treasures that lay within. Much to play with, but nothing to eat.

And then he spied, wedged under the canvas thing, another item, a plastic capsule. Small and light. Brightly colored. He pecked at it hesitantly, probed it with his tongue. He picked it up in the claws of one foot, but as he launched from the ledge into the sky, a strap dangling from the object snagged on a rock and jolted it from his grip.

His lost prize spiraled down and down into the valley below, fluttering fluoro yellow for one, two, three, four, five, six, seven, eight, nine seconds. It hit a boulder with such force that it instant- ly snapped the pin obstructing its activating mechanism, a pin so carefully inserted many weeks ago by a saboteur with dreadlocks.

And it skittered and banged and came to rest wedged among rocks, its radio signal winking into life, its strobe lights flashing and flashing and flashing at the big empty sky so far above.

**

IT WASN'T THAT SHE SAW WATER. THE TERRAIN HERE DIDN'T ALLOW for that. But what she did see was a widening of the sky to the east. For days, they'd seen nothing but mountains in every direction, lurking in groups, jostling for a better look at the Lost. Crowding around, obstructing their view, tripping them up at every opportunity. But now, pausing on the brow of a hill as she brought up the rear, Callie could see a gap ahead, narrow but definite. An absence of mountains.

It had to be the lake.

"Hey, you guys!" she called. The three ahead of her stopped concentrating on their feet and turned back to look at her. "It's more open down there."

They peered towards the east, and Erica clambered onto a rock for a better view. "It has to be the lake, surely?"

"I think so. I hope so. I hope this wilderness isn't going to throw us another curveball—a swamp or an impassable river, or one of those smaller lakes you need a boat for, like we had the very first day."

"The only way to find out is to go and see," Erica said.

"How long do we want to push on?" Jack said. "We've got maybe three more hours of daylight left, and we've been walking a long, long time today. We don't want to be making camp in the dark if we can help it."

Callie looked at Rachel for her opinion, and saw her massaging her temples with fingers that betrayed the telltale tremor.

"Rachel, sit down." She fished in her pocket for the energy bar, broke off a chunk and gave it to her friend. Everyone found a place to perch, and took a rest break. *Please God, whoever you are, don't let my best friend die,* thought Callie.

After a few minutes, Rachel seemed more settled. "I really want to keep moving," she said. "If we can possibly get to the lake today, I want to go for it."

"You'd better hang on to my pack all the time now," Jack said. "And we can carry you if we have to. I mean it. We have to make those carbs last as long as we can." He turned to Erica. "How are the knees?"

She shrugged. "Like pumpkins. I'm sure they'll feel brand new though, if we get to the lake. I say we go for it too, while ever there's light. And even afterwards. We've still got some battery power in our headlamps."

He looked at Callie, and raised one eyebrow in question.

She nodded. "Yep. Let's do it. Onwards and upwards. Or downwards, as the case may be."

"Onwards and downwards!"

He turned and plunged back into the rainforest, Rachel's weight dragging down on his pack. Erica followed, and Callie slotted into her place at the back.

51

"NO SURVIVORS?" BARKED PETER INTO THE RADIO. FURY
rippled along his arteries and he wondered if he might
actually have a stroke. When the call came through from Wellington
that a Personal Locator Beacon registered to Bryan Smithton had
been activated, hope had surged through the search room. Even
though his very next thought had been: *If they've got a PLB, why the
hell didn't they activate it a week ago?* It had taken only four hours
from the first appearance of the signal to the search team's arrival on
the spot. You just couldn't do it any faster than that. And whoever
had activated the thing hadn't stuck around to wait for the rescuers
they'd summoned. Just an orange body bag on a ledge. There were
precious few hours of daylight left, and so much wilderness to
search. He swore in technicolor, but kept it clean when he turned
on the radio again. "Do the retrieval, while the other crew starts to
search a radius. We'll get another fixed-wing over there. Keep me
posted."

"Ellen!"

Peter wheeled around in time to see Amber putting a chair under Ellen's backside to stop it sliding to the floor. He swore again,
and strode across the room—just a couple of steps for a man of his
height. "What's the matter, Ellen? Have you eaten today?" His voice
was harsh, a combination of frustration with the missing trampers
who'd shot through when they should have stayed put, and regret
that he'd ever allowed Ellen into the search room now that things
were hotting up and it was so hard to ask her to leave. Amber, in
the middle of getting Ellen to put her head between her knees, shot
him a reproachful look. It didn't work.

"This isn't a romance novel. If you're going to be swooning all over the place, you'd better wait back at the hotel. I need my staff to be doing their jobs. We're stretched to the limit." The next look from Amber had moved well beyond reproach to sheer poison.

But the rebuke seemed to have a reviving effect on Ellen, a bit like the smelling salts of old, and she sat up and gathered her wits, her spine long and straight. "So, is she dead?" Her voice was carefully controlled.

"I don't know."

"But I just heard you say there were no survivors."

"Oh." He lost a little momentum, suddenly on the back foot. Perhaps not so unreasonable for a woman to faint if she thought she'd just heard that her daughter was dead. "That's not what that meant. They haven't found six bodies in a row." He didn't mention that they had found what appeared to be one body—it wasn't helpful, especially when he didn't even know if it was male or female yet. "But whoever activated the beacon didn't stick around. That's what I meant by no survivors. Whatever survivors there may be, they have not stayed with the beacon."

There was a pause. "So is it possible that she is still alive?"

"With what I know at present, it's possible. I can't guarantee it though."

"Possible is enough for me right now." She paused again. "So you're probably pretty cranky with them for not staying with the beacon." There was just the slightest challenge in her eyes. Gotcha, it said, or something similar. You're angry with them, and you took it out on me.

He conceded to the challenge with the merest twitch of the corners of his mouth. "That would be a reasonable assumption."

She stood, a fluid and elegant movement, and reached for her shoulder bag slung over the back of a chair. "If I'm at the hotel, is there any way for me to know how things are progressing? Could I phone here, or would that be too disruptive?" She was all business now, professional, respectful. Leaving the awkward moment behind them, ignoring it, not rubbing his nose in it. A seriously classy woman, and way out of his league, by anyone's measure.

"We'll contact you the moment we have news of Rachel."

"Thank you." She turned and left quietly, her posture dignified but not stiff.

Amber shot him another glance, this one loaded with razor blades, and returned to her post.

Peter watched the assistant's prickly back for about a second, and then followed Ellen down the corridor and out onto the street.

"Ellen!" She turned and waited politely for him to reach her. She didn't remove her sunglasses.

"Listen, Ellen, I'm sorry that I was rude to you just now. You're right that I was reacting to other stresses when I spoke to you in that manner. I apologize." He didn't believe in beating about the bush when it came to apologies.

"Thank you Peter. I did feel insulted by your attitude"—she didn't pull punches either—"but I'm not going to take it to heart in such a circumstance. It also gave me some clarity about how things have changed in the past couple of hours. I don't belong in there this evening. My presence there is no longer helpful, even to me. Things are extremely intense now, and you all need to be able to speak quickly and without restraint."

"Thank you for understanding that."

She did take her sunglasses off then, and looked intently into his eyes. "Peter, I have a natural desire for reassurance and hope—any mother would. But anyone can do that for me—someone down the coffee shop, for instance." She waved her hand down the street in that general direction, but kept looking at him. "What I need above all things from you right now is for you to do your job. I have enormous confidence in your ability to do so. It is my daughter's very best chance for survival." She smiled slightly, and nodded once. "Go with God."

52

IN THE FADING LIGHT, JACK COULDN'T BE SURE, BUT IT LOOKED like a roof. A man-made structure. Was he just hoping for a roof? Growing delirious with the stress of it all?

The last break had stretched from five minutes into twenty-five, when he saw more fish in the river, quite a group of them clustered in a shallow stretch. The spear fashioned from Adam's hunting knife, duct-taped to the end of a sturdy stick, had proven effective not just once but three times. Dinner was now dangling from the back of Erica's pack, swaying silver in the evening light. He felt like a proud caveman.

When Rachel started to show warning signs of another hypo an hour later, he worried that the delay for the fish had been a huge mistake. It had cost them half an energy bar to bring it under control.

He was still fretting about it now, as he labored over a slimy boulder, hanging moss slapping at his face. Rachel was strapped by the shoulders to the harness of his rucksack, Callie and Erica supporting one of her legs each. She had objected to being carried, but they had insisted. They had to stop her burning energy so fast.

Callie was somehow also managing the weight of Rachel's rucksack clipped to her front, and he could hear the ragged breathing of the others even over the pounding and roaring in his own head.

But that was surely a hut that he could see ahead, through the trees.

53

TWO BODIES, BOTH MALE. THAT LEFT A MAN AND THREE WOMEN still unaccounted for—out there somewhere. But the light was too far gone and the team were on their way back in. There'd be no more searching tonight.

Peter turned and picked up the phone. No answer from the pathologist. He glanced at his watch. No wonder. It was well past business hours. He drew a finger down the list of numbers taped to the wall, and dialed Jonesy's cell phone. It rang eight times, but he finally answered.

"Sorry to call so late. I've got a couple of incoming for you."

"A couple?"

"Two males. One appears to have a gunshot wound to the head."

As expected, he heard an appreciative whistle in his earpiece. "A gunshot wound! What do you make of that?"

"No idea. It's certainly a game-changer. But then, I didn't really know what game we were playing before."

"Definitely murder though now. You can't argue with a bullet."

Peter paused, uncertain how much he could ask of the man on the other end of the line. It was irregular, and he couldn't have explained why it seemed so urgent. Just an instinct that he needed to be fully informed before he confronted the survivors, which could be as soon as tomorrow. "Jonesy, I don't know if you could do them tonight?"

"What, and miss this? Can't you hear that angelic singing in the background? I'm at the school musical—my oldest girl's in the chorus."

"Kids are important, trust me. You need to stay at that."

He snorted dismissively. "By the time your two bundles of joy get down here, it'll be over. I'll congratulate the star, give the necessary hugs and kisses, and head on down to the crypt."

"Thanks mate. I really appreciate it. Call me any time you have anything to report."

"Never fear, I'll call you every hour till dawn."

Peter laughed. "Can't wait. Talk to you then."

***

PETER HEARD THE FRONT DOOR OF THE POLICE STATION SWINGING open, and heavy footsteps scuffing their way down the corridor.

He turned in time to see Hemi walk in, and gave him the best smile he could muster. "Big day huh?"

"You betcha," Hemi said, grinning. He rummaged in a plastic bag he was carrying, and tossed a paper-wrapped burger down on the desk, where its meaty aromas exploded into Peter's nostrils, then rummaged again and drew out a bag of greasy hot chips, which he dumped on the desk between them. Lastly, he extracted a burger for himself. He pulled a chair out, its back towards him, and straddled it, then began to eat the burger without ceremony, one big bite after another, grabbing chips to add to the mix as a kind of chunky condiment.

Peter followed his excellent lead. "Mate, I'm going to get the mayor to commission a statue of you," he said between bites. "You're seriously a lifesaver."

"Yeah mate. That's what they say." He grinned again. "We managed to get the PLB," he added around a mouthful of bread roll, a smudge of tomato sauce at the corner of his mouth. "They weren't gonna bother, but I said we had to give it a try. I'm gonna have a look at it tonight, see if it was faulty or anything. Must have been some reason they didn't activate it."

"Anything obvious?"

"Nah. But I reckon a kea dropped it. They'd been at the guy's rucksack—big hole in it, and stuff spread out everywhere."

"So simple a kea can activate it." *But not a group of humans with opposable thumbs.*

"A kea and a seven hundred meter drop."

Peter's eyebrows went up. "That big?"

"Yep. If it was jammed, that might have released it. I'll give it a check. Not sure if I'll find anything, but it's worth a try."

The meal concluded, Hemi stood, held his fist to his breastbone, burped deep and resonant, batted his eyelashes, pursed his lips and in a sweet voice said, "Excuse me." He moved to the large-scale topographical map on the wall, and Peter followed, still chewing his own burger.

"We found the first body here, on a ledge," he said, pointing. Peter handed him a red-headed pin, and he slid it into the map. "And the second one was here"—another pin—"just above a landslide. That's the one with the hole in his head. Much bigger landslide bit further downstream, about here. Full-on tree avalanche, goes all the way to the ceiling. Look's like God's waterslide." He looked at Peter. "Not easy to get past that one. You'd have to cross the river, but even if you did, not a friendly slope the other side."

"Where do you reckon they're headed?"

"Well, we know they were up towards Poison Bay, because of where we found the girl's body, right?" He pointed at the other red pin to the north. Peter nodded. "I reckon they were trying to head east—which is what I'd do too. They have to know Lake Te Anau is back thataway, even if they've got no maps. But they had to keep finding walkable passes. They're not climbers. So I reckon they've come up here along the Burnley, and maybe had trouble with those landslides. Shoulda happened day before yesterday, I'd say, when they had the big rain event over that side."

"Makes sense."

"Most important thing is, the guy on the ledge, now I'm no Gravedigger"—his nickname for the pathologist—"but it looks to me like he fell from a much narrower ledge above it. I think they were heading up Mount Paice. I managed to track them into a boulder field below Gunpowder Pass. Probably could have found more signs up in the tussocks, but we had to keep moving before we lost the light."

"Where would they go from there?"

"Two alternatives. You can get into the Rossmay valley or the Altham over that pass. I hope they took the Altham—it looks harder at first but it leads all the way to the lake, and there's even a conservation hut at the end of it. The Rossmay just leads further back into the wilderness. It's a horrible valley for newbies."

"Could they do the length of the Altham in a day?"

"If they were motivated, and they started early, I reckon they could. Depends if they're injured, and how sick that girl is with the diabetes. There was no rain out there today, so it would have been a pretty sweet run if that's where they are."

Peter stared at the map. "I'm thinking we'll take the cavalry to Altham Hut, see what we find."

"Sounds like a good place to start."

But can I bet my career on it? thought Peter, as he continued to stare at the map. Altham Hut. A lovely big pebbly apron jutting out into the lake in front of it, well and truly wide enough for a helicopter, or even two. A beautiful spot for a night rescue if you had a chopper with the right equipment. It was time for some fast and confident talking. He picked up the phone to Invercargill.

***

BEYOND THE MAP, THROUGH ONE THICKNESS OF WALL, LAY THE lockup. Tom had his ear pressed hard against the smooth surface. He'd been listening ever since he heard Hemi scuff-thumping down the corridor. He continued to listen, and when Peter eventually put down the phone, he moved back to the narrow bunk and sat, silent, thinking.

54

IT WAS AMAZING HOW GOOD A SURVIVAL MEAL OF FISH AND FERNS could taste, if you ate them in a warm, dry hut while a gentle rain pattered onto the corrugated iron roof and fizzled in the undergrowth outside. Fish and ferns that had been cooked over a fire that crackled and hissed inside a cast iron potbelly stove, while flickering light seeped out the stove vents into the hut.

There was even a pile of dusty firewood on the little veranda, provided by some gracious previous user months ago, or perhaps a conservation worker. It looked like it should be enough to keep the fire burning all night. They had to keep that column of smoke streaming up into the sky. Their "bat signal" as it were. Here we are, rescue us.

Jack had declared that they must collect more wood in the morning, to keep the fire alight. But he could tell that his message was falling on mostly-deaf ears. The urgency seemed to have gone out of everything, now that they had the lake and shelter. Nothing to do now but wait for rescue. Nowhere to walk tomorrow.

Rachel was tucked up in her sleeping bag on one of the hard wooden bunks. Callie checked on her regularly, and had pledged to continue doing so every half hour all night. There was no way to predict what the night would bring.

They lingered around the fire, strangely reluctant to sleep. There were a couple of chairs in the hut, but they didn't seem to know how to sit on them after weeks in the wild, so they lounged around the floorboards on their sleeping bags instead.

"We've really won lotto with this place," Callie murmured. "So very glad we followed your hunch and came down this valley today."

Jack smiled. "Not sure I'd call it lotto, but I'm glad too."

Erica said, "Probably better not to talk to me about lotto. We'll be back in the land of scratch-its and slot machines any day now."

"Oops, sorry," said Callie. "How did you get sucked in to that stuff in the first place? I don't remember you being into it at school."

Erica sighed and stared at her feet. "It was after Kain dumped me, back at uni."

Callie inhaled sharply. "You used to go out with Kain before? I never knew that."

Erica raised her eyes to Callie's face in the dim light. "Yes, for more than a year."

Callie shook her head, and looked away. "I'm such a bitch." Her tone was full of regret. "I had no idea you had history with him. I thought you were just..."

"You thought I was a slut." There was no judgment in the statement. They all seemed to be beyond recriminations—except perhaps against themselves.

"Well, no, it wasn't that. It was..." She sighed. "Yes, I guess that is what I thought. Did you love him?"

Erica merely nodded.

"I'm so sorry." Callie's eyes looked moist.

"I pretty much had the bridesmaids' dresses picked out." There was self-hatred in Erica's tone, and her gaze slid away from Callie's face to the shapes of light flickering on the floor. "I thought he loved me too, but then it turned out a simple nurse wasn't really prestigious enough for the future he was designing for himself. He dumped me for another law student. No idea what happened to her. When I saw him again here, I thought maybe he'd realized his mistake, and wanted me back. So stupid of me. I was just convenient. Liana is probably the only woman he ever really loved, and she fancied him too, but she loved Bryan's money more." She crossed her arms and hunched her body close to her knees. "Being in that tent with Kain was like a prison by the end."

There was a pause before Callie spoke again. "You must feel horrible now he's dead."

Erica nodded, fighting back tears. "How dumb is that?" Her voice broke on the words.

"It's not dumb at all. Your grief is based on your feelings, not his." Her voice took on a bitter edge. "And I'm not going to judge you for falling for a man who was totally absorbed by himself. I'm just trying to recover from the same thing myself."

"Are you?"

"Yeah. I work with him too, so it's even worse. I have to see William every day, and everyone else has to see me seeing him."

"You went out with William Green?" interjected Jack. He'd been keeping out of the girlie chat, but surprise brought him into it suddenly.

Callie looked at Jack, and nodded. "Yes. The King of the Newsroom bestowed his favors upon me, if only for a short time." She glanced back at Erica. "I wasn't quite glamorous enough for him in the end. So he moved on to a sassy little blonde. I was the last one to know about it, of course." She snorted. "She was a bit like you, actually, Erica."

"No wonder you hated me then. Why do we do it to ourselves? Break our hearts over these men who are all style and no substance, and ignore the really nice blokes who might actually make us happy."

Jack was interested to hear the answer to this one, but none was offered. Callie just sighed and nodded. After a longish pause, he gave up waiting, and asked the question that had been left hanging earlier. "So, the breakup started you gambling?"

Erica hauled her mind back from wherever it had gone. "I went out and got drunk that night. I played the poker machines, and I won big. Three thousand dollars. It made me feel so much better. Powerful. Free. So I went out and did it again." She shrugged. "Before long, I was dropping into pubs for a quick play of the pokies, or stopping by the casino on the way home from a shift at the hospital. Always a secret from my family and friends. It just grew and grew. A bit at a time. It took over my life."

"I'm so sorry." Jack's tone was compassionate.

"You don't gamble at all, do you Jack?" Callie said. "Not even the Melbourne Cup sweep, if I remember rightly."

He shrugged. "It was the way I was brought up. No raffles or anything. I guess it was the Protestant work ethic thing—that it's wrong to want something for nothing."

"But isn't that actually the core of your belief, getting something for nothing?" Callie's tone had become suddenly intense, but it didn't seem disrespectful. "Don't you get forgiveness without having to earn it, according to your religion?"

Jack pondered the question. It was quite insightful, actually. "In a way I suppose you're right. Forgiveness is a free gift that I don't deserve. It costs me nothing." His tone became earnest. "But it cost Jesus everything—even the love of God for a short time. And you don't take lightly the sacrifice of someone you love."

"It really is real to you, isn't it?" Callie seemed mystified, and yet intrigued.

"It's the anchor of my whole existence," he replied simply.

"Can you believe in forgiveness for me?" Erica said, her voice small.

"Yes. I can."

A fat tear slid down Erica's cheek. "I'm not sure that *I* can believe it."

"What about Kain?" Callie said to Jack. "Can you believe in

forgiveness for Kain?" There was a challenge in her eyes.

Jack sighed. "Yes, even for Kain. I've been thinking about it on and off all day in fact. If only I'd reached out to him, shown him kindness instead of judging him and trying to catch him out, maybe he'd still be alive. But the fact is, I've always hated him simply because *you* loved him." He couldn't believe he'd said that out loud, and he looked at it hanging in the air between them.

Callie turned her head away.

Jack had more that he needed to say. "If I'd helped him to hope that he could go home, do his time for Sharon's death, and then start again... maybe the despair wouldn't have overcome him."

"You might need to forgive yourself for that," Erica said.

"Yeah. But that's the hardest one of all to do."

55

PETER FOUGHT TO KEEP THE FRUSTRATION OUT OF HIS VOICE. "Every hour matters for the diabetic. We could retrieve her as much as six hours sooner if you send it tonight."

"You can't be sure she's there, and we can't risk a gunman taking potshots in the dark. But we'll have it there at 5.00 a.m."

Peter resisted the urge to slam the phone down. It made sense. They couldn't risk several lives on the off-chance of saving one. Even if that one belonged to someone who'd become important to him.

***

HE FOUND ELLEN SITTING IN THE HOTEL LOUNGE LISTENING TO the pianist, a half empty glass mug on the coffee table in front of her. Hot chocolate, at an educated guess. Her posture in the enfolding armchair was supple and relaxed. But from only one week's acquaintance he was certain there was an iron discipline forcing her to release the tension in the muscle fibers, distract the brain synapses from the endless circuit of worry worry worry.

When he entered her peripheral vision he saw her detect him instantly, sitting forward in the chair, alert and focused, shedding the air of relaxation like an unwanted overcoat. "Peter."

"Ellen." He nodded in greeting, and took the chair at right angles to hers. He didn't toy with her by using euphemisms or empty encouragement, but he wanted to start on a positive note. "We may have a result in the morning. I'd like you to be ready."

"Of course." She nodded, and waited.

"Two more bodies were found today, both male. We believe the relative location of those bodies has shown us the direction the group was heading. If they've taken the better option, they may have reached the lake this evening, at a point where there is a back-country hut they could have taken shelter in."

She considered this a moment. "How certain can you be of their direction?"

"Not certain. But we've narrowed it down to two valleys of the hundreds out there, which is very positive. We'll start at that hut first thing in the morning, and we've been able to secure a medivac helicopter, with a specialist doctor and paramedic on board, due to arrive here about five in the morning."

Ellen's eyebrows went up. "So you really do think she's alive?"

"At this stage, I have nothing to indicate otherwise."

"It's just that your body language is telling me some negative things. I was wondering what you're hiding from me." It wasn't stated as a verbal challenge; she was just puzzled.

His face split in a grin. "Tell me, if I put a paper bag over your head so you couldn't see me, would it help you to believe what I say?"

She laughed, a spontaneous lightening of her heavy mood, a fleeting relief. "It might work. Or you could put it over your own head."

"Probably the better solution." He became serious again. "One of the men we found today had been shot, and I don't know what that means."

"Shot?" She was shocked, and it showed.

"Yes, it was a shock for us too. How do they come to have a gun, and how do we interpret it in light of the fact that they had a locator beacon and didn't switch it on? It's different to the smothering of Sharon Healy—that could have been simply an opportunistic killing, based on her 'drag' on the team if she wasn't well. This looks more deliberate. Planned. I don't know if they're being marched at gunpoint. Or if they've turned into an outlaw gang. I don't know if they're trying to be found, or hiding out from us. Or even lying in wait for us. It's a puzzle, whatever way you look at it."

"Do you know if any of them owned a gun?"

"Bryan owned both a rifle and a small handgun. We couldn't find either one at his house." He shouldn't be telling this woman everything about his investigation, but with Tom off the team he needed the sounding board, and there was no point shutting the stable door at this late stage. That particular horse had bolted days ago, and probably joined the circus by now.

"So it's probably Bryan's gun. But who'd be using it, now that he's dead? Who would he have given it to?" Light dawned. "Kain Vindico, I suppose."

"Perhaps. We can't be sure. Since Bryan had Tom as backup out here, he may well have had another plant in the group itself. And Vindico is now dead, unfortunately."

"Oh! How awful." She stared at him. "But not the one who was shot?"

"No. Probably a fall. Perhaps Vindico shot the other man, and then the others pushed him off a cliff. Who knows? I'm hoping for post mortem results by morning."

A waiter came by at that moment, asking Peter if he'd like coffee. He looked at Peter's police uniform with the open curiosity of a seasonal worker who doesn't need to keep his job for long. In this little town, you had to be dead or senile not to know about the big search that was underway.

Peter was going to refuse, but Ellen gave him what could be termed "an old-fashioned look". "You might as well," she said. "Have you eaten tonight, by the way?"

"As a matter of fact, I have." He felt a need to be scrupulously honest, and added, "Thanks only to Hemi, of course." And to the waiter, "Can you do a caramel latte?" He kept his face deadpan.

As the waiter withdrew with the order, Ellen spoke, a smile in her voice. "I wonder if you'll regret that, once you taste it."

"The worst thing would be if I found out I liked it, and had to order it all the time."

She smiled and got back on topic. "So, what if there's an ambush waiting for you at that hut?"

"That's one of the questions on my mind, and one that you'll need to make a decision about too. The invitation is there for you to be on my chopper in the morning, but you have to know the risks. The medical crew will follow us up there. They'll keep their distance until we've established it's safe to land. I'd have a difficult time wangling a seat for a member of the public on the medical chopper, but there's a spare chair in mine. Once you're up there, it's a different matter to persuade them to give you a seat on the chopper taking your daughter to Invercargill. You're just a member of the public right now, but once Rachel is their patient, you become a relative."

She pondered a moment, and he could sense her desire to resist a hasty decision. "I'd like to go. My feeling is that we won't get shot at, and I'd like to be there for Rachel, either way."

"You need to be ready for the fact they may not even be there. We could be wrong about the whole thing. We could be wrong about lots of things." He didn't need to say: your daughter could be dead after all.

"I understand that. You are making no guarantees. I appreciate you sticking your neck out for me and my daughter in this situation, and I won't be taking that privilege lightly, no matter how it all works out in the end."

***

DESPITE THE DEPTHS OF SLEEP, HE WAS AWAKE BEFORE THE SECOND ring, grabbing for the phone in the dark. It must be the post mortem results. "Peter Hubble."

"It's Hemi." Peter's brain backpedaled, rearranged itself for different news. "There was a tiny metal pin in that beacon, mate. I reckon someone put it in there deliberately to stop it activating. It would have stopped the switch sliding. It's sheared off—probably in the fall."

"Wouldn't they have seen it?"

"Nah. Especially not if they hadn't seen a PLB before. They wouldn't know what it was meant to look like, would they? And it was a strong little pin. You'd need to belt it with a hammer to try to break it. It's not the sort of thing you could do with bare hands, especially if you didn't know what was wrong."

He thought a moment. "Would Bryan Smithton have been able to figure out how to do this?"

"Too right, mate. Real geek he was, always getting into the works of things."

So that accounted for the beacon. Sabotaged by the owner. But it still didn't explain the gunshot wound.

***

When the phone rang the next time, it was harder for Peter to fight his way up from unconsciousness. Disorientated, he fumbled around for the phone in the dark and stabbed at the illuminated answer button, but the beeping continued. He rose and headed towards the doorway, tripped heavily on his discarded shoes, swore liberally, stumbled into the wall and finally found the light switch.

It was his wake-up alarm that was beeping. And the call was live. So the caller had heard the whole charade. He only hoped it wasn't Invercargill.

"Peter Hubble."

"Nice to hear New Zealand's finest are on top of their game as usual." It was Jonesy the pathologist, appallingly chipper for four o'clock in the morning. "I hate to interrupt your beauty sleep. I know you need it more than most."

"Very funny. How many energy drinks have you had tonight?"

"I never have more than four in one night," he said, his tone prim.

"So, what did you find?"

"Contestant Number One, Adam Andersson. Died of a gunshot wound to the head around forty-eight to sixty hours ago. Small caliber. A lot of general bruising around the time of death, and some significant compression bruising to the right side of the body caused after death."

"We found his body next to a landslide."

"A lot of the injuries are not inconsistent with being crushed in a landslide."

"Could any of the bruising be punches, or being belted over the head with a log, that sort of thing?"

"Hard to be sure, they'd look much the same."

"Can you tell how close in time the gunshot and crush injuries were?"

"Very close, some of it. If I were a betting man, I'd say almost simultaneous. The compression bruising took place over several hours."

"Who shoots a man who's about to get cleaned up by a landslide?"

"Someone who hasn't seen the landslide coming."

Peter paused and thought about that. "Or possibly even someone who had a gun in their hand when they got hit by the same landslide. It could have been a threat that turned into an execution. Okay. And the other one?"

"Contestant Number Two, Kain Vindico. Died about

twenty-four to thirty-six hours ago."

"So he's more recent." That meant Hemi's interpretation of the trampers' trajectory was correct. It increased the likelihood they'd entered the Altham valley, and Peter's plan would work.

"Fatal injuries consistent with a fall from height. Broken spine, broken neck, broken head—his skull was pretty much flattened on the back. Died almost instantly. The most likely explanation for the injuries I'm seeing is that he fell backwards while wearing a rucksack, and landed arched across the rucksack."

It was an uncomfortable mental picture, and Peter wriggled his shoulders. "No way to tell if he was pushed, I guess?"

"Nothing obvious like finger marks on the shoulders. But that doesn't prove anything."

"No, of course."

"He also had a belly full of tutu berries."

"What?!" Peter swore. Another complication. "I hope they haven't all been eating them. Was it enough to kill him, if he hadn't fallen?"

"I'd say so. There was a fair bit of the toxin in his bloodstream as well, so he'd been eating them for a while, an hour or more. He'd have been unsteady on his feet if not actually convulsing yet."

"Could be why he fell."

"Indeed. And I've got more. I checked the gloves in his pack, and they're an exact match for that fiber we took from Sharon Healy's nostril."

"Possible someone else has the same brand, I guess?"

"Yes. Andersson's gloves weren't a match. Different color. But it doesn't prove anything unless we test all the gloves."

"We'll sort that out when we find them."

"Righto. Hard to prove who was wearing them the day the girl died, of course."

"Can't you test for DNA in the sweat or something?"

"You watch too much television."

"Ha. Did you happen to check if he's fired a gun recently."

"I did. No residue on his hands, or on the gloves."

"Okay."

"There's something else you'll want to know about Vindico."

"Yes?"

"You know how I told you Smithton didn't have the right blood type to be the father of the suicide girl's baby? Well, Vindico did."

56

Sunday, Eight Days Lost

AMBER WAS FLUSTERED AS SHE RAN UP THE RAMP INTO THE police station. Ten minutes late, all because she couldn't get her stupid car to start. And Peter couldn't leave for the airstrip till she relieved him. The whole rescue mission on hold.

"I'm sorry…" she began, but he walked straight past her, urgent, focused.

"Tell me about it later," he said as the door swung shut behind him. His voice was brisk, but not angry. He would assume there was a good reason she'd let him down on this most important of days, and somehow that just made it worse.

She watched his taillights disappear into the pre-dawn darkness, feeling close to tears, and then pulled herself together and went to check on the prisoner.

"Amber, I've got to call Nyree. There's something wrong with Lily. I can just feel it. She was so sick yesterday. Please, you've got to let me call Nyree."

It was fair enough. Prisoners were allowed to make phone calls. She'd have offered him her cell phone, but the battery was flat. Another stupidity. She'd let him use the office phone. It was only Tom after all.

It happened so quickly she was going to have trouble describing it later. He was so much bigger than her, she didn't stand a chance. But the result was that within two minutes she heard Tom driving off in her car, running traitorously smooth now, while she rattled uselessly at the door of the cell. From the inside.

All she had for company was a dead mobile phone and the

memory of Tom's words: "I'm sorry Amber. I have to do this."

Maybe Tom really was just planning on going home to check on his family. Maybe, but she doubted it. There were ways to make contact with them without forcing an escape and putting himself in even more trouble with the law. No, he must be planning something else. She had to warn Peter. She ran to the ventilation strip in the window and began shouting for the neighbors, with every particle of air in her lungs.

***

PETER WAS IN THE AIR, TEN MINUTES DOWN THE LAKE. THE MEDI-vac helicopter had been a few minutes late arriving at the airstrip, and then there had been the general kerfuffle of discussion and organization. He had briefed them on the risk of a possible gunman at the hut, and they'd formulated a plan for how to approach the situation. The medivac crew would hang back until Peter secured the site—whatever that might take—and cleared them to land.

The medivac crew seemed to him almost reluctant, but it was probably just that they'd been briefed to a different level of urgency than the one Peter was feeling. It irritated him beyond all reason, but he kept it to himself. After all, he could hardly insist, when he in fact had no certain knowledge of the location of the trampers or the condition of the diabetic woman. At least Invercargill had arranged the specialist as agreed, and he had to be satisfied with that concession. It could make all the difference to whether Rachel Carpenter lived or died.

Peter sat alongside Hawk in the small lead helicopter, his eyes straining ahead as light started to creep across the vast length of the lake, creating soft curves and woolly outlines of trees on the foothills of the mountains that lurked to their left. The overnight rain had washed the sky clean, and some fading stars still hung in the indigo now bleaching above. Sunrise wasn't far away. He concentrated on relaxing his stomach, looking far ahead and not down, imagining he was moving in a boat, not suspended in a Perspex bubble a long drop above a deep lake, with only a spinning rotor between him and a fire-and-water grave. Helicopter policing was all kinds of hell for a man who hated to fly, but no one was teasing him about it this morning.

They had a stretcher pod mounted on the skids, in case there were more casualties than the two the medical chopper could carry. His service pistol, unearthed from its hiding place in the safe in his patrol car where it usually rested year-round, was holstered on his hip. A rifle was propped on the floor at his feet. So much armory in his quiet little town was jarring—ugly and yet necessary on this day of uncertainty. More lives could depend upon their superior firepower than simply those of the trampers. His binoculars, still capped, were cradled loosely in his hand. No point in using them yet.

Behind him sat Ellen, less than a meter away and yet it could have been a thousand miles. The distance created between them by his outburst yesterday had healed slightly when he sat with her at the hotel, but she seemed to have withdrawn from him again, and he didn't know why. He might never get a chance to find out. The few possessions she'd brought with her to New Zealand were in the duffel bag crammed under her seat. If Rachel was indeed at Altham Hut, and an extra seat could be wangled from the medivac team, Ellen could well be leaving his life forever within the hour.

Next to Ellen was Hemi, who had brought his portable paramedic kit as instructed. There could be other injuries or illness among the survivors, and having Hemi on hand would allow the medivac team to focus all their immediate attention on Rachel. Plus, Hemi was an all-round useful person to have aboard in any kind of crisis. He must be fatigued by the rigors of yesterday's search and body retrieval, not to mention his midnight dissection of the faulty PLB while Peter slumbered on the camp stretcher in his office, but he didn't show it.

The radio squawked into life, startling the team in the chopper.

"Peter, it's Amber, Tom has escaped. Repeat, Tom has escaped."

Peter swore, and then activated the transmission button. "How long ago did this happen?"

"About twenty minutes. He asked for a phone call and then overpowered me and locked me in. I've just managed to get the neighbors to let me out."

"Do you know where he went?"

"He took my car. I've called Nyree and he's not there."

"Do we believe her?"

"I believe her. She sounded frantic when I told her what he'd done."

"Who's Tom, and what does this mean for us?" It was the medivac pilot. He'd heard the transmission too.

Peter had to think fast. Te Anau's finest must look like the Keystone Cops to the metropolitan crew thanks to what they'd just heard, but that was the least of his worries. He also had to be careful with his words, because he couldn't be sure who else was monitoring this frequency. Every redneck in the district seemed to have a radio scanner.

"He's a person of interest in relation to these missing trampers. We'll discuss options and get back to you, pronto. Keep following for now." He swung round to talk to Hemi, and glanced at Ellen. She'd heard it all through her headset, and her eyes were like saucers. No time to deal with that now. He looked at Hemi and spoke to him through the closed circuit that communicated only within the chopper, the only way to be heard above the rotors. "What do we think?"

"Why is he doing this? He can't get Bryan's money now anyway, can he?"

"It was left to Lily, not Tom, and the terms of the trust looked pretty solid to me. Any challenge would be a fight for the lawyers." His eyes slid to Ellen's terrified face for half a second, and then back to Hemi. "And what matters right now is what Tom believes, which is probably whatever Bryan told him." *If only I'd thought he might do this*, he added silently, *this could have been prevented.*

Hemi began to swear, decided to stifle it in Ellen's hearing, and then got back to the task. "He's got that crazy hunting mate with the little toy chopper, lives halfway up the lake. Thinks the US government is running all our lives and there are aliens inside ATMs, that sorta thing. If I was Tom and I wanted to get to Altham Hut in a hurry, that's where I'd go."

"You think his mate would help him launch a direct attack on the trampers? Paranoia isn't the same as murder." This conversation must be excruciating for Ellen to listen to, but it must be had.

Hemi shrugged, and narrowed his eyes in thought. "He might, if he didn't know exactly what Tom was planning. He might put him on the ground there and Tom could approach on foot. Or he might even let him shoot from the air if he believed Tom's hokum about how evil they are."

"Why not get to us first? That gives him all the time in the world to get to the trampers."

"Harder to persuade a friend to let you shoot down a rescue chopper and a medivac, even if the friend is a sandwich or two short of a picnic."

Peter nodded and turned to the front again, uncapped the binoculars, and began searching the eastern shore of the lake for any sign of movement, while he thought a little more. At his side, Hawk increased speed without having to be asked. It increased the tilt at which the chopper flew, so that most of the bubble of the cockpit was facing down into the lake, right below his feet, had

Peter cared to look there. But he steadfastly kept his eyes up. The pilot kept a firm grip on his controls, his posture relaxed. He'd flown in Vietnam, and Peter was thankful for that. Some of his superiors questioned whether Hawk was too old, but Peter knew the eyes were as sharp and the reflexes as fast as they'd been forty years ago. And the combat experience was priceless. One loon in a play-helicopter was nothing to this man.

Peter continued searching while he activated the radio transmitter again. "Medivac, keep following us at a safe distance. Please ask your passengers to keep a watch to both sides and behind, particularly at the edges of the lake. We believe we are looking for a small two-seater helicopter, but also beware of any boating traffic approaching fast. The wake will be visible, even in this light. If you see anything at all, tell me immediately."

"What are you saying? Is this guy a threat to us? We didn't sign up for that!" The medivac pilot's answer was harsh and rapid.

"We believe it is unlikely there will be any threat to you. Please remain calm and keep your eyes open. And keep pace with us for the time being, but remain at a safe distance in case we change direction suddenly." This could get messy, fast. *Damn, why did I bring Ellen?*

The radio crackled to life again. "Peter, it's Amber. I've just had a call from a farmer driving into town, reporting a dangerous driver. My car. Hard to pin him down to exact details because he was so cranky, but he passed it about twenty minutes ago, about thirty k north of town. Reckons it was doing at least 180, which I find hard to believe."

Peter snorted, a brief sharp laugh, and his tension eased just a little. He knew the morning's failures had hit Amber hard. She must have regrouped if she could joke about her useless car. "Copy that Amber. Well done. Stay by the radio." He swung around to look at Hemi again, and spoke on the closed circuit. "Any idea how far away that makes his mate with the hunting chopper?"

"Not sure, he must be close. At least we know which way to look now."

"Exactly." He looked front again and addressed the trailing chopper. "Medivac, did you hear that? The missing suspect appears to have headed north. Please fall back, but keep us in sight. And keep watch behind and to the side, just in case."

He continued to scour the sides of the lake, looking for movement, a flash of color, a navigation light—anything that might signal another helicopter on the move. He searched with the binoculars, and then took them down to get a wider fix on the lake shore, then put the binoculars to his eyes again. He stared at trees and hills until they blurred and morphed and doubled in number, and he had to blink and look again. The seconds passed, stretched into minutes, and still he searched till his eyes grew dry.

"Two o'clock! Maybe ten k ahead." Hawk saw it first. The man wasn't named after a bird of prey for nothing.

Peter scanned with the binoculars and there it was. How Hawk could see it with the naked eye was nothing short of miraculous. He adjusted focus, and could see it clearly, though at this distance it was still tiny even with so much magnification. Brightly colored, a little dragonfly. "Can we outrun it?"

"We can try. We're already at maximum speed. But we're bigger than they are."

In the back, Ellen was weeping. No matter how hard she tried to stop, tears just kept leaking out of her eyes and dribbling down her face. Hemi noticed, reached out his big paw of a hand, and enfolded her right hand within it. The human touch was immensely comforting, even though he immediately resumed staring down the lake, towards whatever the pilot and now Peter had seen. She didn't want to look, and besides, her vision was being refracted through the prisms of liquid filling her eyes.

So much terror that she wanted to vomit it out of her stomach. Not even just fear for Rachel any more, but for herself, and the other three people in this little fluttering craft. Tom was a loose cannon. Literally. She knew he was a crack shot. They'd told her that days ago, before they knew how much it mattered. And if he'd gone to a hunting friend, that would mean a gun, probably a hunting rifle with a nice long range. If it had occurred to Peter that Tom could just shoot down the rescue helicopter, it had to have occurred to Tom. She hadn't thought she could fear for her own life while her daughter was in danger, but now she found she could. And these good men alongside her—the rumpled paramedic, the enigmatic pilot and the big, calm policeman—she so very much didn't want their breath to be taken from them. All because of mental illness and bitterness and money.

But the deep dragging undertow of dread had been pulling since her eyes had first snagged on the weaponry Peter was toting this morning. He didn't normally carry a gun, but clearly this was considered a situation requiring an "armed response". The metal turned her relationship with him inside out, peeling back the skin and exposing the muscle and gristle and sinew. For the first time, she was confronted with the knowledge that he was a law enforcement official first, her protector second, and her friend… somewhere down the list. Should it turn out to be her own daughter who was armed and dangerous among the hiking party, he would not hesitate to deal with her for the safety of all.

They were closing on the little dragonfly, a meter of airspace at a time. But the dragonfly was closing on Altham Hut. Hawk said, "Smoke. Eleven o'clock."

Peter knew there'd be no point in him trying to see it with the naked eye, so he adjusted the binoculars and there it was: a thin column rising above a fold in the hills, not far from the lake shore, in the small bay that led to the hut. Proof of life. It had to be the missing trampers. No one had used that hut since last summer.

He swung round to look at Hemi. "Smoke rising from Altham Hut. Looks like you were right about the direction they went."

"Yeah, it's great. Be even better if Tom hadn't overheard me."

It wasn't the kind of comment that needed a reply. Peter glanced at the hand Hemi was holding, and felt a flood of longing to be in the back seat with her. For an endless second his gaze locked on her eyes, wide and dripping with tears, and then he swung back to the front. He closed his mind to all but the job in hand. He pressed the radio transmission button. "Medivac, hold back and hover. We'll let you know when we need you. And keep your wits about you."

***

IN THE HUT, JACK WAS PUTTING ANOTHER PIECE OF WOOD ON THE fire. He'd kept it stoked all night, rising every couple of hours to add more fuel. "We have to keep the bat signal alive," he'd told the others.

It had been a long, unsettled night, with Callie's wristwatch alarm beeping every half hour so she could check on Rachel. When the hypo finally struck about 4.00 am, they needed no beeps to wake them. Rachel groaned loudly, thrashed in her bed and shouted nonsense. It had taken the last of their energy bars to fix it. *Please God, let them come soon.*

Jack had already been outside in the pre-dawn twilight, gathering more wood to dry over the stove, so it would be ready to burn when the hut's store of firewood ran out. He was wearing his camera in the headstrap—ready, just in case. After all the horrors his little lens had captured, he didn't want it to miss out on rescue and resolution.

Suddenly, Erica wriggled from her sleeping bag and ran to the window, every line of her body alert. "Did you hear that? It's an engine!"

Callie was awake in an instant and began struggling out of her bag on the floor alongside Rachel's bunk. "Can you see anything?"

Jack scooped up her orange jacket to wave in the air and flicked his camera into Record. Erica shoved her feet into boots as he slammed open the door and ran outside. He pounded through the trees circling the hut, splashed across a small creek and onto the shingly beach that spread out into the lake, wide and level. He could hear the noise getting closer now. A boat or a helicopter? It had to be a helicopter.

Erica arrived beside him, panting. "Can you see it?"

"Not yet."

Callie stood at the window, peering out, holding Rachel's hand. She wanted to be out there helping flag down help, but she couldn't bear to leave Rachel alone. "What is it?" Rachel said.

"I'm trying to see, but the trees are in the way."

On the beach, Erica said, "We can't let it get away. They have to see us this time."

At that moment a tiny helicopter was unveiled by the slope of the foothills, swinging around the curve of the steep shoreline, so close, maybe only five hundred meters away. Jack began swinging the orange jacket overhead, and Erica waved her arms and jumped and jumped. It was such a small helicopter, Jack couldn't believe it could be a rescue aircraft. As the first rays of the new day's sunshine slanted across the beach, it blinded him, and he struggled to make out the details. Only two seats by the look of it, and no doors. Heading straight for them, low and direct.

And then he saw something that made his insides go cold. "Erica! Run! Run!" He dropped the jacket and grabbed at Erica's arm as he turned.

A slow half-second later, she saw what he'd seen, and turned to follow him, trying desperately to make it back to the tree cover, running, running, her heart in her mouth and her breath on fire. She reached forward for the hand Jack was holding back towards her as he ran and ran.

***

ON BOARD THE DRAGONFLY, THE WIRY LITTLE PILOT WAS PARALYZED by disbelief. Tom had eased out onto the skids, and was lifting his rifle, lining up the sights. A man and a woman on the ground, running for their lives. Murderers, Tom had called them, but this wasn't what the pilot had expected to happen. His reflexes made sluggish by shock, he pulled hard on the joystick as the rifle exploded into deadly life.

***

THE RESCUE CHOPPER ROUNDED THE CURVE IN THE LAKE BEHIND the dragonfly just in time for Peter to register the ugly tableau before them. Two people running across the pebbly beach towards the trees, the second one small and pony-tailed—a woman. The hunting helicopter surging towards them, Tom hanging out on the skids, rifle raised. The muzzle flash just as the forward runner reached back to grab the woman's hand and tried to lift her bodily, but too late. Her body jerked and she fell, but the man just kept pulling, dragging her behind him like an out-of-control water skier, and they disappeared under the tree cover.

"She's hit!"

Ellen heard those horrific words and opened her eyes. Rachel? She closed her eyes again, and sent up a wordless, incoherent prayer.

They couldn't do anything about the gunshot victim until they dealt with Tom. Hawk understood that without being told, and swung in a wide arc around the sweep of the little bay, keeping a safe but watchful distance from the dragonfly now reeling back across the lake.

Peter raised the binoculars, fiddling with the focus as he tried to lock onto the erratic movements of the aircraft and see what was taking place inside.

***

"TAKE ME BACK THERE! THERE'S MORE OF THEM." TOM ROARED AT his friend, his face mottled purple.

"You shot that woman!"

"They're murderers! I told you that!"

"Then we take them to the police. We don't shoot them. They're people, Tom, not animals!"

***

INSIDE THE HUT, THERE WAS SO MUCH BLOOD. ERICA WASN'T screaming this time but Rachel was. "Where are you hit?" Callie said, searching desperately up and down Erica's blood spattered body. Jack was wrenching items out of his pack, looking for something to use as a bandage, his breath roaring in and out of his lungs.

"My leg. It hit my leg. It's the artery. We're so close and now I'm going to die, and I deserve it for what I did to Adam."

"Shut up!" Callie said.

"Pressure," Erica said. "You have to apply pressure or I really will die."

Jack grabbed a wadded t-shirt and rammed it against Erica's thigh. "That poisonous, crazy psycho." He bit out the words, fury clenching his teeth. "What else has he got lined up for us?"

"It's still bleeding," Callie said. "We've got to stop the bleeding."

"Hold that. Hard. I'll find something to tie it on." He began rif-fling through their packs, but it was taking too long, so he grabbed Adam's knife from where it lay beside the stove, snatched up his own rain jacket, and sliced off one of its sleeves.

**

THE DRAGONFLY HOVERED A FEW HUNDRED METERS AWAY, REASON-ably stable, but Peter could see a raging argument taking place be-tween the occupants. It would seem that the pilot had not been a willing participant. Suddenly, the radio sprang into life, and they could hear it all. Accidentally or on purpose, someone had flicked the transmit button.

"...don't understand. We have to get them all. It's useless if we don't get them all."

"I'm not taking you back there, so put the gun down."

"It has to be this way. I have to do it for Lily."

"They're Australians. They've never met Lily. What's it got to do with Lily?"

"My daughter will die if you don't take me back there now. My sweet little girl or those murderers. How can you put them first? Do it now, or I swear, I'll shoot you."

"You crazy..."

Even without binoculars, they could see Tom raising the rifle, pointing it at his friend. Stupid to kill his pilot—they'd both die. Even with Tom's limited piloting skills, they didn't have enough altitude for him to have time to seize the controls. Peter glanced at Hawk, but he was already adjusting their position, pulling them away, increasing the distance. Out of the path of any stray bullets.

**

THE PILOT OF THE DRAGONFLY SHOVED THE CONTROLS, TIPPING HIS aircraft as far to the side as he could without crashing it. Floored by fear and grief, he was looking down the barrel of a gun, and beyond it to a man he didn't recognize. A good friend to so many for so many years, but turned into a stranger by emotions they could not share. As Tom's finger tightened on the trigger, he lost his grip on the helicopter and fell through the doorless opening. His outline was lit golden by the rising sun as he dropped towards the black water of the lake. Even as he fell, legs peddling thin air, his mate could see him trying to control the angle of the rifle, still trying to get off a shot, his last act of defiance on this earth.

***

PETER GLANCED AT HAWK, BUT HE WAS AHEAD OF HIM AGAIN, GUID-ing the chopper back towards the beach near the hut even as Tom hit the water, the splash rising up around him with a whoosh, and then closing over him as he disappeared till the end of time. Hundreds of meters deep, with black ice on the bottom.

Peter removed his headset, unclipped his seatbelt, and handed his rifle through to Hemi all in one continuous movement. He was already opening the door as the skids touched the pebbles, unhol-stering his pistol and slipping the safety catch off as he ran towards the trees. Instinct made him crouch low as he passed beneath the whirring blades. Behind him, Hemi slipped out the other side of the helicopter, and followed Peter at a distance, ready to back him up, rifle held in a shooting grip but with the barrel pointed to the ground.

Watching them in horrified fascination, Ellen couldn't believe such big men could move with such catlike grace. Drawing on abundant reserves of common sense, she remained firmly strapped in her seat, and Hawk kept the blades spinning for a quick getaway should it become necessary.

As Peter drew level with the hut, he could see the trail of blood leading across the pebbles, becoming hidden by undergrowth as it went through the encircling trees, and then emerging again up the wooden steps of the hut and in behind the closed door. It was a lot of blood. Someone was in serious trouble and they'd need to act fast. At the window, he could see the pale oval of a face, but through the trees it was impossible to discern detail.

"There's more of them!" Callie said. "They're on the ground around us now. There's even one in a police uniform." Realizing she'd been spotted, she ducked instinctively below the glass, even though she knew the thin wooden walls would not stop a bullet.

"Is there nothing money can't buy?" Jack's fury was white hot. The bleeding had slowed thanks to consistent pressure on the wound, but Erica was so pale. Shock or blood loss, or both, he couldn't tell, and he could do nothing to fix it with danger circling.

Peter knew he'd been sighted, but there'd been no shots fired from the hut, and he decided to take the risk. He looked at Hemi. It was a direct look, and he received a nod of affirmation in return. I've got your back, the nod said. He stepped through the trees into the small clearing in front of the hut, his gun held at shoulder height, trained on the door.

"You in the hut! Come out with your hands up."

Jack erupted. "I've had a gutful of this. I've had it with being scared." He stood from his post beside Erica and looked at Callie. "Keep the pressure on her leg." Startled by the look of righteous anger on his face, she moved swiftly to Erica's side and began pressing, but her eyes followed Jack as he flung the door open so hard it bounced off the wall, and stalked down the steps.

Peter saw a ragged-looking man emerge defiant and stand less than five meters in front of him. His clothes were liberally splashed with blood, and his hands were drenched in it. He held his arms not up in surrender, but wide, out straight to the side at shoulder height, fingers spread, a position that said: *Here I am, shoot me.* Off to the side, Hemi had raised the rifle and was staring down the sights, ready to do just that if necessary.

He wasn't a big man, but the roar that came out of his mouth could have stopped traffic, and his eyes were steely. "Come on, shoot me! I'm just lost, but apparently that's a criminal offence in this country. Or maybe shooting hikers is a national sport." He turned his head sideways and looked straight at Hemi, and when he spoke again his volume was much lower, but the words still carried. "If you've got enough money, it seems you can buy anything you want."

Peter leaned a little sideways and peered around the man into the dim interior of the hut. He could see a woman crouched, staring at him, her expression mostly fear with a gram or two of feisty. It took him a moment to discern that she was pressing on the blood-ied leg of a second woman, the one who'd been shot. He'd studied the collection of passport photos so often in the past few days it was as though he was seeing old friends. Neither of these women was Rachel, and he felt that absence as a blow for Ellen. But relevant to the current crisis, neither appeared dangerous.

He lowered his gun, slipped on the safety catch, slid it into the holster, did up the clip, and crossed his arms over his chest in a slow, deliberate movement. "You must be Jack," he said, his voice mild. Hemi still held the rifle cocked and ready, and kept scanning for attacks from other directions.

Jack let his arms fall to his side with a sigh. "Yes, I guess I must be." The anger had all leaked out of him now, and he just looked tired.

"We understood there to be a gun somewhere among you."

The anger flared again for a moment. "So you shoot at us?"

"That wasn't us." He paused a moment. No time to explain Tom now, but he needed to be certain the situation was contained before he summoned the medical team. "I'll explain it later. Tell me about the gun."

Jack was frustrated by the delay. "We've got two women dying in there!"

"Two?" The crouching woman didn't look sick. Was Rachel still alive then after all?

"Erica was shot and it hit an artery and we're having trouble stopping the bleeding. Rachel is diabetic and she needs help *now*."

Peter felt his spirits surge, but kept his face still. "We have the resources to help, but I must know about the gun before I bring more people in here."

Jack could now understand the policeman's perspective, but what to say? He went to rub his face but saw the blood on his hands in time and stopped, went to put them in his pockets and then thought he'd better not do that either. So he just flapped them uselessly. "It's such a long story."

"Give me the synopsis."

"Bryan gave it to Erica. He expected her to use it on us but she couldn't. It went off by accident in a landslide and killed Adam. She lost it in the landslide." He added, in the interests of full disclosure, "The only weapon we have is a hunting knife that belonged to Adam, and we're not interested in using it on anyone, but I can go grab it if you want. We just want to be safe. We want to go home." His voice broke slightly on the last word and he brought himself under control with an effort.

Peter gave Jack a measuring look, nodded, and whipped his radio from the holster on his belt. "Hawk, power down and bring

Hemi's paramedic kit here, stat, we've got a bleeder. Bring Ellen too, and tell her Rachel is alive." He knew she'd hear it from him, if she'd kept her headset on, and he wished he could have told her to her face, looked in her eyes. But there was a lot of work to do.

"Medivac crew, do you read me?"

The pilot responded in the affirmative.

"The situation is now safe. Proceed to Altham Hut immediately and land on the beach. We've got some customers for you."

57

ELLEN SAW THE SPLASHES OF BLOOD AS SHE HURRIED TOWARDS the hut, and tried not to step in it. Was it Rachel's blood? Hemi had already met them at a full run in the middle of the beach, grabbed the paramedic kit from Hawk, and sprinted back through the trees with it.

Peter appeared in the doorway as she mounted the steps, and held out a hand towards her. She took it gratefully, and his grip was warm and strong. It was dim inside, and seemed to be full of people, all busy. As she entered, she reeled from a rank, caged-animal odor—it took a moment to register that it was the smell of human bodies unwashed for weeks, and constantly assaulted by fear.

In the confusion it was so hard to make out Rachel. Hemi was busy with someone on the floor on one side of the hut, and she caught a glimpse of blood and surgical gloves. Peter steered her towards the other side of the hut, to a bunk against the wall, and a blue sleeping bag with someone in it. The face emerging from that sleeping bag. Oh that face. So dear, so very dear.

She knelt on the floor beside the bunk. "Rachel. Oh my darling. Rachel."

"Mum? Is that really you?"

"Yes it's me. Here I am darling. I'm right here."

Arms fumbled out from the sleeping bag and reached for her. "Mummy. Oh mummy." The childhood endearment pierced Ellen's heart and she was overwhelmed. Always she'd been able to be calm and strong when her child was sick, not show her own fear, whatever the crisis. But not this time. Deep, guttural sobs burst from her as they clung to one another. Rachel wept too, a weak mucousy noise, catching in her throat. "I'm so glad you've come."

Standing behind Ellen, Peter felt his eyes moisten, and took a slow deep breath, composing his face. He turned and headed outside, looking for the medivac crew.

On the beach, Peter joined Hawk, and saw a small wiry man he didn't recognize, hanging off at a distance, fidgety and uncertain. His senses went on full alert, but then he caught a glimpse of the little dragonfly chopper parked round the far sweep of the bay behind their own machine, and the man's presence made sense. He looked at Hawk and inclined his head in the direction of the other man, a questioning look in his eyes.

"He's just killed one of his best mates," Hawk said. "He's gutted. Hovered out there for ages waiting for Tom to come back up. Wants us to start a search, even though he knows it would be a useless exercise. And he's worried about the woman Tom shot."

As soon as he'd briefed the arriving medical rescue team, Peter left Hawk to lead them through to the hut, and went to talk to the dragonfly pilot. He would take his details, tell him they'd question him formally later, instruct him to go home. Lift the burden of any further action from the man's shoulders by a display of uniformed authority.

But from there, the burden wouldn't be carried by the uniform, but the shoulders inside it. The shoulders of a flesh-and-blood man who had failed to notice the pain and fear of a friend and colleague, and how despair had disorientated his moral compass and turned him into an enemy. Had seen the breath of that friend and colleague snuffed as swiftly as a church candle, and would later this day face the task of telling a wife and mother what had happened to the center of her family's life.

Peter felt the heaviness of it within him, pushing his feet down further into the gravel as he crunched his way across the beach.

***

CALLIE SAT CLOSE TO JACK ON ONE OF THE BUNKS, KEEPING OUT OF the way, watchful and tense. It was like being in a backwoods emergency room. They'd stopped Erica's bleeding, but she needed fresh blood supplies. Rachel's condition needed to be assessed before they moved her. And so Hemi pumped IV fluids into Erica while the doctor and medivac paramedic working on Rachel connected a drip, tested her blood, asked questions. Ellen moved to the head of the bunk to give them access, and stroked her daughter's forehead tenderly.

Hemi glanced up, saw the mood of the two healthier hikers, and grinned his trademark grin. "You guys did a great job with this one, no joke."

"Really?" Jack said, astounded.

Callie said, "But it looks like a massacre in here."

"A wound like that, the first couple of minutes are vital. You did everything right. That's why she's gonna be fine." He grinned down at Erica now, who opened her eyes and gave him a weak smile. The morphine was doing its thing. "No dancing for a coupla days though, okay?"

The other paramedic noticed the exchange and looked over from his station near Rachel's bunk, and said, quietly, "This one's doing much better than we expected."

Callie's face crumpled and she began to weep softly as a swirl of emotions went through her. Relief was dominant but there were so many undercurrents. So many losses—of lives, of opportunities, of innocence. She fought to keep the noise down, so she wouldn't disturb the others.

***

JACK GATHERED HER INTO HIS ARMS AND ROCKED HER GENTLY, JUST
letting her weep it out. The encouraging words from the two para-
medics seemed to have lightened his body by about a hundred kilograms. Maybe the four of them really were survivors. Maybe they
really were safe. He grimaced at his red hands around Callie's shoulders, but the blood had dried now, so he figured it didn't matter
much, and besides, she was liberally splashed with it anyway. He
caught a glance from Peter, who'd paused from sorting the contents
of their rucksacks in the corner. "It's probably not the best holiday
we've ever had," Jack said.

Peter quirked an eyebrow. "We might not get you to star in the
next tourism ad then." He went back to his sorting.

Callie grew quiet as her tears ran their course, and she sat back
and started fishing for her t-shirt underneath her fleece, looking
for something to wipe her face that didn't have too much blood on
it. "I'd lend you the team hankie," Jack said, deadpan again, "but I
don't know where it is. I think Erica had it last."

Callie stifled a giggle and looked at the dried blood on her
hands. "You know what, I think I'm going down to the lake to wash
this lot off." She looked at the policeman, inquiring. "Is that okay?"

"Sure. Anything in your pockets before you go?"

She turned them all out, both pants and fleece, and all she found
was two curly fern tips. She placed them carefully on the edge of
the bunk near the policeman, and gave him an impish look. Her
spirits were reviving. "You can have one of those if you're peckish,
but you have to leave the other one for me."

Jack did the same with his pockets, then followed her down
to the water. By the time he'd crunched his way across the gravel
beach, she'd already shed her boots and walked shin deep into the
clear frigid water, and was sluicing water up her arms, and then her

face. She paused a moment, and then immersed her scalp in the water and began washing her hair, even though the cold water must have been agony for her scalp wound.

By now, Jack was alongside her, joining in with gusto, washing his hands and face, and then his hair. The cold was both numbing and exhilarating. He then hauled both t-shirt and fleece off over his head and plunged them into the water, scrubbing with his fingers at the blood, and all the other stains.

Somewhere along the way it stopped being about hygiene and became a ritual, a symbol—washing themselves free of much more than blood and sweat.

She watched him, considering. "Won't you get cold if your clothes are all wet? We're still a couple of hours from civilization."

"Have you forgotten already what Ranger Bryan told us? Merino t-shirts, polyester fleece, so they dry fast and keep you warm even if they get wet. That doesn't just apply to rain."

"Well then. You'd better look the other way or pretend we're at the beach." She quickly stripped down to her bra and began to wash her own shirts.

Jack flushed to his hair follicles. He didn't know where to look. But he knew where he wanted to look. So he definitely must be feeling better.

They washed and scrubbed and wrung and laughed, and then made their way back to the hut, their clothes damp, their faces clean and shining, their spirits more alive than they'd ever been.

***

THE MEDIVAC HELICOPTER WAS LOADED WITH ITS PRECIOUS CARGO. Two patients, both stable now. Two lives that would always carry scars, but would nevertheless go on from here. Two futures retrieved from the cliff edge of death.

Ellen's duffel bag was stowed, and she turned to Callie and Jack, finally able to give them a moment's attention after the long minutes of tunnel vision while Rachel was being treated. "Thank you for getting my little girl out of there." She reached for a hand of each one, squeezed hard, and gazed into the eyes of first Callie, then Jack. "We'll talk more before long, but I can't leave without saying thank you. From the depths of my soul."

"You're so welcome, Mrs C," Callie said, a schoolgirl again, addressing a friend's mother, her voice thick with emotion. Jack just smiled sheepishly and returned the squeeze of her hand.

Ellen turned to thank the rescue team. A quick peck on the cheek for Hawk, who looked awkward but pleased. Another one for Hemi, who said, "Aw, come on," and turned it into an enveloping hug.

A long, speaking gaze for Peter, her eyes full of relief, thanksgiving, hope, even forgiveness. She held out both hands to him, and he took them, squeezed her fingers, and then enfolded her in a fierce hug. It wasn't a very professional thing for a uniformed police officer to do, but he could count on Hemi and Hawk to be discreet. "Let us know how you get on," he muttered as he released her.

"I'll tell you all about it over a caramel latte one day," she said, with a teasing smile. "Soon." She turned and stepped aboard the helicopter, and the others moved back as the engine began to hum.

58

THE LAUNCH CHUGGED DOWN THE LAKE, CUTTING A WIDENING white trail through the upside down hills and peaks sealed into its mirror surface. The sun was well up in the sky now, but the wind had not yet risen. The mountains clustered around to watch them go, whispering. When they were lost and fearful, Callie had struggled to keep hope alive with thoughts of civilization, a square meal, a hot shower, a soft bed. But now she felt a strange reluctance to go back to the hum of traffic and the buzz of machines, the glow of her laptop, the burble of her phone, the ceaseless workplace obsession with trivialities and beat-ups and prying into other people's traumas. Whatever else these last few weeks had been, they had been utterly real. After week upon week of numbness after William's defection, she had felt something again, really felt it, more than she'd probably felt anything in her life. It could be addictive, that sort of intensity.

The big tall sergeant who seemed to be just a little bit sweet on Mrs C had sent the pilot home—not enough room for all of them in the helicopter. He'd brought the amiable paramedic with them on the boat, even though they'd already received first aid for their cuts and bruises and muscle strains. At first Callie had feared he was present in case the pain in her side turned out to be more than just broken ribs. He'd said a full medical check later in the day would be soon enough, after a shower and some clean clothes, but was he secretly concerned? But she became calm again as the realization dawned that they were probably going to be questioned, informally at least, and the policeman would need a witness to whatever they said.

She was content to sit next to Jack opposite the other two, and quietly nibble sultanas from the ration pack she'd been given—slowly, as instructed, so as not to overtax her unaccustomed stomach. She didn't need to control or guide anything now. Things could just unfold.

***

JACK HAD NO DESIRE TO BE PASSIVE. HE COULD EAT COLD OAT PORridge out of a bag with a plastic spoon, and be blunt at the same time. "So I guess you'll want to ask us some things," he said, feeling only mildly silly in his one-armed jacket. It's missing arm, soaked in Erica's blood, lay on the floor at Altham Hut awaiting a cleanup team. "You should get the details before we get among other people. Otherwise we'll hear rumors, make wrong connections, get confused, forget."

Peter nodded, his expression wry. "Have you done this before?"

Jack shrugged. "I interview people for a living too." *And there's quite a lot of things I'd like to ask you.*

Peter said, "Do I need to say that this conversation is 'off the record'?"

Jack laughed. "Anything that would be sub judice is obviously off the record anyway."

Peter apparently caught the implication, and so did Callie. "Are you thinking of writing about this?" she asked, curious.

"Not today. But I reckon I'll want to eventually. Won't you?" He looked at her, and his face darkened. "People have to know how toxic money can be when it's used to manipulate people. What's happened to us will be a quick blip in the news, forgotten tomorrow. But the lives of Sharon and Adam—and even Kain and Bryan—can't mean so little as that."

***

"SO YOU SEE IT AS BEING ALL ABOUT MONEY?" SAID PETER, INTER-ested. He had a hunch he'd get better results if he discarded his professional persona and just conversed with these two.

"No, money was just the tool. The problem was bitterness. Unforgiveness. At first I thought Bryan was acting as some sort of impartial judge and jury because he was nuts and he blamed us for Liana's death. Do you know about Liana?" Peter nodded, and Jack continued. "But he wasn't quite as deeply nuts as he seemed, and he definitely wasn't impartial. I'm convinced he dressed it up as the scales of justice to make himself feel righteous, but really he just wanted good old-fashioned revenge. Revenge on Kain and maybe Adam for sleeping with his girlfriend, revenge on the rest of us in case we knew about it all along, revenge on us and the world for being friends with his money instead of friends with him. If he could have forgiven us and himself for failing Liana, and gotten on with his life… none of this would have happened. His wealth was the best weapon he had, and it turned out to be a powerful one. Erica didn't take the bait quite the way he'd have liked her to, but he was a good judge of character with Kain."

Callie said, "I'm not sure if that's completely true. I think Kain had trouble deciding how to respond to what happened. And then he regretted what he did."

"When did you become aware Kain was involved in Bryan's plans?"

"We didn't know for sure until we found that survival gear in his rucksack after he was dead."

"Why did you leave the locator beacon behind?"

"It didn't work," Jack said. "I wrestled with it for a couple of minutes."

Callie looked at Jack. "I think they might be telling us it did work."

Jack stared at the two men opposite, then sighed and leaned on his knees, his head in his hands. "You've got to be joking." His voice was muffled. "I probably should add that I'm terrified of heights, and I was about to wet myself on that ledge. Perhaps it interfered with my fine motor skills, or just, you know, my general sanity." He looked up again.

Hemi grinned at him. "I'm not scared of heights, mate, and I was about to wet myself on that ledge."

"The PLB activated yesterday afternoon," Peter said. He smiled. "We weren't best pleased when we found it with no one beside it, I have to say."

"Yesterday afternoon? But we were miles away by then."

"We think some keas got at it."

"Oh great. So a parrot could turn it on, but not me."

"A parrot and a seven hundred meter drop," Hemi said. "I took it apart last night. It'd been sabotaged. A strong metal pin straight through the mechanism. You'd never have managed to activate it. Not without a sledgehammer."

"And it's just as well you left it behind for a parrot to drop, as it happens," added Peter. "A survivor from a rock fall once waited seven days at Altham Hut before a boat came by. We found you today partly because the beacon helped us work out where you might be heading."

"Oh. Well that's a good thing then." He thought a moment. "So why torment me with it?"

"Didn't mean to do that. But we were curious why you left it and kept the other gadgets, if they weren't working either."

"They're a bit more complicated. I didn't know if I might be doing something wrong and the others could get them to work. The instructions on the beacon were so simple a trained monkey could have followed them."

Hemi grinned. "Or a parrot."

Jack laughed.

Peter handed the satellite phone and GPS to Hemi from a bag at his side. "Can you tell what's wrong with them?"

Hemi looked towards the bag, expecting more. "Got the battery for the phone?"

Peter in turn looked at Jack, and Jack frowned. "Isn't it in it?"

"Nah, mate. This is an old model. Has a separate battery about the size of a house brick."

Jack looked at Callie and raised one eyebrow. "More of Bryan's mind games."

"Looks like it. That's definitely the way the phone looked when Bryan showed it to us that first night and told us how wonderful it was," she said. "There was nothing else with it." She sighed. "I guess he could count on us not to know what it was meant to look like. We were so passive in so many ways. We put ourselves completely in his power." She shook her head, rueful and reflective.

Jack said, "Yes, but we weren't to know how he was going to use that power."

Hemi was fiddling with the buttons of the GPS. "Completely stuffed. It's like there's a virus in the software. I can have a closer look at it when I get home if you like."

"No doubt it will turn out to be sabotaged too," Peter said. "So it seems Bryan gave a set of survival gear to Kain that didn't work. Any idea when Kain found out it didn't work?"

"We're not sure, but it may only have been in the past couple of days that he tested it, after Adam turned up with a bullet in his head. Kain would have suddenly realized Bryan must have had a Plan B, if there was someone out there with a gun. And then later he realized Bryan might know he'd slept with Liana, and whatever

Bryan had promised him took on a different light."

"Bryan did know he'd slept with Liana," Peter said. "He'd checked the post mortem report a few months ago. The blood type of the baby didn't match Bryan, but it matched Kain."

"I see. And you probably know Bryan asked for our blood types on the emergency information form he sent with the invitation." Peter nodded. "Well, not long before Kain died he found out we suspected him of killing Sharon."

"So you knew she was murdered?"

"Not straight away, but Callie realized later what the bruises on her face meant. I assume that's why you've taken all our gloves." Peter nodded and Jack told him Erica's fears about that night and what she'd seen.

Callie took up the tale. "Our gloves were one of the things Bryan supplied when we got here. And we all had the same brand and color except for Kain. Bryan said the shop didn't have enough pairs in that brand. Kain joked about how his were better than ours—the lining was softer. I bet he thought he was getting special treatment. Imagine how he must have felt when he realized Bryan was just creating an evidence trail in case Kain did anything criminal with gloved hands."

"As a lawyer, it's surprising he didn't think about that," Peter said.

"When you're in that situation out there, it gets very primal," Callie said. "You start to feel as though none of the normal rules apply."

"Callie also thinks Kain might have committed berry suicide when he realized Bryan had set him up, and he wouldn't be able to get away with it," Jack said. "The more I think about it, the more it explains the way Kain looked and acted that afternoon. You know, it was Bryan who recommended those berries in a private chat with

Kain back at the beginning of the hike. Told him they were 'almost a perfect food'."

Peter looked grim. "That's an especially sick thing to do. They're probably the only deadly plant out there."

There was a lull in the conversation while each member of the group absorbed the new information they'd learned.

Callie said, "Have you found out how much Bryan offered Kain for being his henchman?"

Peter made a quick decision to be open with them, even about this. "Kain had a copy of a will in his house leaving Bryan's estate divided equally between the seven of you who went on the hike, or however many of you outlived Bryan by thirty days."

Callie and Jack stared at him as they processed the implications, then looked at each other. "No wonder he wanted to get rid of the rest of us," Jack said. "Although it's strange he wasn't more proactive about it."

"Maybe he didn't have the stomach for it, after Sharon," Callie said.

"Or it might have dawned on him that the will would make him a suspect, so the other deaths had better be natural."

Callie said, "But it was a fake will of course. Another trick."

"Not fake," said Peter, "just superseded. He made another one a few days later."

"Leaving it all to Greenpeace."

"No, not Greenpeace." He weighed up whether to tell them, what to tell them, and how to tell them. "Leaving it to the six of you, excluding Kain, and if none of you outlived Bryan by thirty days, it all went to a little girl called Lily Granton. She's the daughter of the bloke who shot Erica this morning, and she's dying of cancer."

Jack and Callie stared at their feet as a few more pieces slotted into place.

"It doesn't justify Tom's actions," Peter said, "but I've known him eight years, and he's always been a good guy. He thought there was a treatment in the States that might save Lily, but he couldn't afford it. And Bryan told him you lot had murdered a girl ten years ago and got away with it. I think he lost the plot."

Callie shook her head sorrowfully. "I can see how someone could get sucked into a thing like that, especially when they're desperate. And now he won't even be around to help his daughter."

Jack's voice when he spoke was low with anger. "Bryan really knew how to tap into the weakest and the worst in everybody. I felt sorry for him you know, but some things are just plain evil."

"The puppet master," Callie said. "He pulled the strings and everybody danced."

Jack said, "Strings with hundred dollar bills twitching on the end of them."

"So what will you do with the money?" Peter said, watching closely for their reactions. "If you live a few more weeks, you become two of the four heirs."

They stared at him, shocked. It was obvious that neither had comprehended that part of the situation.

"As if we'd want his money." Callie almost spat the words.

"Speak for yourself," Jack said.

She swung on the bench seat to face him. "You're not seriously going to take his filthy money?"

Jack's expression was mild, as was his voice when he spoke. "It might help Sharon's little boy. And there's Adam's fiancée. They had a business together. How will she cope in the next little while? Plus there's the organizations that helped search for us—I imagine they run on donations. And there's the little girl with cancer."

Callie's indignation deflated like a punctured balloon. "Oh. I hadn't thought of any of that."

Jack shrugged. "It's probably all academic anyway. There's probably no money left, or his aunt will challenge the will, and so she should, when the whole purpose behind it was so immoral. But in any case, the money itself isn't evil. It's just a thing that can be used by people whose motives might be good or bad. Or a mixture of the two."

Callie was gazing off into the distance. "Just like those mountains. I really thought they were evil some days, and Bryan certainly tried to use them as a murder weapon, but they don't actually have a morality. They just did what mountains are meant to do."

***

WILLIAM GREEN, TELEVISION STAR, STOOD IN THE PARKING LOT AT the head of the jetty with his camera operator, watching the launch approach. A young police officer had asked them to wait there, but he knew there'd be no difficulty slipping past him when the time came. There never was, in these country towns. Unsophisticates always yielded to the boldness of the media. *If you act like you have the right to be somewhere, most people believe it.*

He glanced at his reflection in the window of their hire car, and gave his hair a refining tweak. It had been an effort to get the boss to agree to this particular overseas excursion. In these times of budget cuts, it was a long way to go for an uncertain story. Who knew if they'd ever even find the bodies?

But the missing included one of their own. And so the boss had approved it, though he gave William only three days on location, and no sound engineer.

They'd done the shots of aircraft and search teams, and interviewed experts. Most importantly, they'd got William's face on screen—windswept on the lake shore, and in pseudo survival mode over in the dense rainforest (he hadn't needed to go more than a few meters in).

Their three days had expired, but William had called Sydney and persuaded the boss to extend that by just one more day, and *voila*! The story had happened, just in time, and his "exclusive" was moments away.

There was a slight commotion at the gangway and William said to his cameraman, "Here we go!" They walked forward, the red "record" light already showing in the camera viewfinder.

William saw Callie Brown coming towards them, some unremarkable guy in a strange, one-armed jacket limping along beside her. He narrowed his eyes, gave her a considering look. The hair was a fright, but nothing a couple of hours in a salon couldn't fix. And he noted with approval that she was supermodel thin, even thinner than the blonde he'd taken to Italy. For a few weeks at least, she'd be quite the celebrity. Perhaps he had missed her after all.

***

AS SHE EMERGED FROM THE GAGGLE OF PEOPLE HELPING THEM OFF the launch, Callie looked up along the jetty and saw William Green, with a little power-socket-shock of recognition. How unfamiliar he looked, even though his face had been so dear for so many months. Had he actually been worried about her?

Then her eyes shifted to the camera beside him. Oh. She was News now. And he'd want to exploit their previous connection to get the story that might just win him an award, or at least get him a gold star from the boss. William was wearing moleskins with an outdoorsy jacket and shirt—obviously his interpretation of wardrobe for a story set in the wilds of New Zealand. His beautiful hair was just slightly mussed—another outdoorsy touch. The corners of her mouth twitched in the tiniest of smiles.

William stepped forward with his television face and voice on.

"Welcome back, Callie Brown. How does it feel to be safe at last?"

Callie felt rather than saw Jack step away from her side and edge past the television crew. Getting out of the firing line of the camera lens, yes, but also an emotional withdrawal. She could see him now past William's shoulder, standing at a slight distance behind William, his body angled away from them, his hands in his pockets, gazing up the lake.

Their relative positions made it easy to look from one to the other, comparing the two men. Two journalists. One gorgeous, successful and supremely confident. The other not very tall, not very good-looking, not very anything.

The strength of her own reaction took her by surprise, and brought with it self-knowledge. She held William's eyes in a steady gaze, and spoke to him, just two words, then pushed past him.

William stared down the jetty after her, uncharacteristically speechless. It was hardly the first time he'd ever heard those two words, but to get them from this woman, and now, of all the times! "No comment." Had she actually said that? To him?

As Callie drew level with Jack, she lifted her hand toward him, hesitantly, suddenly unsure. Jack reached out and grasped it in his own strong hand, and looked her in the eye for a long moment. They turned together and walked down the jetty towards the shore, and Jack's face split into an enormous grin.

***

In Poison Bay, dark water seethed and hissed over boulders, in and out, in and out, as though the ocean was breathing. Above, mountains stood back, watchful, brooding. And then they hid their heads behind a cloak of silent cloud.

THE END

About the Author

BELINDA POLLARD IS AN AWARD-WINNING FORMER JOURNALIST who loves mountain hiking despite bad knees and a fear of heights. She has been a professional writer/editor for decades, and a contributor to the *Closer to God* series since 1999. The words "Poison Bay" on a map triggered her journey to the sinister end of the bookshelf. Spooky and remote, it was a location just begging for a mystery. *Poison Bay* is her first novel, and won a Varuna Publisher Fellowship in 2011. Belinda lives in Brisbane, Australia where she undertakes ball-throwing duties for a dog named Rufus, and turns on the air-conditioning so she can dream of snow...

If you enjoyed this book, please review it on Amazon or your favorite bookstore, and share this link with your friends and social networks:
http://www.belindapollard.com/poison-bay

For updates on the sequel to *Poison Bay*, subscribe to Belinda's blog, Real Life on a Beautiful Planet:
www.belindapollard.com

Follow Belinda on Twitter at:
https://twitter.com/Belinda_Pollard